About the author and th

So here we are wit ller
from C.M.Vassie, a ? -
While Whitby Sleep s
known as *The Whal*

We are still no closer to knowing much about the author other than the self-evident fact that they love Whitby.

Sometimes in life we find a place that captures our imagination. Sometimes that place finds us. It sneaks into our dreams, haunts us, whispers gently until we are obliged to return.

This may be what happened to C.M.Vassie, trapping them in that web of narrow streets and lacklit yards where footsteps echo and seabirds shriek.

Where SCRAVIR creates a contemporary gothic horror tale set very much in the present, the 21st century characters in *The Whitby Trap* slip through cracks in the timeline first to a moment 200 years ago and then back millions of years to a beach on the Jurassic Coast.

Has the author made that journey themselves? Who knows? Stranger things have happened in Whitby.

C.M.VASSIE

The WHITBY TRAP

injini press

Back cover art: Dominique Vassie

A catalogue record for this book is available from the British Library

ISBN: 978 - 1-7391132-1-6

www.injinipress.co.uk

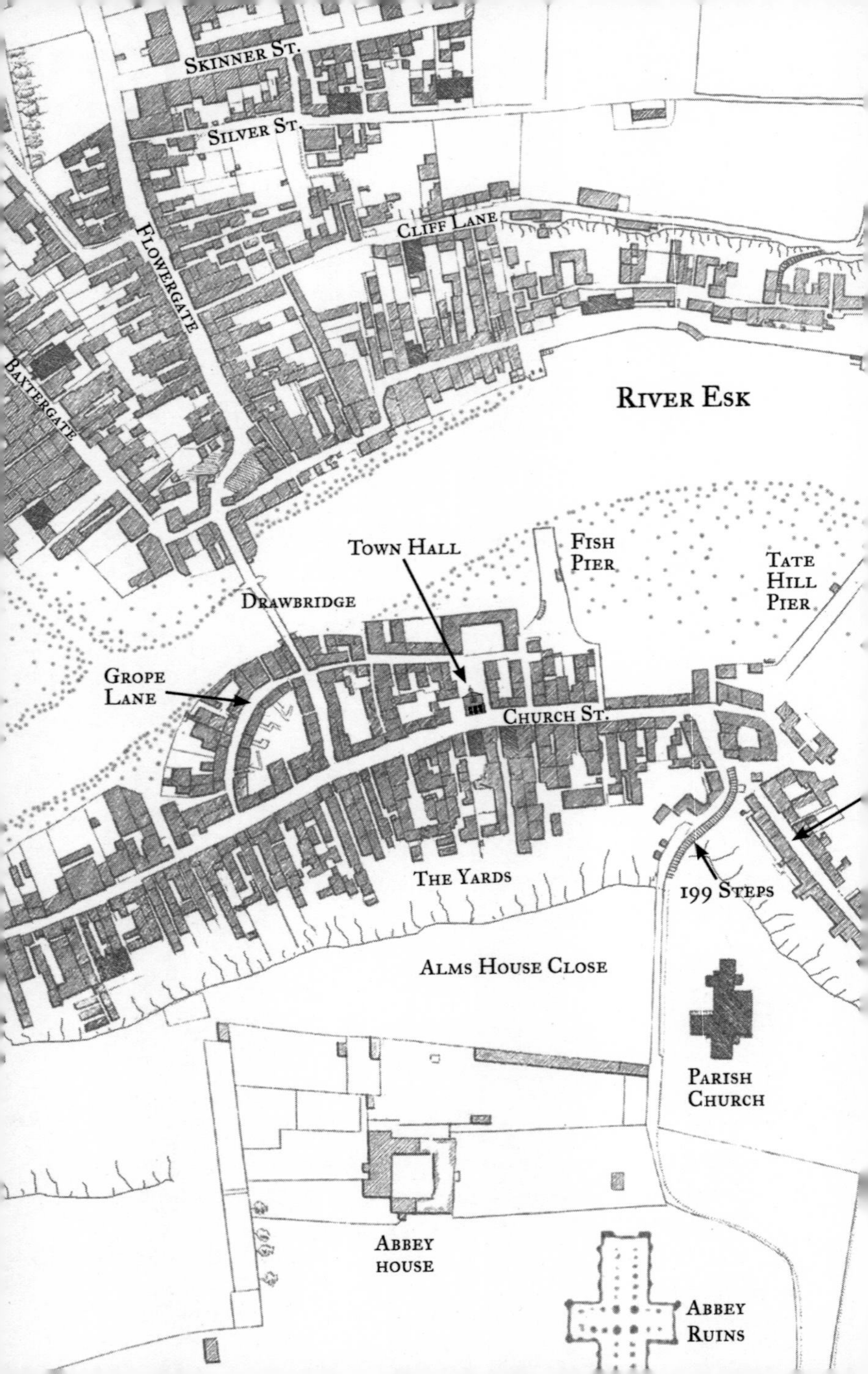

Skinner St.
Silver St.
Cliff Lane
Flowergate
Baxtergate
River Esk
Town Hall
Fish Pier
Tate Hill Pier
Drawbridge
Grope Lane
Church St.
The Yards
199 Steps
Alms House Close
Parish Church
Abbey house
Abbey Ruins

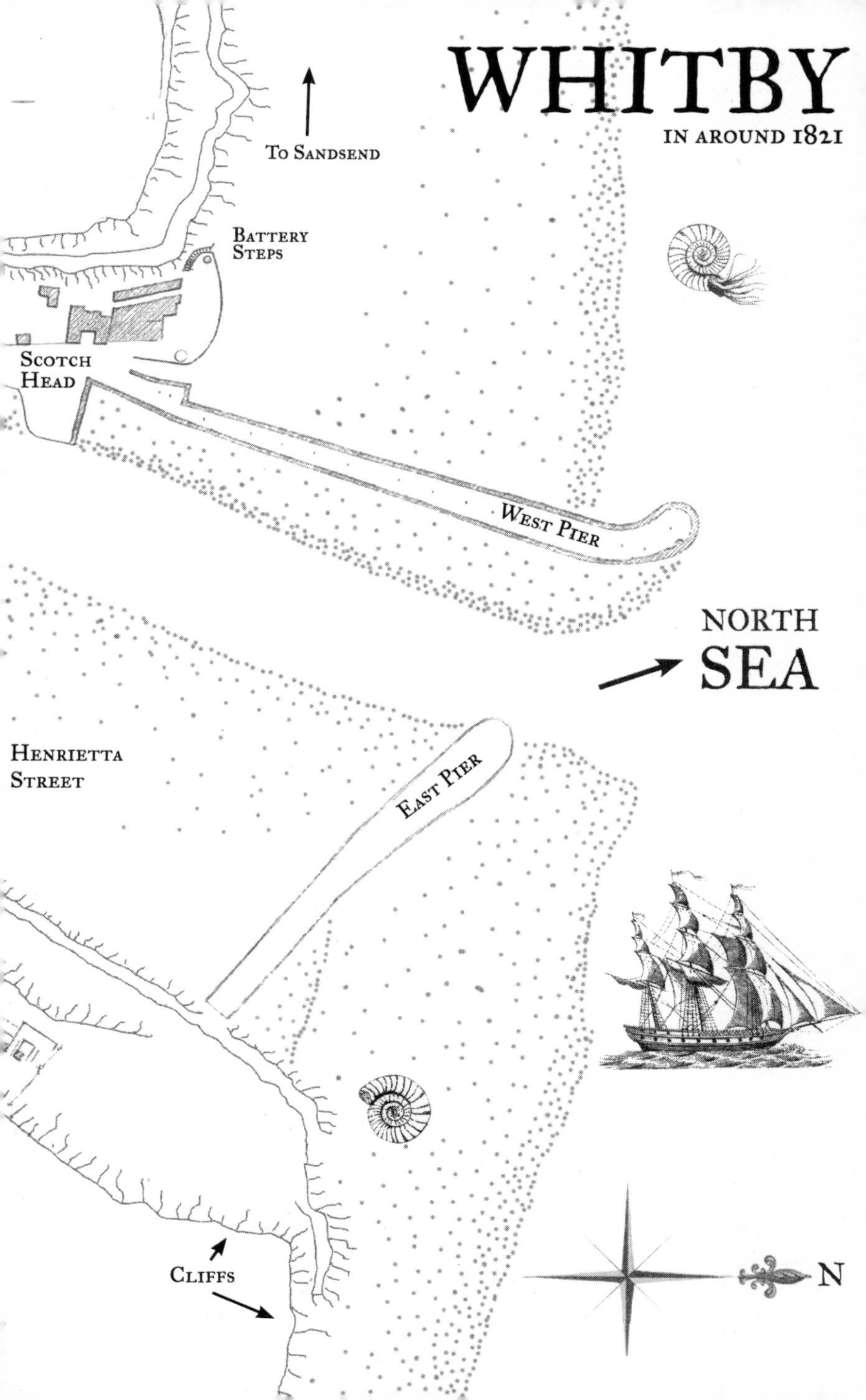
WHITBY
IN AROUND 1821
To Sandsend
Battery
Steps
Scotch
Head
West Pier
NORTH
SEA
Henrietta
Street
East Pier
Cliffs
N

CHAPTER 1

‘Wow, is it always like this?’

‘I told you it was gothic!’

The electric storm is directly overhead as they turn onto Church Street. The car rattles the cobbles. In the dusk gloom, the shop fronts are bright as birthday cakes: jet jewellers, photographers, bookshops, cafés, pubs.

Fork lightning rips the sky. The old town hall in the square is thrown briefly into silhouette as a thunderbolt smacks the bell tower with several hundred million volts, knocking out the power supply across the neighbourhood and plunging the window displays into darkness.

And, finally, the clouds break.

Hail hammers the car roof and bounces on the cobbles in a reverberating cacophony. People huddle in shop doorways or race for shelter beneath the town hall.

Sarah advances slowly, windscreen wiper blades beating frenetically. Arguments Yard on the left, they squeeze along the narrowing street, past the foot of the 199 steps and onto Henrietta Street.

She stops right outside the cottage and cuts the engine. Just ahead is another car with its boot open. A mum, dad and two kids are running in and out of a house a few doors up, shouting and carrying armfuls of stuff. The boy, maybe fourteen, looks happy enough, but the girl, maybe the same age, has the slumped shoulders of someone being forced to visit the Beige Room in a thimble museum.

The girl breaks away and walks straight towards Sarah, the dad coming after her. He grabs her arm just as she reaches the car.

‘I don’t care if it’s bloody hailing!’ the girl shouts above the noise of the downpour. ‘Stay indoors all weekend if you want, but I’m going fossil hunting.’

‘Calm down,’ pleads the dad, his hair plastered down on his head by the elements. ‘Mum is worried about Nan so …’

‘No! Sod off. Jurassic Coast not Geriatric Coast. You promised. I’m here to look for dinosaurs, not bore myself stupid with puzzles and card games.’ With that she turns and storms off back up the street with the dad in pursuit.

Up ahead the mother is holding up an umbrella to escort the grandmother into the cottage.

‘Well, here we are!’ Sarah says brightly. ‘Welcome to Whitby!’

No one moves. Sarah sets a good example, throws open her driver’s door and steps out. Bombarded with hailstones the size of peas, she hurries round the front of the car to the door of the cottage, and shoves the key that arrived in the post into the lock.

Since the whole street is in darkness it comes as no huge surprise that the light switch doesn’t work.

Doesn’t matter; you’ve got a torch.

Back outside she opens the boot and starts transferring luggage inside. Suitcases and half a dozen carrier bags. The others are still sitting in the car, hoping the weather will give up. By the time everything is in the front room, the lights have come back on up and down the street, the hail is relenting, and the others finally venture out of the vehicle.

Lights are thrown on in every room and discoveries are made. The cottage is warm and Sarah reassures everyone that everything will quickly dry out.

‘Cup of tea?’

‘It says you can turn the car round at the top,’ Stephen says.

‘Can you bring back some chips, love?’

The front door closes.

Feet run back downstairs.

'You can see the harbour jaws from the bedroom!'

'You can see them from down here too.'

'Is he always like this?'

'Did you bring coffee? He won't drink tea. Calls it cat-lap.'

A whole weekend in Whitby old town. Sarah fills the mugs and carries the tray to the through lounge that looks both onto the street and down to the harbour. Someone has switched on the television. She bites her lip and counts to ten and hopes it will be left off once they all have been for a walk. She rummages in the bags and finds the hot water bottles. It feels warm and cosy in the cottage but it's still nice to have something to snuggle up to in bed. Besides Stephen, of course.

She stacks the bottles on the kitchen windowsill beside the kettle and heads up to the bedrooms.

The wooden stairs creak. Sarah persuades herself that it doesn't really matter that Derek and Amy have clearly already taken the room that faces the harbour; the bed is just as nice in the other bedroom, even though it only faces the street. A boat enters the harbour, lights flashing, ploughing the thick water. Why hasn't she ever noticed before that boats have windscreen wipers?

Amy enters behind her. 'Have you ever seen such retro ugly mugly décor? Brown curtains with a stripy pink bedspread. Meh! But it is a lovely view, isn't it?' Amy collapses onto the bed. 'We'll just have to keep the light off,' she laughs. 'Oh!' she says innocently, as if the idea has just dawned on her. 'You don't mind us having this bedroom, do you? We can always swap if you really want to and …'

Sarah shakes her head, no point making a scene. She leaves Amy to her little victory.

The other bedroom will do. She hears people laughing in the street below as she empties the suitcase and hangs things up in the wardrobe. The toothbrushes and soap can stay here on the dressing table. Seeing her reflection in the mirror, Sarah ruffles her brunette boy bob to stop it looking too tidy. Yes, they have all had their lateral flow tests and are COVID-free but no point tempting fate, is there?

The front door opens downstairs.

'Grub's up!'

Stephen has found plates and the small dining table is covered in fish and chips. Derek has at least muted the television so that they don't all have to listen to the commentary. Sarah is profoundly disinterested in rugby.

'The lights are all off in the basement,' Amy announces. 'Took ages to find the toilet. Do you think it's a fuse?'

'The spring roll is for Sarah,' Stephen announces. 'She's vegan. Cod for the rest of us.'

'Spring rolls don't sound very traditional, mate,' Derek says. 'Don't they do pickled onions and eggs? A vegan egg. Do vegans lay eggs?'

Sarah ignores Derek; she has heard it all before.

'Ta-da!' Amy deposits drinks on the table. Newcastle Brown for the boys and Theakston cider for the girls. 'No one's driving are they?'

'I left it in the long stay beyond the station,' Stephen tells Sarah. 'Could be fog later.'

'That's miles away.'

'We don't need the car.'

'Fair point. Wrap yer soup coolers round that, Stevo.'

'Cheers everyone!' Amy and Derek click bottles together.

Sarah pours her cider into a glass and does the same with Stephen's beer. 'Oh, I promised to show you photos of the Arnold Palmer crazy golf course, didn't I?' she laughs, handing her iPhone to Amy. 'There's a space rocket, and a watermill without any water in it! Can you imagine! And a hilarious little man who takes your money. He's always so grumpy. No idea why. A real jewel in the crown, isn't he, Stephen?'

'If that bloody rain stops for a few seconds we can all troop down to the pub for a few jars later,' Derek says. 'On Tripadvisor it says that …'

Amy glances at a couple of photos and places the phone on the table beside the chips.

'Have they all got vinegar on them?' Sarah asks, putting a brave face on the lack of interest in the crazy golf.

'None of them have. You brought vinegar with us,' Stephen replies. 'She prefers balsamic,' he explains to the other two.

'Good job you didn't ask for that in the chippie,' Amy giggles. 'Can you imagine?'

'Anyway,' Stephen says, changing the subject. 'Here's to Henrietta Street and a wonderful weekend. Cheers.'

'It's really good they don't use those horrible polystyrene trays anymore, isn't it?' Sarah explains as she shovels her chips onto a plate. 'And the chippie we found last time cooks in vegetable oil instead of beef dripping. Stephen, you did …'

'Yeah, yeah, they fried them separately.'

'Poor old Stephen can't smell anything. COVID,' Sarah tells the other two. 'Says everything is just fresh air, don't you?'

'Must be awful,' Amy sympathises. 'Don't know what I'd do without my nose. Do you come here every year then?'

'We used to before …' Stephen starts.

'Hang on! Hang on! … No!' Derek shouts at the television. "He should have scored. Three metres from the line! For fuck's sake. They're a bunch of blouses. Sorry mate, you were saying.'

Stephen shakes his head, it doesn't matter.

Outside hail has turned to rain. Lightning illuminates the lighthouses that stand on the piers like sentries against the North Sea.

'Well, this is gothic,' Amy says staring out of the window. 'Anyone fancy a séance in the graveyard?'

'You're mad. She's mad. Still, if it gets you in and out of that purple corset.' Derek flashes his eyebrows up and down suggestively at the other two. 'You know what I mean?'

Amy giggles.

Sarah is beginning to wonder if she will survive two days with Derek and Amy.

They open all the cupboards and find half a dozen games. Derek, who is on his third bottle of Newcastle Brown, declares he doesn't do board games. Stephen suggests cards. Derek suggests strip poker.

They play knock-out whist. At eleven o'clock Derek declares himself desperate for a bevvy.

'You can all stay here if you like but I going to find a pub and have a couple of proper pints, assuming they sell proper pints.'

He throws on his coat, grabs an umbrella from one of the carrier bags and throws open the front door. Water falls like a power shower out on Henrietta Street. Derek mouths an insult and steps out, slamming the door behind him.

'Oh Stephen, aren't you going to keep him company?' Amy says. 'We come all the way from Dorking.'

Before Stephen can reply, the door flies open and a broken umbrella is tossed into the cottage. The door slams a second time. Stephen looks at Sarah and sighs.

'There you go,' Amy coos. 'He'll be so happy. Don't stay all night!'

The two women watch Stephen leave, his hat pulled down hard over his ears.

'Men. Fancy watching Strictly on catch-up? I missed last week's.' Amy channel hops the television.

Sarah crosses to the window and stares out into the night, allowing the curtains to fall behind her to cut the reflections of the room. Across the harbour the lighthouses flash red and green in the darkness. She wants to open the window and hear the wind and waves and feel the salt air on her face. She senses infinity in the light shifting on the water.

Every ripple unique, from now until the end of time.

'Lovely, isn't it?' Amy says, squeezing in beside her. 'Looks just like an amusement arcade, all lit up like that. Derek and I love going down Hastings on bank holidays. All those big bikers on their machines, and the one-armed bandits.'

Sarah grits her teeth. Why are Amy and Derek so unspeakably dreadful?

Make an effort, Sarah.

'Shall we go for a walk?' she says. 'Down to the pier. You know this is where Dracula's ship landed in the story?'

'I just had my hair done.'

'Dracula won't mind. You can wear Stephen's anorak. I don't know why he didn't take it himself. You'll be dry as doughnuts.'

Amy hesitates.

'Mustn't let the boys have all the fun,' Sarah says.

Two minutes later the women are heading up Henrietta Street, the breeze at their skirts. The cobbles glisten slip with rain. Above them, the wind winds the chimney pots and rattles Amy's bling grade gold earrings. Sarah immediately feels more alive.

Amy grabs Sarah's arm. 'It's cold.'

'Really wakes you up, doesn't it? Oh, Sorry, Amy. You all right?'

'I'm fine. Have you got a hankie?'

Sarah gives her a tissue and Amy wipes away the tears.

'Sorry, I'm just a bit emotional.'

The path down to the pier is steep. They can hear the waves now, crashing the rocks, water sparking into the air. The lower notes of the undertow dragging the water back.

A lacklit night with no moon. Above them the serrated blade of the cliff rips apart the speeding clouds, bringing more rain down upon their heads. A crackle of lightning sparks the sky. The streetlights stand guard, fragile beacons in the noisy dark. Rain peppers their faces.

As they climb up from the low point and onto the harbour wall a creaking sound distracts Sarah. She turns this way and that, looking to locate the source.

'You sure it's safe?' Amy asks. 'Maybe we should …'

'It's absolutely fine. Come on.'

If it is fine, why is she hearing the creaking of wood against wood, rope tightening a noose, and shackles raw-rubbing ankles to the bone?

Back in the dark basement of the cottage, all is not well. A strip of wallpaper in the corridor beside the bathroom has started to tear. Quietly, fractionally. Fibre by fibre, stretching in a line from floor to ceiling then yielding like a paper zip.

Then the process starts again further along the wall.

CHAPTER 2

The east pier is broad as a sandstone tennis court and hundreds of metres long. Sarah has walked its length many times, and crossed the new bridge linking to the pier extension that juts out into the North Sea opposite its sister on the west pier to form a beetle's mandibles against the waves.

Compared with the pier, the bridge ahead is wafer-thin, taut as a high wire act, tough as a spider's web. Crossing it above the heaving water is exhilarating.

But right now, crossing the pier, she is apprehensive. Why does she feel that tonight the pier is not a bulwark to the sea? Tonight, it takes just a thimble of imagination to see the waves are not moving towards the pier but passing beneath it, as if the pier is the deck of wide tanker floating far from land.

Sarah breathes deep the salt air; the restless sea gives her wings.

She says nothing of this to Amy who is walking with her eyes glued to the floor, watching her every step, clutching Sarah's arm as if at any moment the wind might scoop her up and toss her into the harbour. Her leather trousers are soaked through and will stick to her thighs like Velcro when she tries to get out of them later on.

'Why are there all these square holes?' Amy asks. 'Look! Cut into the rocks. Why would someone do that?'

Sarah doesn't tell Amy that they are Lewis holes carved into the huge blocks to enable them to be hoisted into position when the pier was created. Nor does she tell her that they are the nests gouged out the solid rock by sandstone petrels, diminutive birds with the toughest beaks in the world. Amy doesn't want to know why the holes are there; she simply wants to talk, to know she is not alone.

Sarah leads Amy to the lighthouse and the two women sit in silence on the steps, looking back across the harbour at the town, its houses cradled between the cliffs like eggs in a nest.

The pink noise of the sea cocoons them, soothes them. The rain eases. The breeze wanes. A dog barks and headlights sweep up Khyber Pass, across the harbour, the vehicle hidden from view.

'Do you think he found Derek?' Amy asks.

'They met at the rugby club, didn't they?'

'I wouldn't want him to get lost. He'd already had a few when he left.'

'Stephen says they hardly see each other at work.'

'Different departments.'

'Forgive me for asking, Amy, but what do you do? For a job, I mean.'

'I'm having a year off. To sort out the curtains and things.'

Sarah doesn't really know how to respond. What can you say to someone who sees picking curtains as a meaningful way to pass a year?

'That's why I am so hot on décor,' Amy continues. 'It's a gift, I suppose. And a lot of work, obviously. Derek says he trusts me to make sure everything is tasteful.'

'There's only three or four pubs on Church Street,' Sarah says.

'I hope they do traditional Surrey bitters. Derek is very particular.'

'Amy, you are two hundred and fifty miles north of Surrey. The pubs will not be selling London beer.'

'Maybe we should be getting back.'

They all arrive back at the cottage at almost the same time.

'That's lucky!' Derek says, his words echoing up and down the street. 'We were about to knock the door down!'

'Shh,' Sarah says.

'Oi, fancy running up and down the Abbey Steps, Sarah? Stevie always says you have plenty of energy, if you know what I mean.'

'Please, love,' Amy pleads.

'It's the north, Amy! Nobody minds shouting on the street. It's part of the culture.'

Sarah opens the door and ushers them all inside. Stephen's face suggests that he has had enough of Derek for tonight.

'Where's the booze, babe?' Derek walks into the dining table, sending the place mats to the floor. 'Whoops-a-daisy.'

'I think it's time for bed,' Amy says, steering him back toward the hall.

'Need the john. The old can-a-rooney.'

'It's downstairs.'

'What's the point of that?'

'It's just the way it is, Derek,' Stephen says, in a voice that betrays his fading patience.

Derek staggers down the steps.

'Bloody light's gone!' he shouts at the bottom.

'We know,' Stephen says. 'I'll sort it in the morning. There's a torch on the last step.'

A loud bang. Stephen and Sarah exchange glances. Amy shrugs apologetically. Muffled garbled singing drifts up from the basement.

'A thousand quid deposit,' Stephen mutters. 'If he breaks anything …'

'He'll be all right in the morning,' Amy suggests. 'Just a little nervous, that's all.'

Twenty minutes later both couples have retired to their bedrooms and the cottage is dark. No one has noticed the rectangular rip in the wallpaper in the corridor beside the bathroom. Sarah has noticed the smell, like melting animal fat, but for want of a better explanation has decided that the source must be Derek. She will wash and disinfect the bathroom floor in the morning.

'They're saying sunshine from 8 o'clock until around 10.' Stephen is in bed checking the weather on his phone.

'Maybe we can go for a walk and leave them a note.'

'We can't just ignore them. We invited them.'

'*You* invited them, Stephen.'

Stephen sighs, puts his phone on the bedside table and switches off his bedside lamp. 'Night.'

He is snoring after just a few seconds. Sarah envies him. It will take her an hour to get to sleep. It always does, worrying about the morning. Is everything organised? Did they bring enough food for sandwiches? Is the front door locked?

The light from the street cuts into the room above the curtains, casting a thin stripe across the ceiling. If they were in the other bedroom, she would have the curtains open and the window too. They aren't as close to the water's edge as they were in the hotel at Robin Hood's Bay where the waves lulled them both to sleep but she knows the night air will be full of sound.

Abruptly the streetlight outside cuts out. More lightning. Another power cut. Sarah hopes it comes back on quickly before the cottage cools down.

In the basement the smell is thickening. The air tastes of hot meat and the wallpaper is becoming greasy.

CHAPTER 3

By the time Derek staggers drunkenly downstairs to empty his bladder, sometime after 2am, the basement is in a curious state of flux. The only light source is a faint blue wash spilling through the frosted glass of the bathroom window that gives onto the alley beside the house. Derek stands to urinate, his shoulder leaning against the wall, his back to the open bathroom door, his head throbbing.

Out in the corridor behind him the wallpaper continues to rip, a whispering hiss like a skater etching a groove on a frozen lake. Wisps of mist emanate from this jagged line, curling, drifting, folding. Thin tendrils of smoke probe the lacklight.

Searching for something.

The groove rises then turns then turns again until, all at once, it becomes a panel of ripped paper that curls and buckles to reveal behind it … a door. A door that is opening for the first time in two hundred years. Dark voices whisper hoarsely in the shadows beyond the door. Metal grinds over metal and someone stamps his boots against the cold.

Derek is almost done. He catches sight of himself, a shadow in the dark monochrome reflection in the mirror over the sink. The mother of all hangovers throbs the tendons of his neck. Why has he drunk so much? Why does he always drink so much? Why is it so bloody dark?

The air stinks. Has he pissed himself? That's all he needs. Smells like a fat fryer but nastier. He fills a cupped hand with cold water from the tap and drinks it. Tastes weird. How can something as boring as tap water taste different depending on where you are? What he would give for a pint of Dorking's finest H2O.

Footsteps in the corridor.

Shit, he forgot to close the door.

'Out in a minute,' he calls.

A last handful of water, splashed across his face this time. He crosses the bathroom, each step rattling the vertebrae beneath his skull. On the threshold into the corridor a wide rough hand slaps him full in the face, muffling his cry. Other hands grab him and pin his arms behind his back.

'March him out lads. If he squeals run him through.'

A gnarled hairy face thrusts itself in front of Derek. 'You'll not try anything stupid.'

The other man's breath is fetid. He raises a lantern to peer up into Derek's eyes. Dirty smoke rises from the flick-fluckering flame. Burning grease in a saucepan.

Derek is so drunk he doesn't even register that he is being pushed towards a door that wasn't there moments ago. He does glance up the stairs and shake his face free from the limpet hand over his mouth, but before he can shout for help he feels a blade at his throat.

Out in the alley, Derek's hands are pulled behind his back and tied together. He shivers, he isn't wearing shoes. He is in the clothes he had on when he collapsed on the bed; shirt and trousers. He can see his breath.

Four men, two of whom are carrying old-fashioned lanterns. A pungent smell. Not the smoke stink of the lanterns, something else. A weird blue glow hangs by the back of the house.

'Move.'

They're walking along behind the houses and then down narrow irregular steps down towards the harbour. Muddled-headed, Derek complies, assumes that this is all part of some stupid festival stunt or a Whitby initiation thing. That's why they're in costume.

And if Stephen …

… oh, now he gets it. It's Stephen and his stuck-up wife Sarah! They're behind this. It's all 'matey, join us for a perfect weekend in t'North' while secretly organising the mother of all humiliate-a-thons.

They're probably in the cottage laughing like drains.

Well, he will not give them the satisfaction of shouting out. Let them worry. Let them end up dialling 999 when he doesn't reappear and then get sued for wasting police time. Teach them a bloody lesson.

A painful kick in the back of the thigh brings him back to the here and now.

'Shall we truss him up like a turkey?' a rough voice laughs behind Derek.

'Tar and feather the bugger!' said in a strange accent.

At the bottom of the steps a rowing boat, piled high with boxes and barrels, is waiting in the rippling shadows. In it sits a scruffy girl with large dark eyes and thick curly hair poking out from beneath a black tarpaulin hat that is several sizes too large. Maybe nine years of age, she holds a lantern and looks deadly serious.

The men bundle Derek aboard. He stumbles, cracks his head against something and ends up face down spluttering in a puddle of dirty harbour water as the boat is pushed away from the steps into deeper water. One after the other the men scramble aboard and the boat slip slides the liquid darkness, its momentum juddering to the rhythm of the oars.

Derek struggles to understand the conversation - the accents and the vocabulary leave him at a disadvantage - but he does learn that they are heading towards "the ship", that they "lose the tide" in an hour, and that there is a "good breeze out on the drink". He feels the cold in his feet and hopes that the *entertainment* is soon brought to a close. Though it pains him to admit it, the whole thing is very realistic and is clearly well organised but, if he catches a cold, or worse, he will sue.

The harbour is dark, there must be a power cut. Presently the boat bumps up against a second vessel; a hollow thump of wood against wood. Thick ropes and a net drop from above and the boxes and barrels hoisted aloft. Without addressing him directly, the crew manhandle Derek onto the net and he is lifted into the air and dumped unceremoniously onto the deck of a ship and there's that pungent smell again coming directly from the planks under his nose. Suddenly it comes to him; tar. The smell of road repairs. Everything stinks of it.

A rat peers at him from the shadows beside a hessian sack.

'Does someone want to tell me when this bit of fun finishes?'

No one is listening. The men scramble aboard and the boat is lifted up out of the water with the young girl still in it. Low voices are exchanged, there must be twenty people busying themselves on the deck, shifting stuff around, tying boxes down.

Derek has had enough. 'Hey! Hey!' he shouts. 'Yes, you with the hair. Untie me and take me to the organiser. Right now.'

He feels the vibration of the planks behind him but before he can roll over, his wrists tied behind his back, a hand grabs his face from behind, pulls open his jaw and stuffs a rag into his mouth. The smell of tar is overwhelming and Derek starts to gag helplessly.

Running footsteps. A screeching hinge as a hatch opens on deck.

'Quick lads, haul anchor, lower the sails, man the boats and haul us away,' hisses a new voice. 'We must be gone or we'll be grounded!'

Derek's shouts have not passed unnoticed on the shore. A distant voice starts to shout. 'Pressers! Bastards are back! Wake up, wake up!'

The ship comes alive as some of the crew race up into the

rigging to attend to the sails, while others lower two boats into the water. A chain rattles. The anchor is hauled up. Ropes are dropped and attached to the boats, and the crew, six in each boat, pull their oars to drag the ship into motion.

The noise grows on the shoreline as half a dozen locals gather to hurl insults at the ship. Stones are raining onto the deck and Derek finds himself dragged quickly, on his back, to the safety of an overhang.

The ship approaches the constriction of the harbour jaws to a raucous chorus of jeering from the piers but now the sails catch the edge of the wind and start to fill. The boats, no longer needed, come alongside the ship and the men scramble back aboard doing their best to dodge missiles, mainly stones, from the pier.

'Heave men, heave!'

Water drips beneath the keels as the rowboats are lifted out of the harbour. A man shouts as a rock catches him on the temple and fells him. Two women rush out from beneath a tarpaulin to grab the victim and drag him to safety.

Now between the harbour jaws, the ship starts to ride the swell, rocking and yawing in the waves. In seconds the ship escapes onto the open sea. Cheers erupt around the ship; they have made it by the skin of their teeth.

Amy sits up in bed and wonders where Derek is.

Utterly bewildered by unfolding events and hidden from view in the shadows of a tarpaulin, Derek falls into a drunken slumber on a wooden ship sailing out of Whitby.

It starts to snow.

CHAPTER 4

It is late afternoon. A sharp wind rattles the rigging and billows the sails. Derek has absolutely no idea where he is or, for a second, even who he is.

He does know that he has a hangover. His head lies at right angles to moving feet and legs. He is lying on a ship's deck, frozen to the core, and lucky that someone has kindly covered him in blankets or he might not have survived. A thin coating of snow covers every surface.

The sound of laughter. Male and female. The smell of food.

'He's awake!' shouts a child's voice.

A young girl stops in front of him and bends down to peer into his face. The girl from the rowboat.

'Now then,' she says, her face as serious as when he first set eyes on her. Was it last night?

Derek stares back, lost for words.

'You'll need your wits about you. We crossover soon,' she says. 'Shall I sit you up?' She takes the gag from his mouth.

Cross over?

Derek makes a pathetic effort to sit up. 'Can't do anything with my hands behind my back.'

The girl produces a long knife from the folds of her clothing and steps over him. Derek flinches. The girl laughs. The knife slices his ropes effortlessly. Derek immediately dreams of escape.

The girl shakes her head, second-guessing him. 'There's nowhere to go, lad. Dost thou need water?'

Derek sits up and looks about him. Whitby has disappeared. They are out at sea. Some distance away are snow-covered cliffs. A large gull glides into view then out again. Bird calls, harsh as rusty hinges, and all around them the muttering of waves.

Why has she called him 'lad'?

The sun bursts the clouds, low on the horizon, blinding him in golden light.

'We're heading north,' he observes.

'Aye. For a short while yet,' she agrees. 'I'll be back.'

'Wait, what's your name?'

'Lizbet.' And she is gone.

Derek stretches his legs, swings his head back and forth. The hangover isn't as bad as it might be, all things considered, though the movement of the ship is making him nauseous. He decides to stand up and, as the tarpaulin slips from him, is immediately shocked at how cold it is on the deserted deck.

The ship is in full sail and moving more quickly than he would have imagined possible. The stiff breeze is invigorating. He crosses unsteadily to the port side and wonders if he has the strength to swim to shore. They are maybe a mile out. He has swum a mile more than once.

In a swimming pool. How long would I last in these waters? Five minutes?

One way or another he must escape this ridiculous pantomime, or demand that the organisers drop him ashore. Amy will be frantic if he doesn't …

I've still got my phone!

He feels its weight in his trousers. Thank God for technology! The Goths can keep their top hats and brass goggles. The re-enactment societies can indulge their fantasies of a purer life free from plastics. The rest of us love the modern world, even if the broadband signal can be shitty and ready meals all taste the same and the country is going to the dogs because of little Englanders and their obsession with being Johnny-no-mates … At least we have our smart phones.

The phone is dead.

Not *your battery needs recharging icon* dead. Not *switch it off and on again* dead. Just dead.

Bloody bloody bloody hell!

Derek is not used to being denied. He is classic road rage material, especially when drunk or hung-over. Losing all sense of proportion, he almost hurls his phone in the sea then thinks better of it and shoves it back in his pocket. Instead he grabs the nearest object, a barrel of some sort, and walks to the side of the ship to throw it into the waves.

'Leave it, lad!' shouts a voice above his head. 'Or we'll throw thee in after it!'

Derek looks up and sees two pairs of eyes looking back. Two women up in the rigging, one holding a telescope, the other a tankard. They are both in loose brown clothes, their hair scraped back in ponytails. One wears a red kerchief.

'Throw that whisky over the side and it's a one-way journey to Davy Jones' locker,' says the second woman.

Who the hell are they? Hippie tarts playing at sailors? The whole situation is insane.

Derek puts the barrel back down on the deck and looks around. He could do with a drink.

A hand tugs at the sleeve of his thin polyester shirt. It is Lizbet. In one hand she holds a tankard, in the other a thick overcoat.

'Captain says I've to keep thee keep warm while we reach crossover. He wants thee fit for work. I've put a drop in t'water,' she winks.

Derek takes the coat and puts it on.

Her intense brown eyes study him from beneath her mop of dark tightly-curled hair as she hands him the tankard.

'Where can I charge my phone?' he asks.

She stares up at him quizzically, decides he isn't talking in English, and saunters off, disappearing down the hatch in the middle of the ship.

'And can someone find me some bloody shoes?' he shouts after her. 'Or is frostbite all part of the experience?'

The sun disappears as quickly as it arrived. It is time to find out where the captain is hiding. Derek follows the girl down the hatch.

The steps are steep and at the bottom Derek discovers that the ceiling is less than five feet above the floor. As he bends down, he is grabbed by two thickset sailors and pinned to the floor.

'Fetch Captain, Lass. This one's going walkabout.'

Lizbet, who is warming herself in the galley by the cook, nods and runs off towards the back of the ship. The food smells good. Derek is ravenous and would eat almost anything right now.

Footsteps drum the wooden boards and the captain appears with the girl at his side. Even without the extraordinary contraption upon his head Captain Jean-Jacques Elmo would appear remarkable. He is in his mid-forties, Derek would guess, tall and of slender build. His dreadlock hair and skin tone suggest that he is of mixed race. Unlike the rest of the male crew, he is clean-shaven. Derek cannot see the man's eyes; they are hidden between sets of brass eyepieces that are arranged in circles like the objective lenses mounted on the revolving nosepiece beneath a microscope. These lenses are fixed to a metal band that is in turn fixed to a leather helmet. The overall impression is of the compound eyes upon an insect's head.

As the captain gazes down to scrutinise Derek, the lenses rotate to afford him views of different magnification.

'Shall we throw him in the brig with the others?' asks one of the sailors holding Derek.

'No, Master Chisholm,' replies the captain. 'We are but a few minutes from crossover and need all hands on deck.' The captain turns towards the galley. 'Cook, feed this man a bowl of broth. He will need his strength. Where is Noah?'

'In the store, Captain,' Chisholm answers.

'I need him on deck to take instruction and steer us in.'

Chisholm nods. The captain departs, climbing the steps, leaving the cook to feed Derek. The two crewmen follow the captain. Lizbet gives the bowl to Derek along with a chunk of bread and indicates that he is to sit on the floor.

The soup rocks back and forth in the bowl as Derek raises it to his lips, there being no spoon. The ship has changed course and is fighting the waves rather than riding them. He is mopping up the damp patches of spilled broth from his shirt with his hunk of bread when the girl dumps a pair of worn boots in front of him. She doesn't wait to be thanked.

'Ahoy! Crossover ahead! All hands on deck!' shouts a woman's voice.

Half a dozen men emerge at speed from the fo'c'sle (a word Derek has yet to learn) and rush up the steps and out onto the deck. The air fills with the tumultuous grinding of wood against wood and the squeals of the rigging, unlocked, loosened, twisted, as instructions are barked back and forth.

'Hurry, lads! Drop the mizzen!' It is the captain's voice. 'Heave her round or we'll smash against the rocks! Pull! Pull, you miserable beggars!'

There is a loud bang followed by a blood-curdling scream.

'Free him, lads, or he is a dead man, mark my words!'

Cramming the last of his bread into his mouth, Derek shoves his feet into the boots given him by the girl, crushing a family of woodlice that have made their home in the right boot. Miraculously the boots fit. He heads up the steps.

The scene that awaits him takes his breath away.

CHAPTER 5

'Oh bloody hell!'

Sarah wraps the pillow round her head to block out the noise on the landing and get some shut-eye. Quite what Amy is doing out there sniffing and muttering is anyone's guess. Sarah does not want to become embroiled in a domestic; Derek is Amy's problem.

Sarah turns over and tries to think herself to sleep.

With limited success.

With zero success.

'Right,' she says, trying to create the sense of resolve and purpose that is eluding her.

She sits up and smashes her hand down on the quilt, this weekend is going to be a total washout and Stephen should have listened to her. Never ever book a whole weekend away with people until you have at least tried an evening together somewhere. She swings her legs out from under the quilt and reaches her toes out to find her slippers.

Stephen turns over and carries on snoring.

'What on earth is the problem?' Sarah hisses at Amy as she hauls opens her bedroom door and steps out onto the landing. 'It's the middle of the night.'

The lights are back on in the house. Amy stands in her pyjamas and slippers, shoulders slumped, her hair a tangled mess. Weirdly still wearing all her jewellery: earrings, necklace, rings, bracelets.

Who wears jewellery in bed?

Amy's face looks more natural without 20 coats of slap, so that's something, and Sarah decides Amy would be pretty if she wore less makeup and if her cheeks weren't drowning beneath a curtain of tears.

'The smell,' Amy says. 'Downstairs.'

'Where is Derek?'

'I went down but the smell. Sorry, Sarah. I really am. This weekend was meant to be so special.'

Sarah sniffs. Tar. Back at home the whole house stank of it for days after the workmen had fixed the garage roof. She grabs Amy's hand.

'Come on.'

The two women descend to the ground floor where the smell is noticeably stronger.

'Why build a house and put the toilet in the basement?' Amy sobs.

'None of these houses would have had inside lavatories when they were built. They were sailors' cottages.'

Sarah flicks the lower landing light switch. Nothing.

'Wait here,' she instructs Amy.

She returns from the bedroom with her smartphone in hand. Amy is in suspended animation, like one of those mechanical toys where the key has stopped turning and a wind up is necessary. Sarah lights the torch on her phone.

'You sure he isn't in bed?'

Animation finally in Amy's eyes. 'You think I wouldn't notice if he was in the bed?' she pouts.

'Only asking. Come on.'

It isn't just the smell of tar. The air tastes meaty and sweet. Both women wrinkle their noses. A cold draft is blowing.

'Does he have intestinal problems?' Sarah asks.

'Not like this!'

They see the muddy footprints before they see the door.

Sarah hesitates.

'Oh God!' Amy blurts standing behind Sarah. 'See if he's in the bathroom.'

You go and see if he's in the bloody bathroom, he's your sad excuse for a partner.

There is no way but down. Sarah descends, avoiding the mud, with Amy in her wake. The carpet is cold. A section of the wall has swung aside to reveal a black void like an open jaw. Sarah approaches cautiously.

'Where is he?' Amy groans from the bathroom.

As she emerges, she slips in the mud and falls to her knees, almost taking Sarah with her.

'Shh!'

There is sound emanating from the void beyond the door and a faint blue glow. Voices and what might be music. Sarah's heart is racing.

There wasn't a door there. There was a wall.

This is not normal.

Oh bravo. That's genius, Sarah.

'He's out there, isn't he?' Amy hisses. 'Oh God. Why has he gone outside? He's drunk. He could fall into the harbour and …'

'Right,' Sarah says, getting a grip. 'First we get dressed and wake Stephen. Then we decide what to do. Okay? We can't go out in our pyjamas.'

Amy nods helplessly.

'Agreed?'

Another nod.

'Right.' Sarah turns and heads upstairs with Amy in her wake.

Only when they are halfway up the stairs to the ground floor Amy decides she has not agreed. She about-turns, runs back down, crosses the muddy carpet and disappears through the open door into the night.

CHAPTER 6

It isn't funny anymore. If indeed it ever was funny.

Derek has never felt so afraid. He is stuck on board a ship heading straight at a cliff. The keel is scrapping noisily over hidden rocks, jagged limpet-covered stones ripping at the ship from beneath. Above the waves the vessel appears to be breaking up; the masts collapsing backwards towards the deck one after the other. Worse still, the captain is clearly insane, standing at the front of the ship, his coat tails flapping in the breeze, his telescopic lenses covering his face, urging his crew onward as they throw themselves towards certain catastrophe. If he stays on board, Derek is a dead man. If he jumps ship, he will be torn to shreds. As they enter the long shadow of the cliff, the whole crew is excitedly accelerating their certain demise.

'Heave, lads, heave! Wind the masts! Clip her wings, my hearties!'

Men and women loosen the rigging and haul the foremast back down towards the deck to lie upon the mainmast as they sing.

And when we reach the crossover
We haul the masts and sails
And ploughing fast toward the cliff
We stand as hard as nails

No fear or lily-livered frit
Will whimper in our eyes
As flushed with lion-hearted grit
We stay fixed on the prize

We'll take the ride
And hold our pride
And reach the other side!

Maybe fifty metres from the rocks and all the masts are now flush with the deck, the wood lost beneath a tumbled sea of rigging and white cloth. Moon sails, sky sails, royals, top gallants, top sails, jibs and spanker, all lying about, the yards, from which the sails hang, spun round to ensure nothing trails over the sides of the ship.

A crewwoman barges Derek aside as she passes, gripping a rope that springs up as tension is applied, almost catapulting Derek into the waves.

Captain Jean-Jacques Elmo is a man possessed, arms flailing in the spray of water that rises over him as the ship slaps the surface of the sea. And still the crew sing, like a death cult embracing the end of time.

Forty metres. Thirty. The light fading with every passing moment. Derek's eyes are adjusting to the darkness and he sees now that the black of the cliff is graduated; there is dark and there is darker still. An open maw of blackness darker than the pitch of night lies right ahead of them.

The ship's keel rough rumbles and scrapes the serrated seabed.

How can they be accelerating without the wind in their sails? Is a water current propelling them towards their deaths? Or dragging them like a river rushing to the waterfall's lip?

Is that a cave?

It is a cave! Derek can see it now. A large void the size of a house gouged into the solid rock, maybe ten metres wide and five metres high. It's insane. The captain is taking a whaling ship into a cave! To what end? And, if they do manage to avoid the sides, what next? Their speed will surely smash them to flotsam and jetsam.

His life about to end, Derek finds himself muttering sweet words to his mother; he has always loved her and will see her soon. He thinks briefly of Amy, a union made in a shared love of designer gin and leatherwear rather than in heaven but none the worse for that. He forgives himself for having become drunk; it wasn't his fault, his father should have shown him more affection and apologised for stepping on his model of the space station that Christmas. A career in insurance wasn't exciting and he should never have listened to Mr Small, his careers advisor. And the boss at Dorking Rugby Club always was and always will be a bigoted little shit who wouldn't recognise real talent if it bit him on the butt.

Derek is spared further self-indulgent introspection by a smack to the back of the head that sprawls him to the deck where he is hopelessly entangled in a sail as the ship crosses the threshold from sea to cave and begins the crossover the crew have been anticipating.

The noise is overwhelming. From wide open sea to narrow enclosed space screaming with grinding wood against stone, stone against iron, iron against wood. Derek braces himself for impact or rather he grabs armfuls of sail and blubs pathetically into the rough fabric, cursing his bad luck with a relentless stream of *Why me? Why me? Why is it always me?*

Two seconds. Five. Ten. Twenty.

The end does not come.

They are *not* in a cave … but in … a tunnel.

And the temperature is changing fast. The frozen winds on the North Sea are being replaced with warmer air. Around him in the darkness the crew hold lanterns that light patches of the rock speeding past the bows. The singing has been replaced by excitement, cheering and laughter.

'Hold fast! The crossover draws night!' The captain's shouts boom and echo in a glowing blue fog that grows with every passing second. 'We shall dine in style this night!'

A rush rumbling rumpus as the ship barges and bounces on wave after wave of water helter-skelter round corners in a furious waterfall wash of noise that takes them careering onwards until Derek gives up trying to make sense of anything and instead abandons himself to the ride.

The air is now positively warm and charged with scents and odours Derek cannot name. He lifts his head.

The captain still straddles the ship's prow, his telescopic eyepieces silhouetted against a golden light spreading along the roof of the tunnel. Elmo barks out orders 'Left … left … right .. left …' to persons Derek cannot see. The tunnel is growing and Derek cannot help but imagine the ship being a gobbet of food travelling upward along a vast subterranean oesophagus to be vomited somewhere as yet unknown.

All at once the journey does end and the ship is indeed regurgitated, flying out of the rock face to land back in the sea in front of the very cliff face it entered. For a few minutes the entire crew are silent, drained, overwhelmed, grateful to have survived.

Gentle rippling waves lick the ship's wounds.

Derek blinks and rubs his eyes. It is early evening. The cliff is still the cliff, sky above and water below. Aside from that, everything is new.

The air is balmy in sunset's afterglow. Some distance away large birds are diving into the sea. Gannets perhaps? Derek disentangles himself from the sail and clambers to his feet. The crew are busying themselves, working purposefully like a colony of ants.

One of the birds is flying towards the ship.

Derek swallows hard. He's been to museums and watched television and he knows what he is seeing. But it's just not possible. It must be a weird drone of some sort.

CHAPTER 7

Sarah stands at the top of the basement stairs, arms akimbo, ready to scream in frustration.

Count to ten, Sarah. That's it.

How stupid can a person be? Sarah does not know what lies beyond the open door but she does know that only an idiot would imagine that the best thing you could do is to run through it. And only a double idiot, or Amy, would run out without even any flipping shoes on! In November!

While she feels the urge to protect Amy from herself, Sarah is not about to sign fate a blank cheque.

Should she close the door? How can a door suddenly appear in a house? What is Stephen going to say? He was already terrified about losing the deposit. The mud on the carpet will freak him out, never mind the wallpaper disaster. She buries her face in her hands in frustration.

You can't leave them out there.

The whole thing is a nightmare. Checking first that her feet are clean and that she isn't treading mud all over the cottage, Sarah goes back upstairs to the bedrooms. Stephen is still snoring happily.

Men.

She gathers her clothes and gets dressed. Thermals, fleece, geography trousers, hat. She makes no attempt to be quiet, hoping that Stephen will wake up and ask what is happening. But no. It's the same every morning as she gets up to get ready for school. She's up at ten to six while he sleeps. She's been at work for a couple of hours before he trundles into the office.

In her rucksack she finds her torch and penknife, and spots

her personal safety alarm. Might as well take it. You never know.

She pauses at the bedroom door. I suppose it makes sense him staying in the house, it's best that someone stays to keep an eye on everything. Even if he is as much use as Rip Van Winkle.

The door to the other bedroom is ajar. While Amy's clothes are piled up on the dressing table, her leather trousers hanging weirdly over the back of the chair like a flailed skin, Derek's are nowhere to be seen. The quilt bears the impression of his body and his pyjamas are folded and untouched at the foot of the bed; he must have collapsed in a drunken stupor on the bed and so may still be dressed.

Which is something.

Down in the entrance Sarah finds her walking boots and … sees Derek's shoes beside them. He's also gone out in bare feet! Checking her phone is well charged, she writes a note to Stephen, which she pops against the pepper pot on the table, and heads down to the basement.

Nothing has changed. The lights are still dead, the mud is still on the carpet. The door that should not be there is still open.

Sarah zips up her anorak and crosses the threshold, pulling the door to behind her. Upstairs the note to Stephen is caught in a gust of air and floats to the floor, landing face down under the sofa.

Sarah sniffs the air. It is thick with coal soot. She recognises the smell from having visited the Beamish Museum near Durham as a child and from the crusty coal tar soap bar her elderly grandmother has festering in her downstairs lavatory.

No lights anywhere, other than the faint blue glow in the air, there must be another power cut, which is strange because the lights were on upstairs. But most unpleasantly there is the smell, like an open sewer but worse, fetid and sweet, like crap, vomit and caramel all rolled together. Sarah gags, buckled over. Should she go back inside? But who will rescue Amy and Derek? Walking behind the houses until she reaches the alley she is again overcome by the stench and turns back towards the open door, but can no longer see it.

Just get on with it. Find them and bring them back.

Down to the beach or up onto Henrietta Street? She has no idea where Derek will have gone, but Sarah is pretty certain that Amy will have chosen the street in preference to fumbling her way down a dark alley towards the sea.

At first glance everything looks comfortingly normal on Henrietta Street, except for the lack of lighting. The houses and cottages all look the same. Most of them. A few look better than fine. Good as new, in fact. The town must have a renovation programme.

To her right are the 199 steps up to the abbey. Amy is looking for Derek. Will she assume he has wondered off to find a late-night pub?

The sound of approaching footsteps clatters the cobbles and echoes in the lacklight. Instinctively, Sarah presses herself into the shadows beside a wall. Hard hobnailed boots perhaps. A couple of people, maybe more, approaching from Church Street. And not just footsteps. Something else. Maybe wheels turning?

'I tell thee, she won't budge while her man's not back.'

'We've four bairns. They'll not survive on fresh air.'

'Try Angry Bob. Won't he lift finger?'

'Don't be daft. He's in his cups from dawn to dusk. And has troubles of his own.'

The voices are almost upon her. Black silhouetted against dark grey, three forms appear. Two women, breathing heavily, are bent over, pushing a rough wooden cart with a dodgy wheel that jumps and clicks as wood grinds against wood. The cart is piled high with boxes and what looks like cloth, though it is so dark Sarah is unsure quite what she is seeing. The women wear long dresses, aprons, and headscarves. Oblivious to Sarah's presence, they continue up the street.

Sarah wonders what business they have on the street; they are plainly locals and not tourists. All the houses are now holiday lets.

None of your business.

When they are a safe distance away, Sarah emerges from the shadows and hurries down the street in the opposite direction, glad of her quieter footwear. She is keeping a grip on her emotions; it is hard work. Something is plainly very wrong. The shops are unfamiliar. The tourist nick-nack shops have all changed their window displays and that smell is everywhere, her nose is choking with it. Meaty, sweet, sickening, putrid. She is torn again between the urge to run back to the cottage and the determination to find Amy; however dumb the woman is, she does not deserve what will surely happen to her if she stays out here.

Torch in one hand and her personal protection alarm in the other. She daren't switch on the torch for fear of drawing attention to herself. As she makes her way down Church Street, at once reassuringly familiar and yet utterly different, Sarah's conscious mind will not allow her to admit where she is, but her subconscious has already adjusted. In some impossible unfathomable way she has found herself in …

No, it's not possible. Don't be stupid.

Through the open maw of a side alley leading to one of a dozen yards that lie behind Church Street, she hears screaming, followed by a cacophony of voices calling for quiet.

'Let sleep, the pair of you!'

'Beat her in the morning, John, I'm up at dawn,' shouts a second voice.

A loud clanging sound, followed by a male howl of anguish this time.

‘Take that, you drunken shit,’ screams a woman in the darkness.

‘I’ll come and give the pair of you black eyes if you don’t shut up!’

Sarah moves on, having replaced her personal alarm with her open penknife.

In a doorway by Arguments Yard, two skinny children stare fearfully from beneath a pile of rags, as she passes. A rat scurries out from beneath an ill-fitting door and hurries off up the street, a blur of fur hugging the shop fronts.

How far can Amy have got? Will she be cautious? Will she have seen enough of Whitby on their arrival to properly understand how wrong everything is?

‘Derek! Derek!’

Amy’s voice echoes in the cold dark up ahead.

Oh Amy, you stupid cow!

As if to underscore the risk to life and limb, the drunken laughter of a group of men erupts somewhere in the lacklight to her right. Sarah surges forwards, desperate to arrive before it is too late.

CHAPTER 8

Arms akimbo before his crew, the telescope helmet finally off his head, Captain Jean-Jacques Elmo breathes deep the evening air and smiles.

'Ah, the sweet spice smell of home! One day, lads and lasses, I promise, all of ye shall dine with me in Port-au-Prince!'

The crew cheer and stamp their feet in celebration. Derek, who is standing at the back of the ship, is confused. As well he might be. Twenty minutes ago he was on the North Sea, a few hours before that he was in a cottage in Whitby, and now they've dropped anchor in the West Indies? He sort of understands that this has to be some kind of theme park experience but cannot for the life of him work out how it is done. For maybe the first time in his life, he decides the best course of action is to keep a low profile and say absolutely nothing to anyone. Maybe he can clamber over the masts, riggings and sails that are spread across the deck, sneak through the open hatch to the lower decks and wait for the show, or nightmare, to pass.

No such luck.

'Blood and thunder! Does thou sleep, friend?'

Derek spins round to find himself face to face with Master Chisholm, the man who would have thrown him in the brig, whatever that is, if the captain had not directed otherwise.

'Tis time to rebirth the ship, haul the masts, right the rigging, and span the sails. To the bowsprit and make lively or I'll slap thee in irons.'

Derek nods constructively. Chisholm strides off to organise the works, with Derek trailing along behind; he has no idea what a bowsprit is but being slapped in irons sounds painful and best avoided.

They start at the front of the ship and work towards the back, reversing the sequence of mast lowering that preceded their arrival at the cave for the crossover. It is backbreaking work, even with the windlass and capstans to winch the ropes that lift the masts. First the bowsprit, which was retracted into the body of the ship, is pushed back through, then each mast, each as tall as a tree and heavy with sails and rigging, must be lifted from horizontal to vertical on massive hinges, bolted and locked into place against the submasts that rise up out of the deck.

Tilting a mast from horizontal to vertical one degree at a time requires almost superhuman effort from twenty of the crew. Derek thought he was fit, he plays rugby for Dorking RFC second fifteen, he's a big guy, but twenty minutes man-handling the foremast of a whaling ship leaves him feeling as weak and useless as pedalo at a speedboat race.

There are maybe forty crew, if you include everyone from the brawny sailors to the young girl Lizbet, plus himself and two others who have been brought from the brig to help. They work in shifts - every last man and woman - some heaving, others turning the windlass, all singing as before, in English but in half a dozen different accents. Captain Elmo leads by example, working as hard as any. Soon it is fully dark and still they toil, tensioning the rigging by lantern light, till the deck is slick with sweat.

Finally the job is done. The anchor is raised and the sails lowered. In a tumultuous racket of creaking, the breeze fills the sails and the ship begins to move! Those who know the stars know the ship is hauling south.

Water, whisky, and rum flow freely and the crew recover from their arduous labours. Squeezeboxes, a violin, flutes and drums are produced. One of the drummers plays what looks to Derek like the djembe drums he played at school. Shanties are sung. Space is cleared and the deck timbers pulse to the rhythm of jigs and hornpipes. Some of the songs have a decidedly African feel, one of the squeezebox players, known as Haitian Pierre by some of the crew and simply Pierre by everyone else, is black and sings in what almost sounds like French but isn't quite. Someone produces a set of bagpipes. Someone else a banjo. The crew and the music seem to come from half a dozen different countries, the West Indies, North America, Scotland, France, Scandinavia, Ireland and England. Derek is happy to gulp down pints of water, and a fair amount of spirits, sit in the shadows and observe. He has no idea why he is here, wherever here is, and even less idea how he will get back to where he should be. But *here* is, at least for the moment, less frightening than it has been. He keeps his mouth shut and his eyes open.

Human resilience in the face of adversity is a story as old as time; it's funny how one small detail can lift the spirits and, for Derek, the discovery that two of the people thrown in the brig are clearly like him is the best news he has had in hours. They exchange brief smiles. A youth of around fourteen and a girl of maybe the same age, both in ordinary twenty-first century clothes, jeans and t-shirts.

He recognises them! The kids carrying stuff from the car parked in front of them when they first arrived on Henrietta Street! The bright colours of their clothes stand out, even in the lamplight because, aside from the captain in his bright blue jacket with gold brocade and epaulettes, everyone else wears the same drab beiges, greys and browns.

Emboldened by the discovery that he is not alone, Derek gets to his feet and begins to copy the moves of the hornpipe dancers, much to the amusement of Lizbet who rolls about helplessly as she points him out to her neighbours.

'He dances like a drunken octopus!' laughs a woman.

'Maybe it's the tightness of his breeches,' wheezes Irish Joe, a short man with a scruffy beard, and a twinkle in his eye.

'Go on, Beth. Put the giant through his paces,' a second woman, Alice, shouts above the music. 'Hey, Pierre, play something dazzling fast from the Indies.'

Egged on by the crew, Beth, as tall as many of the men, her red hair tied back, her green eyes sharp as an eagle's, her face a carpet of freckles, finishes the tankard of rum she is holding, crosses the deck, grabs Derek's hand and hauls him to the centre.

The dancers form two lines and bow, and the chaos begins. Derek has never before brought so much happiness to so many people. They watch him flounder about, attempting to dance a hornpipe to a music that blends the sinuous melody of a hornpipe with the intricate rhythms of African drumming. Laughter fills the balmy night air. Aside from folding your arms, something that Derek accomplishes effortlessly, the simplest of moves requires strength, coordination and precision. Within seconds he has given all the other dancers bruised toes and shins, inadvertently shoved a man headfirst into the mainmast, caught his shoe on a rope and slammed himself to the deck, and nearly given Beth a black eye. He also learns that dancing takes the wind out of you. He spins round gasping for air, desperately trying to catch up.

'No! *Turn* the toe and *pull* the heel, Fool!' Beth barks at him. 'Now the other side. The *other* side! Oh, may the Lord protect us!'

'You were wrong, Beth. Even an octopus in his cups dances better than this cod's bladder!' Irish Joe is on his knees, slapping the deck to the music in rapturous glee.

'Enough. Enough!' laughs Captain Elmo, above the noise. 'Let's the poor fool catch his breath. We cannot have half the crew injured by such pudding-headed buffoonery.'

The music drifts to a stop. The dancers stagger off, clutching whatever needs clutching and, head spinning from the exercise and the alcohol, Derek sinks to his knees and crawls to the side.

A kick in the ribs brings him to his senses. Derek looks up to find a thickset sailor with a broken nose and three missing teeth glowering down at him.

'You'll leave Beth be, if you have any wits about thee,' he snarls. 'I catch thee with her and you're shark food. Understood?'

A second man leans into view and smiles malevolently. He is clutching a long serrated cutlass that he brandishes in Derek's face. 'We've seen off bigger men than thee. Shall I spill his guts, Bill?'

'He'll keep,' replies the first man, treading on one of Derek's hands.

The second man glances to his right and tugs Bill's sleeve and they slope away.

The captain approaches. 'What did those two want with thee?'

'Nothing,' Derek replies, climbing to his feet.

No one likes a snitch.

'They're hard workers, but bear too many grudges. Bill Stanway has his eye on Beth, though she has sent him packing more than once. Like his lickspittle associate Silas, he is all brawn and no brain. If either give thee trouble, come to me. Work hard and I'll look after you.'

Derek nods.

'We'll need our wits about us when the sun rises,' Captain Elmo shouts, for the benefit of all on deck. 'Thank the Lord for our good fortune this day and prepare ye thy hearts for the morrow! Though we be born of earth we must be brave as lions in our work. Wrap yourselves in beauty sleep and sweet dreams, my hearties, and savour this good night!'

With that the captain disappears to his quarters. In the

twinkling of an eye the crew are transformed from rowdy revellers to competent company, each person setting themselves to the task of tidying the deck with a seriousness of purpose that takes Derek by surprise.

'Hey.' A hand tugs at his shirt.

Derek turns to find the two kids from the brig.

'You have to help us,' says the boy.

'Where are we?' asks the girl.

'You were in the car ahead of us,' Derek says. 'You probably didn't see me; I was in the back of the car.'

'The red Toyota?'

Derek nods. 'You've a good memory for detail.'

'She's a swot.'

'I'm Aleka and this is my twin brother Nat. So you were kidnapped too? Last night? It's your height and clothes that give you away.'

'I told her it's not a kidnapping, we've been pressed. The pressgangs, you know?' Nat presses his hands together to illustrate his point.

'That's ancient history, not the 21st century,' Aleka corrects him.

'Oh, smart. 21st century? Yeah, I get it. The 21st century that has pirates and whaling ships and no electricity or phones or anything. And sodding pterodactyls?' Nat flaps his arms like a giant bat. 'Let's not forget them. *That* 21st century, yeah?'

'It's pterosaur, not pterodactyl, Dumbo. Pterodactyls are a type of pterosaur.'

'Swot.'

Derek watches the pair of them squabbling and smiles. Pterodactyls? As mad as it sounds, he is comforted to learn that he is not the only one mistaking the drone that flew above the ship for a pterodactyl.

'I wonder why they threw you both in the brig,' Derek muses.

Before either kid can answer they are all distracted by the sight of a sailor scrambling up the rigging in his bare feet faster than if he were walking on the deck.

'Guess,' Nat says, getting back to business.

'Asking too many questions?' Derek ventures.

'Will you help us escape?' Aleka changes the subject.

'She was demanding to know where the toilets were and kicking off about having to go over the side,' Nat sneers. 'So we got locked up and she had to use a bucket.'

Aleka looks daggers at Nat. 'Not cool, bro.'

A crunching sound followed by a scream that rips the air above them. Hanging by his feet from the rigging, the sailor is tangled up in one of the flapping drones, his head caught and his body shaking violently from side to side.

'No shit!' Nat shouts.

The kids scramble to safety under a sail while Derek looks around for somewhere to hide. He spots a pile of potatoes on the deck, grabs a couple, and throws them at the drone that looks remarkably like a living creature. They hit their target but have no effect on the situation. Finding a long metal bar propped up against the mainmast, Derek takes it, crosses to the side of the boat and swings up onto the rigging. It is hard enough climbing a web of ropes with two hands. With one hand it is all but impossible.

'Here, use this!'

Nat is standing beneath him on the deck, offering up a short sword. Derek drops the bar, grabs the sword and slips it into his belt. As he climbs, his face and upper body are quickly drenched in blood pouring from the screaming man above.

It must be three metres across from wing tip to wing tip, its dark leathery wings flapping noisily. The rigging is shaking about making it even harder for Derek to climb up. Gripped in its jaws or beak …

It can't be a drone.

… blood pouring from the side of his head, the sailor looks pleadingly at Derek.

Derek is finally almost level with the mayhem. Wrapping one arm in the rigging to secure himself, he draws his sword and lunges at the beating wings.

Miss.

Miss.

On the third attempt he catches a wing. The blade cuts into the thick fabric …

Skin not fabric.

… and the creature's movement does the rest, ripping the blade through the canvas-like membrane. The beast howls and flaps, smacking Derek hard against the rigging and ripping the sword from his hand.

Derek has done enough. As the sword falls into the sea below, the animal releases the sailor from its jaws and backs away, shrieking into the night sky. Derek closes his eyes momentarily and catches his breath. Suddenly the rigging is shaking violently again. Derek looks abound desperately, expecting to be ripped to pieces himself. But no, the shaking comes from two other sailors who are coming to the rescue, racing up the rigging. They grab the sailor and help him to sit up, relieving the pressure on his feet and ankles. Having checked that Derek is able to hang on, the sailors accompany their injured comrade down, shouldering his weight and helping him to plant his feet safely.

Other hands grab him and lift him down onto the deck where his wounds are washed and first aid is administered. By the time Derek steps down onto the deck the captain is waiting.

'Well done, lad. A crewman lives thanks to thee. What is your name?'

'Derek.' As he says his name, he thinks to himself how unspeakably stupid it sounds, how out of context.

But Captain Elmo doesn't think so or, if he does, passes no comment. 'Let us all go below, Derek. It is safer there. Tomorrow we have much to do and I will talk with thee. You may dance like a drunken octopus but thou hast shown courage this night. And strength.' He turns to those gawping. 'Someone fetch this man a pot of rum, he has earned it.'

They are all safely below deck with the hatch closed, the cramped space lit by three or four lanterns, when they hear a series of large objects land on the deck above and begin walking about, poking and pulling at things as they shriek among themselves.

With the crew's thanks ringing in his ears, an empty tankard in his right hand and now drunk as a skunk, Derek lies down with a sack of flour for a pillow and a sack of questions to ruffle his brain. Is it Saturday evening? What's happening in Whitby? What's Amy doing? Are the police looking for him? Where is he? Is any of this real or did someone put something in his rum? What are those weird lamps floating inside metal spheres that keep the flame upright however much the ship rocks?

And it's not just him, somewhere on board there's two kids in jeans. What about their parents? They all have to escape, but how? And where to?

Derek is lying against a wall close to a passage that leads towards the back of the ship. A conversation is taking place in the passage and fragments of it are reaching Derek.

'... and if he keeps off the grog the gollumpus may be of use but why the other two? They are too young to ...' A woman's voice.

'I didn't ... because we sent ...' A male voice. The captain?

'Horse feathers! If they can swim ... If not, throw them back.'

'... into the interior once more then leave this place for good.'

‘Wasting more lives? Have we learnt nothing from …?’

‘Her knowledge saved us. Anyway we must sleep. Enough!’

Derek sags back upon his sack of flour, as tired as dad jokes. For the first time in as long as he can remember he finds himself praying.

Please let me wake up in that little cottage beside my dippy, expensive and well-meaning girlfriend and spend the whole day shuffling round Arnold Palmer's sodding crazy golf course in the snow with boring Stephen and his sanctimonious vegan treasure, Sarah. Amen.

CHAPTER 9

'Take five steps back, turn round and be off with ye!' shouts a middle-aged woman, raising a wooden staff above her head. 'I'll not tell ye twice.'

She is a stout woman, strongly built and used to hard work. And she's seen off tougher men than this rabble.

'And I'll tell thy wife, John. For shame,' she adds for good measure.

The three men mutter and stagger away into the darkness. Sarah and Amy relax a little. Amy is shivering, her teeth are chattering. The mud clinging to her pyjamas shows she has fallen at least once. Sarah removes her anorak and wraps it round Amy's shoulders.

'Follow me,' Rebecca tells them. 'You'll not survive long out here in whatever it is that you are wearing.'

'We're looking for someone.'

'That's as maybe. But I'm not stopping out here in rain. I'm Rebecca.'

They follow the light of Rebecca's lantern out of the town square back into Church Street. A little way along she steps into an alley that leads to one of the yards. Sarah has visited many of the yards before on previous visits to Whitby but she has never seen them looking, sounding and smelling as they do tonight. She and Amy hesitate, wrinkling their noses.

Rebecca turns back. 'You're not from round here. With your strange attire and turned up noses. Have you never smelled trying-out before?'

'What?'

'Trying-out.'

'It stinks,' says Amy.

Rebecca looks at the pair of them and laughs. 'If you don't like the stench of boiling blubber, why have ye both come to Whitby? It's what we do. That and fishing. There's a trying-out pot in every yard.'

'Whale blubber?' Sarah asks.

'Is there another kind?' Rebecca retorts. 'Come, I'll not dawdle all night with pair of you.' She grabs Amy's sleeve and tugs her forwards through the dense miasma of coal smoke and steam that billows out into the alley.

It's like drowning in thick fish soup Amy decides, wriggling free from Rebecca's grip to linger by the open door, in spite of the smell, because the stones flags are wonderfully warm beneath her bare feet.

Sarah pushes her forwards, Rebecca is already five metres ahead, her shoes clattering on the stone flags. A couple of lanterns create yellow pools in the darkness.

The Whitby woman is waiting for them outside one of the cottages. Tin baths hang on hooks by the front doors.

'Mind pots and boxes. We brought them in because of the rain.'

The hall is piled high with so much junk it is almost impossible to get through. Metal buckets, wicker baskets, wooden boxes, clothes, rags, sticks, nets.

Everything stinks of fish.

'Almost there.'

Sarah and Amy fumble forwards, trying to keep their balance, trying not to touch anything. Through an open doorway they glimpse a family gathered around a table upon which burns a single candle. Small children and a dog sleeping on the floor. A woman threading glistening things onto a line in the half-light. Her man smoking a pipe. A youth picking his nose. A baby crying somewhere out of sight.

The next room, busy as the first, four adults drinking

and talking loudly while two children are fighting beneath a window, their faces lit by a lamp hanging from the latch.

'There we go,' Rebecca says welcoming them into her room. She unhooks the lantern hanging in the middle of the room and places it on a large box that clearly serves as a table. 'Budge up, Rosie, we've guests.'

A young woman cradling two small children looks up bleary-eyed.

'I know, love, but I need space. These two strange looking creatures are out looking for someone and I intend to help them.'

Rosie sighs and shifts herself. The children grumble a little as they're moved along the floor. Rebecca finds a blanket and covers them gently. 'Goodnight, my sweet loves,' she says.

Boxes are dragged across the floor to serve as chairs.

'Ladies,' Rebecca says, sitting down and turning up the wick to bring a little more light to the proceedings. The flame splutters in the cold current of air that races in through the broken windowpane. 'So you're looking for someone?'

Sarah sits down while Amy continues to stand. The windowpane, grimy with soot, is streaked with tears of rain.

'Derek, her boyfriend, has gone missing,' Sarah explains. 'A door opened in our cottage and there's mud all over the floor and we think he may have been kidnapped.'

She doesn't try to make sense of why the woman in front of her is dressed in such rough clothes, or ask why everyone is in costume. Or query why the alley stinks of fish and blubber. Or why the street lighting is down. Or any of the other extraordinary things she is witnessing. Her conscious mind has decided it is all part of some kind of weird festival that she and Stephen should have noticed when they made the cottage booking.

'Pressers!' Rebecca says, immediately very agitated. 'You saw them? Is there a ship or have they come overland? Bastards!'

'Derek got a bit drunk. He went downstairs to the toilet and just vanished,' Amy says, on the edge of tears. 'I was looking for him and those men surrounded me. Is there a power cut?'

Rebecca looks confused. 'We've had pressers twice this year and twice we sent them packing. The whole town hates them. They took Emma's lads last time. Sixteen- and fifteen-year-old. No sight nor sound since. If I catch the buggers I'll kill them with these bare hands!'

'How long does the festival go on?' Sarah asks, a little concerned that the acting is becoming uncomfortably realistic.

'Where will they take him?' Amy asks Rebecca. Amy has no thought of any festivals and is currently finding Sarah as confusing as Rebecca. A small voice in her head is telling her that she should have stayed in Dorking, she had literally no idea how primitive people were in Yorkshire or how far behind the rest of the country they were in terms of their standard of living.

'If they have a ship, they'll have gone as soon as the storm abates. They keep boats on the piers and smuggle the men out as soon as they set hands on them. There were noise on the piers an hour back and rumours on Grope Lane that a ship had snuck in and out.'

'So it's too late?' Amy asks.

'No, maybe not. If they came overland they'll be in one of the inns where they will await the soldiers. When we catch pressers we break their backs. And beat landlords that give them shelter, though in truth some can do no other lest their own families are taken from them.'

'Will the police help?' Sarah asks.

Rebecca looks confused.

'Oh my God!' Amy begins to lose it. 'Are there no police in Whitby? Sarah, did you know this?'

'Of course there's police,' Sarah snaps back. 'Calm down.'

'I am calm!' Amy shouts in a voice that clearly isn't.

'Let's find Tobias,' Rebecca says. 'The harbour master. If there's news he will have it. But first you must put on proper clothes.'

Rebecca goes to the back of the room and rummages in a pile of fabric, handing items back over her shoulder as she finds what she seeks. The clothes are of coarse cloth and in need of a good iron, Sarah decides but says nothing.

'I'm lending these,' Rebecca says. 'I shall want them back. Understood? And you'll be needing shoes,' she tells Amy.

Ten minutes later the three women, all in long loose skirts, aprons and shawls, head outside, squeezing past the junk in the hall. Back through the town square and along Sandgate, past the bridge and onto Grope Lane. Rebecca leads them into another narrow alley and, halfway down, knocks on a broken door. The person approaching from the other side has a bad cough and a foul mouth. Dogs are barking. With much heaving and cursing, bolts are drawn back and eventually the door, or what remains of it, creaks back to reveal a large old woman with grey hair beneath her bonnet.

'E's not here. So bugger off or I'll set the dogs.'

Before the old woman can close the door, Rebecca has the tip of a long knife beneath the woman's throat. 'You'll tell me where I will find Tobias, and keep a civil tongue or I will cut it out and feed it to the fish.'

They find an irritable Tobias Jeffers in the Freemasons Tavern across the river Esk on Baxtergate. The landlord walks them down the corridor toward the backroom.

A furious argument is taking place on the other side of the door.

'Shipbuilding is finished!'

'We've had a bad year, that's all.'

'Blather! They're dropping like flies. We've lost Holt and Richardson. Fishburn about to close, Eskdale and Cato just behind them. It's over, Thomas. And the same with whaling.'

'A temporary reversal of fortunes.'

'That what this catchfart is telling you, John? Face reality. We diversify or we drown.'

The landlord knocks and the argument stops. He pushes the door open.

Three men are seated at a table that is covered in empty glasses, a collection of gaming dice, and two piles of coins. Two of the men are well-dressed and looking lively. The third is Tobias. Slumped in his chair, he has consumed copious quantities of snuff and ale and lost all the money he earned during the week, by foolishly agreeing to play hazard with men who have deeper pockets.

'These ladies wish to have a word,' the landlord explains.

'Have pressers been about?' Rebecca asks Tobias.

Tobias shakes his head.

'Any ships left in last few hours?'

'Two. The *Londonaire* and the *Inevitable*.'

'Did you check them?'

'It were lawful business, woman. *Londonaire* were stopping on route back south. Left after midday. In spite of the storm. The *Inevitable* had come to trade. Left a short while back.' Tobias puts more snuff onto the back of his hand and sniffs loudly.

'Are these wagtails here for sport?' Thomas Watson pats his expansive paunch and leers at the women. He belches loudly.

'Why hide their colours then?' Rebecca asks Tobias, ignoring Watson. 'Why skulk about in the dark?'

'Any gentleman going about his business is routinely set upon by your rough rabble, woman,' sneers John Kidson, adjusting his yellow waistcoat. A vain man, Kidson hides his bald pate with a forward-brushed Caesar haircut. Also known as a comb-over. 'Is it any wonder they try to avoid your charms and graces, Madam?'

Rebecca continues to ignore the interruptions. 'So they might have taken a hostage or two?'

'All I can tell thee is that I've heard nowt of pressers in town,' Tobias insists. 'My lads would have squawked. Crews are all alert.'

Thomas Watson stands from the gaming table and limps towards a mahogany dresser upon which is a silver platter bearing the remains of a large pie. 'Damn this gout!'

'Would these fine ladies like to sup with us?' asks the landlord, stroking his beard with one hand and miming giving Sarah and Amy a pat on the bottom with the other. 'Not often we see wenches with a full set of teeth in Whitby. We'll make it worth their while, won't we, Thomas?'

Thomas smiles suggestively. 'Indeed we will.'

Rebecca snorts. 'And give them both the pox.' She turns to Sarah and Amy. 'Come. Let's leave these *gentlemen* to their wickedness.'

Crossing the bridge back to the east cliff, Amy can't stop asking questions. What pox? What are the *Londonaire* and the *Inevitable*? What were the men shoving up their noses? What does hiding their colours mean? Who is Tobias? Are cars and lorries banned from the old town 24/7? Rebecca isn't listening or, if she is, does not to respond.

When they reach the town square Rebecca stops beneath the open ground floor of the town hall and allows Sarah and Amy to catch up. The skies have cleared and the women can just make out each other's faces.

'That's as much as we'll discover tonight. I'll help you tomorrow but I'm up before dawn and busy while the tide is out. Return to your lodgings and meet me here at midday. Chin up, Amy. If your man is still in Whitby we'll find him.'

'What if they are on a ship?' Amy asks.

'One thing at a time, love.' Rebecca spins on her heels and is gone.

Sarah and Amy look at each other in the gloom. Now what?

'She has no idea what's going on, does she?' Amy says.

'To be honest, I have no idea what's going on,' Sarah answers. 'Let's head back to Henrietta Street. With any luck we'll find Derek in the cottage waiting for us.'

They head back up Church Street, past the sleeping shops, past the two children still crammed beneath a pile of rugs in a doorway, past a silent Arguments Yard and on to the foot of Abbey Steps. Sarah is dog-tired but with the clothes Rebecca has given them, or lent them, she is no longer cold. The moon has emerged from behind the skating clouds and, on a whim, she heads up the steps.

'Sarah!' Amy hisses. 'It's this way, not up there.'

Sarah doesn't reply but beckons Amy to follow her. They stop maybe seventy steps up and turn. The town is dark, all shadows and blacks except for the moonlight painting the rooftops, the air so cold that their breaths bloom in front of their faces. In the distance luminous waves roll in to spend themselves on the west beach beyond the pier. Smoke drifts up from a hundred chimney pots. The air still stinks of boiling whale blubber and coal and fish and sewage but, in a curious way, Sarah is exhilarated, almost moved to tears by the intensity of the moment.

'It's … it's …' Amy struggles for words.

'Amazing. Yes, it is, isn't it?' Sarah smiles. 'Come on let's get home.'

They run down the steps as quietly as they can and turn right onto Henrietta Street. The cobbles mutter and turn in their sleep. With growing excitement the two women take the alley that leads down to the beach then turn right behind the cottages. A seagull stirs beside a chimney pot. One cottage, two, three …

They stop and stare. Feel the bricks with their hands. Feel again. Count the cottages. They must have made a mistake.

'Over here!' Amy whispers.

She has found the door. Sarah grabs the handle and pulls. The door opens one centimetre and jams. With the light on Sarah's phone (the charge has dropped to thirty-nine percent), they discover the door is secured top and bottom by two large padlocks.

'Damn, damn!' Sarah says aloud in frustration. 'Maybe we can rip off the padlocks.'

'Shhh,' Amy whispers, but it is too late.

Close by, a dog growls, its paws banging repeatedly on the other side of a door.

'Shut up!' shouts a muffled male voice in the darkness.

The dog does not shut up; on the contrary it escalates its tide of complaint. Sarah and Amy have not moved a muscle since the noise started but the dog can smell them.

Amy finds Sarah's sleeve and pulls; they have to move. The two women withdraw slowly, quietly. When the dog stops barking, they stop.

'We can't get back,' Amy whispers simply.

The nightmare isn't over; it has just begun.

A posse of fat snowflakes yaw and gimbal in the lacklight air like gulls riding thermals. The two women sink to the floor at the back of one of the cottages, huddle together for warmth and, like the children in the doorway on Church Street, await the cold light of dawn.

CHAPTER 10

Another morning, another hangover.

It is still dark. The smell of cooking is in the air. A familiar odour. Derek turns over and tries to return to the world of dreams. Eventually he gives up.

The cook, Samuel Solander, is busy at his stove, with the girl Lizbet standing at his side, running errands as required. Sam is loved by all on board. In his late forties, he has been retired from arduous duties following a fall from the rigging a few months ago. The fall, which broke his leg badly, has left him missing a foot but, being a long serving member of the crew, he is glad to have work and ensures that everyone is well fed. This morning, as every morning, breakfast is porridge. Lizbet measured everything out and left the oatmeal soaking last night so everything could be ready by dawn. Each member of the crew receives a bowl of porridge with a spoonful of sugar or molasses, as they prefer.

Derek accepts the bowl Lizbet places in front of him and wolfs it down. He watches the girl help the cook pour ladles of porridge into the crew's bowls as they stand in line. It is funny how some people move clumsily while others do everything with natural grace and poise. Lizbet moves like a dancer, every gesture coordinated and precise. A smile for each of the crew along with a *good morning* spoken softly and sweetly in half a dozen languages.

The sun shines through the open hatch, lighting the smoke and steam that curls above the fire, and bringing a glow to Lizbet's face. Laughter and gentle chatter fill the air. There is a general sense that today is a good day. It must be twenty degrees warmer this morning than it was in Whitby yesterday.

'Well done saving Ezekiel last night. There's a few here that wouldn't have joined thee up in the rigging.'

Derek turns to find himself face to face with Beth.

'You're less flat-footed that I thought,' she continues, looking him straight in the eye. 'Though my ankles will take a few days to recover.' Dimples form in her cheeks as she smiles.

Derek grins. 'I have some questions, Beth. Like where are we and when …' he starts then, over her shoulder, he spots two figures at the other end of the deck: broken-nosed Bill and his lickspittle sidekick.

'The sooner the pair of them fall in the drink and are swallowed by sea monsters the better,' Beth mutters, having turned to follow the direction of Derek's gaze. 'Don't let them bully you, Derek.'

Derek's confusion is evident.

'Lizbet told me your name.' Beth winks and moves away to collect her breakfast.

Derek finishes his porridge. Still no sign of Nat or Aleka. He wonders if they are still asleep or maybe they are already on deck. As he climbs up to the deck, Derek's primary interest is to relieve himself. Seeing some members of the crew hurrying towards the front of the ship, while others are ambling back from the same location, he decides to follow the hurryers. Sure enough steps take him down below the figurehead, a beautiful black mermaid who stares out to the horizon, carved in Brazilian ebony, to an area below the bowsprit sail. A couple of crudely drawn signs direct men one way and women the other and in a couple of seconds he is settled on what he later learns is called a seat of ease. His work done, he searches in vain for paper to wipe his cheeks.

'For the love of God,' says a man waiting behind him, 'use the tow rag and make way for others, landlubber.'

For Derek, who has often called someone a toe rag without

ever knowing what he was saying, hauling the frayed rope out of the sea to wipe his behind is a revelation. He will pass the good news onto Nat who can explain everything to his sister.

Belly full, chores done, except his teeth, he'll have to ask for a toothbrush, Derek is ready to meet the day.

CHAPTER 11

Sarah is stiff wi
huddled togeth
tage that two h
to allow them

The silho
blue pre-dav
melting wha

As she h
Sarah sees her breath cloud and
Suddenly worried that she may have frostbite she
heels, getting the blood circulating once more. Amy begins to stir.

‘What time is it?’ Amy’s eyes open, register her circumstances and fill with tears.

‘It’s okay,’ Sarah consoles her. ‘In a little while we’ll go and find Rebecca. She’s a good woman. She’ll help us. Things could be worse.’

‘How the hell could anything be bloody worse than this, Sarah? If you can think of something, please do let me know because right now this feels like the shittiest thing I could possibly ever experience.’

‘We could be stuck at a *Bring Back Pounds and Ounces* conference in Luton.’

Twenty minutes later the air is no longer silent. Sarah and Amy climb to their feet keen to find somewhere to relieve themselves before the streets fill with people. There are already clear signs that Whitby is waking. Lanterns glow in windows across the harbour. A fishing boat heads out towards

oices, now calling loudly as
roosts beside the chimney pots
out over the soft harbour waters.
nd edge of the beach, turnstones shuf-
pecking for scraps and crumbs. Up in
onkeys are braying, the staccato spasms of
g off the dank ruins of the abbey. Cats wind
ong walls and round shadowed kegs and barrels
s in search of prey or fight among themselves in a
umble of spitting fur. A cormorant perches immobile
mooring post, its eyes blank as an empty shop's windows.

As Sarah and Amy come back up the alley from the beach and out onto Henrietta Street they watch and then follow a cart piled high with rags rattling the cobbles on its way to Kiln Yard.

The two men taking turns to push the cart, Charles Grier and Michael Connelly, are dressed in little more than rags themselves. In their sixties, this is their only way to earn a living. They are one missed meal from the workhouse. Unfortunately for them, the rags they push are not only dirty; many carry lice and fleas and disease. Any garments that might have further use as clothing have been removed, the cottons and linens have been separated and the linen rags on the cart are the very dregs of the dregs on their way to the paper mills.

Sarah and Amy know nothing of this as they follow the cart onto Church Street, at a respectful distance. The children have gone from the doorway. A woman is sweeping the pavement in front of her shop.

In the cold light of day, Sarah is slowly processing the possibility that she is not part of a festival put on by the council and that she and Amy have, by some impossible quirk of fate, found themselves thrown back in time. This reality is all the more shocking and confusing because so much of the material world before her eyes is so utterly familiar. She recognises all but a handful of the buildings. The road and pavement she walks is the same as she walked yesterday, the same surface as they drove over on their way to their rented cottage.

'That's Rebecca's alley,' Amy announces.

They squeeze into the alley, pass the trying-out pots, which don't smell as bad as last night. Maybe a night outside has blunted their sense of smell. In the busy yard three children are splashing about in one of the tin baths that was hanging on the wall, the steam rising around them. People are coming and going as the poor head off for another long day of drudgery. Sarah and Amy enter the cottage and squeeze their way down the corridor towards Rebecca's room. When they get there they find the two children on the floor, alone, in the clothes they slept in, playing with marbles.

'Is Rebecca here?' Amy asks brightly.

'Mum and Nanna Bec are working,' says the little girl, picking her nose. 'I'm Vera and I'm four. And he's Simon. Who are you?'

'Do you know where they are working,' Sarah asks.

Simon rolls his eyes. 'Where they always work.'

'Which is?'

Simon sighs as if this is the most stupid question he has heard in all his five years. 'By the pier.'

'Have you had your breakfast?' Amy asks. 'My tummy's rumbling.'

Vera points at a hunk of bread resting on one of the boxes. Beside it are a knife and a bowl that appears to contain some kind of congealed fat.

Amy looks like she just might, until Sarah grabs her arm and shakes her head. 'That's not vegetable spread,' she whispers. 'It's not even butter.'

'I don't care.'

'And it's probably all they have to eat. Let's find Rebecca.'

On the threshold Sarah turns, the children have returned to their game of marbles. Beyond the grimy windowpane, someone dumps a black kitten on the windowsill and laughs.

In the space of a few minutes Whitby is transformed. Church Street now bustles with activity. Horses pull carts laden with barrels on the way to the White Horse Inn. Half a dozen children rush pell-mell out of one yard and into another, laughing and yelling as they go. A gentleman in light-coloured trousers, high-collared shirt, cravat, frock coat and top hat carries a leather pouch as he hurries past on his business.

'Oh what! Is he the Mad Hatter or the White Rabbit?' laughs a wide-eyed Amy. 'All he needs is a teacup or a pocket watch the size of a plate.'

'I guess he works at a bank or a solicitors.'

'Really? What do you think Rebecca does for work?'

Sarah shrugs. 'She's on the pier, so something to do with fish.'

It does have something to do with fish and the sea of barrels crowding Tate Hill Pier. Hundreds of them. Some ends up and stacked two or three high, some on their sides wedged in so they cannot roll away. Men are busy nailing down lids while others load and unload the barrels onto two ships.

The women, gathered in groups of up to a dozen, are sorting fish in long wooden troughs. They chatter as they work, their coarse fabric aprons encrusted with fish scales, their hands thick and slick with slime. It is hard physical work. The smell of fish is so strong that it blocks out both the odour of burning coal and the stench of boiling whale blubber.

Sarah and Amy watch their feet as they make their way to the heart of the toiling.

'We're looking for Rebecca,' Sarah explains to a large woman in a brown headscarf.

The woman looks Sarah and Amy up and down, with barely concealed contempt. She doesn't answer but instead gestures with her head; Rebecca is further down the line.

'There's one has never done a day's work,' mutters someone behind their backs as Sarah walks away with Amy in her wake.

If Rebecca is pleased to see them she hides it well. She is up to her elbows in cod, sea bass, and whiting and working as fast as her arms can move, throwing fish this way and that as another wave is poured into the trough for sorting.

Above them the gulls swoop and turn and cry, dropping in to steal whatever scraps they can find from between the fisherwomen's feet.

'It didn't work out,' Sarah explains. '

Rebecca puffs her cheeks. Two of the young women on the other wide of the trough look annoyed; they are paid piecework and can ill afford anyone slacking.

'I'll give thee two minutes but that's all. We've work to do here and I've bairns to feed.' Rebecca says, stepping back from the sorting trough.

She leads Sarah and Amy away between the barrels, to get out of earshot of her workmates.

'We need your help,' Sarah begins.

'And we're really hungry and don't have any money,' Amy adds. 'We're hoping that …'

'Stop right there.' Rebecca holds up a hand. 'I'm not your mother. Last night I were happy to help, there's not a woman in Whitby who hasn't found herself at wrong side a bunch of drunken men. But I have to work and I certainly don't have money to feed two extra mouths.'

'Could we work here? With you? Just to get money for some food while we sort ourselves out.' Sarah says.

'You said that …' Amy starts.

Rebecca laughs out loud. 'Look at pair of you. Work? With your pretty little fingers? I don't think so.'

'Well what can we do then?' Amy asks.

Rebecca looks her up and down. ‘You can always entertain the gentlemen on Grope Lane, love. Or if that isn’t to your taste, and it certainly isn’t to mine, you could pawn some of your baubles.’

Amy is confused.

‘This lot,’ Rebecca indicates her earrings, necklace and bracelets. ‘If that’s real gold, you have enough for a year’s lodgings and food. Sell it before it’s taken from you in one of the alleys. And I’ll need back those clothes. They’re not mine, I’m adjusting them for someone.’

‘Where do we …’

‘Cross the bridge and ask in one of the banks.’

‘Which bank do you go to?’ Amy asks.

‘What! Me? What would I do in a bank, flither-brain?’

‘What time do you finish here?’ Sarah asks.

‘We work while one o’clock. Why?’

‘Could we meet then?’

It is Rebecca’s turn to be confused.

‘We’d like to talk with you. About what to do. You’ve been so kind and …’

‘When I finish here, I’m on to the next job, love. An hour after you left last night I were up to go flithering on the scaurs. When we got back I came straight here, and when this is done it’s back to the yard for skaning and baiting.’

‘What does any of that mean?’ Amy starts. ‘I couldn’t understand a single …’

Sarah grabs Amy’s arm. ‘We’ll leave you to get on, Rebecca. Can we maybe come to see you later on? If we are still here. Is that okay?’

‘Oh kay?’ Rebecca repeats the word; she has never heard it before. ‘What do you mean?’

‘Doesn’t matter. By the way, what’s the date?’

‘The 28th of November.’

‘I meant the year. What year is it?’ Sarah asks.

'1821.'

Sarah's head is spinning. She walks briskly away with Amy in her wake. Rebecca returns to her work.

Back on Church Street Amy, catching up with Sarah, feels self-conscious and is now painfully aware of people looking at her. She reaches up and removes her earrings and stuffs them, along with her bracelets, rings and necklace, into one of the pockets of Sarah's anorak that she is still wearing beneath the clothes Rebecca lent her.

'Do you believe her?' Amy says. Her voice is fragile, pleading. 'Are we really in 1821?'

'Makes as much sense as anything else.'

CHAPTER 12

'It's mad. It sort of looks like Whitby but it can't be, can it?'

Aleka is right. The shape and lie of the land, the river, and the beach all look familiar. There are no piers or houses, no hotels, no bridge or lighthouses, the cliffs have all shrunk but in some crazy way, somehow you'd still swear it was Whitby.

But the issue isn't just what is missing, of course, the problem is also what shouldn't, by all that is reasonable and rational, be there but somehow is there. The conifers and other tall trees growing right down to the beach in a green carpet that covers everything, thick as a jungle.

And the noise. Animal cries and shrieks emanating from the forest, so loudly that they can be heard from the ship. It's a cacophony straight out of a rainforest documentary. All that's missing is David Attenborough emerging slowly from behind a ginkgo tree in his khaki shorts, whispering about the courtship dance of the lesser spotted something or other.

Derek and Aleka cannot pull themselves away. Holding the handrail, they gawp slack-jawed towards the shore. The ship is maybe a hundred metres from the beach sailing a turquoise sea towards this weird Whitby that cannot possibly be Whitby but somehow is.

The air hangs heat heavy and spice sweet. It smells of exhilaration and trepidation …

… and adventure.

'Magnificent morning, eh?' says Pierre, walking past with a huge rope slung over his shoulder. 'Some days it feels almost like home.'

'Where are we?' Aleka asks him. 'And can someone give

us toothbrushes?'

'I already asked and was given this.' Derek produces a twig from his pocket. 'A *chewing stick*. Best they have.'

Aleka grimaces, deeply unimpressed.

'The happy hunting grounds,' Pierre answers her first question.

'Where do *you* think we are?' Aleka asks Derek.

Derek smiles and shakes his head, he has absolutely no idea, and it has to be a trick question.

'Oh what!' Nat shouts. 'Look at that! Down below!'

Aleka and Derek join Nat further down the ship. Beneath the surface of the waves is a forest of what might be kelp, its fluctuating fronds rippling yellow-green in shafts of sunlight that are themselves shifting to the folding rhythm of the water and above it …

'An octopus!'

'It's massive.'

The octopus is swimming alongside the ship above the kelp, half-hidden in the shadow of the keel.

'Maybe it's hunting,' Derek suggests, 'using the ship as cover.'

A cloud of purple and yellow fish appear and disappear.

'Or being hunted,' Aleka points at a vague shadow moving beneath the octopus, hidden in the kelp.

They watch in fascinated horror as a head, more than half a metre long, rises sleek from the parting fronds of the kelp. The neck, thick as a telegraph post and several times longer than the head, disappears back into the depths, keeping the rest of the animal hidden from view. Panicked, the octopus accelerates but the head, opening to reveal an army of serrated teeth, closes the gap in a forward rush of movement. The jaws grab and grip its prey. The octopus' tentacles writhe in a desperate kaleidoscope of colours as the head sinks slowly beneath the kelp taking the octopus from view.

'Shit! That is some shark!' Nat laughs.

'No, it isn't,' Aleka corrects him. 'Maybe it's a plesiosaur.'

'Yeah, right,' Nat sneers. His eyes light up. 'Oh, I get it! This is because I said pterodactyl yesterday. Right?'

'Pterosaur. Remember?'

They are distracted from their bickering by the arrival on deck of Master Chisholm who bangs a metal bar. 'All hands on deck! Raise the sails and drop anchor!'

A dozen crew race up the rigging to raise the sails. With a huge splash the anchor drops and the ship comes to a stop. In ten minutes the entire crew, with the exception of Sam, the cook, is assembled up on deck. Derek counts forty-three including himself, Nat and Aleka: seventeen women and twenty-six men, all standing in two lines, men on one side and women on the other. The crew chat quietly among themselves. Chisholm strikes the bar three times. The chatter stops and, moments later, Captain Elmo steps on deck.

He walks up and down the lines inspecting his crew, starting with the women. Not for the first time Derek appreciates that the men and women who dance and drink hard are also a disciplined body of seafarers. Elmo pauses from time to time to lean in close to an individual and whisper something quietly in their ear. Sometimes he gets a smile, other times, as with Beth, a short serious nod. Aleka stares straight ahead as the captain addresses her. Elmo pauses in front of Lizbet. After a second she glances up briefly to look the captain in the eye. Derek fancies he sees a faint smile cross the captain's face.

Next the men.

Elmo stops in front of Ezekiel, who is standing upright but plainly in some discomfort. His cheek and nose are bruised and very swollen from last night's attack. The blood from the pterosaur's attack is clearly visible on his shirt. Elmo whispers a few words. Ezekiel nods gratefully, steps back and sits down.

The captain also has a few words for broken-nosed Bill and

his sidekick, Silas. Bill's jaw clenches as the captain addresses him. For a second it looks that he might answer back but the moment passes. Silas breathes heavily as he receives words of advice and Derek sees the hatred in his eyes as the captain carries on up the line. Seeing all the men together at once reveals the presence of a pair of twins on board, both bearded, wiry men with dark tans, blue eyes and easy smiles. The captain exchanges a joke with Pierre who laughs loud and long and slaps his thigh and shouts *Oui, Bravo!* Finally, Elmo reaches Derek and Nat at the end of the line. He leans forward between them.

'You will witness wondrous new and dangerous things, as all of us have before you. Apply yourselves with courage and we will be here to support you. You are both fit and healthy men. The crew on this ship all share in the spoils that accrue from our enterprise so work hard and you will both be rewarded for your labours. When we are finished here, Derek, I would like to talk with you in my cabin.'

Nat basks in being called a man for the first time as the captain marches to the middle of the deck and faces his entire crew.

'Welcome all to New Whitby! Once again the Good Lord has blessed us with this opportunity to fill our boots with the bountiful products of his creation. Once again we will face trials and tribulations as we go about our business but be strong of heart for our cause is good. We will fill the hold with the bounty of this place. We will hunt and dive.'

'With our sweat and our blood we rose against the cruelty of our masters. We beat back the press gangs, those mountebanks who tricked us onto their whaling ships, those who sent us to feed the canons in pointless wars, and those who told us women were too weak to haul a sail. We shunked and cheeved those who beset us like vultures. We have dared be free and our labours shall reward *us* and not *them*!'

'Now we toil as free men and women who have rid

ourselves of the sorry shackles of shame and cruelty. We are lions and leviathans and we shall strike fear in the hearts of the monsters that await us! When we have plundered the treasures of this place we will return with God's Speed to the crossover and cash in the fruit of our labours. And conspire further voyages! Though I tell you we have all but cleared our debt and will soon be free to sail our ship where we please. We are the *Inevitable*, let us fulfil our destiny!'

'Come, my valiant heroes, let us set to! This day shall we make our fortune!'

Captain Jean-Jacques Elmo throws up his hands. The crew cheers long and loud. Hats are tossed into the air!

Derek feels he has just attended the team pep talk before a rugby match. He guesses that there is far more at stake here than ever there is on a strip of grass on the outskirts of Dorking. But there is much he didn't understand.

'Why did he say we were the inevitable?' he asks Pierre who is still beside him. 'The inevitable what?'

'It is the name of our ship,' is the reply.

As the crew busy themselves, Derek descends below deck and asks Sam Solomon for directions to the captain's cabin.

He knocks.

'Come in, Derek. Tell me what you know about soraudines,' Elmo says as he scribbles in a ledger.

'Sardines?'

'No, you fool. Lizards. Big lizards.'

Derek is confused. He shrugs.

'Ah.' Elmo looks up, disappointed. 'I thought you would know this.'

'Komodo dragons?' Derek suggests, trying to sound both intelligent and helpful.

'No.' Elmo drums his fingers on the desk.

'Why do you ask?'

'It doesn't matter.' Elmo returns to his paperwork.

‘What year is it?’

‘Seventeen years since Haiti declared its independence,’ Elmo replies without looking up. ‘Now go up on deck. You are going ashore.’

All of which leaves Derek none the wiser.

Ten minutes later the ship’s cranes, known as davits, lower three fully crewed whaleboats onto the turquoise waters. Derek is in the third boat with Master Chisholm and four other sailors, three men and one woman. He has been instructed to row, to watch and learn.

The boats, around five metres in length, move in formation towards the shore. Up on deck Nat and Aleka watch them pull away.

Chisholm stands at the back of the boat to issue commands and to handle the steering oar. Beside him lies an assortment of weapons: flintlock pistols, harpoons, and cutlasses, and a collapsed metal frame that Derek guesses may be a basket or box. Everyone else rows, their backs to the shore. The earlier euphoria has disappeared and there is now a seriousness of purpose and quiet introspection.

Derek, still unclear how he has ended up in this place or how he will get out of it, pulls his oar in silence in time with the others. He thinks of the huge head that rose up out of the kelp to snatch the octopus. What lurks beneath the boats?

Between strokes, as they lift their oars and bright water drips from the blades, he hears the noise of the forest, a cacophony of unfamiliar sounds: shrieks and yelps like bird-calls and the chatter of monkeys.

Some ten metres from the shore, the crew recite the Lord’s Prayer together.

‘… and deliver us from evil. For thine is the kingdom, the power and the glory, for ever and ever. Amen’

Five metres from the shore, at a signal from Chisholm, they all raise their oars and, in silence, let their momentum and the waves carry them in. Water glides and slips beneath the hull, the waves reflecting fractal fragments of a golden morning sun.

Derek glances left and right as the boats beach simultaneously in the hot sand. For a minute or so, no one moves a muscle. The forest falls silent.

The oarsmen and women are all facing out to sea. On the ship, the rest of the crew and the captain are on deck, watching. Very slowly and deliberately, Chisholm leans forward and lifts a telescope to his eye. He scans the beach and the treeline. He takes his time; no rush. Only when he is satisfied that all is safe does he lower the telescope and nod to his crew and those in the other boats.

Still in silence, the crews climb out of the boats and wade ashore, dragging the vessels up onto the sands. Each member of the crew then collects a weapon, as directed by Chisholm.

Two of the men, Noah and Toby, are assigned to carrying the collapsed metal boxes up the beach; there is a second box in one of the other boats. Noah carries ugly deep scars down his left arm, all the way from shoulder to wrist.

CHAPTER 13

Stephen is alone in the cottage on Henrietta Street. On the television is an advert for the thrills and excitements that await at a zoo, some twenty-five miles away, where you can watch bored penguins swallow dead fish. He paces up and down as he has for the past two hours. Checks his phone, still no messages.

Back to the window that gives onto the street, maybe they are coming up from the Church Street end, just a few metres from the front door.

They aren't.

Over to the window that looks out onto the harbour, maybe they are coming up the alley from the beach. Maybe they are across the harbour on the west pier. It's almost eleven o'clock. Maybe they walked up Khyber Pass to the whalebone arch; the view is great up there. Or maybe they are playing a round of crazy golf. Maybe they're having a cup of coffee.

He goes into the kitchen and boils the kettle, makes himself a cappuccino.

Why did no one wake him? Why would Sarah walk out of the cottage with two people she barely knows and leave him sleeping in bed? Has he done something to annoy her? Why didn't she leave a note? What's he meant to do, just sit around all day doing sod all, waiting for someone to bother to ring or message him?

Derek's shoes are by the front door, which means that he must also have walking boots. Or flippers. He wanders upstairs to the empty bedrooms to see if there is any clue as to where they might have gone. What clothes have they taken?

He tries all their mobile numbers for the fifteenth time.

Another message to each, followed by a phone call. But the messages are not delivered to Sarah's phone or Derek's. Amy's phone is apparently taking messages but she's not responding.

Hang on, what's that?

He follows his ears into Derek and Amy's room.

There.

His eyes scan the room. The muffled sound of a phone.

It's under a pillow, vibrating and buzzing. So the only phone that is actually receiving messages hasn't left the house. The frustration finally boils over. Stephen hurls a pillow across the room. Inconsiderate gits.

Right. I'll just go for a sodding walk then. And they can bloody try to find me. If or when they can be bloody bothered.

He runs downstairs, grabs a glass of water in the kitchen then down the second flight to the basement. No point counting on public toilets to be open.

The mud on the carpet does not pass unnoticed.

Selfish bastard. Couldn't even clean his shoes.

Stephen doesn't notice the smell however. He hasn't smelled a thing for three months, ever since he succumbed to the virus. Hasn't even smelled his own farts. If it weren't for Sarah gently suggesting, from time to time, that it might be time to change his vest, God only knows the aromas he'd be trailing about.

Stephen never really thought about his sense of smell until he lost it. Your nose is just a smoke detector he has always said to Sarah when she bangs on about essential oils, karma, and wellness. It's there to warn you of danger. No point in smelling flowers, unless you're a bee.

Now the chickens have come home to roost. Stephen senses no danger down here in the basement. He does not smell the coal, the burning whale blubber, the fetid miasma that poured through an open door that has now disappeared. To him the air is fresh and clean; he might as well be standing on top of the

West Cliff pointing his nostrils at Denmark.

The front door keys are all hanging on the hook beside the door. They've gone out without even taking a key. Zipping up his anorak, Stephen curses them all.

They'll just have to wait then, won't they?

A bracing wind whistles Henrietta Street. Tourists wander beneath a mackerel sky clutching kippers wrapped in last week's Whitby Gazette. Stephen turns the car keys over in his hand. Should he go for a walk or drive out onto the moors?

Choices, choices.

On Church Street he decides he has earned a treat and pops in to Justin's for a crinkling cellophane bag stuffed with chocolate fudge.

Half-expecting to bump in to the others at any moment, he ambles along munching and nosy-parkering other people's conversations, but his worries cling to him. Either the other three are all fine and busy enjoying the day somewhere. In which case it's not fine at all. Sarah doesn't even like the others. She barely knows them. What is she thinking?

Or they are not fine, and something has happened to one or even all three of them. In which case, and on one level, it is fine and serves them right for driving off or walking off or whatever selfish thing they have done that has ended up with one or all of them having an accident.

He crosses the swing bridge, passes tourists fishing noisily for crabs in the upper harbour, passes the replica of the Endeavour with its tannoy animals depicting a life on a whaling ship, passes the raised beds with last summer's wildflowers, now empty skeletons shaking in the breeze, and the brave souls sitting outside cafés clutching cups of hot chocolate.

The car is in the long stay car park where he left it.

So they can't have gone far.

Retracing his steps he returns to Henrietta Street picking up a brace of kippers at Fortunes to poach for lunch.

CHAPTER 14

'What are they doing?'

'Talking.'

The boat crews are at the top of the beach gathered close to the forest's edge beside a massive fallen tree. They've hauled the boats right up the beach, well away from the water's edge.

Master Chisholm is gesticulating with one of the flintlocks, pointing up and down the sand, while the crew listens attentively. The sun is hot as a furnace even though midday is still sometime away.

Derek, a good six inches taller than anyone else, has been given a cutlass or a machete; from the ship it isn't clear which.

'They'll stay on the beach if they have any sense,' Aleka says.

'Maybe they're hunting crabs or something,' Nat suggests.

'With guns and swords?'

'I dunno. Oh, I get it! They're retrieving sunken treasure. Rubies and diamonds. Yaargh! Pieces of eight!'

Aleka shakes her head pityingly.

'What?' Nat feigns disappointment.

On the beach the crew splits into two parties. A fresh racket of animal shrieks and alarm calls follows them as they walk along the beach. Derek is in the group heading west. When they are maybe a hundred metres apart, they stop and wait in silence.

Finally Chisholm is satisfied. He raises a hand and both groups step forward and disappear quietly into the trees.

'Looks bad,' Aleka says. 'Like they are going in to ambush someone.'

'Or steal something,' Nat suggests.

'It isn't what you think,' says a voice behind them.

The twins turn to see Lizbet standing behind them. 'The captain asks if the pair of you can swim.'

Nat and Aleka look at each other, both thinking the same thing; what happens if they admit they can swim?

'I'll tell him yes.' Lizbet is already walking away.

'Shit,' Nat says simply.

Aleka's eyes are drawn back towards the beach. Half a dozen creatures the size of chickens, dark in colour and with long tails have gathered around the deserted boats.

But that is not what Aleka is looking at.

To the west of the point where Derek and the others entered the forest, the top of the tree canopy is moving, leaves and branches bending in a rippling wave.

A second wave of creatures, quadrupeds the size of deer emerge from the undergrowth to gather in the shade of the fallen tree. Their defensive positions, in a circle, twitching their heads left and right, suggest they have been startled.

'Those animals aren't normal. We have to warn them!'

'No noise!' Captain Elmo is now standing behind them, accompanied by Lizbet, Beth, and two other members of the crew. 'Their mission is dangerous enough already. Come, I have work for you.'

Aleka and Nat hesitate, what does the captain mean by dangerous?

'You'll be safe,' Beth reassures them.

They follow her to the other side of the ship where two other boats are being readied for lowering onto the sea.

The boats are piled high with wicker baskets, knives and curiously fashioned goggles. Three men and two women in each boat. Taking command is Beth.

'Lower away,' she says.

As the boats drop down, Nat notices that the sun will not

last long, out to sea a swathe of dark clouds is gathering on the horizon.

'Where are we going?' Aleka asks Beth.

'Where the diving is easy and treasure lies thick as snow-drops,' Beth smiles.

The giant ferns and horsetails that form a palisade at the edge of the forest have given way to marginally more open terrain beneath the tree canopy. If he thought it might be cooler beneath the trees, Derek was wrong. It's like a sauna and in less than ten seconds he is dripping with sweat.

The soft ground is thick with tracks. Derek grips his machete more tightly. The tracks run in all directions; almost all are three-toed and maybe eight to ten centimetres long, the kinds of marks made by large birds. Derek's arm itches like hell where he brushed against the vegetation as he stepped out of the sunlight and into the shadows. The horsetails are massive, nothing like the straggly weeds he is familiar with on derelict land in Dorking. Here they grow in dense thickets like bamboo and, from what he can see, they seem to be ten metres high or more. They must have serrated leaves because his arm looks like a cat has used it as a scratching post.

The crew walks in single file and Derek struggles to keep up, still none the wiser as to what they are doing here or what they are looking for. He is also far from happy at being assigned to a crew that includes Silas, Bill Stanway's sidekick, and he knows he will have to be on his guard.

'Are we looking for something?' Derek asks Phin who is walking immediately ahead of him and has been instructed by Chisholm to "*keep an eye on the tall fellow*".

No answer. Phin was talking with Bill's sidekick Silas earlier on the ship and Derek wonders if he is being deliberately ignored.

Chisholm leads from the front and marches purposefully,

slashing the vegetation with the machete in one hand while gripping a flintlock pistol in the other.

The trees species are changing. Now the air smells not of the sea but of conifer resins; sweet and lemony, clean and invigorating.

Maybe fifty metres on, much to Derek's relief, Chisholm stops, allowing the crew to catch up and regroup. The job of carrying the collapsed metal frame is reassigned to two other men. The leader whistles a short fragmentary melody, like a birdcall and everyone waits in silence. After a few seconds, the whistle is answered. Chisholm smiles and heads off again along gently rising ground.

They all follow the sound of Chisholm's machete up ahead. Derek notices the light is fading; the sun is no longer making silhouettes of branches in the tree canopy. The undergrowth becomes denser as they climb, huge clumps of ferns and horse-tail slowing their progress. The rest of the crew appear well aware of the plants' defences and take care to avoid brushing against the vegetation.

A constant shifting sea of animal noises surrounds them. Insect calls stop as the crew approaches then resume once they have passed. Sporadic bursts of grunts, howls and alarm calls. Derek wonders how quickly they can retrace their steps to the beach if they have to.

The heavens open.

At first there is only a hollow drumming way above the heads, a sound you might mistake for distant applause. Then the first fat drops fall from the tree canopy as the volume of water overwhelms the leaves. Derek is looking up when some-thing smacks against his thigh. He staggers back as a dark shape disappears into the undergrowth.

'Psst!' Phin in front of him beckons him forward.

Derek does as he is told. Just in time as four or five other animals emerge from the ferns, cross the path and vanish along the route taken by the first animal. Long muzzles and tails. Maybe the size of sheep, but muscular and more aerodynamic in shape.

The rain finally bursts the canopy and falls in hot drenching sheets, harder than a power shower. Thick with noise, the air strobes with lightning. Derek peers back down the path, gripping his machete.

A tap on his shoulder.

The group are moving off again, slipping and sliding in the mud that has formed in less than twenty seconds. Steam is rising around them reducing visibility to little more than four metres. Still the path rises. Derek wants to grasp the branches on either side to steady himself but dare not. He is amazed at how quickly the others are moving, he is obviously not as fit as he likes to pretend. They must all have skirted the line of trees ahead of him. He picks up his pace to avoid being left behind but the many lateral roots running along the ground make the going treacherous underfoot. Scrambling up past a massive tree trunk, something yanks his collar from behind. He staggers back, catching his boot in a root and losing his balance.

In a second he is on his back, aquaplaning down the slope, out of control on a shifting carpet of thick mud. He calls out but can barely hear his own voice in the clatter of the rain. Like the ball in a pinball machine he smashes against various objects, trees and bushes, stuck for a moment then flipped or bumped and on his way again, relentlessly downwards until, finally, the air punched out of him by the impact, he comes to a tumbling stop hard against a tree where he lies in a foetal position, gasping for breath, head throbbing, visuals spinning as the rain obligingly rinses the mud from one stinging eyeball.

Eventually he finds the strength to roll himself over and climb to his feet. The mud is still slurping down the hill. Gingerly, Derek makes his way round the tree, that must be three metres in diameter, and seeks shelter on the other side on a patch of almost dry ground. He sinks to the ground with his back to the tree trunk and notices two alarming things.

He no longer has his machete.

An iridescent two-metre-long centipede is crawling across the largest footprint he has ever seen.

CHAPTER 15

'It's theft! How dare he! Those are real diamonds, Sarah. I have never been so insulted.'

'Shhh! Not here out on the street. Zip it. Let's find somewhere quiet.'

Amy doing her bright red angry face is something new. Sarah wants to laugh out loud but she is acutely aware of how vulnerable they are out on the street.

The greed in the jeweller's dark eyes was a warning. The way he looked at them as Sarah showed him her bracelet; him in his fancy clothes, them in their fisherwomen's rough dresses and aprons. His tallowy face betrayed suspicion and interest in equal measure. He was sensing an opportunity, wondering how they could have got hold of such riches, wondering how he might seize the bracelet and send them packing.

But she also saw fear. The man could see that she and Amy were plainly not local women, their accents and the way they conducted themselves gave them away; maybe the jeweller feared a trap.

They leave Baxtergate, narrowly avoiding being run over by a stagecoach thundering past and turning onto the bridge over the Esk. They reach the bridge in time to see the horses turn onto Church Street. On a whim they follow its route to see where it stops and find the passengers disembarking outside the White Horse and Griffin Inn.

'You're early,' shouts a man from a first floor window.

'The road's been clear all the way from York. Even in Malton!' replies the driver, stretching his legs.

'Well that's a first,' laughs the first man.

Sarah and Amy walk back across the bridge, along St. Anns Staith and Haggersgate and on, all the way to the beach. The tide is out and the sand soft. Huge clouds squat over the grey sea. Finally the women can talk freely.

'I know how much that bracelet is worth, Sarah. And the necklace. I saw an article about it in Tatler magazine at the dentists. Dazzling December diamonds for your Christmas wish list.' Bottled up too long, the words tumble in a torrent from Amy's mouth. 'Derek would be mortified if I sold it for thirty pounds. It's worth three thousand and the necklace is worth even more and …'

'Stop,' Sarah raises a finger in front of Amy's face. 'Have you listened to anything anyone's said since we found ourselves in this mess?'

Amy pouts and sighs heavily. 'I don't believe any of it.'

'You don't believe this is 1821?'

'It's impossible.'

'I agree, it is impossible but, unfortunately it is what has happened. Look around you, Amy. Do you see anything that tells you we are still in the twenty-first century? Cars, electric lights, plastic bottles, pushchairs, a *Welcome to Whitby* mug, women in trousers, anyone holding a smart phone, a fish and chip shop, boats without sails, bicycles, a bloody supermarket? Anything at all.'

Amy shakes her head sullenly.

'No? So, where do you think we are?' Sarah asks.

'It's impossible.'

'Yes, you said that. Let's pretend for a second that we really are in the beginning of the nineteenth century. How much do you think things cost?'

'Don't care. It's my jewellery. Not selling. I'd rather…'

'You'd rather what? Die of hunger and cold on the streets? Earn a few pennies on Grope Lane?'

Amy's resolve is crumbling. Her eyes fill with tears.

'Where's Derek?'

'Let's do some homework,' Sarah adopts a softer tone, putting an arm round Amy's shoulders. 'Let's sort ourselves out.'

'Why don't you sell *your* jewellery?' Amy says, between sobs.

'I'm wearing a cheap pair of sleepers and that's it. Sorry.'

'I only kept everything on because I was worried someone might break into the cottage and steal it in the night. I don't usually wear it in bed.'

'Come on.'

The two women head off back towards Baxtergate. They pause to look in shop windows. The grocer, the butcher, the candlestick maker. Drapers, gunsmiths, haberdashers, booksellers. They stop a couple of women and enquire as to where they might find lodgings to rent.

An hour later they have learnt that meat and fish cost 4 1/2d a pound (*that's 2p a kilo, Amy*), beer just 2d a quart (*1p a litre*), and vegetables for two cost 2d a day (*You could stuff yourself stupid on onions, potatoes, carrots, cabbage, leeks, turnips and all the bloody rest of it, all day, and still not spend a penny*). They have discovered that they can rent lodgings for three shillings and six pence a week. A week's provisions will cost them less than five shillings. Thirty pounds could last them a year.

'I don't know if they have public toilets anywhere but if you want to spend a penny here you can probably do it every day for four years and still not spend a bloody penny!' Sarah explains, losing any semblance of patience with Amy.

'But we may only be here a few more hours,' Amy protests one last time.

'If we don't quickly get food in our bellies and a roof over our heads we may not survive even that long,' Sarah retorts. 'Maybe it is time we did what the leopard can't do; maybe it is time for us to change our spots.'

Half an hour later, around noon, they visit a second jeweller.

'Good afternoon. My name is Phoebe and your establishment has been recommended to us,' Sarah introduces herself to the man behind the counter. 'Are you the proprietor?'

'I am John Camphor. Yes.'

'Excellent. My friend Maud and I arrived some little time ago on the stagecoach from York, Mr Camphor,' Sarah continues in the poshest accent she can muster.

Rubbing his bald head, a feature offset by long and very thick sideburns, John Camphor attempts to make sense of the jarring disconnect between the women's clothes and their strange accents.

'We have travelled from London to surprise our husbands. You may have met them. Tobias and Gordon, solicitors employed by Pelmet, Soffit and Grout, of Piccadilly? They are working in the town and we wish to surprise them,' Sarah explains. 'Hence our lowly attire. Maud, will you show this gentleman the bracelet?'

Amy, now Maud, smiles and produces the item. The diamonds sparkle obligingly.

'We wish to sell this item to generate some funds for our big surprise,' Sarah says.

'It's eighteen carat gold, all hallmarked, with sixty-five diamonds. Four carats,' Maud explains. 'Also from Piccadilly. Where Gordon works.'

Mr Camphor takes the piece and holds it up to his loupe. It is indeed a beautiful piece.

'Do you handle items of this quality or shall we …' Sarah asks.

'Of course, Madam.' Camphor puts the bracelet down on the counter. 'A fair piece. Good setting, nice stones.' He strokes his chin. 'I'll give thee twenty guineas for it.'

Sarah feels Amy's blood rising. 'That's a shame,' she says.

'Maud was expecting thirty, weren't you?'

'Pounds or guineas?' asks Camphor. 'You'll not get London prices up here, Madam. I can stretch to twenty-three guineas but this is a difficult time for …'

'Surely, Mr Camphor, it is only weeks until Christmas. There must be ladies in Whitby who would appreciate such a singular item as a gift, and gentlemen minded to demonstrate their affections at such a time. Shall we say twenty-seven pounds?'

Camphor hesitates.

'Come on, Maud,' Sarah says, collecting the bracelet and passing it back to Amy. 'There's a couple of other places recommended to us and …'

'Twenty-five guineas,' Camphor says, drawing himself up to his full five feet and four inches. 'My final offer.'

Sarah glances at Amy, who is clenching her jaw and looks far from happy.

'Please, Maud. It will be such a treat. Can you imagine their faces when we spring our surprise? The poor loves must be so tired of vexatious litigants, disputes, and deeds of covenant.'

Amy sighs and nods reluctantly.

Sarah claps her hands happily and beams at Amy then turns to the jeweller. 'Mr Camphor, I believe we have a deal.'

CHAPTER 16

'Just follow me and you'll both be fine,' Beth says.

They have waited for the rain and clouds to pass. Beth crosses herself and checks her knife, goggles and diving belt, a rope carrying four rocks with holes drilled through the middle. The boat rocks as she jumps into the turquoise sea.

Nat looks at his sister and shrugs. 'No point waiting till she's out of sight.'

Aleka nods. They dive. Beth is already at the bottom some three metres beneath the boat. Clinging to the rocks is a thick carpet of molluscs interspersed with all sorts of different algae; red, green, yellow and brown. Beth and another member of the crew have their knives out and are prising oysters from the rocks and placing them in a wicker basket. They work quickly, each taking maybe thirty oysters before swimming to the surface to take a breath.

The molluscs come in all shapes and sizes, most are the size of your hand but some are much bigger. The twins let themselves rise to the surface for air.

'You need knives and a basket,' says Thin George who is the scout, keeping an eye out for danger, 'and a diving belt.'

Properly equipped, they dive down a second time and join Beth on the reef.

The molluscs cling to the rock with a kind of stone glue. Some need a sharp bladed knife to prise them away but others can simply be twisted off. To begin with the twins are gathering just five oysters in a single breath but, young and fit, after twenty minutes and once they have learned the knack, they are soon keeping up with Beth and the others.

The sea is not just oysters and seaweed of course. There are corals, starfish, brittle stars, clams, mussels, and sea urchins in profusion. Weird-looking crabs, lobsters, and squid meander over the oyster beds. Then there are the ammonites.

So many of them.

Nat knows immediately what they are because they are featured on all the Jurassic Coast websites he and Aleka have looked at over the past couple of weeks as they planned their trip to Whitby. But those were old fossils on a beach, not large blooms of living creatures, in clouds as dense as a smack of jellyfish. It is strange to see them frundling past, always in reverse, their tentacles waving behind them like streamers.

Nat is fairly sure that they are meant to be extinct.

If the molluscs and crustaceans are familiar, the same cannot be said of the fish. The small stuff close to the reef is okay, just a collection of shapes, sizes, patterns that are as varied as the fish he has seen when snorkelling in the south of France but the big stuff, the stuff loitering in the middle distance on what they imagine to be the edge of the reef, is freaking out both Nat and Aleka. It's hard to be sure because the water distorts the size of everything but, if pressed, Aleka would say that some of the fish out there in the open sea are as long as buses and, alongside these megafish, there are other creatures with bodies the size of cars, four huge flippers, long necks and tails.

The reef is alive with sound: chirping, clicking, booming sounds, and the liquid gurgling of the sea while waves wash, fold and tumble overhead.

Their catch baskets, once full, are taken up. Reaching the surface is an explosion bright light and brittle noise, water drops, splashes, reflections and the hollow wooden sounds as the baskets are tipped into the boat. In little under an hour the boat is full and it is time to go.

'We're fishing for pearls, right?' Aleka asks as they row back to the ship.

'Of course,' Beth replies.

'And each oyster contains a pearl?'

Beth almost loses her oar as she rolls backward laughing. 'No, child. If that were true we would already be millionaires! If we are lucky we may find one or two in this pile.'

'Are we really in the Jurassic?' Nat asks. 'Like why are there ammonites swimming about?'

Beth does not understand the question.

'Maybe they're not actually extinct everywhere.' Aleka suggests.

'Do you know how stupid is?' Nat replies. 'What you just said.'

Beth leaves them to it. The boats come and go between the reef and the ship and, shortly after midday, there is a small mountain of oysters and clams on the deck of the ship. The boats are hauled up and work begins to find the pearls.

Between them the three boats have harvested a pile of oysters the size of a large car. They are so busy shucking the oysters, prising them open with knives to see if they contain a precious pearl, that it is almost mid-afternoon before Nat and Aleka remember Derek. At that point the eighteen members of the crew have found a total of seven pearls. Nat climbs to his feet and looks towards the shore. The boats are still on the beach. The green wall of the forest still presses the edge of the sand. The occasional howl or alarm call still drifts across the water. But there is no sign of the men and women who stepped beneath the trees.

'Come away Nat. We have work to do.' Beth has appeared at his side. 'We must clear this pile and go back to refill the boats before the sun sinks. It is safe diving by daylight.'

'But the others. What has happened to them?' Nat asks. 'Why have they gone into the forest? Are they hunting?'

'They're on a rescue mission. If they are not too late. Pray God is on their side. Now come and work.'

'But who are they rescuing? What is out there?'

Beth doesn't answer.

Nat tries to question Beth a second time but again she ignores him and Aleka shakes her head at her brother, warning him off.

By the time the boats are being readied for lowering back again onto the sea, the pearl pot contains seventeen pearls. Lizbet, who has been summoned by Beth and charged with taking the pot to the captain for safekeeping, allows Aleka and Nat to peek at the fruits of all the hard work.

The pearls are between a large pea and a small grape in size. Two of them are black, all of them have a magical iridescence.

'Wow! How much are they worth?' Aleka asks.

'The captain has a *bucket* of pearls in his quarters!' Lizbet confides in them. 'And when it is full we are ready to leave.'

Nat hopes the bucket isn't as large as the one in his grandfather's shed or it will take month's to fill.

Derek takes very shallow breaths, aware that each one might be his last, and keeps quite still. His ankle is throbbing but, as far as he can tell, nothing is broken.

The rain has stopped, the centipede has moved on, and the sun is once again beating down on the tree canopy. As the heat rises, the waterlogged ground releases fresh billowing clouds of steam and the horizon of Derek's world shrinks until it is not much further than he can spit.

But while the forest mist conspires to thwart his vision, it does nothing to limit his hearing. The symphony of insect chirrups, buzzes and scrapes hangs heavy and, masked beneath it, other more alarming sounds. In particular a low booming interspersed with a vibration that Derek feels in his chest rather than hearing it with his ears.

Someone tried to kill me. They pulled me back.

For the hundredth time Derek hopes he is dreaming, that

his body is lying on the bed in the cottage on Henrietta Street, Amy snoring gently beside him, and that he is safe. The booming sound is just the sound of the central heating kicking in. Maybe his beer was spiked by one of the locals.

But if he is dreaming then he must be lucid dreaming since he is conscious. Which means he must be able to change the dream or wake himself up, like he used to do when he started secondary school and had nightmares.

Try as he might, he cannot wake up.

The booming sound gets louder.

Then stops.

Derek feels himself beginning to panic. Fight or flight?

Flight, flight, flight!

The gentle sound of big breathing close by, accompanied by the sickly stench of putrefaction. He feels the air brushing his right cheek.

Don't look.

Fight or flight?

One .... two ... three .. four . five six seveneightnineten

A bang away to his right.

The stinking breath moves away from his face as a huge shape in his peripheral vision turns towards the noise.

Don't move, don't move.

Derek's heart is racing. The fragments of what he has seen and heard over the past twenty-four hours are beginning to make an insane kind of sense.

The booming returns. So close now. Rattling his ribs. The ground sinks gently as whatever it is beside the tree leans forwards, crushing something brittle underfoot.

Another bang and a human shout. The ground shakes and a huge animal lurches forwards and charges in the direction of the sound. Its haunch, as large as an elephant's, scrapes the tree trunk. A foot the size of a dustbin lid smacks the ground and a blur of colour fills half of Derek's field of view before disappearing, crashing and crushing the undergrowth.

Derek is taking deep breaths is a futile bid to keep calm when the hand grabs his shoulder. He recoils, cracks the back of his head against the tree trunk.

'Get up!' a voice hisses.

Chisholm hauls Derek to his feet, looks into his eyes to check he is all there, and hands him the machete he lost on his slippery descent.

'Follow me!'

Derek doesn't need to be told twice. He scrambles up behind Chisholm, who is plunging his own machete repeatedly into the mud bank as he climbs so as not to lose his footing. Derek copies his action only too aware that whatever distraction it was that diverted the monster, he cannot yet call it what it is, must long since have run away to safety. Every single inch of his skin is caked in mud. His ankle aches. His eyeballs are aflame, red raw from the grit trapped beneath his eyelids.

Chisholm is using the exposed tree roots and flattened vegetation like the rungs on a ladder, and Derek copies him. More giant footsteps and trampled bushes. Chisholm stops to allow Derek to catch up.

'Halfway, lad,' Chisholm says under his breath. 'I'll not lose more men to this hellhole, if I can help it. But neither will I sacrifice the entire crew for one man. You must use your brawn and your wit from here.'

'Someone pulled me over,' Derek says, catching his breath. 'Tried to kill me. What are we looking for?'

'A fool's errand. But the captain saved my life I cannot refuse him. Come, the others are waiting. '

And with that Chisholm turns and climbs the slope between the trees. They finally stop and Derek collapses to the ground, muscles on fire, lungs heaving the hot humid air.

On his hands and knees, then on his side, and finally eyes closed on his back. Voices around him.

'Slid all the way down.'

'Nothing broken?'

'They made it back.'

'Which way did the beast take?'

'You did well, lads. Thank God those monsters can be distracted.'

Derek feels something soothing his face; water dissolving the mud caked to his forehead, flushing the silt from his eyes. He blinks. The pain is excruciating but the water is doing its job. The seconds pass. He blinks again. This time he sees blue sky. And a strange, darker line arcing over his head.

A hand gently pushes away the mud from his face as the water falls and the pain subsides.

'You may open your eyes.'

Derek sits up. He is in a jungle clearing overlooking the sea, maybe fifteen metres above the beach. A gap in the trees afford him a view of the ship below, anchored some fifty metres from the shore. Bright sunlight bears down on the crew around him, busy cleaning equipment, checking the flints on the pistols.

Which of them tried to kill me?

Phin has tied a flag to a pole cut from the stem of a tall horsetail and is waving it to and fro. Someone up in the crow's nest on the ship waves a chequered flag in response.

'Ahoy!'

All heads turn towards Noah, who has climbed high up a tree on the edge of the clearing and is looking out over the jungle canopy along the beach towards the river.

'I see their flag! All is well!'

The crew cheers the good news that the other landing party are safe but Derek is only half-listening. Behind him is an object he recognises from the photo on the postcard Stephen sent him on a previous weekend in Whitby.

'Magnificent, is it not?' says a woman's voice beside him. 'It were the captain's idea. To mark our presence in this place.'

‘It’s not from here,’ Derek says. ‘How can it possibly …’

The woman laughs. ‘Indeed not. We brought it with us. We’ve yet to catch a monster in this sea; they’re a different breed. Fearsome brutes. We’ve lost a boat and four of the crew in pursuit. Chisholm it were who persuaded the captain of the *Mary* to sell us the jawbone. He served with Oyston before joining Captain Elmo on the *Inevitable*.’

The jawbone in question is maybe seven metres high and forms an arch above the clearing. Though no mariner, Derek knows enough to tell it is the jawbone of a huge whale. It is beyond curious to see it sticking up out of the soil in a jungle clearing overlooking a turquoise sea.

‘Leave him be, Alice. We’ve work to do,’ Chisholm says. ‘By sunset we must have a palisade and a fire. Derek, go with Phin and Jack and cut wood. And this time keep your wits about you.’

‘Is this a good moment to ask if there’s a pub nearby? If we’re spending the night here.’ Derek asks. ‘I’m dying for a pint of Pilcrow pale ale. Well, several pints, if I’m honest.’

Chisholm shakes his head pityingly and chuckles. ‘Get to work, landlubber.’

Derek glances back at the sea below as he joins Phin and Jack. The ship suddenly looks a haven of safety.

The three men re-enter the forest to a chorus of alarm calls.

CHAPTER 17

Three hours later the transformation is complete. The two women have rented an apartment in a pleasant new house on Silver Street for three months, bought new clothes, groceries and provisions and are standing at the window watching the dusk arrive on a cold Whitby day in November 1821.

'So what do you think?' Sarah asks.

'Absolutely awful. There's a shop on Baxtergate selling quite nice fabric. We have to change the drapes. In the morning I'll …'

'I don't mean the bloody curtains, Amy!'

'Colour makes all the difference,' Amy continues, ignoring Sarah's unpleasant tone.

'I mean our circumstances.'

'Well, since you ask, and since it's my money we're spending, the drapes are part of our circumstances. And what I think is that if you insist on buying beeswax candles, we'll soon be back on the streets.'

'I'm sorry, but the smell of burning tallow is stomach churning, and I am not prepared to have spermaceti candles in the house. The whale trade is disgusting, and they may not know it here in Whitby but what they are doing almost brings the whales to extinction.'

'I get it, Sarah, but that one beeswax candle is probably a week's wages for Rebecca.'

'If you say so.'

'It's my bracelet so you can't just ignore me. And I don't want to be a vegan, I need to eat meat and I need to be eating well.'

'Can you imagine the diseases? And the extra cost?'

They stand in silence for a few moments.

'Let's light a fire and have coffee and cakes,' Sarah says in a more conciliatory tone. 'The bread is delicious, isn't it? I guess you're right, we need to adjust to our circumstances.'

Amy isn't quite sure what Sarah means but decides not to pursue the matter. Ten minutes later they are sitting in wing-back armchairs before a roaring fire with a hot pot of coffee, half a dozen slices of parkin, and a notebook to plan how they will find Derek and make their way back to their own century.

'This is delicious,' Amy licks her fingers. 'What's in it?'

'Parkin? Oats, molasses and ginger. And butter,' Sarah adds, suddenly hoping the fat really is butter and not lard.

Too late, I've already eaten it.

Thankfully, Amy offers no comment; she appears to be less interested in cooking than curtain fabrics.

Sarah is just about to put pen to paper when there is a knock on the door, startling both women.

'Why would anyone be knocking?' Amy says.

'It may be one of our new neighbours.'

'It could be anyone. They can come back in the morning.'

'They may have heard us dragging the furniture about and wondered …'

'Are you blaming me?'

'I am not blaming you for anything, Amy. I am simply saying that …'

Another knock on the door followed by a theatrical cough.

'Forgive my impertinence,' says a reedy male voice, muffled through the door, 'but there are informations that I must relate to you as a matter of some urgency.'

Sarah and Amy look at each other in the shifting light of the fire and the weak glow of their single candle. The speaker is very definitely not a Yorkshireman, but a southerner like themselves.

'I will leave my card,' the voice announces after a few seconds, 'and pray that no injury occurs to your persons during the night. My name is Robert Seeker. You may find me at the White Horse and Griffin. I shall await your visit and beg your forgiveness for my intrusion.'

Footsteps retreat down the corridor. Amy sighs with relief but Sarah leaps to her feet, grabs the poker from the fire.

'No, Sarah, it may be a trap!'

Sarah flings open the front door. The candle flame gutters behind her in the rush of cold air causing shadows to dance upon the ceiling.

'Mr Seeker, wait!'

Sarah stands in the open doorway. It is dark out in the passage, the only light being a weak moonglow whimpering at the window. The boots in the stairwell have turned and are heading back up towards the landing. A large cloak or coat traverses the window light as footsteps tread the rough hessian rug towards her. She grips the poker tightly.

A broad-chested thick-set man appears. He nods politely, awaiting permission to enter. Robert Seeker has an incongruously thin face, long straight nose over thin lips and a weak chin. His eyes look excited but not threatening.

For his part, Robert Seeker spots the poker in Sarah's hand. 'You are right to be cautious, Madam, but I assure you I come with the best of intentions.'

'Come in, Mr Seeker, but know that we are armed and will defend ourselves,' Sarah says.

As he crosses the threshold, Robert Seeker removes his top hat and hangs it on the stand by the door.

Amy still looks deeply suspicious as Sarah takes a chair from the dining table and positions it closer to the fire.

'Please take a seat, Mr Seeker.'

Seeker removes his coat and both women are amazed at the transformation. It is as if a soldier were vacating his sentry box because from the coat emerges a much thinner man. The light from the fire and the candle reveals him to be wearing two waistcoats, yellow over blue. The collar of his shirt is so high as to completely hide his neck.

His pale clean-shaven face is topped with a chaotic mess of curly red hair. The overall impression is perhaps of a moss-covered boiled egg sitting in its cup. As he takes his seat, Seeker produces from his yellow waistcoat a small silver box with a snakestone embossed on its lid. He opens it and places a large pinch of snuff on the back of his hand, between thumb and forefinger, raises it to his nose and sniffs enthusiastically.

'I must explain myself,' he says. 'But first, thank you for graciously allowing me to prevail upon your time. My ears took the liberty earlier today of hearing some fragments of your conversation in the street. These same fragments, combined with other words heard about the town during the course of the day, have given me to conjecture that providence has thrown us together.'

He pauses to let his words sink in and to take another snort at his snuff as Sarah and Amy exchange glances.

'I am, dear ladies, an explorer, an investigator of arcane mysteries and it is this interest that has brought me to Whitby where these two months past I have been studying a curious phenomena. I believe that you may have direct experience that may inform my studies and that I, in turn, may be able to provide you with information that might benefit you in your current predicament.'

Amy is looking bored.

'Can you cut to the chase, Mr Seeker?' Sarah says. 'I'm worried that we may still be here at sunrise waiting for you to get to the point. We are both quite tired.'

Seeker reaches into one of the many pockets of his waist-coats to retrieve his fob watch. 'Good heavens, yes! The chase, indeed, Madam.' A deep breath. 'How did you get here?'

Which stops his monologue dead and leaves both Sarah and Amy speechless. What can they say? What does this strange man actually know? What can they in all honesty say to him that won't either freak him out or have him writing them both off as insane or, possibly even worse, have him shouting *Aha!* before going off on some fantastical stream of madness like those mad scientists in Frankenstein movies?

The three of them sit in silence around the crackling fire, watching the flames dance and coals gleam and glow in the iron hearth on a cold November night in Whitby. The year is eighteen-twenty-one and two of the three people are two hundred years out of sync and lost, and the third is looking at them both with the hungry curious excited anticipating delirious pleading eyes of a man who has just found a treasure without price.

'In which case,' Seeker says quietly, 'maybe *I* can tell *you* how I think you got here. I believe, dear ladies, that you are both victims of the Whitby Trap.'

CHAPTER 18

Stephen has had enough. The sun has set and he has still not heard a thing from anyone. It just isn't possible that they have all gone for a walk and forgotten about him. It's been at least seven or eight hours. He has to do something.

The phone rings four times and is answered by a mechanical voice that, in between dollops of cheery mechanical music, informs him that he is sixth in a virtual line of people waiting to be ushered in to speak with someone at a virtual reception desk beneath a virtual clock that is turning so lethargically that it may be the same clock that Einstein imagined on a moving train, the one that charts the way time shifts and slows to stop when you approach the speed of light, as observed from the other side of the universe.

'North Yorkshire Police. How can I help?'

'Sorry?' Stephen who has been clutching his phone to his ear for thirteen minutes and twenty-seven seconds is momentarily confused by the interruption to his thoughts. 'Oh. Yes, sorry. I was hoping to speak with the police about possible missing persons.'

'You can either complete a report with me over the phone or, preferably, come into the police station. Are you in Whitby, Sir?'

'Yes.'

'In which case, we are on Spring Hill, behind the railway station. Can I take a name, Sir?'

Minutes later, Stephen is crossing the swing bridge for the fifth or sixth time since he woke up.

He sits in the non-virtual reception area. The real clock

above the reception desk tells him he has waited thirteen minutes and six seconds when a door opens and he is ushered into an office by a grey-haired and overweight police officer who has a cold and looks like he has had a very long day.

'Take a seat, Sir. I am Sergeant David Pannett.' The policeman folds open a note pad and checks his pen is working. 'How can I help?'

Stephen sets out as best he can the events of the past twenty-four hours, while the sergeant scribbles on his pad, asks the occasional question and blows his dripping nose.

'Right,' says the sergeant when Stephen finishes. He taps his pen thoughtfully on the notepad. 'Henrietta Street. I was about to go off shift but I'll walk up with you, Mr Bootle, and we'll have a quick look round. Does that sound all right?'

Stephen nods gratefully.

Crossing the swing bridge again, this time walking beside a policeman in uniform, Stephen has mixed feelings. A slight concern that passers-by might think he is a criminal being taken into custody. A feeling of importance that he is 'helping the police with their enquiries'. A wish that the other three would appear and be confronted with the selfishness of their actions and obliged to apologise to him in front of the policeman. A shiver at how cold it's getting now the light has gone and a sea breeze is whistling through the bridge's ironwork.

Sergeant Pannett doesn't do small talk so the two men walk in silence, save for the policeman's stout footwear clattering the Church Street cobbles. By the time they reach Henrietta Street it has started mizzling and a damp dark clings to every surface.

Stephen shows the sergeant around the cottage, upstairs and down. The open suitcases in the bedrooms, shoes by the door, bags of groceries in the kitchen, cans and bottles of booze by the bin.

'You say it is your first time in Yorkshire, Mr Bootle?'

'No, no. My wife, Sarah, and I have visited Whitby many times. Four or five. But it is the first time that Derek and Amy have come north.'

'And you think that Derek may have left the house without his shoes? In this weather?'

'I could be wrong about that. He may have packed other footwear. But those are his shoes by the front door.'

'Let's take a look in the basement, Sir.'

'The muddy bootprints were there this morning when I got up. No idea how they got there. Derek might have … but then why aren't there muddy prints on the stairs and why …?'

'Quite. Would you like to put the kettle on while I have some space? Coffee, white.'

Sergeant Pannett is better able to focus without the yabbering in his ear.

Besides the muddy bootprints there are a number of other interesting details in the corridor. Soot on the ceiling. Small drops of what might be wax or tallow on the floor, a thicker density of them interspersed with the busiest area of bootprints. He imagines a scuffle. Lanterns shaken in the hand. He inspects the walls carefully but other than the soot there is nothing to be seen.

'Did anyone take a candle downstairs last night?' he asks standing in the doorway of the kitchen.

Stephen jumps and turns away from the sink. 'Sorry, did you want sugar, Inspector?'

'It's sergeant, Sir. No sugar, thank you. Candles. Did you use candles during the power cuts?'

Stephen shakes his head. 'I certainly didn't. We didn't pack candles. We're only here for the weekend, you don't think to …'

'I understand. Can you check the cupboards?'

Stephen opens the kitchen cupboards. 'There's these.' He shows the policeman a small glass jar containing half a dozen birthday cake candles. Are they important?'

Pannett laughs then smothers his nose in a handkerchief. 'Not to worry, Sir.'

He blows on his coffee and takes a sip.

'What will you do?' Stephen asks. 'What can I do? My wife has never ...'

'I've got all the details I need, Mr Bootle. Let's talk again if you've heard nothing by the morning.'

'But this is serious,' Stephen says, beginning to lose his cool. 'They might be in real trouble. We've got to do something.'

'Mr Bootle, if I may? I don't want to sound disrespectful, Sir, but these kinds of disappearances are not unheard of at holiday destinations. The change of scene, the break from routine. Disagreements bubbling to the surface, a spat perhaps. Relationships under strain.'

'No, nothing like that,' Stephen protests.

'Sometimes people get carried away. Stress. Matters coming to a head.' Pannett's voice is calm and measured. 'Temptation becoming too much to resist. Sharing a cottage. Excitement. A group of adults. Liaisons, if you follow me.'

'Ridiculous! I can categorically assure you than nothing, absolutely nothing of that kind will have entered my wife's head!'

Sergeant Pannett has seen it all before. 'In my experience Mr Bootle, it is better to assume the least worst options and go from there, if we have to. They might be lost at sea, or fallen into a sinkhole on the moors, or abducted from their beds, but let's not get ahead of ourselves. There may have been a furious argument here last night that resulted in things getting out of hand.' He pauses and looks long and hard at Stephen Bootle. Lets the words sink in.

'I was sleep,' Stephen splutters. 'I would never ... I explained that ...'

'Yes, you did. Shall we speak in the morning?'

Stephen's shoulders slump and he acquiesces. Sergeant Pannett finishes his cup of coffee and hands it back to Stephen.

'I'll let myself out. Try to have a quiet evening, Mr Bootle, and let's both hope that your wife and friends turn up soon. I do appreciate that this is a real worry to you, Sir. I have your mobile number; we'll speak in the morning.'

'Will you contact the media to let them know?'

'In the morning, we'll talk again. Oh, to be clear, you won't try to leave Whitby, will you Sir? Goodnight.'

CHAPTER 19

The sun has set. Nat and Aleka are sitting on the deck beside Beth, working their way through the third pile of oysters. The work is mechanical and rough; their pampered 21st century hands are blistered and sore. The oysters contain digestive juices that have the cumulative effective of burning the skin. The others don't seem to mind, their rough hands are used to the daily grind of manual work, singing shanties as they force their blades between the shells, twisting and turning to prise the oyster apart and check for pearls.

According to the girl Lizbet, they now have sixty-one pearls safely stowed in the captain's quarters. The twins aren't listening, they're more concerned about the three boats that are still on the shore. It will be dark soon and there is still no sign on the beach of the nineteen men and women who climbed out of the boats and stepped into the jungle.

They barely know Derek but he nevertheless represents a lifeline, a link with the world they have lost, proof they belong somewhere else, the hope that things might return to normal.

And now he is gone.

'Look!'

Aleka follows Nat's line of sight. In the gathering gloom the jungle is turning from bright green to a monochrome dark grey. A light breeze animates the leaves of the tallest trees. As they watch an orange glow blooms between the trees throwing some of the leaves into silhouette and colouring others.

'A fire! Someone has lit a fire,' Nat says.

'Over there too!' Aleka points to a spot to the west where a trail of smoke is rising in the middle distance.

As they watch, the glow becomes brighter and the smoke thicker. The rest of the ship's crew are now paying attention. Someone cheers, another tells Lizbet to inform the captain.

'Are they staying out there?' Nat asks Bill who is sitting between him and Beth. 'Is it safe?'

Bill sneers. 'Why? Does thou want to join them, lad?'

'Leave him be, Bill,' Beth shouts.

'Why don't you tell him why they have gone ashore, wagtail? Maybe he will …'

Bill doesn't get to finish his sentence as he is sent flying into the mountain of oysters by a well-placed kick in his back.

'Enough! For the love of God!' Captain Elmo stands over Bill. 'Wretch! We should have left you in Whitby, if it weren't punishment enough for that town that you had ever set foot there.' Elmo turns to the crew. 'Throw this vermin in the brig and slap the irons on him. If he gives any trouble we'll toss him to the beasts. I curse the day I ever took you on board!'

Bill is hauled to his feet and marched to the hatch by two of the men. As he starts to climb down into the belly of the ship Bill looks up with a sly grin and mutters something to the men. The taller of the two says nothing in reply but kicks Bill so hard in the shoulder that he loses his balance and falls back, clattering onto the deck below with a howl of pain. The crew scramble down the ladder after him.

'Bastards! You'll pay for that!' Bill shouts as he is dragged away to the brig.

At which point another of Bill's acolytes, Frank Dent, a ferret-faced man with a torn ear and only a third of his teeth (and those that remain yellow and black from chewing tobacco), appears from the front of the ship, where he has been availing himself of the seats of ease. He studies the scene, the captain, Beth, the twins, Lizbet.

'Unless you wish to join Bill in irons, you'll back off and hold your tongue,' Captain Elmo says.

Dent shakes his head pityingly. 'Pay me my share when we return to Whitby and I'll gladly jump ship. Rather that than serve with worms, wenches and half-breeds on this floating wreck.' He spits on the deck and turns away.

Lizbet has moved to stand closer to the captain, who now puts his hand on her head. 'Back to work. Let's clear the decks, eat and rest. Lizbet, ask Sam to give every man and woman a tot of rum with their meal, you have all earned it this day.'

Lanterns are brought out to light the work, and the crew continue the task of shucking the oysters, every woman and man now paying extra attention, 'seeing' the contents of the belly of the mollusc with their probing fingertips, to ensure that no pearl is missed. By the time they finish it is quite dark and another eighteen pearls have been collected.

While the shuckers have hunted the iridescent jewels that hide within the meaty folds of the oysters, Lizbet has collected the flesh and given it to Sam Solander who has used it to produce a hearty meal. The smell has been wafting up from the open hatch.

The pearls are gathered up and taken below deck as Beth collects the shucking knives and lanterns and everyone heads below. Pausing by the hatch Nat looks toward the shore. The fire is now very clearly visible in the jungle. He tries to imagine what it is like out there for Derek. The air is still warm and now alive with the relentless scratching and singing of insects and what he assumes must be frogs. He imagines the crew sitting in a group around a bright fire, not for warmth but to keep predators at bay. He imagines the flames lighting up the tree trunks and the faces of the crew. Do they have food and water? Why are they staying in the jungle? What was Bill referring to?

'They'll be fine,' Beth tells him. While her voice sounds confident her eyes tell a different story. 'Down below, the pair of you, and take these lanterns with you.'

CHAPTER 20

The candle is half spent and twice they have fed coal to the fire and still Robert Seeker's tale is not done. Sarah and Amy are both torn between dismissing the man as lunatic and the uncomfortable reality that, however insane his theories and confabulations may seem, the simple fact remains that somehow here they are, stuck in lodgings on a Whitby street one hundred and seventy years before either of them was born.

A church bell has rung the hour, the quarter, and the half as Seeker has set out the peculiarities of the harbour and river mouth. The only town on the Yorkshire coast where the sun both rises and sets over the sea. The propensity for terrible storms. The sacred history of the old abbey. His own research into temporal displacements and arcane phenomena. A closed conspiracy of silence. The nefarious activities of secret societies sponsored by rich patrons and outsiders.

'And seventeenthly, I must touch upon the exploitation of electricities. You have seen the splendid town hall on Church Street. Pray ask yourselves why such an edifice has been constructed here in this town. So strange and so singular in its construction. Why no rooms on the ground floor? Is not the purpose of a building to provide internal spaces to protect its occupants from the ravages of the environment? And yet this building, created at considerable expense, is open to the four winds. Does it not remind you of another place?'

Seeker's eyes gleam in the light from the fire. He pauses to reach into his waistcoat for his silver box from which he takes another pinch of snuff. His extravagant hand gestures remind Sarah of the Italian tour guide who had accompanied them on their tour of Naples. She is suffering information overload as Seeker runs his hands through his tousled mop of red hair and the barrage of conjecture recommences.

'… his father met John Wood on multiple occasions and you will recall that Wood it was who created the first accurate plan of Stonehenge. A coincidence? Possibly, but then he, Jonathan Pickernell also attended the great Piccadilly debates of 1780 in London, shortly before designing the town hall which, as you will know, was completed just thirty-four years ago in 1788. And the subject of those debates? Indeed! None other than *electricity*, ladies!' Seeker says triumphantly, then falls back in his chair, exhausted.

It is Amy who, after a couple of minutes, breaks the silence.

'So the town hall is somehow responsible for everything? Is that it?'

Robert Seeker slaps his thigh and beams at his audience of two. 'Bravo! Exactly! The building has been designed to do precisely what we are witnessing! And with your assistance, ladies, I believe I shall prove it. The scoundrels responsible will be taken to court and made to pay for the grave danger their diabolical construction is visiting upon the town. It must be dismantled stone by stone before more harm is done.'

'How would that help us, Mr Seeker?' asks Sarah. 'How are we to escape this *trap* you have described at such extraordinary length?'

Seeker is stopped in his tracks. He has no reply; he has not considered for an instant the possibility that his hosts might not wish to remain in 1821 Whitby. For a second he looks completely out of his depth. Could the portal he has described operate in reverse before being destroyed? Would he, by agreeing to help the two women, become as degenerate and evil as the men he is attempting to bring to book? Is it a crime to seek to alter the laws of time and space, however noble the cause?

'I must confess you have me at a disadvantage,' he says

eventually. 'I had assumed …'

'If you want our help, Mr Seeker, then you must …'

'Quite, quite. I understand.' Seeker consults his fob watch. 'Until now I have applied myself only to the materialisation of artefacts and persons that have been transported to the old town by this infernal construction.'

'And we did not arrive in the town hall. A door appeared in the cottage on Henrietta Street when ...' Amy adds.

'Yes, yes,' Seeker cuts her off in mid-sentence, annoyed that she has caused him to lose his train of thought.

'And what about my fiancé who was kidnapped and …'

'Please be quiet!' Seeker holds up a hand to shut Amy up. 'More important than ever,' he mutters to himself. He stands and crosses the room to the hat stand and rummages in the pockets of his voluminous coat from which he retrieves a small pouch and his Francotte Pinfire revolver.

Sarah and Amy gasp aloud at their abrupt change of circumstances. Are they to be held hostage?

'What?' Seeker says. 'Oh. No. Please, forgive me. There is no need for alarm.' He empties the pouch on the chair he has occupied. A collection of tools tumbles out, which he checks carefully. 'It is clear that I must immediately carry out the investigation that I have hitherto postponed,' he announces. 'I shall take my leave of you and, with your permission, return tomorrow evening when I hope to have further news.'

With that, Robert Seeker replaces the items in his coat, which he then puts on, he takes his top hat, and stands by the door waiting to be let out.

'Ladies,' he says as he crosses the threshold.

'What were those things he had in that bag?' Sarah muses as she closes the door on his fading footsteps.

'I saw tools just like those on an antiques show,' Amy says, happy to know more than Sarah for once. 'Mr Seeker is about to pick a lock.'

CHAPTER 21

Robert Seeker hurries back to the harbour, crosses the bridge and passes down Sandgate to reach the town square. It is still early evening and there are too many people about but, as he makes his way back to his room, he loiters long enough to take note of the sightlines around the square. Satisfied with his research, he makes way back to the White Horse and Griffin Inn where he avails himself of an evening meal and a couple of drinks to stiffen his resolve. Sitting by the window overlooking the yard, he transfers to his diary the mental notes he made while conversing with the two women. He replaces the diary beneath the mattress then stretches out upon the bed for an hour or so to relax.

Some little time after eleven o'clock Seeker emerges from the Inn and heads along Church Street to the town square. A mist has rolled in off the sea and the chill damp dank has driven everyone indoors. Everyone except the rag men and women whose poverty obliges them to continue to trudge back and forth through the night pushing their wooden carts laden with textile detritus, the tired women on Grope Lane hoping to exchange their favours for enough money to buy breakfast, and the two children huddling together for warmth on the doorstep close to Henrietta Street.

The moon is hidden. Whitby old town lies deep in shadow. There being no electric light there is nothing to pierce the lack-light gloom, no bright windows, no illuminated shop window displays, no street lights, no passing vehicle headlights. Seeker is practically feeling his way along the wall and, when he reaches the town hall, he is literally doing so. Passing between the Tuscan columns that mark the perimeter of the undercroft used by market traders during the day, Seeker fancies for a moment that he is entering a petrified forest. Remembering that one of the paving slabs is loose, having witnessed a fellow catch his heel and measure his length a few days ago, he treads carefully.

The town hall measures eleven yards by nine yards. In the centre of the space between the forest of columns is a larger trunk some three yards across. Round as a lighthouse. Round as a mighty oak. Rough to the fingertips. Seeker fumbles his way round this obstruction, his shoes scuffing the sandstone flags at his feet. Eventually his fingers feel the wooden frame and, beyond that the door. He creeps forwards until he stands squarely before the door. Fumbling in a pocket of his voluminous coat he finds his tools. He has spent days familiarising himself with the tools in his pouch to the point that he knows them all by feel: picks, hooks, half diamond, saw rake, snake rake, and more. He has practised on a dozen locks and more.

Keeping his eyes fixed upon the gloom of the square, Seeker lets his fingers 'see' and select the tools then gently probe the lock. There is something almost magical about the task in hand. He imagines himself a prestidigitator upon a stage before a swooning audience, bending the very laws of physics, defying the rules of mechanics. He is a catfish hidden in the silt on a riverbed probing the mud with his whiskers to find its prey, forcing hidden things to divulge their secrets. He feels the tiniest click, the hint of give, the sly slip of levers unseen, the play in pins. Can he bounce the pins to the shear line or does he have to be more subtle? Must he scrub the lock or jiggle it?

Incrementally the lock reveals its secrets, like a rose bud pulled apart before it has chosen to bloom.

And he is in!

He pushes open the door and steps inside. With the door

closed and locked behind him Seeker feels safe enough to light a candle, nurturing a spark into a flame in his tinderbox. A spiral staircase winds clockwise up towards the room he has wished to enter these past two months. He climbs quickly, extinguishing his candle as he nears the top, and emerges in the middle of the room. He knows from his earlier external inspection that the room has windows on three sides and that he must take great care to give no hint of his presence to anyone in the adjoining buildings or crossing the square below.

It would be fair to say that Seeker is disappointed at what he finds in the monochrome gloom. The room is almost empty: a dozen chairs; a large desk; various lamps upon a shelf; a ledger bearing the words 'meetings diary', and a box containing petrifications, principally snakestones collected, Seeker assumes, on the beach. And that is all. The desk drawers contain only an assortment of broken quills, an empty ink bottle, three pencils and a ruler.

Seeker paces the room in frustration. He peers into the fireplace and feels around for a hidden shelf. He checks every floorboard, drags the desk off the rug upon which it sits and rolls the rug, looking for a hint that one of the boards might be loose or contain a lock.

Nothing!

How can there be nothing here? It doesn't make sense. He has been reliably informed that this is where an esoteric society meets, supported by various important and influential figures, to pursue those esoteric, malevolent and acroamatic activities that are causing such chaos in the town. How can there be no trace of their operations?

On either side of the fireplace there are doors. The first opens onto a retiring room containing a commode complete with chamber pot. Behind the second door is a narrow staircase. Seeker lights his candle and hurries up the steps, his hand around the flame to prevent it from going out.

The shadows dance as the flame of his candle settles down. The attic is considerably more cramped than the room below as it is contained within the pitch of the roof. At the centre of this space are the timbers that support the bell tower. Seeker notices pipes emerging from the bell tower, running the length of the roof ridge to disappear into the wall close to the chimney. Aside from that the attic is empty.

Back downstairs in the main room, his candle once again extinguished, Seeker opens the ledger. Maybe the list of meetings will contain clues as to what is happening here aside from occasional court hearings, but it is too dark to read, even beside the large window that overlooks the square, so Seeker takes the book with him and descends the spiral staircase towards the exit. Reaching the bottom he relights his candle, drips the tallow on the fifth step up, positions the candle securely, then sits on the bottom step with the light behind him to read.

Infuriatingly, the ledger is as dull as the building that houses it: containing only a list of formal meetings of the court of pleas for the recovery of small debts (every third Monday), and the annual court leet (held at Michaelmas).

Seeker shakes his fists in frustration and, in short order, both creates a current of air that extinguishes his candle and drops the ledger that clatters to the floor in the darkness. Some little while later, when he has produced his tinderbox for the fourth time and again coaxed a spark from his flint, while muttering *Damnations!* repeatedly under his breath, he lights the candle and looks to retrieve the ledger.

But it is not on the floor in front of him. For the first time Seeker's frustration is overtaken by another emotion.

Fear.

Has he, in his foolishness and hubris, underestimated his opponents? He has thought only in terms of science; he is after all the product of the age of science, the glorious 18th century that has transformed mankind's understanding of the natural world. But what if he has misunderstood the powers at play? What if the forces of nature are harnessed not by the reasoned advancements of scholarly men but, rather, by the ugly machinations of souls engaged in the pursuit of evil?

He peers more closely at the stone floor and gets on his hands and knees to inspect the flags.

The ledger bounced on impact and has come to rest in the void beneath the spiral steps. He can see it now and reaches to retrieve it. In doing so he notices something rather odd. Whereas the majority of the flags are of roughly similar size, similar to those on the pavements outside, in the shadows there is a strip of stone the length of a flag but only three inches in width. Seeker crawls forward to inspect it and is surprised when, pressing upon this strip of stone it tilts towards him, as if on a hinge, to reveal two brass handles set into the stone beneath. He reaches out and grabs them, feeling the click of a mechanism within each handle. The stone, now released drops down on a pneumatic piston to reveal a lacklit void.

Eureka!

Fetching his candle, Seeker is able to see a ladder leading down into the very bowels of the earth.

The town hall has a basement!

CHAPTER 22

Stephen is at his wits' end. It is midnight and he is still alone in the cottage, going round and round the small living room like a shark trapped in an aquarium.

Still no call or explanation from Sarah or the other two. Still no news from the police, though a police car drove up and parked further up Henrietta Street with its lights flashing for fifteen minutes earlier in the evening.

Stephen's anger has evaporated. All he has left is worry; he just wants Sarah home and safe. He cannot bear the thought of her being out there in the darkness, either alone or with Derek and Amy.

Why did the bloody police not take him seriously? The arrogance of the man. What was his name? Punnet, Pannet? What was it he said?

'Temptation becoming too much to resist. Sharing a cottage. Excitement. A group of adults. Liaisons, if you follow me.'

How dare he insinuate such things instead of doing his job?

Impulsively, Stephen throws on his jacket and steps out onto Henrietta Street. For the next three hours he pounds the streets, the east cliff, the west cliff, along the harbour, up and down the 199 steps. All the way to Pannett Park. Up the Khyber Pass and along North Terrace, passing the ridiculous Arnold Palmer Putting Course and the empty outdoor swimming pool. Round the Royal Crescent and down through the streets of Victorian Whitby to Skinner Street and Flowergate and back to the swing bridge.

Nothing.

He has forgotten the beach so he rushes back past the blind shuttered frontage of the clairvoyant's shack and amusement arcades where the lights have finally stopped twinkling and on to the pier. He runs to the lighthouse and on along the planks until he is obliged to stop or fall into the sea. He looks between the planks at his feet to see if she is on the lower level, dreading what he might find.

Nothing.

Down on the beach, the clatter clamour chaos of the folding waves wraps his ears like tinnitus as he races along the foot of the cliff peering in the darkness, slipping on the rocks, exploring every void. Behind him the sand stores the record of his footsteps. In his haste he ignores the evidence that there are no other steps set in the sand. He runs until his lungs are burning, past the brightly coloured beach huts. Upgang Beach all the way to Sandsend Beach.

Nothing.

What a fool he is! Why would anyone be out on a beach after midnight? Now the policeman becomes Iago in his ear, sower of doubt and jealousy, insinuator of infidelities. Of course they aren't on the beach. They are ensconced in a hotel or a cottage back in the old town just metres from Henrietta Street. All three of them. Drunk on champagne, locked in each other's arms, mocking him for being so naive. They probably booked a second cottage before they even got into the car to drive north. It was all planned.

Stephen runs back towards the harbour, thick with rising rage. The tide is coming in and the broad beach has narrowed to a strip as the waters wash over his shoes. His footsteps have disappeared and the wind has picked up. He should get off the sand and follow the path back up the cliff past the Pavilion but he is not about to allow the sea to tell him what to do. Sod it, sod her, sod them, sod bloody Whitby and all it stands for.

He runs his splashing shoes, the whispering waves licking

his ankles, still a thousand metres from the pier and the safety of the ramp up to Pier Road. Stephen wants the fight. He wants to take on the sea and the rest of the world if he has to. Why has she left him? What did he do to be treated so badly? Why could he not see it coming?

The water is up to his knees as waves meld and merge.

A larger wave crashunders in, surging the sea up halfway up his thighs. Stephen loses his footing and falls, splash down in a freezing face full of salt water. The shock wakes him, drags the self-pity out of him even as the water slyly sucks him down the beach towards the sea. He rouses himself in a frantic tangle of limbs, pulls his head out of the water and tries to climb to his feet but the water is moving too quickly.

'No!' he shouts into the night as he slides helplessly towards deeper water.

The wave dragging him down is confronted by a second wave coming in and, in the brief moment of respite, Stephen finds his feet and lifts himself up and staggers pell-mell up the beach, blind to anything but his own survival. Towards the steps beside the gun battery forty metres away. His clothes heavy with the sea, sticking to his limbs, he prays there are no more hidden rocks to catch his feet. In the periphery of his vision he sees a figure to his left, standing at the railing up on the pier.

A wave ambushes Stephen from behind. Again he falls. Now he is swimming. He must reach the steps before the wave changes course and drags him back. With a roar he uses every ounce of his strength to close the gap.

There! A rusty rail set into the stone. He lunges forward. Misses. He feels the water shift beneath him. Another desperate lunge. This time his fingers scrape the rough surface. He grasps it with all his strength. As the wave retreats so does his support. His body falls heavily onto the stone steps winding him and crunching his shoulder painfully. He is not yet safe.

Somehow he pulls himself together and scrambles up out of harm's way before the sea flings itself at him. The wave shakes at the jaws of the steps like a great white shark come to snatch a huge serrated mouthful from the belly of a whale.

But Stephen is safe. For a while he sits on the cold steps, clutching the rusty rail, eyes closed, heart racing, lungs heaving, ears sloshing with the chaos of the sea.

'You all right, lad?' A gruff Yorkshire voice. 'I said, are you right?'

Stephen opens his eyes and turns to look up the steps. An old man in a thick coat and with his flat cap pulled down hard on his head is studying him.

'What were you thinking? She doesn't need asking twice.'

'Who doesn't? What?' Stephen says, confused.

'The sea. She's had her share of Whitby folk over t'years. You'll need to get inside. You'll freeze out here, lad.'

Stephen nods. 'Yeah, you're right.'

'Do you need help?'

'No, I'm fine.' Stephen stands up. His legs give way. He falls and tries again. 'We're in … I'm in one of the cottages. Across the harbour.'

'Didn't think you were local. I'll walk with you, if you want.'

'That's kind but I'm okay.'

'Suit yer sen.' The old man smiles. 'Anyroad, you're better doing that in summer with trunks on. Goodnight.'

Stephen watches the old man walk to the narrow passage that leads between the fish restaurants up to Khyber Pass.

Teeth chattering, Stephen takes the other route, to the bandstand. He squelches his way down Pier Road and St Anns Staith, and crosses the swing bridge where the wind on his wet clothes chills him to the bone. As he trudges up Church Street past the closed shops and pubs he suddenly has the most curious feeling. A tingling sensation that ripples up his back, causing all the hairs on his neck to stand on end. To his right is the narrow entrance to one of the yards. It is as if someone is whispering to him in the lacklight. Beckoning him.

'Sarah?'

He steps into the passage.

There is a foul smell in the air like boiling fat. Emerging into the yard the sensation is even stronger. A single light in one of the houses. The yard is empty. In a dusty bay window is a collection of jumble, boxes and trinkets. He listens to the night air but all is silent.

He heads back down the passage to Church Street. Three minutes later he is back at the cottage where he strips off all his wet clothes, leaving them in a pile on the kitchen floor. The lights are back on through the entire house. He stands under a hot shower for fifteen minutes then having found his dressing gown, a couple of hot water bottles and a quilt from one of the bedrooms, Stephen falls asleep on the sofa in the front room with a cup of cocoa and the comforting trivia babble of an all-night radio show.

CHAPTER 23

Sarah waits until Amy is snoring gently then pushes back the blankets and gets up. She gathers her clothes and creeps out of the bedroom.

She dresses quickly in front of the dying embers in the fireplace. It is hard to know what she should wear. Should she dress as a well-to-do respectable woman of means or dress like the hard-working fisherwomen? What will keep her safe at night? She plumps for fisherwoman with an undercoating of 21st century jeans and fleece. She wears the shawl Rebecca gave her as a headscarf to hide her modern haircut.

The visit from Robert Seeker was as interesting as it was unexpected but Sarah does not wish to leave all her eggs in one basket. Seeker is an eccentric and Sarah knows making sense of her curious predicament will require more than the theories of a subterfuginous conspiracist.

She unlocks the door quietly and lets herself out into the passage. Once outside she hurries through the empty streets, down to the bridge, along Sandgate, and through the town square onto Church Street. She walks briskly and confidently as she has seen the local women do. The two men she passes don't seem to notice her, which is just as she wants it.

She pauses at the entrance of the yard, wrinkling her nose. The smell of whale blubber being rendered does not get any better. The yard is quiet, it is past eleven o'clock. No rain expected tonight, so baskets, tables and fishing lines are all outside. Pushing open the cottage door, Sarah fumbles her way in the gloom and knocks on the door at the end of the corridor.

'Go away,' says a sleepy voice.

'Rebecca, it's me, Sarah. Sorry to knock so late but …'

The door opens. Rebecca is dishevelled and clutching a blanket. The room is quite dark. 'What do you want, Sarah?' she whispers. 'I am back at work in a few hours and I need my sleep, love.'

'I know, I'm sorry. I wanted to give you this.' Sarah grabs Rebecca's hand and presses a fistful of coins into it.

'Bloody hell, have you robbed a bank!'

'We did as you suggested and sold one of Amy's jewels. Her bracelet.'

'Keep your voice down. Does she know you've come here to give me this?'

'We've found lodgings up on Silver Street.'

'You won't be wearing those rags up on top hat hill.'

'That's what the money is for, Rebecca, for the clothes and for all the help you've given us.'

'Those rags are worth but a few pennies. I cannot take all this brass from thee. I'm not a beggar.'

Sarah had not considered Rebecca's pride. Behind them her daughter and the children are stirring.

'All right, my loves. Back to sleep.'

'How about this then?' Sarah says. 'Can Rosie cook? How about we pay her to cook and look after our lodgings?'

'You'll get two months' work from her for that,' Rebecca says.

'Will that help you?'

'You addle hat blunderbuss, of course it will help!' Rebecca smiles.

The two women hug.

'Where can we find you tomorrow afternoon?'

'I'll bring Rosie up to your lodgings around ten. Will that do?'

'Perfect.'

As she steps from the yard passage back onto Church

Street, Sarah has the most curious feeling. As if she is passing through another body that is standing invisibly in the road. As if she is embraced in a lover's arms. She pauses briefly overwhelmed by emotion, tears welling up.

She calls out, 'Stephen?'

The street is empty.

Twenty minutes later Sarah is back in Silver Street and climbing into bed. She lies back and closes her eyes. For the first time in twenty-four hours she feels she has been of some use in the world.

'Where have you been?'

Damn. Why did you have to wake up, Amy?

'I couldn't sleep,' Sarah tells her. 'All that stuff Mr Seeker told us. I've been sitting by the fire thinking.'

'No, you haven't. I got up and had a look. You've been out.'

'I'll tell you about it in the morning, Amy.'

'You could have been killed.'

'But I wasn't.'

'If you leave me here all alone I will never forgive you.'

'It's not what you think. Whatever you think. Let's just get some sleep.'

For an hour they do get some sleep.

Out in the kitchen a couple of mice have found the bread and are breaking small chunks away to hold and nibble. Down in the harbour wooden boats knock against each other gently as the water shifts them forth and back. Poverty snores in the workhouse while in the yards whale blubber simmers in burnt black cauldrons. Frost paints the windows and Whitby sleeps.

Suddenly Amy is awake, sitting bolt upright in bed, shouting blindly, incoherently into the darkness. 'No! No! Don't leave me! Mum, where are you? Why are you hiding?' Tears stream down her face.

Sarah's eyes open in the lacklight of a damp and unfamiliar

room, the smell of smoke and floor polish in the air. Someone is sobbing. Heavy bedding is pressing down on her. She shakes her head as if to rid it of cobwebs and pinches herself. But she is not dreaming, she is awake and it is Amy who is sobbing. Sarah throws off the blankets and crosses the cold rough carpet to sit on Amy's bed.

Switch the light on and find your clothes.

You can't, there are no light switches. Remember?

'Shh. It's okay,' she says softly, putting a gentle hand on Amy's back.

'No, it's not okay,' Amy replies. 'This is a nightmare and we are stuck in it and we are never going to be safe again.'

CHAPTER 24

The flames are probably of more use than the palisade, Derek has decided.

Wild animals fear flames, don't they?

He has seen no other ships but what if there are settlements inland? If they are on a rescue mission then, by implication, somewhere in the jungle there are people awaiting rescue. Might some of the crew have mutinied and taken others hostage? Why will no one tell him what is really going on?

On the other hand, two defences may be better than one. Having returned from collecting wood with Jack and Phin while the others enlarged the clearing, it has taken the whole crew the best part of an hour and a half to erect a circle of what are effectively thick spears facing the jungle in all directions. Seventy or more of them, all cut from giant horsetail plants, maybe fifteen centimetres in diameter at the base and cut to sharp points with their machetes.

They are a crew of ten. Two women: Alice and Flora. And eight men: Chisholm, Jack, his twin brother Noah, Phin, Silas, a whale of a man called Big George, Newt, and Derek. There are no slackers, everyone knows the job they have to do; they depend upon each other for survival, here in the jungle or out at sea.

Buried half a metre into the soil these upright stakes serve to hold the thick fronds of vegetation that are woven in and out between them to create an impenetrable barrier a metre and a half in height that will repel anything smaller than an elephant. Not that they have seen elephants in this jungle. Or tigers. Derek has seen the rear end of a large creature but he still cannot bring himself to name it. In fact he has convinced himself he was hallucinating as a result of being in shock.

There is no gate or opening in this palisade, having completed it the crew are as locked in for the night as surely as any potential predators will be locked out. Looking at their handiwork, Derek is proud of himself. He has played his full part in the creation of a defensive wall far stronger than any line of prop forwards on a rugby pitch. The two women, Alice and Flora, both forty centimetres shorter than Derek have shown themselves as strong as the men, but they are used to this work so he feels no shame.

Within the palisade, that is maybe seven metres in diameter, they have built a large fire that burns brightly. Given the downpour earlier in the day Derek was sceptical that this could be done, imagining the wood must surely be soaking wet. The others have proved him wrong; they know which trees to cut and which to leave. Behind Derek is a large woodpile containing a mixture of logs, branches, leaves, and long trimmed stakes cut with machetes to create sharp spikes. Away from the fire the metal structure they carried up the hill has been assembled: it is a cage the size of a small shelving unit, with two hooks at the top, presumably intended to accommodate poles to carry it.

'Sit down, Derek. Watching thee pace about makes me tired,' says Alice.

'Me too,' laughs Phin.

'Are we safe?' Derek asks.

'As long as we keep fire fed and bright they'll keep their distance,' Jack explains. He produces a set of dice from his pocket. 'Who's for Hazard?'

'With those dice?' Silas replies. 'You'll not flutter-filch me twice, you fishmonger's fleapit.'

Jack pokes Silas with a stick. 'There speaks a yellow tow rag.'

'Gentlemen,' barks Chisholm, using a term that applies to neither man. 'Civil tongues and keep your wits about you. We have twelve hours of darkness ahead of us.'

The bickering stops.

'We'll have two keeping watch, the rest will sleep. Phin and Derek, you'll go first.' Chisholm checks his watch. 'Rouse me in two hours.' With that he lies down, a log for a pillow, and is asleep in less than a minute.

Derek sits crossed legged by the fire. As night has fallen so the temperature has dropped and he is glad of the warmth. Phin sits opposite him staring over the flames and Derek's shoulders at the forest beyond.

Now properly sober and with time to think, Derek is lost with his thoughts. Who tried to send him to his death earlier? Is he sharing the clearing with the men who abducted him in Whitby? Who can he trust?

The gentle crackling of the fire, the dancing shadows and the smell of the smoke eventually combine to undermine Derek's defences. After an hour, in spite of himself, he starts to feel drowsy. How can he escape back to his own time? Is he hallucinating everything? Maybe when he wakes up and …

His chin drops to his chest.

'Hey! Hey! Keep your eyes open.'

Derek lifts his head. The sky is clear. No moon, no clouds. The Milky Way is brighter than he has ever seen it before. So many stars.

Something is not right.

He lifts his hands to shield his eyes from the light of the fire and, for the first time since his kidnapping he feels real terror. It catches him in his throat, leaving him barely able to breathe.

The enormity of what has happened to him is written in the sky above his head. The constellations have fallen apart! He can see what he is sure is part of Orion's Belt, but why is half of it missing? The night sky represents permanence; the stars of your birth are the stars of your death. In a universe billions of light years across, a human life is so short as not to register in the night sky. For Orion to have fallen apart he must be millions of years in the future, or the past. Maybe hundreds of millions of years! It is as if he has fallen through a black hole; the sky above proves that he is in a completely different moment in time.

Where the hell is he? When is he?

'Hey! Hey! Wake up!'

Derek looks across the fire at Phin who knows nothing of light years or the Big Bang.

'The stars,' Derek splutters, 'they're all wrong! You have to trust me, the universe is …'

'We navigate by the stars. There is nothing to fear,' Phin replies. 'The captain explained it is God's plan for us in this place. A reminder not to travel far when we crossover, lest we become lost forever.'

'You don't understand. We are millions of years from …'

'We're here to work,' Phin says, 'and that's it. I don't want to ...'

'But what if …'

They are interrupted by a low booming sound in the trees. Instantly Phin is on the alert. He grabs his flintlock and looks towards the source of the noise. A second booming sound, from a different direction this time.

'Rouse the crew,' Phin hisses as he gets to his feet and collects firewood from the pile to feed the fire.

Bright sparks fly up into the air and the fresh timber crackles and spits as it catches fire. Derek hurries round, shaking shoulders and prodding backs and in seconds everyone is awake. Alice and Jack grab long branches from the woodpile and thrust the spikes deep into the fire. The others check their weapons: four flintlocks, cutlasses, two axes, machetes and a row of glass bottles, containing what looks like shards of metal and a long fuse, that have come from one of the men's packs.

The air smells vaguely of rotting meat.

In the dappled shadows are three juvenile creatures. The only indication that they are alive is found in their ballooning necks flaps that swell then collapse to create the low booming sounds that fill the clearing. They are opportunists, bipeds, fast and intelligent, as comfortable scavenging bodies on the beach as hunting their prey. Being juveniles they are still on the small side, around two metres tall, but already weigh as much as large tigers. Their bodies are covered in a hazy down of unpigmented protofeathers. By day their feathers reflect their surroundings allowing them to meld into the background. In the darkness their feathers reflect nothing.

The leader of the group has one large clawed foot resting on the carcass of a smaller creature, one of the quadrupeds that Aleka and Nat saw from the beach earlier in the day. Satisfied that each member of the group is in position, they stop booming.

Within the palisade the change does not pass unnoticed.

'I think we have frightened it away,' declares Newt. 'They hate fire.'

'Frightened *what* away?' asks Derek.

No one answers. Alice and Noah arrange the glass bottles close, but not too close, to the fire. Jack runs a finger down the blade of his cutlass, checking its sharpness. Chisholm cups his hand to block the light of the fire as he slowly scans the treeline beyond the palisade. Silas glares sourly at his companions while muttering under his breath. Newt relaxes, shakes the stiffness from his shoulders. Big George stares blankly into the flames, his face grim.

The minutes pass. The jungle remains silent.

'Right men,' Chisholm says eventually. 'Stand down. Feed the fire. Jack and Alice, take second watch. The rest of you grab what sleep you can. Phin and Derek, good work.'

Sighs of relief.

'Wait,' says Flora. She is one of the quieter members of the group and generally just gets on with whatever she is asked to do. Tough as nails she has demonstrated many times that she is capable of handling herself. There is some talk that she might replace Chisholm if ever he retires. 'Something's not right.'

'If you want to do a double shift on watch, be my guest,' sneers Silas. 'But don't expect special treatment.'

'Hold thy tongue, Silas!' Chisholm grabs Silas' arm and spins him round.

Silas is gripping his cutlass. For a second he locks eyes with Chisholm and it looks like trouble, then the challenge fades. Silas snorts contemptuously, backs away and sits on the ground with his back against the woodpile.

'Join them on second watch,' Chisholm tells Flora. 'The rest of you grab your beauty sleep while you can, my pretty ones. This night is far from done.'

Derek lies down as close to the fire as he dares, closes his eyes and tries to relax. The cicadas, or whatever insects are up in the trees, have started buzzing again. First one then two, then hundreds of them until the air is vibrating. The insects set the frogs off and in next to no time the clearing is drowning in sound to the point that Derek can no longer hear the crackling of the fire. He lies there trying to imagine he is back at home, watching a rugby match on television, a pile of empty cans on the floor beside the sofa, Amy popping her head round the door to announce that the takeaway pizzas have just been delivered and, yet again, they forgot to include the garlic bread.

It sort of works but, opening his eyes just enough to squint at the dancing flames reflected in the blade of his cutlass and Alice's curves and the flintlock pistol resting in her lap, Derek also realises that he feels more alive than he ever does sitting on a sofa or getting legless in the pub or staring at a spreadsheet on a computer screen in those boring boring offices that suck the bloody life out of you until every day is measured by how long it is until the weekend. He thinks of Beth back on the ship, and the twins, and the girl Lizbet, and the porridge he had with the early morning sunshine streaming through the open hatch while the ship rocked gently on a turquoise sea.

A sickening visceral smack against the stakes. The crunch thud of flesh and bone. The whole palisade creaks from the weight of it and the chaos begins.

In a flash Flora and Jack retrieve burning stakes from the fire and swing them round as the first predator emerges from the jungle and leaps up onto the palisade using the body of the impaled quadruped it has just hurled as a buffer to protect it from the spikes of the stakes. A second bound takes the creature onto the top of the woodpile from which it leans forwards, using its tail as counterbalance, until its open jaws reach and grab Silas' head and twists it violently round. The ripping of tendons and muscles is clearly audible.

Silas' muffled scream is still in the air as Alice and Jack plunge their burning stakes into the animal's face, one tearing at its neck, the other taking out an eye. A shot rings out.

Derek finally admits the truth that has been loitering inside his head.

Dinosaurs!

The sky does not lie. They are tens or hundreds of millions of years in the past and about to be torn to shreds by bloody dinosaurs! Or megalosaurs to be precise.

Derek is still reaching for his cutlass as a second creature leaps onto the carcass of the impaled quadruped and up high into the air to land beside the roaring pain-racked body of its sibling. Chisholm screams an oath and thrusts his cutlass into the creature's chest but, while the blade goes in up to the hilt, the predator seems unimpressed. Small but powerful forearms lash out, ripping into Chisholm's bicep as he attempts desperately to withdraw his weapon.

The third megalosaur has emerged from the jungle. It rushes to the palisade and stops, its chest just centimetres from the sharpened stakes. It opens its jaws to reveal dozens of sharp teeth as its eye fixes on Noah who is standing directly across the palisade. In his hand is one of the glass bottles, its fuse lit from the fire.

'Let him have it!' screams Flora.

Noah throws the bottle over the palisade. As it hits the ground it explodes sending a shower of shrapnel in all directions. The metal shards tear into the dinosaur's legs and tail. It doesn't need a second helping, turning on its heels and rushing away into the jungle.

Within the palisade the battle is not yet done. The first creature has slid off the woodpile, tumbled down and crushing Silas beneath it. Limbs thrashing and lashing blindly, the animal is in its death throes. The second megalosaur is still above the crew, a cutlass embedded deep in its belly. Chisholm lies on the ground clutching his arm in agony while Derek and the rest of the crew lunge at the animal with cutlasses and machetes. Despite weighing as much as three men, the creature is struggling and when Big George starts beating it with a burning stake from the fire it decides it has had enough. It somersaults backward off the woodpile and over the palisade, the embedded cutlass in its chest clattering to the ground as the animal picks itself up and rushes away into the jungle.

It takes seven of them to roll the dead megalosaur off Silas but they are too late. Silas is dead.

Derek helps Alice to tie a tourniquet around Chisholm's shoulder to stem the blood flow from his torn bicep. Half the crew are nursing injuries as a result of the thrashing back legs of the dying dinosaur and the shrapnel from the exploding grenade.

It is an hour before the palisade is secured, the fire built up and a semblance of order descends on the clearing. Phin is for dismembering the dinosaur and throwing it and Silas over the palisade but Chisholm persuades the others that the dinosaurs will not return. Everyone is dog-tired. Four of the crew keep watch while the others sleep, the sleepers trading places with those on watch every hour.

Dawn is an eternity away.

CHAPTER 25

Seeker, having first removed his voluminous coat, turns round and eases himself through the narrow gap and down the ladder. He places his candle on the floor then climbs back up to retrieve his coat and to pull the mechanism that lifts the flagstone above him back into place.

Down on solid ground, he catches his breath and gives himself a moment to enjoy his triumph. He has found the room he has believed must exist and, with it, the proof that dark forces are indeed at work orchestrating the extraordinary happenings that have been occurring in the old town of Whitby!

The room is crammed with esoteric machines. Plans and maps adorn the walls alongside a large slice of slate upon which is a series of calculations. Seeker has never previously seen coloured markings on a slate but he has heard about them and knows that they are created from a mixture ground chalk, coloured pigments and porridge, to a recipe invented a few years ago in Scotland.

On a shelf is a mannequin head.

'Hello!' he whispers excitedly.

Upon the head is a most curious piece of headgear, a helmet made of strips of brass and bearing a rotating brass dial on which are mounted three telescopes of varying length, clearly designed to fit over the wearer's eye.

Seeker is shivering in chill dank air, so he climbs back into his thick coat. Before yielding to the desire to study each object and every paper stacked on shelves he must understand the layout of this subterranean vault and establish a clear route of escape. It cannot be that all its visitors enter via the trap door in the town hall, since that opening can accommodate only the lightest and lithest of frames; there has to be another method of ingress and egress.

Seeker lights one of the lanterns on the large table in the centre of the room and explores his surroundings. There are two doors. The first, as in the town hall above the spiral staircase, reveals a retiring room and commode. The second gives onto a passage with a stone flagged floor that leads, if he has his bearings correct, eastwards towards the abbey side of Church Street. A sharp turn to the south. The air is damp, the walls encrusted with calcification. While the town hall was built only forty years ago, this passage is hundreds of years old.

Another door, painted red and bearing three large locks, each with its own ornate key in situ.

He turns each key. The door opens silently on well-oiled hinges. Another passage, this one carpeted and dry.

Significantly, the door has no keyholes or handles on the other side; it can only be opened from the inside. Carefully wedging the door open with his tool pouch, Seeker advances into the carpeted corridor, revolver in one hand and lantern in the other. He moves cautiously, alert to any sign that his progress has been noticed.

Half a dozen steps lead upwards. A left turn and he joins a second passage. It is warmer here and the air smells of coal fires and food. An archway to his right leads to a basement room piled high with barrels. The passage itself leads to another flight of steps. All at once Seeker is emerging behind the bar of none other than the White Horse and Griffin Inn.

The very building in which he has been lodging these past two months!

Without wasting further time, Seeker turns tail and retraces his steps, hurrying back to the door with the three locks where he collects his tool pouch, pulls the door to, locks himself in, and returns to the chamber beneath the town hall.

For the next half an hour he probes the secrets of this Aladdin's cave, jotting and drawing into his notebook. He scribbles down the equations on the blackboard. They mean nothing to him but may mean something to his employers. He sketches the helmet with its mounted telescopes.

The maps on the wall show the old town, over which a lattice of lines has been drawn linking features and structures. On one map overlaid lines link Abbey House on the hill with a couple of the yards, a building near the harbour, Tate Hill Pier, and Henrietta Street.

Seeker copies the plans quickly in his notebook and turns his attention to the books and papers upon the table. A diary reveals the date of meetings going back nineteen years, giving the initials of the participants at each meeting. Seeker's eyes are aflame with excitement as he scribbles, transcribing the initials into his notebook and muttering under his breath. Who are the initiates engaged in these nefarious activities? His employers in London will surely pay handsomely for the information. After months of frustration and failure, his prospects are at last improving with every passing minute!

And what of those curious goggles with the crystal lenses? He tries a pair on. Immediately the room appears dimmer, the colours muted. What can they possibly be for?

Beneath the table is a waste bin. On impulse, Seeker pours its contents onto the table. Among the discarded packaging materials, strings, spent candles, broken biscuits and empty whisky bottles are various crumpled sheets of paper. He opens and flattens the first sheet and reads:

Commentarius diarium et ephemeris 1819

Beneath the title is a list of names and the words *impensa* and *reditus*, alongside which are sums of money. Presumably monies coming in and going out. A set of accounts?

Seeker is about to start copying when he hears a sound above him. A door swings open. Muffled footsteps. The sound of running. Someone has entered the town hall! More steps. Shouting.

It is time to flee. Seeker trousers his notebook and shoves the crumpled balls and torn fragments of paper into his coat pockets and is grabbing the lantern as the mechanism that operates the hidden entrance clicks above him.

'They may already be inside!' shouts a voice. 'Hurry and cut them off!'

Seeker grabs a pair of the goggles and shoves them in a coat pocket and races out of the room, down the passage to make his escape. In his foolishness he triple-locked the door and now he has work to do. With no time to waste, he turns the three keys. It will only take his pursuers a few seconds to run down Church Street and enter the White Horse and Griffin. Should he return to the basement room? He is armed after all. No one can enter through the locked door and he can shoot each man as he comes down the ladder. But how many of them are there? What if they simply commandeer the town hall and mount a siege? Sooner or later Seeker will be flushed out, or die of thirst and hunger.

The last lock is turned. His mind made up, he hauls open the door and runs up the first set of steps and into the second passage as fast as his feet will carry him. Can he reach the bar of the White Horse and Griffin and disappear into the night before they catch him?

He is almost at the second set of steps when he hears the sound of broken glass ahead of him. Frantically he spins on his heel. He is cut off; they are already in the building above!

A hand reaches through the broken window to find the key in the lock.

'Which way?'

'The passage behind the bar! Hurry!'

Two sets of boots crunch over the broken glass. Two burly men enter the White Horse and Griffin. One holds a thick iron bar, the other a pistol and a lantern. They charge through, dislodging a tray of wine glasses that shatter on the floor in their wake, and disappear down the steps into the basement.

'Not that way! Over here.'

The first thug remerges from the beer cellar and follows his partner down the passage toward the triple-locked door.

As their footsteps become fainter, Robert Seeker, gun in hand, fumbles his way from behind the beer barrels where he has been hiding, passes under the arch and follows the lacklit steps up towards the bar.

He is crossing towards the open door, and the yard beyond, as the landlord emerges bleary-eyed from upstairs.

'Stop, thief!' The landlord grabs a bottle from behind the bar and hurls it at Seeker's head.

Seeker dodges the missile and races out into the night, praying the landlord hasn't recognised him.

CHAPTER 26

Stephen wakes up as tired as he fell asleep, still on the sofa. He checks his phone. Nothing.

It is seven forty-three. The local radio station is burbling in the background.

They have to vacate the cottage by midday. Just the thought of it makes him nauseous. He staggers into the kitchen, puts the kettle on, tears open the bag of croissants sitting on the work surface and eats two or three mechanically, one after the other, his mind racing. A glass of water followed by a cup of coffee. Down to the bathroom, where he does his level best to clean the mud off the floor with a towel, while worrying whether in saving his deposit he is tampering with a crime scene.

Can't waste a thousand quid! I'm the only bugger who slept here!

He dumps the dirty towel in the kitchen then up to the bedrooms, trying to form a sense of what needs doing. He throws clothes, makeup, toothbrushes, alarm clock and books into the suitcases then crosses the landing into the room occupied by Derek and Amy and does the same in there.

Trudging the suitcases downstairs, Stephen goes through in his mind all the things he will need to do in order to avoid losing their deposit. It's not just the mud, it's the whole house. Is it tidy? Sarah would be busy with the vacuum cleaner and a duster by now, giving him his orders. Has the rubbish been taken out? Is the shower clean?

Sod the bloody deposit. Who cares?

Back upstairs. Check all the cupboards and drawers. Down

in the bathroom. Scoop everything up and dump it in a carrier bag, doesn't matter what belongs to who. Suitcases and bags by the door. Another cup of coffee.

The pips on the radio.

'Good morning. It's 8 o'clock on the 29th of November. Welcome. It's Monday in North Yorkshire! Another cold morning but the worst of Storm Arwin is behind us and Whitby is getting warmer as those bitter Arctic winds settle down.'

'The main news in this morning. Five mysterious disappearances reported over the weekend. All in the old town. All visitors. What is going on? Later in the show we'll be talking with the man who has seen it all: Whitby Gazette's veteran reporter Brian Whaler. First over to Fiona for the shopping news. Local traders are desperate to avoid COVID lockdowns in the run-up to Christmas. What can you tell us, Fiona?'

Five people!

Stephen is gobsmacked. How can the media be running a story about Sarah and the others? Have the police leaked the information even though they have refused to investigate? And why five people?

Rather than sitting about to hear the interview with Brian Whaler, Stephen decides to leave the house and find the reporter.

Twenty-three minutes later he has collected the car, dumped all the suitcases and bags into it, shoved the cottage key through the letterbox and found contact details for the Whitby Gazette. Seven minutes after that he is in front of a modern house up on the hill off the Scarborough road. He presses the doorbell.

'Come in. It's just through here.'

Brian Whaler shows Stephen into his back room, opening the windows.

'I'll close the door to keep the heat in. Please, have a seat, Mr ...?'

'Stephen Bootle.'

'I'm not sure how I can help. Have you been to the police?'

Brian Whaler is a gaunt and slightly stooped man with grey hair and sad grey eyes. *Four sticks of rhubarb and some Sellotape* is how Stephen's grandmother might have described him. He wears a pale blue cardigan over a tired cream nylon shirt and maroon tie. Whaler is wearing his facemask and has insisted that Stephen does the same. The dining table is piled high with books, old newspapers. Dark brown corduroy curtains. A clutter of Victoriana on the mantelpiece. Stephen guesses that Brian Whaler lives alone and that the furniture is all inherited from an aged aunt. Only the state-of-the-art iMac and expensive headset on the dresser confirm his engagement with the modern world.

'I know you have been speaking with the police. How else could you be reporting a story about disappearances without *them* tipping you off?'

'You are quite right, Mr Bootle. My apologies. How can I be of assistance?'

'My wife, Sarah, and two friends have disappeared. The news said five people. Who are the other two? They called you a veteran reporter on the radio, what is going on?'

'People disappear for all sorts of reasons and …'

'I already heard that crap from the police. My wife has not run off with my workmate, we have not been arguing recently, and we did not escape to Yorkshire for a spot of kinky hanky-panky.'

Whaler nods and looks away.

'Have there been others?' Stephen asks. 'Does it happen all over Whitby or just in one place? I need to know, I have to find her!'

Whaler holds his hands over his nose, as if in prayer and taps his fingertips together. He sighs. 'I've been a reporter here for forty years. To answer your question, yes, this has happened before.' Whaler looks Stephen in the eye. 'Always on the east side, always in the old town, at night, and during a storm. An electrical storm to be precise. I am aware of fourteen disappearances, going back to 1937, including the five this weekend.'

'Bloody hell! And *none* of them have ever been found?'

'It's a little more complicated than that.' Whaler stands up and walks over to the window. A startled blackbird flees the bird feeder. 'There were one woman who turned up in 2017, I think, claiming to have been kidnapped by pirates. When police interviewed her they couldn't decide whether she was a victim of human trafficking or insane.' He sits back down. 'The trouble were that, according to her, she had travelled alone to Whitby. No close family in this country. Claimed to have stayed in a campervan on a site outside town. No hotel or bed & breakfast receipts. No one could vouch for her presence in Whitby three years earlier, when she claimed to have been kidnapped. In the end the police closed the case.'

'Where was she from? Where did she go?'

'I believe she were from France or Belgium. Angelique Vallar. I interviewed her a couple of times for the paper, she had reasonable English. It only became news because she refused to accept the police's decision and became very agitated. Threw a chair through the police station window. A passer-by got hurt. They had her sectioned. That's when I went to chat with her. Nice lady. Very sad.'

'Do you know where she is now?'

'A housing association flat on Crescent Avenue, if nothing has changed. This were four years ago, though.' Whaler stands and goes to the door.

'Are all the disappearances linked to visitors? Have local people gone missing?'

'Both. That's all I have, Mr Bootle. Sorry.'

CHAPTER 27

It is still dark when Lizbet awakens Aleka and Nat. The twins climb out of the hammocks they have been given and join the others gathered round Sam the cook to collect their porridge.

'Eat well. Today our work will be a little harder than yesterday,' Beth explains.

'When will be going home?' Nat asks.

Aleka gives him the eye.

Beth looks nonplussed. In the background Lizbet is watching the conversation as she helps the cook.

'We don't belong here,' Nat continues. 'You know that. We were kidnapped and I want to know when …'

'I cannot answer,' Beth cuts him off. 'Here we work and I follow orders like everyone else on this ship. If you have questions, talk with the captain.'

'That went well,' Aleka says, watching Beth walk away.

'Shut up,' Nat snarls. 'At least I am trying to get us out of this mess.'

'You said the diving was fun.'

'That is not the point. We've been kidnapped. What will mum and dad be thinking? What happens if we fall ill? Have you seen any medicines on board? This is nuts! We don't know where we are. If you break a leg this lot will just pin you down and saw it off. This isn't a bloody joke, Aleka!'

'Hey! Hey!' Aleka waves her hands to shut him up. In a quieter voice she adds, 'Cool it bro. I'm not blind, I get it. We just have to be smart, that's all I'm saying. I'm guessing that when the captain is happy we have filled his bucket with pearls we'll leave this place and return to Whitby. That's when we can escape the ship. We can't do it now, in the middle of nowhere.'

'All I'm saying is …'

'I know what you're saying but we have to keep our shit together, Nat. Focus on surviving. Okay?'

Nat glowers and sticks out his lower jaw. She's right. Why is she always bloody right?

Twenty minutes later with the sun still not over the horizon, one of the boats is lowered onto the water and they row away. Up on the ship, Lizbet waves them off cheerily. No sign of the captain. These new oyster beds are much further away, four kilometres or more. As they make their way along the coast the twins look at the beach. The tide is going out.

'Look. There's only one boat on the beach,' says Nat.

'Maybe the others came back to the ship in the night.' Aleka suggests.

Beth hears them and turns to look. Her face drops. She turns to Thin George, the scout. 'Two of the boats gone. We don't have time to turn back. Flag the news to the ship.'

Thin George produces a set of flags and sends the message back to the ship while the rest of the crew continues to row towards the oyster beds.

'Message acknowledged,' he tells Beth.

'What's happened?' Nat asks.

Beth shakes her head; she has no idea.

Forty minutes later they reach their destination just as the sun finally heaves itself out of the sea and up into the sky. They have timed it perfectly. The tide is almost out. The water is clear. They are on the edge of a kelp forest. They kit up; each of the divers is given heavier weights than yesterday.

'The beds are one or two fathoms deeper here,' Beth explains to the divers. 'Be careful as you dive. I want everyone safe. You two watch the others and learn.'

The teenagers nod. Ten minutes later as they enter the water

Aleka is on edge. It isn't just that the oyster bed is deeper; the kelp forest means they only have a clear view on one side and while Beth and most of the others are behaving just as they did yesterday Aleka notices that one of the party is not gathering oysters, he is facing the kelp, knife in hand.

The oysters are bigger here and they are not the only molluscs that Beth is interested in. There are clams of all shapes and sizes. Some of them are absolutely enormous. Up to a metre across. Three of the crew have remained in the boat: Thin George, as scout; Paul who has a mop of grey hair and protested at the depth of the oyster beds, claiming they are too deep for his 'old lungs'; and lastly, Henrietta who didn't dive yesterday. She is officially the fastest shucker on ship and can prise open hundreds of oysters an hour. While the others dive and bring up baskets of oysters Henrietta and Paul are shucking the catch at the surface. They are too far from the ship to make repeated visits to this bed and must collect as many pearls as they can in the one visit.

Aleka and Nat are coping with the extra depth but with less time to move around on the reef they are cutting corners. Despite instructions to touch only the oysters, both of them grab at the corals and rocks to get around quickly. They are wearing gloves but jagged edges and sharp spines make short work of penetrating the fabric and cutting into their fingertips.

They have been diving down and swimming back up with baskets of oysters for around an hour when, coming up for air with her basket, Beth is alarmed to see hundreds of shucked shells drifting down beneath the boat, oyster juices and flesh clouding the water.

'We've run out of space,' Henrietta explains.

'I don't care. No more crap in the sea,' Beth says angrily. 'We'll row ashore soon to dispose of the shells, understood?

But the damage is done. Dragged away by the current, the smell of the opened oysters is drifting into the kelp forest.

Beth instructs the divers to switch to the other larger bivalve molluscs they have seen clinging to the rocks while the tide is still out and they can still reach them. Who knows what they might find?

It is harder work, it often takes two people to cut a single mollusc away. Some are twenty and even thirty centimetres across. After twenty minutes they have collected only seventy-seven between them. Which is probably just as well as the weight of them is destabilising the boat. All but the two strongest divers – Beth and Tattoo Joe - scramble back on board and all hands turn to shucking.

The tide is turning and the rising waters mean that the dive site is now four to five fathoms, or seven to nine metres, below the boat. Beth and Tattoo Joe add extra weights to their belts to help them reach the beds below.

It is fair to say that only Nat and Aleka really believe they will find anything in the larger molluscs. The seasoned divers know the odds; to find a pearl in fewer than a thousand oysters is a good result, even in these waters. Nat's hands are stinging from all the cuts he has suffered.

Beneath the boat, and in spite of best efforts, the liquor or juices from the opened oysters continues to leak into the sea and drift with the current into the kelp forest.

The crew have found eight pearls within the oysters, including one that Thin George declares to be at least forty-five carats, so the mood is jolly. They have a good haul. Aleka and Nat have broken a couple of blades opening eight of the larger molluscs and have found nothing. Backs are burning in the bright sunshine and almost all the water on board has been drunk; everyone is keen to leave.

'Where are they?' someone asks.

Aleka leans out and peers into the depths. Beth and Tattoo Joe are blue shapes way below. They are wrestling with a very large clam, trying to dislodge it. Aleka likes Beth, she is strong, brave and focused. A natural leader. Tattoo Joe she hardly knows but she knows both of them sufficiently to wish they forget their giant clam and come back up. The boat is full and it is time to head back.

Aleka is having this thought as something curious happens on the edge of the kelp forest. Some distance below the surface four octopuses fly out from the safety of the kelp and rush towards the two divers, discharging clouds of ink behind them, cloaking the swaying kelp in their wake. The creatures shoot straight past Beth and Tattoo Joe and head away at speed across the reef.

Tattoo Joe signals to Beth but they both look in the wrong direction, at the disappearing octopuses instead of where the creatures have come from.

As the ink clouds disperse Aleka sees a dark shadow emerge from the kelp. Behind the massive crocodile-like head is a thick muscular neck. Water distorts the shape and sizes of things but this creature must be the length of a double-decker bus. Its head alone must be two metres long, its flippers the size of single beds.

Aleka screams.

The boat rocks as the crew lean over the side. They shout and beat their hands on the water to attract the attention of Beth and Tattoo Joe below. The commotion does draw Beth's eye. She grabs Tattoo Joe's arm and signals to him, but they still haven't looked behind them. The monster has now fully emerged from the kelp and is almost within biting distance of the divers.

The crew plunge their knives into the waves and shake them about, desperately hoping Beth will get the message.

Beth finally gets the message. She turns to find herself looking into eyes as cold as a shark's and open jaws containing well over a hundred long curved and very sharp teeth. She barely has time to register all this when the creature, a pliosaur, lunges forward and tears off one of Tattoo Joe's arms. The air bubbles out of his mouth as he turns towards Beth and indicates to her that she must swim to the surface.

Beth shakes her head. Tattoo Joe looks furious with her and mouths the word '*Go*'. It is the last thing he ever does. The pliosaur takes a second huge bite, crushing his shoulder and chest in its jaws. His body disappears into the cloud of bright red blood that blooms from the devastating wounds.

Beth, accepting that she cannot save him, unfastens her weights belt. It drops onto the rocks with a dull thud as she rises quickly towards the boat that is silhouetted against the light rippling on the surface of the waves. Her lungs are shot and it takes all her mental strength not to attempt to breathe. One second, two, three … Close to passing out, she fixes her attention only on *up*, it doesn't matter what is happening below.

As she bursts up into the open air hands grab her and haul her out of the water and she lies gasping for air on the sharp shells of the oyster pile.

The boat is already moving, heading towards the shore as quickly the crew can row but it is so overloaded that they are shipping water.

'Trim the boat or she'll capsize!' Thin George shouts, tossing his hat to Aleka. 'Empty the bilge! Get water out!'

The crew shift stuff around to distribute the weight more evenly. The back of the boat is lipping the waves and water is coming in as quickly as Aleka can throw it out with the hat. They are maybe twenty or thirty strokes from the shore.

'To the shallows! Pull! Pull!' shouts Thin George. 'The monster will not reach us on the sands! For the love of God pull!'

The crews pull with all their strength. They have all seen the monster and they know the fate awaiting them all if they do not reach the shore. They are halfway to the sand when the monster's head appears above the waves in their wake. In that instant Nat and Aleka realise that their situation is even more desperate than they have imagined. Unlike the rest of the crew, the twins know about dinosaurs, exploring the Jurassic Coast is after all the one thing Aleka was looking forward to from a weekend in Whitby, though it is fair to say she was expecting to be looking at fossils rather than attempting to escape from terrifying and very much living monsters.

They both know the creature is a pliosaur and they know that pliosaurs, like turtles, are amphibious. Reaching dry land and hauling the boat out of the water won't be enough; the animal will simply crawl out of the water after them!

CHAPTER 28

Some two miles down the coast the mood among the crew is subdued as they dismantle a section of the palisade in silence. Of the ten who climbed the hill, Silas is dead and two are gravely ill. Chisholm, whose bicep was lacerated by one of the megalosaurs, and Alice, who received a blast of spittle on her face from another of the creatures, both have high fevers and are in acute pain. Flora, Noah and Newt are busy transforming the palisade stakes into two makeshift stretchers.

The sun is beating down on the clearing out of a blue sky. The cacophony of jungle noise is as intense as the heat. The air smells of damp vegetation and corpses. The dead megalosaur is already covered in a blanket of flies and beetles. Big George and Phin have carried Silas' body into the jungle. Small lizard-like animals are gathered on the edge of the clearing, attracted by the smell of death.

Chisholm is delirious. He mutters about the gates of hell and perdition, while Alice is unconscious and breathing with great difficulty. Derek guesses that Chisholm's wound is infected; he remembers a wildlife documentary where they explained that it was the pathogens under the komodo dragon's claws that killed their prey rather than the lacerations themselves. He guesses the dinosaur's spit must have got into Alice's lungs.

A sudden flashback to something Elmo said.

Soraudines. He said Soraudines. It's almost an anagram of dinosaur!

'What year is it?' he asks Jack excitedly.

'Eighteen-twenty-one. What other year could it be?'

'Try going back another sixty or seventy million years,'

Derek tells him. 'I'm guessing that you haven't the faintest idea what penicillin is. We must abandon rescuing the people we came to find and get back to the ship or these two may die. And the rest of us with them.'

'There is no rescue mission,' Jack says simply. 'That's not why we are here.'

'Oh brilliant … so why are we here?'

'Our orders were to capture some creatures and take them back. We were trying to reach the nests.'

'That's what the cage is for? It's insane!' Derek says. 'Who knew?'

'Chisholm, me and Tom Hardlock. The previous mission failed, no one can survive long out there. The captain thought everyone would refuse to go ashore if they believed the last crew dead.'

'And you were going to squeeze a dinosaur into that bloody cage? You're all insane!'

'Babies and eggs, not the adults,' Jack shouts back. 'It's part of the deal the captain agreed.'

Big George and Phin appear at the gap in the palisade.

'The coast is clear! Let's go!' Phin says.

Derek and Jack's argument is parked. They gather their weapons. Noah and Phin take one stretcher, Flora and Newt the other. They abandon the cage. Jack leads the way with Big George and Derek taking up the rear. They retrace their steps from yesterday, their path having been cleared by machetes just hours ago. With the ground relatively dry, their progress down towards the beach is good, though manoeuvring the stretchers round the larger trees presents its own challenges.

Now he has accepted that they are somehow in the Jurassic, there can be no other explanation for being attacked by huge two-legged dinosaurs, Derek is trying to remember the stuff he learned as a child. The rest of the crew have no vocabulary for what attacked them. They haven't yet grasped the concept of fossils or created the name dinosaur. Last night and this morning the crew have spoken only of monsters and creatures.

So how has Elmo heard and misremembered the word?

'Keep thy wits about thee, Derek!' Big George prods Derek with his cutlass. 'No time for daydreaming.'

A set of huge footprints, even larger than the ones he saw while recovering from his fall, keeps Derek focused on his immediate surroundings. The jungle is so alive that if he stops for a moment he will surely see it growing before his very eyes.

Passing the spot where Derek slipped and fell, Big George sees movement between the trees. He points and fires one of the flintlocks. Derek jumps and promptly feels embarrassed. The stretcher carriers stop. The burning metallic sulphurous smell of gunpowder hangs in the air.

For a few seconds the jungle is silent, then the insect shrills and buzzes return. Big George waves the stretcher-bearers forward.

They are safe for now.

A little less than an hour after they stepped out from the safety of the palisade, the crew emerge from the trees and onto the beach, to discover that two of the three boats have been smashed to pieces in the night.

The stretchers are lowered gently to the sand in the shade. Flora runs to the waves to collect water to keep Alice and Chisholm cool, while the others inspect the damage.

'We have but four oars, a little fresh water and two ropes,' Noah announces. 'Everything else is lost.'

'If … when the others arrive,' Jack corrects himself, 'we will draw lots to decide who goes back first to the ship.'

'Why wait?' Newt says. 'Take the injured now, while we can.'

'He's right,' Noah agrees. 'Who knows how long we are safe here?'

‘And the pair of you are volunteering to remain on the beach while Chisholm and Alice are rowed to safety?’ Jack sneers.

‘Draw lots,’ Noah says.

‘Aye, draw lots.’ Newt agrees.

Jack looks round to see if anyone dissents. The rest all have their heads down. He walks to the edge of the jungle and collects a bunch of twigs. They draw lots.

Newt, Noah, Big George and Derek are to go back to the ship with the injured while Phin, Flora, and Jack stay on the beach.

They drag the boat to the water’s edge and lift the two stretchers aboard. Dragging the vessel out into the shallows, the water is warm and soothing. Newt, Noah and Big George scramble up but at the last moment Derek changes his mind.

‘You go,’ he tells Flora, ‘you’re a better nurse than I’ll ever be. I’ll take my chances here with Jack and Phin. Look after Chisholm and Alice.’

‘Hurry!’ Noah shouts. ‘Let’s not waste time.’

Flora smiles at Derek and shakes her head bewilderedly. ‘You are a strange one, Drunken Octopus. Useless flither-brain one minute and knight in armour the next.’

She climbs aboard, grabs the fourth oar and off they go towards the ship.

‘Make sure there’s a gallon of rum ready when I reach the ship, Alice!’ Derek shouts.

He joins Jack and Phin in the shade besides the wrecked boats. They sit in a circle with their backs to each other, weapons beside them on the sand and wait.

CHAPTER 29

A night under canvas. Not in a tent but on a large boat moored in Whitby harbour. It's raining and it is the drumming on the canvas that rouses Robert Seeker from his slumbers. His voluminous coat has kept him warm enough. He consults his watch. Already almost ten o'clock, he is fortunate that no one has discovered him. He hears voices close by and carefully sits up and pulls back the canvas.

A group of men are gathered on the ghaut, or slipway, at the harbour end of Arguments Yard, the rain spattering their caps and shoulders. Seeker watches and waits. They appear to be arguing about money.

Who doesn't?

After a few minutes the men shake hands and head off back into the yard. Seeker doesn't waste time. He is on the third boat out from the shore and must quickly move from one boat to the next to reach land before he is spotted.

Once ashore he hurries to Joseph Hamilton's bakery by the potato market to buy a loaf of plum bread. It is still hot from the oven and cheers him up hugely. From there it is back to his room in the White Horse and Griffin. The landlord's hearty greeting suggests that Seeker was not recognised in the middle of the night while he made his escape. For now he is safe.

Having wedged a chair under the door handle to ensure he is not disturbed, Seeker spreads the evidence he retrieved from the room beneath the town hall and gets to work.

Across the harbour up on Silver Street, Sarah and Amy are also up and about. Sarah has lit a fire and is preparing a pot of tea. Amy is at the table staring at a slice of bread smeared with butter and cheese. It is the bread they bought yesterday at the bakery on Skinner Street but Amy seems oblivious to its qualities.

Sarah pours the tea and sits down. She is having jam. With only butter or lard to spread on her bread she is either going to have to do without fat of any kind or make compromises. But not *this* morning.

'Where will we start?' Sarah asks, standing at the window and looking out at the rain circles animating the puddles in the street below.

'Do you think our Mr Seeker will have learned anything in the night?'

Amy doesn't appear to have heard her.

'Amy?'

'*Our* Mr Seeker?' Amy mutters sullenly and sighs.

'You all right?'

'Deeply weird. Nutty McNutface.'

'Agreed, but given our situation we probably need someone *deeply weird* to save us.'

'You believe all that stuff about dark forces and channelling lightning?' Amy says. 'Out with the fairies.'

Sarah puffs her cheeks. 'Next you'll be telling me that aromatherapy and homeopathy don't work.'

Amy arches an eyebrow. 'I think we should go back to Rebecca and see if she …'

'I already did.'

'When?'

'While you were asleep.'

'You could have been killed!' Amy explodes. 'Promise me you won't ever leave me alone again. I don't want to go through this alone. I can't, Sarah. I just can't.' Tears well up. 'Why? Why did you go?'

'I gave her some money and …'

'*My* money?'

'*Our* money. Or would you rather we went our separate ways?'

'No. Sorry. *Our* money. What did you give her?'

'She wouldn't take it unless she could give us something in return?'

'Which is?'

Sarah consults her watch. 'She should be here in ten minutes. You can ask her yourself.'

'Better do some tidying then,' Amy pulls herself together, collecting the plates and cups and taking them through to the kitchen. 'Where do we empty our chamber pots? It's all so disgusting.'

Amy is spared the trauma as, moments later, there is a knock on the door. Sarah welcomes Rebecca and her daughter Rosie into the tenement.

'I've taken an hour off,' Rebecca explains.

She and Rosie are both in their Sunday best clothes. Rosie getting a job as a maid is a step up and Rebecca is keen she makes the most of the opportunity.

'Let me take your wet shawls and dry them by the fire,' Sarah says.

'Her father would be proud to see her like this,' Rebecca says. 'Bless his soul. She's a new apron and you'll not find her wanting. She can cook and sew and clean.'

Rosie herself is looking a little apprehensive.

'What about the little ones?' Amy asks. 'Vera and Simon.'

'They're with my sister,' Rebecca explains.

They all stand awkwardly for a moment.

'Well, I'd best be back to work,' Rebecca says.

'Please stay,' Sarah says. 'We've a pot of tea.'

'And cakes,' Amy adds. 'You've been so kind.'

Rebecca nods then turns to Rosie. 'You'll not forget this is a special occasion.

Rosie shakes her head vigorously.

Sarah disappears into the kitchen and returns with a tray upon which are cups and saucers, teapot, a jug of milk and four teacakes. For a short while the women are equals, all four in unfamiliar surroundings, all pleased of each other's company. They talk about Christmas, which is only weeks away, and are delighted to learn they all know the same carols – *God rest ye merry gentlemen, Hark! the herald angels sing, While shepherds watched their flocks by night.*

They are not so different after all. Sarah is far from sure that Rebecca and Rosie really believe that she and Amy come from two hundred years into the future, but she and Amy know it is true and the fact that they can sing Christmas carols together across the centuries both delights them and moves them to tears.

'Are you all right, love?' Rebecca asks.

Sarah wipes away the tears and smiles. She takes Rebecca's hands and holds it. 'Sorry. Mustn't wallow. My life and Amy's have been so easy compared with yours. We don't know we're born. It's just that I want to get back to my own time. I cannot bear the thought of never seeing Stephen again.'

'I understand. Rosie's father, my John, were lost in an accident when she were just six,' Rebecca says. 'It were all I could do to keep us out of the workhouse. Pressgangs took my father. And the same with poor Rosie; she were all ready to be married when the pressers snatched her Edward. Life is cruel and hard, Sarah, we must take our happiness where we find it.' Rebecca turns to Amy. 'And you'll be in torment, what with you expecting.'

Sarah spins round to look at Amy and then back at Rebecca. 'What? Amy isn't …'

'Sarah, love. Have you boiled eggs for eyes?' Rebecca smiles. 'It's written all over Amy's face, bless her.'

Amy looks embarrassed. 'I haven't even told Derek yet.'

Sarah, at a loss for words, glowers at Amy.

'I've been trying to tell you ever since we arrived in Whitby,' Amy insists, then changes the subject. 'Do you know Robert Seeker?' Amy asks Rebecca. 'A strange skinny man in a huge coat. Wild red hair.

'He's not the father, is he?' Rebecca laughs.

'No. No!' Amy shudders at the very idea. 'He came here last night with some story about the town hall, evil thunder-storms and a conspiracy involving the richest men in Whitby and …'

'Rosie, take the tray and wash everything up,' Rebecca tells her daughter.

Rebecca waits until Rosie has left the room.

'She has enough to worry about,' she explains. 'Anyroad, no, I have not heard of Robert Seeker but be careful. You'll not want to pick a fight with folk on top hat hill. They're too strong. They own every other house on the east side and can put us all in the workhouse if they choose.'

'We just want to go home. We'll not do anything that puts you or Rosie in any danger,' Sarah insists.

Rebecca looks far from convinced. 'I must get back to work.' She gathers her shawl from by the fire.

Sarah accompanies Rebecca out of the flat and down the corridor.

Rebecca steps out into the rain. 'Rosie has instructions to make you a lovely fish pie this evening.' She hurries to the steps that lead back to the harbour. 'And stay out of trouble!' she shouts over her shoulder.

Back inside, the fish pie becomes two pies: one vegetarian, one with fish and bacon.

CHAPTER 30

Stephen climbs the steps and enters the building. He knocks on the first door and waits. Protected by a security chain, the door opens a fraction and an old man's face appears in the gap.

'Yes?' he says cautiously, his voice weak and frail.

'I am looking for Angelique Vallar,' Stephen explains. 'Does she live here?'

'I live alone.'

'I mean in the building. In one of the flats.'

'No idea, sorry.'

The door starts to close.

'Wait. Please. I have a photo.'

Stephen holds his phone up and shows the old man the photo from the Whitby Gazette. It shows Angelique Vallar in a tatty wing-backed armchair, taken in the secure unit in Scarborough.

'It was taken four years ago; she may have changed. She has a strong French accent.'

The French accent registers with the old man. 'We did have someone like that but I think she left. Blond not brunette though and I'm not sure she spoke much English.'

'Does she … did she have any friends here?'

The old man considers the question. 'You could ask Margaret. At number five. A right busy body. She might know.'

Flat 5 is on the first floor. No one is in. On the stairs back down Stephen crosses paths with a middle-aged brunette woman with blue eyes who glances fleetingly at him as she carries her shopping. Back on the ground floor, it occurs to Stephen that a brunette who became a blond might reconsider and switch back. He races back up the stairs two at a time, skipping the first floor exit, he would have heard the door, and on up to the second floor. He throws open the fire safety door. No one. There are four flats, as on the floor below. Should he try them all?

The decision is taken from him. As he stands there he hears a muffled shout.

'Ah non!'

A front door opens and a cat appears. Stephen hurries forwards as the door starts to close.

'Miss Vallar? Angelique Vallar?

'It's not worth the pain. No one listens.'

They are sitting at the small kitchen table. The old man was right, Angelique has a thick French accent but her English is excellent. The room and the whole flat are absolutely spotless; in fact there is little indication that anyone lives here other than a single geranium in a pot on the windowsill. Through the window, that looks north, the sea is visible, blue-grey and wide as the horizon.

'Will you please tell *me* your story?'

Angelique eyes him suspiciously. 'So you can write another article in the paper about the mad French woman who dreams she was abducted by aliens?'

'I am not a reporter. My partner and two friends disappeared three days ago. On Henrietta Street. I am desperate to find them and I do not believe the police are telling me everything. You might be the only person who can help.'

Angelique sips her coffee while Stephen waits patiently.

'It was a long walk to return to the caravan site and I was tired,' Angelique says eventually. 'Maybe five kilometres. And it was raining since midday. I had visited the museum and then the abbey, in spite of the weather. You know the steps to the abbey?'

Stephen nods.

'It was raining torrents on the way back from the abbey down into the old town and I was soaked so I entered the first pub and ordered a hot chocolate. The weather went from bad to worse and night had fallen so I decided to stay and eat. You can eat quite well in the pubs. One small glass of wine and then another, you understand. Thunder and lightning outside. In the end I decided to take a bedroom in the pub, spend the night in the warm and walk back to my campervan in the morning.'

Angelique pauses to drink the rest of her coffee. She hasn't yet looked Stephen in the eye.

'Sarah and my friends disappeared in the middle of the night, during the electrical storm on Friday night. Does that ...' Stephen starts.

'My bedroom was on the first floor. It was perhaps three in the morning that I heard a thunder strike so loud that I told myself the pub was under attack. At the same time there was a smell, very strange, like burning. So then I was frightened there was fire in the whole building. I left my bedroom to find the landlord or a fire extinguisher. The electricity was cut and it was all black. The smell was stronger in the corridor. All of a sudden I heard exploding glass. At that point I should have returned to my room perhaps and waited for the landlord or the police to act but head-strong as I am I decided to go downstairs to investigate.'

'There were three men in the bar, sitting in the black, drinking. They wore old-fashioned costumes. The outside door was open. It was freezing and I was in my t-shirt and bare feet. It smelled of coal. How does she know this, she is French, you are thinking. But I come from north of Calais where there is coal. Anyway, before I could escape the men saw me and caught me. They dragged me out into the rain and down to the pier. I knew well what was going to happen so I started screaming at full voice.'

Angelique pauses, struggling with her emotions as she relives the fear she had felt.

'And then, all at once, another man stepped in front of us. He held a lantern and a long cutlass and he called out *"N'ayez pas peur, Madame"*. Do not be afraid, Madam. I imagine that I must have been shouting in French. The man ran towards us waving his sword and my kidnappers staggered away, cursing him. Maybe it was because he spoken in French that I trusted him. I know that isn't a reason to trust one man over another but there you are. He offered to escort me back to my lodgings and it was only then that I realised the whole town was dark. No lights anywhere.'

'A woman appeared. They knew each other. He spoke with her in English. It was then that he introduced himself and told me he was a sea captain. The woman explained that I was welcome to shelter on the ship until it was daylight and the storm had passed. I agreed, not thinking that I would find myself in a rowing boat going to a large three-masted sailing ship moored in the harbour.'

'But there are no large sailing ships moored in the harbour,' Stephen interrupts her story. 'Except the replica of the Endeavour.'

'You understand nothing,' Angelique retorts. 'I don't understand how but, one way or another, I was no longer in the twenty-first century, I was in the nineteenth. The air smelled of fish and burning fat and coal. No electricity, no swing bridge, no modern boats, nothing.'

'How did you get back? To the 21st century?' Stephen asks. He is far from convinced by her tale but that doesn't matter. What matters is what she thinks happened and how she thinks she escaped.

Angelique is no fool, she has picked up Stephen's change of tone and knows exactly what he is thinking.

'You have already given up listening. Go. I do not want

to spend my time being indulged by another chauvinist who thinks I have spiders on the ceiling.'

'Sorry?'

'You think I am mad. Please leave.'

'Forgive me, please. This is difficult,' Stephen says. 'I woke up on Saturday morning and they had all gone. Downstairs there was mud on the floor in the basement. I think my two friends had left without their shoes. The reporter for the Gazette, Brian Whaler, told me he knows of at least fourteen disappearances, including my partner and friends. And you. I came to learn, not to laugh. Please, I beg you, please carry on.'

For a moment Angelique is lost in her thoughts and seems to have completely forgotten Stephen is in the room.

'The ship is called the *Inevitable* and the captain is Jean-Jacques Elmo, a Haitian who fought in the revolution against the French. There was a disagreement among the revolutionaries so he fled the country, taking a ship. I spent nearly five years aboard that ship as it sailed between Whitby and a place I will not name because you will consider me insane. It makes its money trading pearls, a trade that earns a fortune for Elmo and his crew and for his sponsors in Whitby.'

Angelique pauses again and turns to look out of the window at the sea.

'How did you escape?' Stephen gently prompts her.

'I promised him I could take better care of her in my own time. I pleaded with him. He is a driven man but not a bad man, you understand? He is earning a fortune in order to one day return to his country and fight for freedom. To return to the West Indies.' For the first time she looks Stephen in the eye. 'Do you have children?'

He shakes his head.

'Imagine an old whaling ship crewed by misfits, adventurers, fortune-hunters and neck-breakers,' Angelique says. 'It is not place for an infant, is it? I persuaded Jean-Jacques to let me bring her here so that she might be safe. And he agreed.' She sighs and her eyes fill with tears. 'We returned to Whitby and awaited a winter storm and after a couple of weeks it came. By then the crew were restless but Jean-Jacques had promised them extra profits. He had negotiated with his sponsors, the men who had charge of the town hall, and when the lightning struck the clock tower we were ready. But on the threshold between times he tricked me. They knocked me out and tossed me over the threshold but kept my child. I awoke back in the twenty-first century. Alone.'

She glances at Stephen then turns back towards the sea. 'I lost her.'

'You had a daughter with the captain?'

'I know, it is foolish to worry about her. Even if she lived a long and healthy life she will have been dead for over a hundred years, but with all my heart I still wish I could have brought her here to the 21st century.'

'What was her name?'

'Eliza Bethany.'

CHAPTER 31

As soon as the boat hits the sand everyone leaps out to haul it up the beach.

'Heave! Heave!' Beth shouts.

Muscles burn and backs bend. Laden with oysters and clams, the boat is heavy and the sun is fierce. In seconds the crew is exhausted. As Nat and Aleka have guessed, the pliosaur does not give up as it reaches the beach, it simply climbs out of the water and continues its pursuit on its huge flippers.

Out of the water, however, the pliosaur is as lumbering and ungainly as a seven-metre-long turtle dragging itself up a beach to lay its eggs. It will struggle to catch any of the humans, but its eyes are fixed on the boat. Beth has retrieved their pearls and stashed them in her pockets. Frantically they grab their knives, ropes, cutlasses and oars before the beast arrives. Like cavemen around a mammoth, they circle the pliosaur and attack it from all sides, Paul, Nat, Aleka and Thin George beating it with the oars, while Beth and Henrietta dodge in and out to stab it with the cutlasses. The pliosaur wheels round, its huge tooth-festooned jaws snatching air as it tries to grab its attackers, its tail thrashing back and forth.

Henrietta mistimes her run. She races in to slash at the animal's back as the tail sweeps in behind her and takes her off her feet. Sensing it has hit something with its tail, the pliosaur spins round ready to devour Henrietta. In desperation Beth throws herself forward and jumps onto the beast's back.

'Leave her be, you bitch!' screams Beth as she plunges her blade into one of the pliosaur's eyes. At that the monster arches its back to shrug Beth off. She falls headlong in the sand. Nat and Aleka drop their oars and run forward, grabbing Beth's feet and dragging her back just as the beast jaws snap shut, on a mouthful of beach. On the monster's blind side Paul pulls Henrietta to her feet and out of harm's way.

Blood is pouring from the pliosaur's eye socket clouding its vision. As blows from the oars continue to rain down upon its back, it has had enough. It turns back towards the sea, its lashing tail smashing down onto the boat, and hauls itself back into the water.

The crew lie about gasping. Slowly, as calm returns, they become aware of the jungle sounds just a few metres away. They are still a long way from safety. It is around midday.

'How far are we from the ship?' Aleka asks. 'Two miles?'

'Aye, all of that,' says Thin George.

'Will the animal attack again if we take the boat back into the water?' Nat asks.

'It will have gone to lick its wounds,' Beth replies, 'but there may be others. We have time to shuck our catch while we decide.'

'What about the jungle?' Nat says. 'There's stuff in there that will kill us.'

'We only rarely see anything venture out onto the beach in daylight,' Thin George says. 'They prefer darkness.'

'But we saw those animals yesterday morning.'

'They were but babies. The big beasts stay out of sight.'

'No, that doesn't make sense. Like I'm not staying here even if you pay me. We have to move man!' Nat's voice is rising as his fear gets the better of him.

'Calm down!' Beth orders everyone. 'Thin George is right, we are not in immediate danger. Let's get to work. We'll leave the shucked oysters on the beach, wash out the bilge in the shallows, wait for the water to clear, then row back to the ship. We only have knives and cutlasses, we are safer on the water than walking all that way on the beach. To work!'

'You let him die,' Henrietta says sullenly. 'Tattoo Joe needed you and you let him die, Beth.'

'Leave her be,' snarls Paul. 'We're none of us out of this yet.'

'She'll betray us like she betrayed him,' Henrietta insists.

'Shut your yapping, I should have left you where you fell and let the monster deal with you.'

'Unless you want a fist fight, right here, you'll hold your tongue,' Beth warns Henrietta. 'Which is it to be?'

Henrietta spits on the sand and backs off.

They find two more pearls among the oysters. The clams are tough as three-year-old ship's biscuits. Two broken blades and forty-three clams have yielded nothing. Henrietta is muttering under her breath.

'Another dozen to go,' Beth announces. 'We are almost done.'

'I'll have nothing to do with them,' Henrietta declares. 'We've lost a man for nothing.'

The others ignore her as she wanders off down the beach in a huff.

Aleka and Thin George are working together on the clams. Aleka's fingers are tired and stiff. Thin George holds the clam.

'Press your blade in there,' he tells her. 'That's the sweet spot.'

There are no sweet spots as far as Aleka is concerned, her forearms are cramping from the effort and the heat and she wishes she could curl into a little ball and drift off to sleep. Her hands are red and itching, her eyes thick with tears as she pushes the edge of the blade between the edges of the shell and twists a fifth time. Finally the mollusc starts to give a little.

'That's it! Again, girl. Twist!' Thin George encourages her.

Aleka grits her teeth and twist the blade with all her strength. All at once the shell falls opens. Inside is the usual soupy mess containing gelatinous gloop and a large yellow sac like a partially deflated football. Just the smell of it is enough to make Aleka feel sick. She pokes around expecting nothing, the same nothing that is it in all the other slime-sloppy mush-filled molluscs. *Meh!* Why couldn't they just leave them alone to live their boring lives on the seabed?

Then her fingers brush something hard. Fighting revulsion and tiredness, Aleka probes further. Thin George is already eyeing up the last clam, ready to discard the one in his hand.

The lump is quite large, tucked away between the slippery folds of the clam's digestive tract or its liver or whatever other disgusting body part she has between her fingers. It's maybe the size and shape of a small satsuma. Do the clams have bones, Aleka thinks to herself. She squeezes at the lump, it is like trying to feel a fish hidden behind a curtain, slipping away from her.

Use the knife.

She uses the knife, cutting gently along the sac to release its lump. It pops out into her hand.

A pearl the size of a golf ball! A perfectly round beautiful pearl, white with a golden pinkish overtone.

'Oh. My. God!' she says.

Everyone turns towards her as she slowly lifts her hand to show them what she is holding.

Eyes as big as saucers. Mouths open like stupid fish. No one speaks as they take in what has just happened.

'We … are … all … very … rich,' Beth whispers. 'That is the biggest and most beautiful pearl I have ever seen!'

She stands up and starts to dance a hornpipe. The others join her. Everyone dancing and smiling like their faces will split in two. No one minds that Aleka and Nat are not dancing a hornpipe but doing a cross between Texas line dancing and some crazy hip-hop vibe, and Henrietta is running back towards them wondering what the hell has happened.

CHAPTER 32

Robert Seeker stands over his desk, looking down at his notes and the papers he has retrieved from the waste bin in the room beneath the town hall. He only sees a fraction of the story but it is enough to grasp the enormity of the enterprise. Eleven individuals, who call themselves *The Architects*, are engaged in an outrageous scheme to enrich themselves and appear to have found a way to slip into different time periods to steal from them.

From the future Seeker thinks they are taking people. He feels sure that this is how Sarah and Amy and others have found themselves dragged from their own time and back into the present: 1821.

What are they taking from the past?

The first of the four crumpled sheets that Seeker has now painstakingly flattened out is written in blue ink and on the best writing paper. It details an agreement between 'The Architects' and a Captain Jean-Jacques Elmo in which the first party are agreeing to:

> *"... supply informations that shall enable the second party to locate persons that he may take as crew members in his enterprise."*

In return for which the second party (Elmo)

> *"shall supply the first party with a harvest collected beyond the crossover totalling not less than fourteen thousand pounds, said sum to be paid in precious stones the value of which shall be determined by J.A, A.S, and a jeweller chosen and advised by M.B., Z.B. of the first party."*

Seeker is impressed at the size of the sum the captain is agreeing to pay. £14,000 is a fortune, the cost of a new 500 tonne whaling ship. Who is this captain and why has he agreed to such a payment? Is he a slave trader, a whaler captain or something else?

The second sheet of paper contains an agenda.

Meeting of The Architects

5th August 1821 at 7 pm

Venue: Town Hall.

In attendance: J.A, A.S, C.T, Z.B, T.W, E.H, C.F, G.P, J.K, H.S, & M.B.

Agenda

1. *Approval of the Minutes of meeting held 23 April*
2. *Accounts*
3. *Mechanics and triangulation*
4. *Security arrangements*
5. *Matters arising*
6. *Any other business*

The third, and torn, sheet of paper contains part of what Seeker assumes to be a set of accounts. Robert Seeker has only the most basic understanding of Latin so much of the document is closed to him but the huge sums of money going in and out are easy enough to understand.

Commentarius diarium et ephemeris 1819

Aprilis - reditus

Seven Voltaic Piles	30 - 11 - 7
Five Galvanometers	13 - 6 - 0
300yds silk-covered silver wire (No.35)	25 - 10 - 0
1 ton bare copper wire (No.2)	120 - 0 - 0

Maius - reditus
*Quercus Robur (£18 5s a ton)*________ 36 - 10 - 0
*Construction work / ironmongery*______ 3 - 7 - 6

The final sheet of paper, assembled from five torn fragments, contains a variation of the drawing Seeker saw on the wall in the basement room: a map of the town upon which has been drawn a series of lines. Looking at it again he sees the lines are far from random, they form a six-pointed star. The points touch the very end of Tate Hill Pier, a cottage on Henrietta Street, a small building to the west of Abbey House, a shop on Baxtergate, a building between Pier Road and Cliff Street and, lastly, a building flanking the harbour not far south of the potato market on Church Street

And at the epicentre of this star is …

... the Town Hall!

That's it! I am right!

While the crumpled papers and his notebook contain but a few details of what is happening, it is enough to gauge the extent of the evil and the greed that has possessed almost a dozen of the town's businessmen and women. Times are hard, the whaling industry is on its knees, profits are down, but there can be no excuse for the inhumanity at the heart of this enterprise.

Seeker is ill-equipped to make sense of the equations and formulae he copied from the blackboard, someone else can unravel them. In any event, he already has enough to think about.

Swelling with pride, nonetheless, at the evident and magnificent outcome of his nocturnal perambulations, Robert Seeker decides it is time to unmask the sordid assemblage of persons involved in this trafficking of goods and persons, and the necromancy that underpins their nefarious enterprise.

Seeker is now a man on a mission!

He checks his weapons, dons his coat, removes the chair he has wedged under the door handle to his room, fairly bounds down the stairs past a bemused landlady and into the fume rich air of a winter's day in Whitby. Striding up Church Street he has but one thing on his mind; a physical confrontation with the perpetrators of the chaos that is disrupting the town, and he will stop at nothing to achieve his ends.

Outside number 89 he stops to gaze at the sign above the door.

PAWNBROKERS, GENERAL STORE
& TALLOW CHANDLERS
Aaron Sly and Joseph Argument

'Hello!' he says under his breath. 'Sly and Argument. Unless I am much mistaken those match the first two sets of initials on the attendance record of the meeting of 5th August. A.S. and J.A. A coincidence? I think not!'

He approaches the door as two gaunt-looking children run out of the shop in terror.

'Come back in here and I'll flay the skin off your backs and twist your guts for packaging string, you little bastards!' A tall stout man with thick arms, a thin mouth, and eyes a little too close together appears in the doorway shaking his fist.

The children race off down the street. Joseph Argument watches them then notices Seeker standing there. 'You are you gawping at?' he snarls.

Seeker is very much on the back foot. 'I was looking to buy … to buy a … a hat,' he mumbles.

'Do I look like I sell hats, cloth head?'

'No. No, indeed not. I'll not keep you any longer. Good day,' Seeker says, backing away.

Argument snorts contemptuously and goes back inside. Seeker, still stepping back bumps into a fisherwoman coming the other way. She drops a wicker basket spilling hundreds of flithers out onto the cobbles. Seeker helps her gather them up. It is a greasy business.

‘Having a few words with Argument?’ she asks.

‘He’s a nasty piece of work,’ Seeker says.

‘Oh, you’ve noticed?’ Rebecca says, lending him a cloth to wipe his hands. ‘Those two bastards have been selling underweight candles and rotten veg for years. Their tea is so weak everyone says they’re selling spent leaves out of their own teapots. And after they’ve screwed you they steal what they haven’t screwed and then they have you thrown in the workhouse. Everyone in the yards hates them. Are you Robert Seeker, by any chance?’

Seeker looks up and down the street. ‘Why do you ask?’

‘My friends described you perfectly.’ Rebecca smiles. ‘Don’t worry, we’re on the same side. Sarah and Amy.’

‘I have to be very careful,’ he explains in a low voice. ‘I have a list. Would you look at it? Your local knowledge will help me decode its secrets to identify each of the gentlemen upon it.’

‘If all the people on your list are like Argument and Sly, I’ll wager you won’t find many gentlemen. I have fifteen minutes, you can buy me a drink, Mr Seeker.’

CHAPTER 33

A sneer loiters on Bill Stanway's face as he watches Noah and Big George relate to the captain the events of the night in the jungle. Released from his night in irons in the brig, Bill stands in the shadows of a sail, his eyes black as bile, while Flora tries to organise medical assistance for the injured who are lying on stretchers on the deck, Chisholm, now unconscious, and Alice who is coughing continuously. A light breeze shifts the sails and cools the air.

'There was nothing to be done,' Big George is saying. 'The beast leapt the palisade and had Silas' head in its jaws before we had time to move and by the time Alice and Jack struck it with burning stakes to fight it off, the deed was done.'

'Who was on watch?' Elmo asks.

'Phin and Derek.'

'Silas will be avenged for their treachery!' snarls Bill.

'Hold your tongue or you are back in the brig!' Elmo shouts. He turns back to Big George. 'Carry on.'

'They roused us and we were preparing ourselves but it was all too fast. Those beasts are smart as devils. They tossed an animal corpse on the palisade to cushion the spikes before they jumped. It's Satan's work.'

'And these two?' Elmo asks, pointing down at Chisholm and Alice.

Bill has heard enough. Silas dead and Phin and that lily-white interloping son of a giant bubo responsible! If Derek makes it off the beach and back to the ship, he'll pay with his miserable neck. Bill's fingers squeeze the hilt of his dagger as he steals away to find the ferret-faced Frank Dent.

Chisholm's arm is black and swollen, the wound stinks of infection. He has a high fever and is racked with uncontrollable spasms.

Alice is very much awake. She looks frightened and is coughing blood and grimacing with pain. Lizbet is by her side, wiping her brow with cool water.

'We must return to the beach and rescue the others,' Big George says.

'Until the pearl boat returns there is but one spare boat on board,' Elmo tells him. Telescope to his eye, he scans the beach. He sees the wrecked boats and Phin, Jack and Derek sitting on the edge of the jungle, flintlocks in hand, two facing the beach and the other the trees. Where is the second crew? Why have they not returned? Surely they are not lost!

'Take the second boat but know we cannot afford to lose another one.' Elmo, says, looking around for fresh bodies to row the spare boat ashore. Bill was on deck, now he is nowhere to be seen. Just as well. 'Pick our strongest crew.'

'Captain! It's Chisholm!'

The captain turns. Flora is kneeling, feeling for a pulse.

'Shall we amputate his arm?' Elmo asks.

'It's too late. The poison has spread. He's dead, Sir.'

'How high the price we pay to adventure upon the seas!' Elmo shouts. 'Hang heavy hearts this dark day. Godspeed, Master Chisholm. A good man, brave, loyal and true.' Elmo pauses and adds softly, 'Go, Big George, and bring the rest back safely, we cannot afford to lose one man or woman more.'

'Aye, Captain.'

Lizbet stands and crosses over to Elmo and quietly touches his hand.

'Someone fetch water and sustenance for Alice here!' Elmo shouts. 'And move her into the shade for pity's sake!'

On the shore Phin, Derek and Jack have seen the boat reach

the ship and the injured lifted aboard. It is such a curious place. They sit upon a golden beach and watch a ship upon a turquoise sea beneath a clear blue sky. Gentle waves lick the beach and the soft drone of insects hangs in the trees. A breeze murmurs the leaves and small animals shuffle along the sand searching for food, just like turnstones and other birds will do on the beach in Whitby millions of years in the future. The early afternoon sun shines bright and hot. It is paradise on Earth, familiar, calm, and achingly beautiful.

But it is also a mirage. Within the jungle's shiny deep green envelope hide teeth and claws that will rip a man in two faster than he can blink, and the same dangers lurk beneath the waves.

'Should we not at least try to follow their path into the jungle?' Phin is asking Jack. 'While the sun is still high and we are safe.'

'There be no safe here,' snorts Jack. 'It were madness to venture inland. And madness the last time we tried. We need a thousand troops and twenty canons to tame just this short stretch of beach. We lost four crew upon our last excursion and will do the same today.'

Derek is torn, haunted by the events of the night and the knowledge that if the situation were reversed and he were stuck in the jungle he would be desperate to be rescued. 'How far into the trees will they have gone?' he asks.

'Further than us,' Phin says. 'We went uphill. They will have followed the river inland on the flat. We found a hatchery two leagues from the coast.'

'What is a league?' Derek asks.

Phin gives him a curious look. 'The distance a man can walk in an hour. Same as it ever was. Do people not walk where you are from?'

'Then let us at least walk a league towards them and meet them halfway, while it's bright.' Derek suggests. 'They would do the same for us.'

'Did you learn nothing last night? Jack says. 'The monsters that attacked us were not even full-grown. And there are other dragons in there. I'll not set foot off the sand.'

'Then you wait here while Phin and I look for them,' Derek suggests.

Phin looks at the tall man. When they kidnapped him just days ago Derek was in his cups, angry, frightened, little more than cannon fodder. Most of them last only a few weeks. Healthy specimens, big and strong but inside they are all soft as jellyfish. This one is different.

'Aye, Derek, I'll go but you will follow my orders. I know this place and will better keep us from harm.'

'Understood,' Derek says. 'Lead away.'

They leave Jack one of the flintlocks along with his knife and cutlass and head off down the beach. The other crew's footprints are still visible in the sand. Being where they are in space and time there is no risk that the feet of other humans have left these marks.

A couple of green ankylosaurs, heavy legged and plodding herbivores the size of small cows with armour-plated backs, are browsing the bushes. They startle and disappear into the thick undergrowth. The beasts look harmless enough but Derek knows that it isn't all about having your head bitten off by large carnivores, like the animal that killed Silas in the night; it is also about the toxins and bacteria animals and plants carry.

The footsteps in the sand come to an end opposite a gap in the vegetation, this must be where the second crew entered the jungle. Phin turns towards Derek and puts a finger to his lips; they must tread quietly.

The drone of the insects continues without a break as they step between the giant horsetails beneath the tree canopy. It is a good sign. The path cut by swinging machetes the previous day is easy to follow and they make rapid progress and in a quarter of an hour they reach the river. Subconsciously desperate for reference points to his previous existence, Derek imagines the river to be the Esk. In his mind's eye, the ginkgoes and giant ferns of the Jurassic are lampposts along the piers, the strange flowers are the neon lights above the amusement arcades and fish and chip shops that he saw across the harbour from the bedroom window on Henrietta Street. Where a herd of strange feathered creatures the size of flamingos are wading the shallow waters, Derek sees cormorants. A huge fallen tree becomes the swing bridge connecting Whitby's east and west sides that he crossed on his drunken pub crawl.

His reminiscences are interrupted by the arrival of a pterosaur (*call it what it is*) that swoops down to snatch one of the 'flamingos' in a chaos of squawking and sharp talons.

Phin has stopped to look at a blue object on the ground. 'Toby's scarf,' he says picking it up and tying it around his own neck.

Further on they stumble across the second proof they are on the right track; signs of a small fire on the riverbank.

'Will they have built a palisade?' Derek asks.

Phin shrugs.

'Who is leading them?'

'Tom Hardlock. Big red beard, no teeth, and a foul mouth. Parish pickaxe.' Seeing Derek's look of bemusement, Phin adds. 'A big nose, red with grog.'

'Blind drunk and clinging to the deck after the crossover?'

'Aye, that's him! Not much upstairs but brave as a basket of bulldogs.'

A group of maybe a dozen small therapods gather on the opposite bank, biped dinosaurs not much larger than chickens Their heads flinch about in staccato bursts, ever alert to signs of danger.

'We should find last night's camp soon,' Phin assures Derek.

They continue along the path cleared by the crew as it heads inland and deeper into the jungle. Intense heat shimmers beneath the tree canopy and, away from the noise of the river, the two men are enveloped in the shrieks, hoots, shouts, yelps, and alarm calls of creatures they cannot see. Without any sense of perspective, a thick wall of vegetation blocking the view in any direction, they feel increasingly vulnerable to attack. An odious odour blooms the air.

A flock of tiny pterosaurs, no larger than blackbirds, bursts from a bush in a cacophony of alarm cries, their bright crests iridescent and glowing briefly in a shaft of sunlight as they fly away.

Skirting a tree trunk, too late to take avoiding action, the two men walk straight into a semi-circle of ten stakes that have been driven into the ground to block the path. Upon each stake is the impaled body of a small dinosaur, similar to the ones that attacked the hill camp last night. Their bodies, covered in a seething noisy mass of insects, are contorted in a way that suggests that they were alive when they were skewered.

They push on past the carnage, Phin cursing under his breath.

'Weren't they meant to be bringing back animals alive?' Derek asks.

'Who told you that?' Phin asks.

'Jack. He said that he and Chisholm and Tom Hardlock all know the previous mission failed.'

Phin is silent.

Abruptly, the clearing is upon them.

It is a scene of devastation. Half the palisade has collapsed. Bits of bodies, human and non-human, all crawling with flies, are scattered about on the soil. Two full-grown megalosaurs lie dead. They are larger than elephants and appear to have died of gunshot wounds. Ash from a large fire covers the ground.

A dozen small green dinosaurs, no bigger than pigeons,

are scavenging, tearing chunks of flesh from the corpses while keeping up a continuous stream of chattering chirps, like a flock of hedge sparrows.

A makeshift cage cut from branches knitted into a lattice contains a dozen large oblong eggs and the bodies of seven baby megalosaurs. They resemble miniature T-Rex with their two powerful back legs, small arms and long tails. All have had their throats slit and have bled out on the ground. The eggs have been stabbed with a blade.

The vegetation all around the clearing is a tangled mess of broken branches as if an army has marched through, destroying everything in its path. Neither Derek nor Phin speak as they look about them for any sign of life.

They count five bodies. Where are the other five members of the crew?

'Let's go back,' Derek whispers. 'We're too late.'

Phin ignores him and continues out beyond the clearing. Some twenty metres on they find two more bodies face down and evidently dead. Phin makes the sign of the cross over them and clenches his jaw. Ten metres on again they spot Tom Hardlock asleep and sitting up against a tree, his chin resting on his chest.

A survivor!

Derek and Phin race forward. Maybe the other two have also survived.

From the front Tom Hardlock looks very different, his belly ripped open, his bowels spread out before him. His dead eyes are half-closed, his face is twisted in agony. In his right hand is a bloodied cutlass. At his feet is part of the lower jaw of a megalosaur similar to the ones that attacked up on the hill during the night.

On the other side of the tree in a pool of blood are the bodies of a butchered dinosaur and a woman. Derek recognises the woman from the hornpipe dance after the crossover, but identifies her only from her clothes. Her face has been eaten away by another of the small green dinosaurs that scurry away as Derek approaches.

Phin and Derek look at each other as a flock of maybe twenty small dinosaurs forms around them, chattering, summoning the courage to attack. The tenth body must be a short distance away but is there any point in continuing the search? If they hurry they might make it back to the beach but, in truth, the odds are slim.

It is clear to both men that Tom Hardlock's crew achieved their objective of capturing a bunch of young dinosaurs, but at a terrible price. Derek imagines the scene. The predators find the bodies of their young impaled on stakes further down the path and are enraged. They vent their fury on the palisade. Several of them die in the assault but they are numerous and easily overwhelm the humans. Hardlock, realising the cause is lost, exacts his revenge. He orders the killing of all the young, or kills them himself. The palisade is destroyed. Some of the crew try to escape and are hunted down and butchered.

'No, you don't!' Phin waves his cutlass at the circle of young megalosaurs.

One of them advances step by step, bolder than the others, its head tilted to one side as if weighing up the odds. Nostrils flaring, smelling fresh meat, it suddenly leaps forwards. Phin swings his blade, slicing off one of creature's arms. It is immediately set upon by the others, in a frenzy of snapping jaws, and torn to shreds. A faint booming sound shakes the leaves.

Derek and Phin are both sick with fear. Derek feels the wet warmth spreading in his trousers; he has pissed himself.

'Dead,' Phin mutters. 'All dead.'

Swinging their blades to dissuade attack, the two men head back to the clearing and on towards the grisly row of stakes. Away from the sickly buzzing of thousands of flies, the jungle is eerily quiet. Maybe thirty metres from the clearing they hear a branch cracking away to their right.

They stop. With trembling hands Phin draws back the flint on his pistol, if they are to die then, like Hardlock, he will die fighting. A second sound. Are they being ambushed?

'Look! Up in the trees. There!' Derek points up.

They hurry forwards.

'Hang on!' Derek shouts. 'I'm coming up.'

Dropping his weapons at the foot of the tree, Derek starts to scramble up. The tree is fortunately fairly easy to scale, no thorns or barbs. A couple of minutes and he draws level with the horizontal branch on which is clinging the sole remaining member of the crew that followed Tom Hardlock into the jungle.

Maybe three metres out from the trunk, one leg on either side of the branch. Eyes vacant, arms scratched and bloody, clothes torn, she looks like she is about to relinquish her grip and tumble four metres to the ground.

'Don't look down. Look at me. Look at me!' Derek tells her. 'You're not alone. We are all going back to the ship.'

Deep in shock, the woman stares blankly, as if she is already dead. Derek swings his body round the trunk to better grasp the branch on which she sits but that immediately causes her to back away.

Another cracking sound from the tree, the branch is beginning to break. Derek retreats carefully.

'You're safe,' he smiles gently.

'We're all dead,' she mutters automatically.

Derek doesn't contradict her. He beckons her forward, all the while looking her straight in the eye. 'The captain sent us. He's waiting.'

'Anna,' Phin calls out from the foot of the tree.

She flinches, almost loses her grip.

'Look at me, Anna,' Derek says, now having a name to work with. 'Come to me. Phin is here. You'll be fine.'

Anna hesitates. She is at least now listening, her eyes haunted but no longer vacant.

'We're going back to the ship,' Derek tells her. 'Together.'

Anna starts to look around and realises she is halfway up a tree. She gasps in fear.

'The captain wants you to come towards me.'

She looks confused. 'Captain's here?'

'On the ship. With Beth and Solomon and Lizbet and the others. They're all waiting.'

The fog is lifting behind her eyes. Anna starts to inch toward Derek who waits patiently, nodding encouragement. The seconds crawl more slowly than a slip of slugs. Now two metres away. Derek wonders if she could survive a fall.

It's not the fall that kills you, it's the lack of medicine.

'Nearly there,' he says softly, his voice barely audible above the buzzing of the insects.

Please keep the dinosaurs quiet a little longer.

One and a half metres away

A sharp cracking sound. The branch judders violently and cracks laterally, dropping Anna maybe twenty centimetres. She stops, gasping and beginning to panic. She closes her eyes.

'Look at me, Anna. Look at me!' Derek urges her.

'I can't.'

'Just a little further.'

She nods and starts to shuffle mechanically, hand over hand, dragging herself towards him. A metre now. Almost close enough. Derek positions himself as best he can; one arm wrapped around one branch, his legs and feet wedged tightly between two others. She is now directly over the broken section of the branch.

The branch gives suddenly, falling with a rush of noise. Derek reaches out and grabs a wrist as Anna starts to drop into the void. It takes all his strength to hold her as she slams hard against the trunk, her legs hanging beneath her.

'Grab my arm with your other hand!' he instructs her.

She does as he tells her.

'Well done! Phin, where can she put her feet?'

Phin, who has been watching everything from the ground, calls out instructions and Anna's feet find a lower branch. Moments later Anna and Derek are safely on the ground.

Phin hugs Anna until she is no longer sobbing.

'Thank Almighty God,' he says, stroking her hair. 'He has saved you.'

Finally Anna pulls away to look over Phin's shoulder toward the broken palisade.

Phin shakes his head. 'No, Anna. We must go. Now.'

She makes to pass him but he grabs her arm.

'Listen! They are all dead. Leave them be.'

And with that, Phin leads her away from the carnage. Derek takes her other arm. At first she resists then allows herself to be led. With every step her reluctance fades; she chooses life.

'Thank you,' she says as, fifteen minutes later, they emerge from the deep jungle and reach the river and the spot where she, Tom Hardlock and the others lit a fire twenty-four hours ago.

They are hurrying now, on borrowed time. A little over a mile and a half to go. They are tired, hungry and thirsty, but dare not stop to drink from the river; the chicken-sized dinosaurs are still there on the other bank. On noticing them, Anna is agitated; they are the same species as her crew caught yesterday. If the babies are out on the riverbank, the adults cannot be far away.

Phin leads the way, his flintlock primed and ready, Anna behind him and Derek taking the rear. The path leads away along the river for a while then back into the jungle.

As they re-enter enter the shadows beneath the trees, something rushes across the path up ahead in a flash of colour.

They stop.

From way over to their right, back towards the river, comes a sound like the alarm call of a bird. But bigger. The call is answered by a second call, in the undergrowth behind them. A crashing sound followed by silence. Are they surrounded?

Anna's shaking legs give way and she slumps to her knees.

How far are they from the beach, Derek asks himself as they bunch together.

'We have to run,' he says. 'It's our only chance.'

Dragging Anna between them, Derek and Phin set off again, scrambling, stumbling over fallen branches. All three dizzy with fear.

The pearl boat still not having returned, only two boats have joined the rescue. Big George, Noah and Newt have gone back on the first boat. Frank Dent and Pierre and Sam Solomon, the cook, take the second boat.

While Elmo does not trust Dent, the man is a fool and easily led, he has every confidence in Solomon and Pierre; Solomon may be missing a foot but his arms are thick as cannons and Pierre fought with him in Haiti during the revolution. It is hard work rowing a boat built for seven with just three men but they need the empty spaces for the rescued.

The six men plus Jack have now been waiting on the shore for two hours. The tide is almost out and it is the middle of the afternoon. They keep moving the boats to keep them close to the water's edge in case they have to leave in a rush. In less than an hour the tide will turn and they will be forced to drag the boats up the beach and then row out to the ship against an incoming tide.

While no large dinosaurs have ventured onto the beach, it is just a matter of time. Half an hour ago a flock of pterosaurs flew overhead, heading toward the river.

'Face it, they are all lost, says Newt for the fifth time. 'Let us return to the ship and save ourselves!'

No reply. All the arguments have been made and no one wants to waste his breath. On a ship you are interdependent. A big family. Leave one man and the ship is diminished. Aside from anything else, aside from common humanity, the reality is that a crewmember's loss means more physical work for those that remain.

But Newt isn't thinking about any of that, he is in shock from the events of last night, of Silas' death, and Chisholm's. When he blinks he sees the face ripping power of the megalosaurs leaping the palisade. The stench of their breath is too fresh in his mind. The rest of the crew know that there will come a point where Newt will no longer be in control of himself.

Someone on board the ship is waving wildly. It is Pierre who turns toward the top of the beach.

'Look, men! They are found!' he shouts.

Emerging from the jungle are Phin and Derek. Derek is carrying Anna on his back.

By the boats the men raise their fists in joy, the others will emerge from the trees in a few seconds.

'Heave the boats into the drink, lads, and grab your oars!' Big George says, slapping Newt on the back.

Phin and Derek have broken into a run, and are racing across the golden sand. They are calling out but too far away for the words to be clear.

The sea feels cool on thirteen feet as the boats are dragged into the waves. The fourteenth is made of wood and feels nothing at all.

'Where are the others?' asks Noah.

Phin and Derek have covered half the ground between the jungle and the boats. Derek is beginning to struggle with the weight of Anna on his back. Pierre leaves the boat and runs up the beach. He reaches Derek as he stumbles and falls.

'I'm sorry,' mutters Anna as she rolls onto the sand.

Pierre offers his hand and hauls Derek to his feet then pulls

Anna up and takes her in his arms. Phin has reached the boats.

'They are after us!' Derek is gasping for breath. 'Quick!'

As he speaks, the undergrowth behind them is broken as two adult megalosaurs burst out of the jungle onto the beach. They must be all of four metres tall, their protofeathers barely visible in the strong sunlight. They pause just long enough to locate their prey and charge towards the boats.

Pierre reaches the nearest boat and hands Anna up to Big George. Behind him Derek is staggering on tired legs as the dinosaurs, with a running stride length of some three metres, are rapidly closing the gap.

Derek stumbles a second time. Pierre again runs back, hauls him up and drags him the final five metres to the boats. As soon as the two men have both tumbled aboard, the oars begin to move.

'Heave! Heave! Heave!'

Even out here, even with the sea breeze, they can smell the fetid stench of the approaching carnivores. The seven men row for their lives while the rescued are lying down struggling get air into their burning lungs.

The megalosaurs reach the water's edge. They turn to each other, back at the boats and then, to the horror of the men, charge forwards in pursuit. Desperately the men pull their oars to reach deeper water. The gap closes.

'For the love of God, heave your oars, men!' Big George shouts again.

The men start to sing to the rhythm of their work.

Pull them hard, lift them high,
ride the waves, lift your blades
Heave ho! Heave ho!

And still the gap is closing. A few more seconds and the dinosaurs will reach them and all will be lost.

The noise takes them all by surprise. One of the megalosaurs slows, blood spurting from an eye socket. Anna has found the pistols. She drops the weapon, picks up a second pistol and fires again. The second shot misses its target but it is enough. Their attackers stop in their tracks, the waves almost around their thighs. One is wounded and half-blinded, the other uncertain what to do next.

And still the men row.

On the ship, the crew roar and cheer the approaching boats.

CHAPTER 34

'And I am telling you that I have no idea what use they have for seven voltaic piles and five galvanometers. In any event such equipment may be bought anywhere in ...'

'Unfortunately not, Mr Dixon. There is but one place in Whitby that sells such esoteric devices: namely your establishment.'

Mr Dixon is a short snub-nosed fellow in small gold-rimmed glasses, with grey hair sprouting over his ears like broccoli. He wears a black laboratory coat over his clothes to communicate the seriousness of his enterprise. He is currently tied to a chair in the backroom of his business premises on Skinner Street. The room is piled high with boxes containing all manner of devices and scientific instruments.

Aside from voltaic piles and galvanometers, Thelonious Dixon sells phrenological heads, telescopes, sextants, ceramic distillation apparatus, apothecary balances, Liebig condensers, and a wide range of other laboratory equipment. He prides himself on following the very latest developments in science and subscribes to journals published by the London Royal Society, and others in Paris and Milan.

Mr Dixon would be screaming for help were it not for the revolver pointed at his chest. His assailants are disguised in hats and scarves that conceal their features but he is certain that one is a man, the other a woman.

'I ask you again, who bought these devices from you?'

Mr Dixon says nothing.

The first assailant steps forward and casually sweeps two expensive-looking devices made of brass and glass off one of the shelves. They fall to the stone floor and smash into dozens of pieces. 'Does that jog your memory?'

Dixon shakes his head; he will not betray his wealthy clients so easily.

'Oh, well,' says his aggressor, looking around the room. 'Quite a few pieces to get through. Mustn't dawdle.' He sweeps an armful of scientific instruments including a mahogany box containing a beautiful barometer off another shelf.

Dixon winces.

Footsteps outside. Someone tries the door handle, but the door is locked from the inside.

'Is everything all right, Thelonious?' asks a female voice.

The gun is raised to point directly at Dixon's face.

'Yes, my dearest,' Dixon says. 'A little accident, that is all.'

The footsteps go away again.

The second assailant, standing at the back of the room, has not yet spoken but does so now. 'Why are you protecting them? You are not a bad man.'

The woman's voice is definitely local, unlike the man's, Dixon thinks to himself.

'I have a family to feed,' he answers.

'Forget the who then and explain to us the why,' says the male assailant who has crossed the room and picked up a curious contraption resembling a small bandstand maybe forty centimetres in height. There is a base connected to a roof or lid by four thin columns of metal. Between these columns is a vertical stack of metal discs with a thin ribbon of copper attached to the bottom and the topmost discs.

'This is a voltaic pile, is it not?' says the male assailant, picking up the object. 'It is my belief that persons unidentified are making use of thunderstorms to collect electricity and that this activity is focused around the clock tower of the town hall. Such energy as is being collected is stored in vast quantities somewhere with the aid of voltaic cells. Is that correct?'

Dixon laughs. 'Halfwit. You have no idea how much power a voltaic pile is capable of storing. You would need thousands of those to store the power required. Alessandro Volta's work is child's play compared with Francis Ronalds' recent work in London.'

Seeker's eyes (for it is he) light up. Dixon needs to show off. 'So a large cupboard in one of the yards is needed. I understand.'

'You understand nothing! Huge batteries are required. You need a warehouse not a cupboard. But storage is not the answer at all. You have to use the power when it presents.'

'So the work is done while the electrical storm is at its peak?'

'Exactly! Did they teach you nothing at school?' Dixon says contemptuously. 'And all that power is worthless without focusing of the lines of force.'

'The six-pointed star on the map!' Seeker expostulates.

Dixon nods then catches himself; he has said far more than he intended.

'Thank you, you have been most helpful. We will leave you now.'

The woman unlocks the door.

'Wait! My equipment,' cries Thelonious Dixon.

'You will be compensated adequately when this matter is brought to a successful conclusion. Oh!' Seeker remembers something and pulls his notebook from his pocket, flicks through the pages and shoves a drawing under Dixon's nose. 'What is this and how did you procure it for them?

Dixon glances at the drawing of the helmet with its hoops of brass and rotating dial on which three telescopes are mounted.

'No idea.'

Seeker throws the chair back, sending Dixon to the floor.

'You have five seconds to remember,' Seeker informs the

hapless Dixon, as he cocks the hammer of his revolver and presses the barrel end against his victim's ear. 'Five … four … three …'

'It came from London,' Dixon whispers. 'Courtesy of SEGTA.'

'Which is?'

'Ignoramus. The Society of Esoteric Gentlemen Travellers and Adventurers.'

'What is it for?'

'The manufacturers claim it assists the wearer to negotiate time portals. I simply placed the order for two such devices on behalf of my clients.'

'Thank you, most helpful.'

With that Seeker and his accomplice leave the room, hurry down a corridor and exit via the back door they used to enter, just as three men armed with cudgels arrive at the front door of the building, alerted by the cleaner, Mrs Wart who has never previously been called 'my dearest' by her employer and knew immediately that something was wrong.

They are too late.

Having negotiated a maze of alleys and passages to reach a shed behind which they remove and abandon their disguises – scarves, overclothes and hats - Robert Seeker and Rebecca emerge from a yard some fifty metres down Church Street and head back northwards towards the town hall and the harbour. It is raining and the wind is picking up. The sky is so dark, it will soon be candle-light and a yellow shine will glow in doors and windows across the town.

There is every chance Whitby won't be waiting long for the next electrical storm.

CHAPTER 35

'Anna, look at me. You are safe,' Henrietta strokes her friend's hand, but Anna, curled in a foetal position by the foremast, continues to stare vacantly into space.

Emotions are running high on the *Inevitable.*

Twelve crew dead.

It is a terrible price and any joy for those rescued is tempered by the collective trauma of their losses. There are no celebrations.

Beth and the pearl divers arrive some little time after the other boats. While they bring a good haul of pearls, they too bring bad news. Tattoo Joe was a popular member of the crew and his death is a blow to morale. Having checked her crew are safe, Beth takes the sack containing the pearl harvest down to the captain's cabin. Neither she nor the Captain have been seen since.

Small groups gather on the main deck, chatting quietly about the day's events in the late afternoon sunshine. Any hope that the hunting party that went missing a month ago on their last crossover might yet be found alive and well in the jungle has been crushed. Derek and Phin are obliged to tell their account of the discovery of the wrecked palisade three times and, while there is anger at the recklessness of Tom Hardlock, only a fool would impale the monsters' young on stakes at the entrance of the camp, there are also murmurings about the decision to put Hardlock in charge of a crew. Whose decision was it? Chisholm's or the Captain's?

There is a sense of betrayal that the expedition was not to rescue missing companions but to make a second attempt to hunt and capture the monsters. Why were they not told?

And now they have lost a quarter of the crew.

The deaths of Silas and Chisholm make matters worse. While Silas was not popular with most of the crew he was a strong pair of hands. Chisholm was a fine second-in-command and much respected. On a corner of the foredeck Frank Dent is seated with Ezekiel, who is still recovering from the pterosaur attack, and with Bill who has appeared from the shadows. The three men are deep in conversation, glancing around them from time to time to make sure they aren't being overheard.

Lizbet and Sam Solomon busy themselves distributing food and drink to the survivors. Water and rum, biscuits, potatoes and stew.

The twins sit by themselves on the quarterdeck towards the back of the ship. Both are feeling unwell.

'You must drink,' Lizbet tells them, placing cups of water in front of them.

'Who is the doctor on this ship?' Nat asks. 'My hand is killing me.'

He shows Lizbet his left hand, it is red and the palm is covered in small cuts.

'We got stung when we were diving,' Aleka explains. Her forearms are swollen.

'I'll tell Sam,' Lizbet says.

'He's not a doctor.' Nat says testily. 'He's a cook. If there isn't a proper doctor then the Captain has to let us go home.'

'I'll bring you some food,' Lizbet says simply and leaves them.

Weary of explaining the events on shore over and over, having drunk water until he was sick of it, Derek has hauled himself up the Jacob's ladder where he has slumped down alone on the mizzen top, the platform at the top of the lower mizzenmast, with a bottle of rum. He is as tired as an ultra-runner's shoes. With the mast at his back he stares out, first over the open sea, a bright dazzling infinity of blue, and then, his hand shielding the sun from his eyes, toward the shore and the jungle beyond.

Derek has always taken life as it comes. Stuff happens and he experiences it. When things get a bit stressful he drinks but, aside from that, he goes with the flow. He didn't actively choose to end up working in a boring office with Stephen, or ever wake up thinking that rugby was the one sport in the world he really loved, or look at Amy and think *that is the woman I want to spend my life with*: stuff happens. Go with the flow.

And so it was when he woke up with a massive hangover a few days ago on a weird ship crewed by a bunch of misfits. On many levels it is insane. The whole thing. How can he possibly be living in the Jurassic on a nineteenth century ship? How has he slipped through time? What was he doing saving a sailor from a pterosaur or whatever it was that attacked him in the rigging, or dancing a hornpipe with Beth, or slashing at a dinosaur with a pirate's cutlass, or any of the rest of it?

Just go with the flow …

… until he saw the dead man in the jungle with his entrails spread out around him.

Derek has never felt so alive, or so close to death, and his value system is …

'Back off or she's dead meat!'

Derek is dragged back to the here and now by an angry commotion below him on the main deck. A sharp howl of pain followed by raised voices.

'Don't be a fool! Let her go!' shouts Phin. 'She's just a child.'

Derek looks down.

Bill has Lizbet in a headlock and a knife to her throat.

'Back off!' Bill shouts at Phin. 'I'll not ask again.'

Beside Bill are Frank Dent, Ezekiel, Flora, Henrietta, Jack

and Newt and three others. Derek is struggling to identify everyone from his vantage point directly above the deck. All are armed with muskets and pistols.

'Find our fancy *Captain,*' Bill spits this last word out as if coughing up a fly that has somehow flown into his mouth, 'and tell him the ship is no longer under his command.'

'Jack,' Noah appeals to his twin brother. 'This is madness! Step aside for the love of God …'

Jack clenches his jaw but stays at Bill Stanway's side.

'Stop whining, catchfart, and fetch Elmo. Now,' snarls Bill, 'or this waif is fed to the sharks.'

Phin holds up a hand and backs slowly away, almost tripping over Anna in the process. He disappears down the hatch steps.

Unseen, Derek observes.

He amazed at how calm Lizbet is. Just a child but in so many ways more of an adult than he's ever been. How did she end up on the ship? Was she kidnapped like himself, Aleka and Nat? Has she escaped something worse?

On the shore, a group of small therapods bursts out of the jungle in a tumult of alarm calls. The size of turkeys, with orange protofeathers, they gather on the edge of the water, clearly very agitated. The horsetail plants on the edge of the jungle are bent back as the therapods are joined on the sand by three ankylosaurs, huge plodding lumps of flesh and bone with heavy tail clubs, also seeking refuge from the jungle.

'So Bill, what irks thee?' asks Captain Elmo stepping up onto the deck, cutlass in hand.

'Keeping cosy, were we?' Bill retorts. 'Counting the treasure and thieving some for yourself? Eh? Or rutting with your Covent Garden nun, Beth?'

'If you have a bone with me, be a man, Bill, and face me instead of threatening a child,' Elmo says coolly.

'My listening to you days are over, hollow man. While you

fancy foot about, thirteen of the crew are dead. We mean no more to you than a sack of fleas. You're too expensive. No one gives a toss about your precious revolution or your promises of good times that never come,' sneers Bill. 'That right, lads?'

His accomplices make approving noises.

On the shore the megalosaurs have reappeared, thundering across the sand in pursuit of prey. The small creatures scatter in all directions, the dull-witted ankylosaurs, unable to move fast enough, adopt defensive positions and swing their tail clubs about.

'So, because I am a fair man,' Bill continues, 'I'll give you a choice. You can enjoy the comforts of chains and manacles, or, if you prefer the tropics, we can set you ashore on the beach to take your chances with the beasts. Which will it be?'

From his vantage point above the action, Derek can see through the open hatch and down below deck. He sees Beth, and Sam and Pierre, weapons drawn at the foot of the steps peering up from the shadows. And just as Derek sees them, so Pierre spots him up in the rigging. With hand gestures, Derek attempts to communicate to Pierre where on the deck the aggressors are standing, how many of them there are, and what weapons they have.

Pierre gives Derek a thumbs-up, he has understood and, with that, he steps back into the shadows below deck.

Jean-Jacques Elmo weighs his options. 'You haven't thought this through, Bill,' he says. 'Slap me in irons if you wish but who will steer the ship? There's not one of you standing there capable of negotiating the crossover? So what's your grand plan? To stay here, in this place, in perpetuity? Is that it?'

Elmo lets his words sink in.

'You say we have lost too many of our crew. Right enough. Will losing more souls help you lower the masts and heave them back?' he shouts for the benefit of those below deck.

'You blunderbuss! It takes more than holding a knife to a child's throat to command a crew, Bill, and you'll need more than flither-brains and hotheads to captain this ship!'

With that Elmo drops his cutlass and allows himself to be seized. Frank Dent and Jack take the captain's arms and manacle him then chain and padlock him to the mainmast.

'When he's fast, go below and slice the necks of any who refuse my command!' orders Bill Stanway, releasing Lizbet.

'Aye, Captain,' says Frank.

Lizbet scurries towards Elmo who shakes his head. 'Don't worry about me, child. Go below and tell the crew, those who understand their duty, not to spill their blood for this!' he shouts, hoping the rest of the crew are now listening through the open hatch. 'This brainless rabble will have to think again or we all die here on this monster-infested coast!'

CHAPTER 36

Robert Seeker has taken his leave of Rebecca, having thanked her for her assistance. He has written a letter to his employers in London, detailing all that he has discovered over the past twenty-four hours and, being unsure that he can trust anyone in Whitby, has sealed it along with several of his drawings in an envelope that he will personally deliver into the hand of the mail coach guard.

Said envelope snug in one of the pockets of his waistcoats, he is now outside, in what cannot be called fresh air, exploring each of the six points of the star marked on the map contained in another of his pockets.

He starts with the end of Tate Hill Pier.

For his troubles he finds only a face full of rainwater, the cold breeze sweeping into the harbour from the North Sea and a sense of being peculiarly exposed to the gaze of the entire town. The tide is in and there are maybe twenty vessels moored in the harbour, rocking gently in the swell. To his right the sands of Collier Hope are drowned beneath the waters. Across the harbour lie Scotch Head and the Battery, and the west cliff.

Half a dozen turnstones walk staccato in single file along the edge of the pier, pecking the ground by the lobster pots, searching for scraps.

If there is a node of force secreted at the end of the pier then Seeker cannot see evidence of it.

He makes his way back onto Church Street and then up Henrietta Street. Ducking behind the houses he seeks the second point marked upon the map. In a back yard is a small outhouse the size of a privy, half-buried in the cliff. He hauls open the door to reveal a space little larger than a sentry box, piled high, from floor to ceiling, with buckets, ropes, nets, an upended table, a tin bath, and other fishermen's flotsam and jetsam.

A dog is barking. Seeker decides to return later; maybe the area he is looking for is within the house.

The third point of the star lies east, up the hill from Church Street, across Alms House Close field and in the grounds of Abbey House, the partially collapsed manor now occupied by an elderly servant of the lord of the manor. This location being not far from the yard in which Rebecca lives and, having learned that she has a good knowledge of how to slip in and out without being seen, to set snares for rabbits, Seeker is leaving exploration of the site until late evening and such time as she may serve as guide.

Which leaves three points. He arrives back at the Inn in time to hand his letter in person to the mail coach guard, and is pleased to wait ten minutes in the street to witness the coach and his letter leave Church Street and begin the journey to York and Leeds.

By now dusk has arrived. Seeker returns to his room at the Inn and, having scribbled copious notes of what he has learnt during the day, enjoys pie and potatoes and a pint of beer at a table in the bar before setting out once more. This time he carries a lantern and is glad of his hat and voluminous coat as he makes his way south along Church Lane past Bridge Street, Grope Lane, the Tatie Market and Cockpit Yard, to Sander's Wharf, and a property that backs onto the harbour.

A narrow alley between the building and its neighbour takes him to the empty wharf. Two heavy iron doors, making up most of the width of the building, stare blindly toward the water. Threaded through holes in these doors is a thick rusty chain, its ends secured by a gleaming and very large padlock. Unlike the rest of its surroundings, the padlock is brand new.

A game is afoot!

Once again Robert Seeker's toolkit is put to good use. Hanging his lantern from a strap on his coat, he picks the padlock, hoping against hope that no one across the harbour notices him.

Padlock removed, Seeker heaves open one of the doors, the thick chain rattling and resonating as the links slip through the opening aperture.

He is inside.

Mr Dixon was not wrong, there are no small voltaic piles here. Instead there is a huge tank connected to thick copper cables that emerge from the ground in a corner of the room. An odour of burning tar and the salty acidic smell of chemistry hang in the air.

The warehouse is thick with dust. A calendar dated 1805 hangs on the wall, its yellowing paper curled at the edges. But like the padlock, the machinery and equipment in the room are all quite new. Seeker scours the room for an explanation. He pulls back the lid of the tank and, holding his lantern aloft, peers inside. The tank is full of a clear liquid and he is tempted to dip a finger to check if it is water but something holds him back. Instead he tears a page out of his notebook, scrunches it up into a ball and drops it into the tank.

The ball of paper immediately shrivels, turns black and disintegrates.

Seeker steps back, seriously alarmed. Acid perhaps? He is out of his depth. He opens cupboards and drawers, explores the office adjoining the warehouse. The building is empty except for the tank, hoists and winches that appear to be for lifting objects into the tank, and a curious pair of boots made from a material utterly unlike anything Seeker has ever seen, save perhaps on the toe caps of the footwear worn by one of those two distressed women up on Silver Street.

He did not comment on her shoes nor ask Sarah if he might

touch them, for fear of causing offence or alarm, but he had been struck by the strange colour and texture. Now as he holds this unusual footwear fashioned from a material that looks almost like the skin of a whale, a smooth flexible dark grey substance that does not feel cold to the touch, he wonders of its provenance and makes a mental note to quiz the two women as soon as practicable.

And with that he leaves the warehouse. If he hurries, he may visit the two points on the west side of the harbour before his assignment with Rebecca.

Further down the street Thelonious Dixon, still shaken from the attack, is seated in his office with two gentlemen who are more than alarmed at what he has told them.

'Good God, man, you blabbered everything to a couple of common criminals!' expostulates the taller of the two, who is none other than pawnbroker Aaron Sly.

'On the contrary,' Dixon retorts, 'my defiance of those scoundrels, in order to protect you, led directly to the wanton destruction of scientific equipment worth some ninety-one pounds and thirteen shillings. For which I will be pleased to learn from yourselves that I will receive complete compensation. I would also remind you that your association is already in indebted to this establishment to the tune of two hundred and thirty guineas.'

Joseph Argument who, strangely, is a man of few words, stands up to stretch his legs. 'I do not believe that our Mr Dixon is engaging purposefully with our predicament.'

Sly drums his fingers on Dixon's desk. 'Indeed. Most unsatisfactory. It appears that we may have made a mistake in our assessment of you as a fit and honourable person, Thelonious.'

'How dare you, Sir!' cries Dixon, red in the face. 'I have discharged my each and every instruction from yourselves to the letter, have I not? We have been in business for twenty-three years and not once, never once, has anyone had reason to say …'

He cannot finish his sentence because Joseph Argument, being a man of few words, has decided that they have all heard enough. As he tightens the garrotte around Dixon's neck, Argument looks almost bored and, when finally Dixon's body slumps, he lets the business owner fall off his chair to the floor. Quite dead.

'We need to find Mr Seeker,' he says, removing his gloves and thrusting the garrotte back into his coat pocket, 'as a matter of some urgency.'

CHAPTER 37

Other than a brief trip to purchase a few novels - Walter Scott's *Ivanhoe*, Louisa Stanhope's *The Crusaders*, and *Roche-Blanche*, the latest romance by Anna Maria Porter - Sarah and Amy have been stuck indoors hoping that Mr Seeker might be true to his word and bring them news as to how they might escape back to their own time.

They have played cards, drunk tea, eaten plum cake, stared out of the window … and are both thoroughly bored. Twice Sarah has made for the door, desperate for fresh air (and a couple of hours to herself) and twice Amy has called her back, pleading with her not to abandon them. *Them* being Amy and 'the baby' who must be a foetus all of eight weeks old.

They have not spoken further on this issue, Sarah because she wishes to avoid a scene, and Amy because she decided that Sarah is possibly jealous.

One the plus side they have a warm fire and have been hearing Rosie singing all manner of songs in her beautiful untrained voice as she has spring cleaned every surface before retiring to the kitchen to prepare the pies, as instructed by her mother.

Outside, the afternoon has grimmed to grey, darkening with every passing hour as rain gorges the gutters and drains in a relentless gloom of gurgling. The two women each sit at a window, Amy squinting and angling the pages of her book to get as much reading done as possible without lighting candles or lanterns; Sarah scribbling mathematical equations on a sheet of paper. She has concluded that light must be thousands of times more expensive per amount of light, she thinks the word is lumen, in 1821 than it is in 2021, and she vows never to take light for granted again. Ever.

The door of the kitchen opens and Rosie emerges with plates, crockery and a lantern.

'Food will be ready in a few minutes,' she announces, setting the table for two and closing the curtains to keep in the warmth from the fire.

Which brings any pretence at reading to an end.

'No, Rosie. You'll eat with us. Won't you?' Amy says, looking at Sarah.

'I can't, Miss.' Rosie says. 'It's not right.'

'If you don't eat with us then we shall all go hungry,' Sarah says. 'We don't care what they do in the posh houses, here we are all equal.'

'Posh?' Rosie has never heard the word.

'Grand. The rich folk. The gentry,' Sarah tries a few words. 'Lords and ladies. Here we will eat together.'

Rosie shrugs. 'Mum's right, you are the strangest couple of chickens we ever did see.'

A few minutes later they are all three seated at the table, enjoying Rosie's excellent pies. Having overcome her shyness and anxiety it turns out that Rosie is quite the chatterbox with opinions on everything. They talk about work and travel (Rosie has once been as far as Pickering and dreams one day of visiting York, forty-five miles away!). They talk about fishing and whaling, and Sarah explains how we have to look after the world and not kill all the whales. And finally they talk about how Sarah and Amy have turned up in Whitby.

'I'm not saying I believe you, mind,' says Rosie, 'but if it's true that you aren't from London but really do come from the future how come you don't know owt about how things work? Don't they have schools? You can't even use a tinderbox!'

'Things are different, that's all,' Amy says. 'We're confused in your time like you'd be confused in ours.'

Rosie gives her a wry smile. 'You're pulling my leg.'

Sarah pulls a small LED torch from her pocket, shows Rosie the button switch at the end and hands it to her. 'Push the button.'

Rosie looks less confident.

'Go on. It won't hurt you.'

Rosie pushes the button and floods the table in a dazzling beam of light. Sarah and Amy burst out laughing.

The young woman shrieks, drops the torch and crosses herself. By the time Sarah has picked the torch off the floor, Rosie has disappeared into the kitchen.

'I'm sorry, Rosie. Please come back,' Sarah says. 'It was a silly trick, that's all.'

But Rosie refuses to come back and insists that she is fine where she is, thank you.

Amy and Sarah are trying to decide what to do next, worried that Rosie may leave and never return, when there is a knock on the door.

'That'll be Rebecca, thank God.' Sarah says.

It isn't. As Amy opens the door, a very dishevelled and very wet Robert Seeker practically tumbles into the room, his top hat rolling away across the carpet. Sarah walks him to an armchair by the fire where he collapses still in his coat.

'Are there any fortifying spirits in this house, ladies?' he asks. 'I am frozen to the marrow, drowning in an excess of precipitation, and have spent the better part of the past twenty-four hours in fear for my life!'

Amy hurries to the kitchen and returns with a bottle of rum, fills a glass from the table and hands it to Seeker, who downs it in a single visit.

'There is food if you want,' Sarah tells him.

'Rum is food enough for now,' Seeker says, holding out the empty glass.

'Shall we at least be drying your coat?'

Seeker removes his voluminous coat but will not allow for it to be hung on the coat stand at the other side of the room. Instead he asks for the stand to be placed beside him, near the fire and away from the front door. Removing several items from the pockets - his revolver, notebook, and an assortment of papers bundled in oilcloth to keep them dry – he sits down, placing the items upon his lap.

'Might I be granted a few precious minutes to compose myself?' he asks, reaching into the pocket of one of his waist-coats for his snuff box, placing two generous pinches on the back of his hand, sniffing loudly, then accepting the refilled glass of rum from Amy.

The two women sit at the table and wait, each lost in her thoughts, as the fire crackles in the hearth and the sounds of washing up drift in from the kitchen. And, welcome sound, Rosie is singing again so all is not lost.

The next noise is less welcome.

Snoring.

'Bloody hell,' Amy says. 'Wake him up, we can't have him sleeping here.'

Sarah gets up and shakes Seeker's sleeve. He awakens with a spluttering jolt, the revolver and everything else on his lap clattering to the floor, looks around him in alarm then realises he is safe.

'My humblest apologies. You are eager to hear what I have discovered and how it may ameliorate your prospects,' he says, gathering the items he has dropped. 'Ladies, I have uncovered an extraordinary conspiracy involving a sinister association that, I believe, are responsible for the incogitable activities that brought you here.'

'What?' says Amy.

'I have also established a link between said association, known as the Architects, and the comings and going of a ship called the *Inevitable*. The captain, a Haitian called Jean-

Jacques Elmo, has entered into a contract that I believe supplies him with persons snatched from the future in exchange for goods of some sort that are procured, obtained or stolen in another time period. Furthermore, said contract leaves Elmo indebted to the Architects for the huge sum of fourteen thousands pounds.'

'Is that a lot of money?' Amy is none the wiser.

'Based on the money we got for your bracelet, I would say around two million pounds,' Sarah says after a quick bit of mental maths.

'Enough to purchase a new five-hundred-ton whaling ship, Madam,' Seeker explains. He lets this sink in then adds, 'We may conjecture that your acquaintance Mr Derek might be upon the *Inevitable* as I have had it confirmed to me that the vessel left Whitby on Friday night during the storm. Press-gangs do not hang about after they have seized new men to join their crews and there is no reason to believe that Elmo would behave with any more decency than the pressers.'

Amy has her head in her hands.

'Is there … would there …' Sarah struggles for words. 'How long might this ship be gone?'

'I have asked a woman known to you both, Rebecca Ann Johnson, to make discrete enquiries on my behalf, and hope to receive informations from her soon.'

'You know Rebecca?'

'I bumped into her on Church Street earlier outside the pawnbroking establishment of Messrs Sly and Argument. I aver she showed remarkable acuity for a fishwoman, unmasking my purpose at once, and offering to assist me in my endeavours.'

'Okay,' Sarah says, nodding slowly. 'Is there anything else?'

Seeker strokes his chin and decides not to tell the two women about the six-pointed star map or of the visit he intends to make to Abbey House with Rebecca in a couple of hours. 'I can tell you that it is indeed the case that the town hall plays a part in the nefarious activities we are seeking to unmask. I cannot say more without putting your lives in mortal danger. Did you say that there was food?'

'I'll fetch him some pie,' Amy says, climbing to her feet and heading to the kitchen.

A second later she reappears. 'Rosie has gone!'

Sarah is unflustered. 'She has worked a long day, Amy. It is natural that she should go home.'

'Where did you find your maid, if I may be so bold?' Seeker asks.

'Who in Whitby produces the weather forecasts?' Sarah asks, choosing to ignore his question.

'Many of the ship owners have barometers,' Seeker replies as Amy appears with a plate of pie and cheese. He leaves his armchair and sits at the table, revolver and papers beside him. 'The fishermen will read the skies before they set sail in the morning.'

'No, I mean a week ahead,' Sarah says. 'Who does that?'

Seeker gives Sarah a strange look as he chews his pie. Not for the first time, he is ill at ease with her bizarre assumptions.

'Why, forecasting that far ahead would require the ability to talk with persons on the other side of the country in order to know what might be heading towards one and by the time the messenger arrived in Whitby the weather would have passed.'

Sarah realises that neither the telephone nor the railways are yet invented; what she is asking for is just not possible.

'Wait! Yes! I do know someone who may be of assistance!' Seeker ejaculates. 'George Merryweather! A young man living in Skinner Street. A man with prospects, fascinated by the natural world and, I hear, aspiring to become a doctor. It rumoured that he conducts experiments involving such lowly creatures as frogs, spiders, and even leeches. He is apparently convinced that they might one day serve as storm forecasters or prognosticators. We can organise an appointment. I have been meaning to pay Merryweather a visit these several weeks past.'

'Let's focus on barometers, shall we?' Sarah replies firmly. 'We need to know when there will next be an electrical storm.'

Seeker makes a mental note that neither woman shows recognition of the value of using animals to forecast the weather.

'It's getting quite late, isn't it, Sarah?' Amy says pointedly.

'Dear me, is that the time?' Seeker consults his fob watch. 'Well, I trust my investigations are raising your hopes of there being a solution to your distressing situation?'

'Yes, thank you Mr Seeker. We are very grateful for your help,' Sarah reassures him.

Seeker climbs into his voluminous coat, retrieves his top hat and pushes it down onto his curly red locks, and takes his leave.

'Bloody hell! He's a weirdo and a half, isn't he?' Amy says once the front door closes. 'I aver she showed remarkable acuity for a fishwoman, unmasking my purpose at once,' Amy mimics Seeker's accent and mannerisms.

Sarah laughs. 'Yes. But he's our best hope, Amy. We now know the name of the ship that possibly kidnapped Derek and have proof that electric storms are important. He is helping and, let's be honest, only a weirdo would entertain the supposition that we really are embroiled in a complex time continuum conundrum.'

'You sound like *him*!' Amy laughs.

'We both deserve a glass of that rum. If it stops raining we shall pay Rebecca a visit.'

Red Weather Warning issued for Storm Beowolf

The Met Office has issued a rare Red Weather Warning as Storm Beowolf is expected to bring exceptionally strong winds on Tuesday 3rd December

The Red Weather Warning covers northeast coastal areas of the UK, where the most significant gusts in exposed areas could be in excess of 90mph from early Tuesday morning. Risk of high impacts and disruption to power, travel and other services. Damage is also likely to buildings and trees, with beach material being thrown onto coastal roads, sea fronts and homes, providing a serious risk on the coastline.

People should check forecasts regularly for the latest warnings and stay indoors and well away from coastal defences, beaches and exposed areas.

Before the thunderstorm

- Lightning can cause power surges, unplug any non-essential appliances if not already using a surge protector.
- Seek shelter if possible. When you hear thunder you are already within range of where the next ground flash may occur, lightning can strike as far as 10 miles away from the centre of a storm.

During the thunderstorm

- Telephone lines can conduct electricity so try to avoid using the landline, unless in an emergency
- If outside avoid water and find a low-lying open place that is a safe distance from trees, poles or metal objects

- Be aware of metal objects that can conduct or attract lightning,
- If you find yourself in an exposed location it may be advisable to squat close to the ground, with hands on knees and with head tucked between them. Try to touch as little of the ground with your body as possible, do not lie down on the ground
- If you feel your hair stand on end, drop to the above position immediately

CHAPTER 38

'So why didn't you bloody tell me that the other night?'

'You were in no fit state to respond in a rational manner, were you, Sir?' Sergeant Pannett answers.

'How dare you?' Stephen is furious. 'My wife and friends have been missing for four days and all you have done is make sneery innuendos. Is there an ombudsman I can complain to?'

'I visited the cottage with you, Sir. No disrespect has been intended, I simply set out the process we have to …'

'Forget that. I've learned that two other people went missing on Friday night. And another ten people have disappeared in Whitby over the past ten years. God help them if you worked as hard to find them as you are working to find my wife.'

'Eight other people, Mr Bootle. I'm not at liberty to say more. All information on missing persons is confidential. We respect the family's wishes unless we believe a crime has been committed.'

Pannett shuffles papers on the reception desk. 'I can tell you that the other individuals who went missing on Friday were also staying on Henrietta Street. Now unless you have new information germane to our enquiries, evidence of where your wife and friends have gone, proof that something untoward has happened, then I have to advise that we are preparing for a major storm. This is only a small police station, Sir. If it is of assistance, I can put you in touch with our professional counselling service. Would that be of …'

'Okay. No one gives a toss. I get it!' Stephen waves his hand dismissively and storms out, where he immediately feels he is acting like an idiot, but what else can he do?

CHAPTER 39

As sun sags into silent sea, Captain Bill and his mates, having seized the ship, are celebrating in time-honoured tradition by drinking themselves into a stupor.

Beth, Pierre and half a dozen other crewmembers who have been unwilling to show the required enthusiasm for their new leader, are locked in the brig. Sam Solomon is manacled to his stove in the galley, under orders to produce food. As encouragement, he has received a beating from ferret-faced Frank Dent.

A dozen others have buttoned their lips and are keeping their heads down.

Aleka and Nat are below deck with the rest of the crew. They are nursing their wounds. Aleka has a fever and both siblings have swollen arms and hands that no amount of hot compresses are able to help.

Lizbet, who is at Sam's side and doing her best to be invisible, sneaks across from time to time with water and food for the twins.

Derek is thirsty. He has spent the afternoon out of sight on the mizzen top platform, a third of the way up the mast. After several hours in the hot sun and having drunk too much rum, his head is throbbing and he is glad to see the day drawing to a close.

Once it became clear that Pierre, Beth and the others would not be able to overwhelm Bill and his acolytes, Derek decided that there was no point in his jumping down from the rigging in a heroic but insane attempt to take on six people single-handedly, armed with only a dagger.

He cannot see Elmo, as the erstwhile captain is shackled to the other side of the mainmast, but he can hear him. Elmo is made of strong stuff. For the past hour he has passed the time singing rousing songs in a language Derek cannot understand but assumes to be a form of creole French.

With the fading of the day comes the increased risk of another visit from the pterosaurs that attacked Ezekiel. They seem to prefer dusk and tend to land once the ship's hatches are closed, crash landing onto the deck like vultures to waddle about pulling open anything that is not securely fastened or tied down as they scavenge for easy food.

Bang on cue, Derek spots two of the creatures silhouetted against the darkening sky over the jungle and realises that he cannot remain where he is. He scrambles down the Jacob's ladder as the first animal passes over the beach and swoops in to land with a heavy thump on the deck. Surprisingly mobile, the pterosaur folds its wings and walks briskly on four legs, claws clicking on the timbers and making straight for Elmo who, shackled to the mast, is easy prey. Elmo calls out at the top of his voice for someone to come to his assistance.

'If anyone tries to go up on deck to rescue the bastard, I'll run him through!' shouts a voice below deck.

Derek jumps down from the rigging and races forward, dagger in hand, hoping his steps will be mistaken below for a pterosaur's.

The monster is in front of its prey, head cocked to one side, its long sharp beak pointing to the right of Elmo's chest. It has almost no binocular vision and has to turn its head to see Elmo clearly, and then only with one eye. Elmo stares back at the pterosaur but keeps quite still, confusing the creature. Elmo has learned from previous encounters that, like a lizard, the animals' vision seems to require movement to trigger action.

The second pterosaur lands and ambles across the deck to join the first.

Derek's first encounter with a pterosaur, as he struggled to fend off the one attacking Ezekiel as he hung from the rigging, was a blur of wings and movement, punctuated by a stabbing beak. This time he has a clearer sense of the animal's anatomy, their huge heads and long necks perched over comparatively small bodies. The wings are enormous even when folded. He guesses the wingspan to be well over three metres.

Curiosity gets the better of the pterosaurs who both step forwards towards Elmo. One of them lunges suddenly, stabbing Elmo in the thigh with its forty-centimetre-long beak.

Wishing he had a cutlass rather than a short dagger, Derek hisses and waves his blade to draw the animals' attention away from the captain. Both pterosaurs and Elmo turn. The two men lock eyes briefly and acknowledge each other. Derek lunges at the nearer of the two predators catching its wing and causing it to retreat. The second animal rushes forwards clambering over Elmo's outstretched leg to get at Derek. It stinks of carrion and even in the gloom it is possible to see that its body carries flesh fragments and other detritus from the last body it trampled about in.

Derek dare not shout in case he alerts the mutinous crew-members below deck to his presence but he stands his ground, dodging the pterosaur's lunging beak and attempting to get close enough to take out one of its eyes.

The pterosaur moves quickly, its sharp hard beak crashing down on Derek's arm. Another blow could snap his arm in half. Human and pterosaur duel like a couple of fencers, back and forth across the deck, advancing, retreating, lunging, parrying.

When the first pterosaur appears ready to re-enter the fray, Derek knows he must act decisively. He is helped by Elmo who, though shackled, is able to aim a hefty kick that throws the pterosaur off-balance. Derek seizes his chance, takes three steps forwards and swipes upwards under the creature's head, ripping into its throat. The pterosaur staggers back, blood pouring from the wound as it collides into its accomplice. The two beasts have had enough. They haul themselves into the air on huge leathery wings and make their escape, shrieking as they go. Barely twenty metres from the ship, the injured pterosaur falls from the sky like a crumpled umbrella and crashes into the sea.

Derek sinks to his hands and knees exhausted and gasping for breath.

'You have saved my life, Englishman.'

'And you must save ours in return,' Derek replies. 'Those youngsters, Nat and Aleka, are both poisoned.'

'Sam will treat them.'

'They need a proper doctor not a part-time cook. You and I don't have children so it doesn't matter to us, but the twins have parents. They need to go back to our time; the century from which you stole us. We want our freedom. And that word you asked me about is dinosaur, not snoreodin or whatever you said. The crew are being killed by dinosaurs.'

Elmo seems about to say something then changes his mind. He beckons Derek to come closer so that he doesn't need to shout. Derek squats down beside him.

'The world rings out with the cries of those who dream of freedom.' he says quietly. 'Freedom from slavery, from poverty, from hunger and oppression. In Whitby, where we found you, some sup wines from silver goblets and crystal glasses and gamble a thousand guineas on a throw of a dice, while others work sixteen hours a day trying to earn a living from the sea and keep their families out of the workhouse. A few in fancy coats, the rest in rags, crowded in damp, smoke-filled rooms, too poor and too tired to light a candle.'

Elmo pauses, gathering his thoughts. 'In my part of the world, people whose grandparents were snatched from Africa, are whipped by men on horseback, forced to grow sugar or produce rum that makes some men rich while others suffer. Men and women dive seven fathoms for pearls and are flogged or tossed into the sea to feed the sharks when they become ill or can swim no more. We are sold like cattle and when …'

'No disrespect, but the history lesson doesn't help. Right now, you've got a mutiny and I want to hear how we can save Aleka and Nat.'

'You must help me.'

'I will once you promise to take us safely back to Whitby.'

'The crew does not order the captain. Not you, not Bill, not Frank Dent, or Henrietta. I command this ship.'

'Suit yourself. Enjoy the pterosaurs.' Derek stands up.

'Sit down and listen,' Elmo barks. 'Or you and your co-travellers will die here in this place as surely as the rest of us.'

Impressed at the bold fearlessness of a man in chains, Derek does as he is told.

'I have survived Rochambeau and Napoleon, and revolution. As a child I witnessed violence, torture and beheadings, you cannot begin to imagine. When Dessalines declared our independence and the creation of Haiti in 1804 I dared to hope the horror was behind us, but the cruelty did not stop. I joined those denouncing the hypocrisy and had to flee for my life with several others of this crew.'

'That is why we are here. But the bad times will one day end. If you are really from the future, Derek, then you will surely know Haiti as a proud and prosperous country.'

As Elmo has been speaking, the full moon has risen pale over the jungle to the east. Muffled sea shanties and raucous drunken laughter drift up from below deck. Derek thinks of what he knows of Haiti, still broken and suffering two hundred years on. The injustices of the world do not disappear because people have invented computer games, mobile phones, cars, rock & roll and oven chips. He says nothing.

If Elmo notices Derek's silence, he does not question it.

'The fortune we have made in this strange land beyond the crossover will be put to the creation of a free and prosperous Haiti.'

'But the ship has been taken over,' Derek points out. 'They have the weapons, they have stolen the jewels, and locked all your best people in the brig.'

'Derek,' Elmo laughs. 'This is my ship. Bill and his grim gallery of gurners have no idea where everything is hidden. They are a box of severed fingers fantasising that they might write themselves a hero's tale with neither hand nor brain nor pen. Even blubberhead Bill and ferret-faced Frank will eventually conclude that, if we are to leave this place of monsters, they will have to release everyone on board to man the ship, and we must plan what we will do when that time comes. Let me explain everything and guide you below deck unseen so no one knows that you and I have spoken.'

CHAPTER 40

Robert Seeker and Rebecca climb the insanely steep Donkey Road, cold sleet pouring down on them like gravel from a concrete mixer. At the edge of Alms House Close, she instructs him to snuff out his lantern and they cross the field above the cramped yards of Church Street in the darkness, dead weeds and grasses snagging their wet clothes.

Below them candlelight flickers the windows of tenements and cottages. Coal fire smoke curls from a score of chimney pots, fogging the view of the harbour. Heaving lungs are hoarse with coughing. A baby cries.

The field as almost as steep as Donkey Road.

'Keep up, lad,' Rebecca calls over her shoulder. 'I don't want out here longer than I must. We'll catch our deaths.'

Robert Seeker breaks into a run to catch up with her. Slides in the mud, falls flat on his face, picks himself up.

'Most grateful,' Seeker gasps, 'and may I interpose a …'

'Save yer breath, it's a long way up, soldier.'

They reach the wall that runs north to south, following the contours of the Esk Valley. A tangled frizz of thorns and brambles hugs the stones. Rebecca heads right, away from St Mary's church on the cliff top. Some fifty metres along there is a gap in the vegetation. Seeker finds Rebecca in front of a broken door set into the wall. She presses her shoulder to the wood and pushes the door open.

'Don't worry,' she says. 'There's nowt up here except an old servant who looks after the ruins. He's caught us rabbiting a couple of times but his running days are behind him, poor sod gets out of breath just shaking his stick.'

Seeker pauses to take in the scene. To their left along the wall is a long shed. Various other outhouses are dotted about in what might once have been vegetable gardens; it is hard to be certain because everything has long since fallen into disrepair.

'Lord of the manor left around time I were born,' Rebecca explains. 'Place is a wreck. Come on, let's find Grouchy Gordon.'

She strides towards the manor.

It is in a pitiful state, half of it collapsed and an empty husk, the other half dilapidated and unloved. Further up the hill stands what remains of the equally forlorn Abbey. Seeker wonders whether it is worth continuing towards so obviously derelict a dwelling.

The sleet peppers them as they pass a thicket of thorns in the centre of which is a statue of what appears to be a gladiator, his fist raised impotently against the ivy that smothers him. Reaching the house, Rebecca turns.

'He has a blunderbuss so I hope you're armed,' she whispers.

Seeker produces his revolver.

A large facade of dark windows stares blindly towards the town as they walk to the southern end of the building and turn the corner.

Weak candlelight flickers in a single window beside the south entrance to Abbey House. Rebecca climbs the steps, knocks on the door and steps aside, pressing herself against the house to shelter from the worst of the rain.

Nothing.

She knocks again and retreats a second time.

This time there is a movement in the light behind the window, a guttering of the flame.

Seeker stands before the entrance, his revolver raised.

Bolts are drawn and the door swings open on rusty hinges to reveal a large elderly gentleman in a coat and hat, holding a lantern in one hand and a blunderbuss in the other.

'Put the weapon down, Sir,' Seeker says, 'or I will be obliged to shoot.'

Gordon MacCrab squints as he shifts his lantern to try to get a better view of his would-be assailant.

'I'll not ask twice,' Seeker says, cocking the trigger of his revolver.

'Thundering Thrallocks! I'll no be intimidated on my own turf, pup.'

Seeker fires at the bell of the blunderbuss. The bullet smacks its target, knocking the weapon from MacCrab's hand and ricocheting just a whisker away from his bulbous nose.

The weapon tumbles down the steps.

'How dare ye?' the old man shouts. 'Come into the light, you pauper's excrement!'

Rebecca collects the blunderbuss while keeping her face turned away from MacCrab.

'I'll leave you now,' she tells Seeker, 'I must protect my family.'

She withdraws into the darkness.

'Return my weapon, you thieving bitch!'

'It will be in the grounds, though it may have rusted by the time you reach it, you lame old fool,' Rebecca says over her shoulder.

'We need to have a conversation,' Seeker says, stepping forwards.

MacCrab leads the way, showing Seeker into his lodgings beside the entrance hall. The main room is sparsely furnished. Coal glows orange in the fireplace, over which hangs a water-colour of a Scottish glen. Mould creeps up the walls and the smell of decay hangs in the air.

The elderly servant fills two tumblers with whisky, hands one to Seeker, then takes his place in the wing-backed armchair before the fire.

'You'll have to make do with one of the other chairs. And you can put your pistol back in your pocket, I'm too old and too tired to take you on. '

Seeker sips and feels the golden warmth of the whisky slip down.

'A fine single malt,' he observes.

'One of the few things I have left from home.'

The two men sit in silence a moment, watching the flames curl over the coals.

'My name is Robert Seeker. I am here to understand how this house is embroiled in the evil that stalks the town,' Seeker says eventually. 'I have, among other items, a map upon which is a six-pointed star that shows …'

'I know what it shows,' says MacCrab. 'Are you alone or do you have assistance? And I don't mean a fishwoman from the yards.'

Seeker does not reply quickly enough.

'Ay, I thought as much. You'll not stop them, laddie, any more than I can stop them.'

'They call themselves the Architects,' Seeker continues. 'I believe the town hall may be key to their operation but I don't know why or what this secret association are trying to do.'

'Do you know when the town hall was built? Let me tell you. In 1788. Were you even alive? You're not from here, I guessing.'

'I'm from London.'

The old man nods and smiles to himself. 'Did you get a good look at this wreck of a manor house on your way here? Half the building collapsed in seventeen-eighty-nine. Just a year after the town hall went up. Some said it was the wind. Titan's Thrallocks the wind! They've been busy with their necromancy since the day that town hall was built and it was their activities brought this fine house down.'

'Do you know their names?'

'Och, I know them all! And if I tell you, the chances are you'll be floating face down in the harbour before daybreak.'

'Do they employ you?'

MacCrab shakes his head. 'The owners of this estate, who live many miles away, pay me to keep this half of the building habitable and free from intruders. To my eternal shame, I have failed on both counts. May God forgive me!'

Seeker stands up and paces the room.

'Your *Architects* come and go as they please,' MacCrab added. 'They may be on their way here right now.'

'Then we are short of time,' Seeker says. 'Don't be afraid of …'

'How dare you!' MacCrab explodes with rage. 'I am a fully qualified engineer. I had a professional career before you could blow your own nose, you turtle's fart!

'I apologise, Sir. What I meant was …'

The old man snorts. 'Save your sweet talk for someone who needs it.' He heaves himself up out of his armchair and buttons up his coat. He lights a second lantern. 'We'll see what kind of man you are, Mr Seeker.'

The house is large. Down one corridor, lined with peeling wallpaper, a dozen doors, and dark portraits that glow briefly in the light of the lantern, then left down a passage that appears boarded up at the end. The threadbare carpet is a faded confection of red, beige and navy blue. As they approach the end of the passage Seeker is astonished to see withered plants in the carpet.

'Nature is reclaiming the house inch by inch,' MacCrab explains. 'The tendrils sneak between the boards and I am tired of purging them.'

The old man pulls open the door set into the boards to reveal the ruin of the house beyond. Ivy and brambles growing rampant up what remains of the walls. The roof long since gone, the first-floor timbers rotted through, the building is open to the skies. Sleet rattles on Seeker's top hat as the two men approach a staircase. MacCrab turns and hauls open a door set into the base of the stairs to reveal steps leading down into the ground.

The smell of damp, decomposition and mould is overpowering, Seeker feels he is wading along a stream not walking in a house. Woodlice, centipedes and slugs cling to the walls. Two rats turn tail and disappear ahead of them. Two further doors, neither one locked, both bearing signs reading:

DO NOT ENTER
upon pain of
DEATH

Beyond this second door the passageway is drier. The walls are painted black.

'Are we still under the house?'

'Aye, but these tunnels continue a long away,' MacCrab tells Seeker as they reach a junction. 'All the way to Saltwick Bay in this direction, beyond the cave, and down to Henrietta Street if you take this passage to the left.'

Thick copper cables wrapped round in cloth run along the floor of the passage towards the harbour. The passage they take continues some twenty metres and opens out on a large cave. Slack-jawed, Seeker looks around trying to make sense of what he sees wandering about, his footsteps echoing, his lamp light struggling to penetrate the smoky gloom. There are two large tanks similar to the one he found by the harbour in Sander's Wharf. Thick ropes of copper cable lie coiled alongside. Winches and tools lie beside the tank.

And there is more.

The floor is covered in painted symbols that are anything but scientific; astrological signs and symbols Seeker has seen only in the grimoires contained within the restricted section of the Cabinet of Curiosities in the annex of Montague House in Great Russell Street in London. Painted on the floor at the very centre of the cave are two equilateral triangles overlapping to create a six-pointed star composed of six smaller equilateral triangles with a hexagon at their heart. Each of these smaller triangles contains a symbol. If Seeker cannot identify these there is no mistaking the image at the heart of the hexagon; the town hall itself with the eye of Horus radiating at its core!

'They've been busy these past few weeks,' MacCrab observes. 'That's the smell of welding in the air; these tanks have been assembled here underground. They bring everything in via the Hawsker Road.'

The tanks and occult drawings are not the only remarkable features. While one half of the floor is a relatively smooth and level, the rest is covered in huge rocks that have fallen from above. The roof of the cave is thick with black soot.

'How long ago was the fire?' Seeker asks.

'There have been several. The first explosion caused the collapse that brought down half the house above. That will be, och, thirty or thirty-three years ago. They removed the small debris but, as you can see, left the larger rocks where they fell. No way of taking them out, do you see? In 1812 they …'

'And have you never challenged them to …'

'Boggin Bambot!' MacCrab explodes. 'One old duffer take on the devil and his work?'

'Are there occult forces at play?'

The old man snorts. 'I cannot answer that. I am a Christian, Sir. They did speak to me once, years ago, about lines of force and their six-pointed star and the energies of the universe. I smiled politely and kept my trap shut. They have long since stopped speaking to me. And I've a care for my own skin, Sir. Look over there. You see those cells?'

Set into the rough stone walls of the cave are the thick iron bars of two prison cells.

'They've locked people up in those. One wretched woman was incarcerated there in the dark for six months.'

'What happened to her?'

MacCrab shrugs. 'They bring me down here from time to time, to put the frighteners on me, you understand. One time she was there, shouting and pleading with me to help her, the next time the poor soul was gone. Was she killed? Did she escape? I canna tell you.'

'When was this?'

'Three, four years ago perhaps.'

Seeker rummages in his pockets for his notebook. 'Can you put names to these initials?' He holds the open page to the light.

MEETING OF THE ARCHITECTS
5th August 1821 at 7 pm
Venue: Town Hall.

In attendance: J.A, A.S, C.T, Z.B, T.W, E.H, C.F, G.P, J.K, H.S, & M.B.

MacCrab studies the list. 'You sure you have the belly for this, my young pup? Once I tell you, there's no going back.

Seeker nods.

Gordon MacCrab sighs.

'J.A.?'

'Joseph Argument.'

Seeker scribbles the name in his notebook. 'A.S.?'

'Aaron Sly. Constantine Featherston, Zachariah Barton, John Kidson, Marmaduke Bovill, Henry Smales, Charles …' MacCrab stops in mid-sentence.

The sound of raised voices, muffled but growing in volume.

'Quick, laddie. Take that exit,' MacCrab points to the far

side of the cave. 'I'll delay them as long as I can. If they see the light of your lamp you're a dead man!'

'Thank you, Sir.'

'Don't thank me. Hurry!'

Robert Seeker dives into the passage. The flame flickers and dances in his lantern as he speeds along. After fifteen seconds or so the passage starts to dip slightly and turn to the right. Behind him all is dark, no longer any hint of light, with luck the same is true in the opposite direction. He is deep in the bowels of the cliff enveloped in thousands of tonnes of solid rock. The ground and the walls of the tunnel are rough-hewn and he is glad of his voluminous coat protecting him from scratches as he runs for what seems like three or four minutes. Finally the air seems to be getting colder and fresher. He smells the sea! Second later he reaches the end of the tunnel and emerges onto a ledge.

Sleet has turned to rain. Steps lead downward but the tide is in. At low tide you can probably follow the beach around the cliff and walk back to Whitby.

But not now. For now the path is blocked by the deafening sea crashing against the rocks below, sending thick plumes of water high into the air.

The noise of the sea is such that Seeker almost misses the shouts from the tunnel at his back! Suddenly he is on the move again, running along the ledge. Cliff above and water below. The voices are getting louder, he has only seconds left. He tosses his lantern into the sea and scours the rock face looking for irregularities. He is no mountaineer but he has no choice. There is no way to reach the top but, with luck, he might just be able to …

The two men reach the end of the tunnel and emerge onto the ledge.

'If the old bugger has lied I will wring his fat neck myself!

All that cock and bull about looking for his cat.'

'Save your breath, John. He has his kept eyes and nose out of our business for 30 years. Why would he lie now?'

'I feel it in my bones. This afternoon Joseph and Aaron almost laid hands on the bastard who broke into the town hall. We'll not be safe until his corpse is feeding the fish.'

'No one has escaped this way. Look at the sea, they'd be smashed to pieces and drowned in seconds.'

'Not if they passed through a couple of hours back.'

'If they passed a couple of hours back they'll be tucked up in bed by now and MacCrab would be in his mould-covered mausoleum.

Clinging to the bare rock above their heads, his fingers and toes aching, Seeker is praying the two men don't look up.

Or down.

His lantern has fallen not into the sea but onto a rock just above the water where it is still glowing faintly.

'There's no cave below this one, is there, Henry? Nowhere to hide?'

'Can't remember.'

Seeker's heart is in his mouth. If either man leans forwards and looks down he is finished!

'I'll hold you so you can take a look.'

'You have a look.'

'Don't be daft, Henry, I'm twice your weight.'

'I'm not leaning over that ledge!'

'Useless shit-sack. Hold your lantern out at least!'

As the bigger man gets down on his hands and knees, a larger wave smacks the base of the cliff sending a thick column of water shooting upwards so high that it reaches the lantern, flipping it over and sending it rolling into the sea where the flame gutters and dies just as John Kidson's head leans out over the lip of the ledge. The rising sea spray drenches the men from head to toe and it takes all Henry's strength to stop Kidson tumbling forwards into the sea.

'What were that noise?'

'Who cares? We're soaked to the skin. Leave it.'

The cold is getting to Seeker's fingertips. He turns his head away from the sea and presses himself against the rock trying to keep his weight on his toes but, in the act of doing so, knocks the brim of his top hat.

Damnations! My hat!

The hat tips backwards incrementally, the slow movement exciting the individual hairs on his head. Seeker leans his body back a little, once again putting pressure on his fingers, so that he can lean his head forwards and down. It is no good, he is lost and might as well announce his presence and take whatever punishment he has coming to him.

The bigger man is back on his feet. 'I think we should see if there's a better view from top of the steps.'

'For God's sake, let it go! There's bloody nowt to see! I'm off back up.'

'I'll not forget this, Henry!'

The men head up the tunnel, back the way they came, the light from their lantern fading just as Seeker's hat tumbles off the back of his head and down onto the ledge. Eyes closed, Seeker counts to twenty, praying the men do not reappear, then slowly reaches down with his left foot, searching for a foothold. He finds one and climbs back down to the ledge where, muscles trembling uncontrollably from his exertions and soaked to the skin, he crawls a few metres into the tunnel. Beyond caring what happens to him, he curls in a ball and falls asleep to the sounds of the surging sea.

CHAPTER 41

It is not yet dawn, and the world is still in monochrome, as he awakens, his cheek pressed against a gritty surface, his body stiff. He can barely find the strength to stretch his legs.

A few steps away is an opening, the source of the noise ringing in his ears. It is brighter over there? His thoughts a reluctant diffuse jumble, Seeker tries to remember who he is and how he got here.

Get up and move.

He pushes himself into a sitting position. Yes, brighter over there but what lies in the opposite direction? A tunnel. Too dark without a lantern. Has he his tinderbox?

He has. And a candle deep in one of his pockets.

Good God, it's cold! Where is my hat?

Cupping his hand to block the breeze, he nurses a spark in the tinderbox, blows gently to create a tiny flame from which he lights his candle.

Colour, the world has colour! And the fatty familiar smell of burning tallow. With the wall for support, he gets to his feet, so numb he cannot feel his toes, and staggers away from the noise and icy wind, back up the tunnel. Has he been here before? Why can he not remember? The tunnel goes on and on. The rough stone walls flicker in the feeble guttering flame that clings to the candle wick behind his cupped hand.

The path leads upward and little by little the exercise brings heat to his legs. The further he walks, the less confident he becomes; the fog is lifting. He came down this way, but why? He was running, from someone.

Or something?

An instinct makes him stop and pat the pockets of his coat, switching the candle from hand to hand.

He finds the revolver. And everything comes flooding back! He is heading in the wrong direction.

Walking directly into danger!

His name is Robert Seeker and he was trying to get away. He must reach the beach. But the tide was in. Maybe the path is now clear.

There is no indication of human presence ahead. Maybe whatever danger there was has now passed. Yes, he should check what has happened. See if the old man, what is his name? Mac … MacCrab! That's it! Check that MacCrab is all right.

Seeker walks more purposefully now has a mission. He remembers recognises the turn in the passage. It is still dark ahead. No sound. A minute later he reaches a cave. The cave. It is empty. There were two men. John and Henry, down on the ledge when he was clinging to the rocks above the tunnel. What did they come for?

He crosses over to the prison cells MacCrab showed him. The doors are unlocked. In each cell there is a bucket and a thin tumble of fetid bedding. And that is all.

Seeker is turning away, the candle flame trembling in his hand, when something catches his eye. He enters the cell.

On the wall someone has carved or scratched notches in bunches of five in the stone. Row upon row. Above the notches are the initials A.V. What can the notches represent? There is no natural light, the prisoner could not possibly have registered the passing of day and night. Were they recording each time they slept? Each time they were fed, or interrogated? Seeker shivers at the thought of the cruelty that was visited here.

He leaves the cell and crosses the cave towards the exit that leads up towards … the house! He remembers now. Something else catches his eye. On the ground behind the metal tanks.

A shoe.

Seeker advances, the hand cupping the flame of his candle now also grips his revolver. He gasps.

The body is face down. Shot in the back. He rolls the body over. The old man's face is barely unrecognisable. Beaten to a pulp. Blood everywhere. Gordon MacCrab is dead.

Seeker feels sick to his core. His own blood ringing in his ears, he looks about for clues as to what has happened. But he knows what has happened. The scoundrels beat MacCrab to obtain information and, not getting what they wanted, they killed him.

MacCrab's lantern lies on the ground. Seeker takes it, lights it from his candle and heads back down the tunnel to the sea. Heading back up to Abbey House is simply too dangerous.

A short time later, still shaken from his discovery but warm from his exertions, Seeker emerges onto the narrow ledge above Saltwick Bay. The sky is now lighter though dawn is still some time away. The tide is out and a strip of beach is visible below. He hurries down the steps; if he is correct then he could be back in Whitby in twenty minutes or so. It is no longer raining and the air is much warmer than last night. Above him, between the jagged edges of the cliffs, dark clouds skitter inland like seabirds seeking refuge from a storm. The moon throws occasional beams onto the beach where rocks the size of elephant seals festoon the water's edge. Seaweed glistens and everywhere the incessant rush of a boiling sea.

The smell of the salt air revives him and he walks briskly. The sight of lanterns up ahead stops him in his tracks. Can they be onto him? If he cannot escape either this way or through the house then he is a dead man. He has no choice.

Advancing slowly towards the lights, having extinguished his lantern, Seeker sees that there are five figures, each holding a lantern, each bending over as if looking for something on or between the rocks. A body?

If they have set an ambush then they are all very much distracted. Seeker wonders if he might make his way round them by venturing out into the water. But that will leave him silhouetted against the white waves.

Drawing closer he can hear them. They are singing, their voices soft and sweet. And suddenly everything makes perfect sense.

'Hey! Over there!'

Whitby's tough as nails fisherwomen are collecting bait before the day has even dawned.

Seeker walks confidently towards them.

'Well, I'll be buggered!' says one of the women. 'Robert Seeker. Has the money gone out of detectivating? We'll not have thee flithering our patch, will we girls?'

'Rebecca, I can explain. After you left I …'

'You know this *gentleman*?' asks one of the other women, incredulously, as she prises limpets from the rock in front of her.

'Told you she had a fancy man!' laughs another.

'Pay them no mind,' Rebecca tells Seeker. 'They laugh like drains over sweet nothings.'

'Sweeting nothings in each other ears, eh?' laughs another, tossing a handful of mussels into her basket. 'Hey, diddle, diddle!'

Unable to think of any clever words that might stop the teasing, Seeker smiles apologetically and makes his way between the women.

'Been up all night, has he?' says a voice.

'I don't know. Ask Rebecca.'

More riotous laughter. Seeker ignores them. Rounding the cliff he sees the harbour wall ahead.

CHAPTER 42

It is just before dawn. The air is warm and moist. Above the vast indigo tablecloth of the sea the sky is streaked with pinks and purples. Gentle waves lick the shushing beach. A thin mist whispers the edge of the jungle and crabs skuttle across the low tide sands as they will continue to do for a billion years.

Three large orange dragonflies with wingspans of over half a metre inspect the ship like helicopter reconnaissance pilots then head to shore in formation.

Captain Jean-Jacques Elmo, who will never see a helicopter, stands on the quarterdeck, breathing the fresh air and enjoying the serenity of the moment, in the knowledge that the day will be busy and complex.

Having slipped below deck unseen thanks to a secret entrance close to the captain's quarters, Derek has had a busy night and is currently grabbing an hour's sleep in a corner beside Nat and Aleka.

The twins are in a bad way. Without access to modern medicine it is unclear whether they are suffering the effects of poisoning from a toxin on the reef, or struck down with a fever. Either way they are fortunate to be attended by the indefatigable Lizbet who passes by regularly through the night to mop their brows and limbs with cooling water from a bucket. Derek is in awe of the young girl, her maturity and composure even after being threatened with a knife by the new 'captain', Bill Stanway.

Derek stayed up on deck talking with the captain until the last of the drunken singing and shouting subsided. When a furious argument erupted below, during which it became clear that Bill was determined to have his way with Beth, it took Elmo's intervention to persuade Derek not to throw open the hatch and join the melee.

'Beth is well able to look after herself, Derek,' Elmo told him. 'No more bloodshed tonight. Your moment will come.'

Eventually raucous laughter and raised voices were replaced by snoring and it was time to make a move.

'Go now, and carry out every instruction to the letter,' Elmo whispered. 'I am giving you my trust, Derek. See that you are worthy of it. Our lives will depend on you.'

Elmo is, like any ship's captain, aware of the risks of mutiny and discontent at sea. A crew are simultaneously free and imprisoned; free of the constraints of a settled life at home and imprisoned together in a large wooden box, stuck in each other's company for weeks and months at a time. A captain has to be smart, balancing discipline and liberty and, above all, being well prepared for those moments when tensions boil over.

Elmo has absolute trust in just a handful of his crew: Chisholm, now dead; Beth; Pierre; Sam Solomon; and Lizbet. Now, he has no choice but to include Derek.

Entering the bowels of the ship, Derek pauses at the door to the captain's cabin and pushes it gently open. In the lacklight gloom he sees Bill Stanway sprawled back in the captain's chair, out cold, a tricorn hat perched on his head, his boots up on the table in front of him alongside an empty bottle of rum. On the floor with their backs against the walls, are Jack and Frank, open-mouthed and snoring like storm gutters. Lying on the bed is Henrietta, comatose, her face lying in a pool of vomit.

Derek pulls the door closed and creeps along to the next door, narrowly avoiding measuring his length as he steps on a bottle rolling along the passage with the rocking of the ship.

The captain's office has been ransacked. Drawers have been ripped out of the mahogany desk and lie broken on the floor. Ledgers, paperwork and all the books from the bookshelf are strewn about. A large chest is open, its locks broken. A jumble tumble of clothes and boots, crockery, three large conch shells, two now empty bottles of rum, and a number of documents in French have joined the rest of the floordrobe at his feet. Derek guesses that Bill Stanway, Frank and others are responsible and wonders if their crime has yielded anything of value beyond the hangovers they will soon be nursing.

The only objects not damaged, still sitting on the desk alongside Elmo's map of the Yorkshire Jurassic Coast, are the navigation equipment that the entire ship's company will rely upon to get them safely back to the nineteenth century: two compasses, Elmo's sextant, and the brass helmet with its disc-mounted telescopes.

All brawn and no brain Elmo has said of Bill and the now dead Silas; the furious and wanton destruction of the office shows he is right. But not so stupid as to destroy the instruments that can see them home.

While the office is small, it is not as small as it seems.

Acting on Elmo's instructions, Derek unlocks the catches that secure the legs of the mahogany desk to the floor and pulls the desk away from the wall, wedging it under the door handle to prevent anyone intruding on what he is about to do.

He explores the room's wood panelling with his fingertips. The task would be easier by lantern light but he cannot take the risk and so makes do with the faint glow from the window.

Beading runs along the edges of the walls. It is almost perfect.

But not quite.

On the wall behind the desk a very observant person might notice that the vertical beading stops a centimetre above the floor and that, on the right side of the wall, the beading is made up of three sections and not one, as elsewhere. This same observant person might also then notice the knots in the wood just three centimetres from the ends of each section of beading.

On his knees, having cleared away some of the rubbish on the floor, his ears alert to any unusual sound beyond the natural creaking of the ship, Derek depresses the two lowest knots and pushes the bead towards the floor. It slides slowly to reveal a gap between it and the section of bead above. He repeats the action with each section of beading all the way up the wall.

Derek remembers an Indian box he was given when he was eight years old. It was called a secret lock box and was made of hardwood. His grandpa told him it was for his special possessions but refused to tell him how to open it. It had taken months to work it out.

As the last section of beading slips down, something gives. So softly that it cannot be called a click. Derek pulls the beading gently and, just as the moon comes out from behind clouds, the wall swings open on silent hidden hinges to reveal the space beyond.

What he sees takes his breath away.

First, on the middle two shelves, are the weapons. In this space, maybe seventy centimetres deep, there are: cutlasses, daggers, machetes, throwing knives, a dozen flintlock pistols, two revolvers, three sawn-off muskets, stacked wooden boxes of ammunition, two sealed boxes marked gunpowder, spare flints, axes, and what look like half a dozen primitive hand grenades.

A veritable arsenal specifically designed to protect the captain in the event of a mutiny.

On a low shelf are various provisions and supplies: food, tobacco, alcohol, tinderboxes, bandages, surgical implements and medicines, a sextant and compass and various other instruments Derek does not recognise, a few items of clothing, paper and writing implements.

On the top shelf are a row of oak boxes, all travelling incognito, and a large ring of keys.

The keys he has been sent to collect. Spare keys for every lock on board.

Derek places them on the desk and turns to close the secret wall.

But he is only human …

… and what he finds shocks him deeply.

Having put almost everything back as he found it, closed the wall and repositioned the desk, Derek steps out of the captain's office and into the corridor, closing the door quietly behind him. On tiptoes he makes his way forwards and opens the next door along. The storeroom is stacked with provisions rendering a clear impression of its size all but impossible. Without a tape measure or a reason to be suspicious, the secret space between the rooms is invisible!

He heads back the way he came and, back out on deck, is relieved to see that the pterosaurs have not returned.

'You have the keys?'

Derek nods and holds them up.

'That one,' Elmo says. 'With the hexagonal bow.'

'And your promise?' Derek asks, holding his ground. 'Shall I trust you?'

'I'll not forget it. You have my word, Derek.'

What else can I do? I have to trust him or … or what?

Elmo has chosen the right key. In a couple of seconds the padlock is unlocked and Jean-Jacques Elmo is able to escape his chains, climb to his feet and stretch his limbs.

'Excellent. Now go back below, find yourself a quiet corner and grab some sleep. With luck no one will realise you weren't there all the time.'

'What will you do now?'

'Don't worry about me.'

Elmo watches Derek head back toward the secret entrance. 'Wait,' he hisses.

Derek stops and looks back.

'You're only human,' Elmo tells him, 'but don't breathe a word of what you have seen while you looked for the keys or none of us will reach Whitby alive.'

A few hours later, having gone back down below and fumbled his way across the darkened deck to Nat and Aleka by following the sound of their coughing, Derek wakes up to the offer of water and a bowl of porridge from Lizbet.

He takes the bowl from the girl and, propping himself up on an elbow, wolfs down the food. He hasn't eaten properly for twenty-four hours and has a headache from dehydration. Such light as there is below deck is finding its way through cracks in the gunports.

'Where were you?' Aleka asks him. 'We couldn't find you.'

She is in a bad way, her arms and hands badly swollen, her face flushed as she struggles with a raging temperature. Beside her Nat is wheezing in his sleep.

The sound of shouting drowns out Derek's reply. Over by the stove Lizbet and Sam Solomon look alarmed and it takes Derek a few seconds to work out where the noise is coming from.

The captain's quarters at the back of the ship. The fight back has begun.

Derek puts a gentle hand on Aleka's shoulder. 'Don't worry, I'm going to get us home.'

The sound of splintering wood and angry cursing greets him as he hurries down the passage and turns the corner towards the captain's quarters. Ahead of him Frank Dent comes flying backwards out of the captain's cabin to slam his head, crunch sickeningly, against a wall. He groans as he attempts to roll his back off the floor, then gives up. Pierre appears in the doorway, spots Derek and tosses a length of rope.

'Tie the bastard up!' he shouts.

Over Pierre's shoulder an epic punch up is taking place, bodies rolling about on the floor. Derek turns Frank Dent over and ties his hands behind his back, as Pierre rejoins the fray in the captain's cabin. The rope is long enough to bind his ankles together too. Derek is finishing the job as a hand grabs him from behind and yanks him backwards. The sharpness of a blade presses against his Adam's apple.

'One false move and thy throat will pour ruby juice like a fountain,' snarls Jack, his knee pushing hard against Derek's back.

Derek smells the sailor's bad breath, thick with alcohol and rough tobacco.

'That will make two fountains then, Jack,' says a second voice.

Elmo!

Derek dare not move or speak. In front of him Frank Dent is wriggling on the floor, attempting to loosen the ropes that were not yet fully tied.

'Damn your stinking soul, Elmo!' Jack cries, his blade still pressing Derek's throat.

'Curb your tongue, Jack, and drop thy blade and ye can rot a while in the brig,' Elmo tells Jack. 'But spill a drop of Derek's blood and this keen steel between your ribs will slice your heart apart and send you to Hell faster than a fellow tossed in sharkish seas!'

His fate being decided behind his back, Derek glances toward the scuffling beyond the doorway to the captain's cabin. He sees the side of Bill's head and the gleam of a raised cutlass.

'Stand your ground, men!' Bill screams. 'These powdered pups haven't the belly for a real fight! The ship is ours!'

With a wrenching splintering of wood, the chart table is

ripped from its floor brackets and hurled at Bill, catching him full in the chest. He staggers backward, catching sight of Jack and Derek through the doorway as he disappears from view.

'Finish him off, Jack! Slice his jaw from ear to ear and run the devil through! They'll see the …'

The wall of the captain's cabin judders as the back of Bill's head smacks against it with a sickening crunch. Jack weighs his options, Elmo's knife tight against his ribs while his own blade whispers sharply across Derek's neck.

'I'll skewer your sweetbreads for that, you miserable runt! By this curse I …' Bill roars.

A single solid syllable, round as a pea and stiff as steel, spits from the mouth of a flintlock, cutting Bill's curse off mid-sentence. A white cloud of gunpowder smoke blooms into the corridor.

Jack turns involuntarily toward the door and Derek seizes his moment!

Pushing his fist up the side of his face, behind Jack's arm, in one continuous movement Derek pushes the knife away from his neck and turns towards his attacker. In the same moment, Elmo rips his blade across Jack's shoulder severing a tendon. Jack howls. His hand releases the knife that clatters harmlessly to the floor.

Frank Dent is still writhing in his ropes as Pierre's boot slams down upon his neck, pinning him to the floorboards. Without a second wasted, Derek quickly finishes the job of retightening and tying the ropes.

The sound of scuffling, oaths, punches thrown, groans and teeth falling from open mouths, continues further along the corridor, but without Bill's urging and encouragement the fight is fading. The mutiny is collapsing.

CHAPTER 43

By seven o'clock Rebecca and her gang of flitherers return from Saltwick Bay, heavy baskets on their heads, ahead of the incoming tide.

As the fisherwomen reach the harbour wall, a maid in a crisp clean apron is opening the front door to the White Horse and Griffin on Church Street. Humming a song about love lost and found, she gets down on her knees to polish the door brass.

'Excuse me.'

The maid turns to find Robert Seeker.

'At least it's not raining,' he smiles.

She nods tiredly. Seeker slips past her and makes his way up to his room. Three minutes later he is tucked up in bed. The door to his room is locked and a chair is wedged under the handle. Revolver in hand, he will sleep a few hours.

On the harbour wall the flitherers chat with couple of the fishermen.

'Those'll need storing,' says Sam Weighell, pointing up at the baskets of limpets. 'We'll not be going out today. Sea's rough and air's too warm. We're spoiling for another storm.'

'You said it were set fair while the weekend,' says Mary, whose husband has been sick for a month.

'Nowt we can do, love. Not sure tomorrow'll be any better. You can send bairns round to ours if they're hungry.' He pulls his cap down on his head to stop it blowing off.

Shortly before ten, Amy and Sarah are walking up Skinner Street looking for the premises of Pennock, Knaggs & Prodham, Instrument Makers.

'We are interested in barographs,' Sarah announces to the sleepy-looking youth behind the counter.

'What?' the youth answers, picking at a spot on his chin.

'It's a barometer connected to a clockwork drum and a pen that records air pressure over time onto a sheet of graph paper,' Sarah explains, parroting the description she learned in physics at school.

'Never heard of it.'

'Is the manager in?'

'No, but he hasn't heard of it either,' the youth sneers. 'Anything else?'

Sarah resists the urge to shout. 'All right, let's try something a little more basic. Do you sell barometers?'

'Yes, we have those. *They* actually exist.'

'Can we view them, perhaps?' Sarah asks, struggling to control her irritation, 'or must we wait for daddy to come home?'

The youth gives her a contemptuous look and disappears behind a curtain.

'So much for the idea that grouchy teenagers were invented in the 1950s,' Sarah observes.

The young man returns and deposits on the counter a large box from which he extracts five barometers.

'Should I write down what they are? For your husband.'

Thirty-all, thinks Amy.

'Let's pretend that I will be buying the device, shall we?' Sarah says.

The youth shrugs. 'This one is a ship's barometer. A French one from Charlet in the Havre. The thermometer reads in Centigrade, which you may not have heard of. This one is from Brabhams in Bristol, temperature in Fahrenheit, of course, and this one …'

'Can I look them over without the explanation?' Sarah cuts him off.

The youth takes a step back, observing the two women with open contempt, while Sarah makes a show of studying each of the devices in turn. One of the barometers shows a completely different assessment of air pressure to the others. She taps lightly to see if it is stuck but the needle stays pointing at *Very Dry*.

'You may need to sell this one in Cairo,' she says. 'Anyway, thank you. Most informative,' she tells the youth. 'Not *much* better than staring at frogs and slugs but it will have to do. Come on, Amy.'

She stops at the door. 'If you're still in business when it's invented, you'll find the barograph is a big leap forwards. Who knows, trains may even exist by then too. Lots to look forward to.'

'That was a waste of time,' Amy says once they are out on the street.

'On the contrary,' Sarah replies. 'Our visit cost us nothing and we learned that five out of the six barometers agreed that we are heading for another storm. We might be able to escape back to our own century tonight! How great is that?'

Amy doesn't answer.

They arrive back on Silver Street to find Rosie and Rebecca sitting by the front door.

While Rosie attends to producing a pot of tea and Amy pops back to the bakery, Sarah and Rebecca talk.

'We were meaning to come to see you last night,' says Sarah.

'By the time I reached the yard I were only good for sleep. I went out on a mission in the pouring rain with Mr Seeker.'

'He told us he had met you.' Sarah says. 'Said you would be helping him.'

'Bumped into him like on Church Street and recognised him from your description. He's a strange one.'

'He is. But I think he wants to help.'

'Worse of it is the girls are out flithering before dawn on the rocks at Saltwick and up he pops like a bad penny. My own fault, I shouldn't have agreed to help him. I can't get rid of him!'

'It's all our fault,' Sarah says. 'We're putting you and your family in danger, I feel terrible.'

'Never mind. Anyroad, I only came to tell you there's to be another huge storm. Sea's already rough and small boats are all stopping in.'

Amy arrives with the cakes just as Rosie arrives with the teapot. They all sit down together.

Besides the cakes, Amy has a second bag that she opens excitedly.

'I've decided that if we are to spend Christmas here we need lots of things to cheer us up!' she says. From the bag she produces an assortment of paper garlands, silk ribbons and gold paper. 'I thought we could make decorations with your children, Rosie.'

'It's weeks away,' Rosie says, confused.

Sarah is taken aback. 'I know, but we can treat ourselves and put them up early!'

'It's a lovely thought,' Rebecca intervenes. 'And the children will have fun, but they cannot go up while Christmas Eve, Amy love. It's bad luck. Still we can make them and have them ready. And if we don't cut those lovely ribbons we can use them afterwards for dresses and aprons.'

'I want it to be the loveliest Christmas. For everyone.' Amy's eyes fill with tears. 'I'm so sorry.'

Rebecca gives Amy a hug. 'It's a lovely thought,' she reassures her. 'Look at me, sipping tea from fancy porcelain and stuffing cake like Lady Muck when I should be on the pier sorting fish!' She gets up and puts on her shawl. 'I'll see thee later, love,' she tells Rosie who collects the crockery and takes it all to the kitchen.

After Rebecca has left, Sarah walks to the window and looks out over the town. 'She says the boats are staying in because a storm is coming, so it's not just the barometers. We need to find our Mr Seeker and organise our escape. Fingers crossed.'

'I'm not leaving without Derek.'

Sarah turns.

'We have to stay.' Amy's eyes are black with rage. 'He's the father of my child. You can't just bat this away, Sarah, or pretend you didn't hear, like you did yesterday.'

'You're a few days late. It's probably just down to stress.'

'Don't patronise me! I've known I am pregnant for five weeks. I was waiting for the right moment to tell Derek. And then this shit storm happens. I'm not moving until we find him. You did get one thing right, Sarah. I can sell the jewellery, a piece at a time. We've enough to last months. A year even. So forget running away and abandoning him. They told us he could have been kidnapped and might be on that ship. We have to wait for the return of the *Inevitable*.'

'Wait for the inevitable? That says it all, doesn't it?

Sarah turns back to the window, anger blooming and bubbling. It never occurred to her that Amy could pull such a stunt. A woman whose idea of a year well spent involves picking curtain fabrics.

'Go on then,' Amy says behind her, second-guessing Sarah's thoughts. 'I'll manage. Find your Mr Seeker and go back to Stephen. I'll write you a note to give my parents.'

Sarah takes a deep breath and tries a different tack. 'We don't even know whether he's alive,' she says quietly. 'We don't know if he was kidnapped, pressganged or killed. He may simply have fallen into the harbour drunk and drowned. He may not even have crossed the portal. What if we have this all wrong, Amy? We can't stay here forever, on the off chance.'

Sobbing.

Amy has sat down at the table, her head in her hands.

Sarah puts her arms around Amy. 'They speak English here but this isn't our world. No police, no tourist information centre, no weather forecasts, no proper hospitals, no phones, no pizzas, no radio. We have no idea what is happening over the horizon in any direction. It takes a whole day just to get to Newcastle. On horseback! London could cease to exist and we wouldn't know about it for days or weeks.'

'We could put an advert in the paper,' Amy insists. 'Or find the mayor. Or ask one of the churches. Someone must have seen something! People don't just vanish.'

'And if it's true that we can only get back to our time during an electric storm,' Sarah continues, choosing to ignore Amy, 'we could be stuck here for years. Tonight might be the only …'

'I don't care.'

'Fine. OK. Well, I am going out to find Mr Seeker. He said he was staying at the White Horse and Griffin on Church Street. That's where I'll be.'

With that Sarah wraps up against the cold and heads out of the apartment. It takes only seconds for her to realise that she is overdressed. The air is so warm it could be spring. Heavy black clouds continue to press down on the town and the light is sickly yellow.

Arriving at the White Horse and Griffin, Sarah finds the landlady behind the counter in the bar, cleaning glasses.

'I am looking for Robert Seeker.'

'I've not seen the gentleman. He must still be in bed.'

'What is his room number, please?'

The landlady's withering glance is enough; unaccompanied women do not wander about upstairs.

'Could someone please go and knock on his door?' Sarah changes tack. 'He was due to meet us an hour ago and …'

'Harry!' the landlady shouts.

A youth appears.

'This *lady* wishes to speak with Mr Seeker,' she tells the youth. 'Go up and knock on the gentleman's door.'

The youth gives Sarah a funny look and disappears through the open door to the hall. His feet echo in the stairwell as he runs upstairs.

Sarah has all but given up when Robert Seeker steps into the bar, his red hair in chaos, eyes thick with sleep, his blue waistcoat now over his yellow waistcoat, his voluminous coat draped over one arm. He stares about him and spots her.

'Ah ha! Mrs Munion. What a wonderful surprise!' he exclaims. 'The legal papers arrived on the stagecoach from London yesterday afternoon, some scoundrel had waylaid them in York, I am told.'

Sarah has no idea what he is talking about but notices that the nosy landlady appears satisfied that all is above board so, for now, she is happy to be Mrs Munion.

'Good morning, Mr Seeker,' Sarah says. 'I was getting worried.'

'I can only apologise for my dismal dispunctuality,' Seeker continues, talking loudly for the benefit of others. 'Our solicitor is on Baxtergate, just a few minutes' perambulation. Shall we?'

'Yes, thank you. I am keen to have everything signed.'

And with that they both step outside.

'If you will forgive me, we must first stop at Newhams,' Seeker says, putting on his coat.

Sarah doesn't enter the shop, preferring to observe the comings and goings out on Church Street. Two young men carrying a table between them. An older man in a bloodied blue apron hugging a leg of beef to his chest. Three fisherwomen chatting and laughing as they pass down the side of the town hall towards Sandgate.

'Thank God!' Seeker emerges from Newhams sporting a

new and very grey top hat.

'I thought all top hats were black.'

'A most unfortunate incident at high tide under cover of darkness. My faithful chapeau from Christy & Co. in Gracechurch Street is, regrettably, bobbing in the waves and halfway to Rotterdam. If you will forgive me once again, I venture that we find somewhere quiet for the purpose of colloquy, Madam. Much has happened!'

Sarah is not sure what colloquy is and even less sure that she wishes to participate in it with Robert Seeker.

'A conversation, Madam,' he explains, registering her confusion.

OK. That sounds OK.

Sarah nods.

They head not towards the bridge and over the river to Baxtergate but in the direction of Henrietta Street, slipping into one of the yards off Church Street. Two children are playing with a kitten and some string. The yard is otherwise empty, all the adults at work down in the harbour. Seeker takes a tin bath down from the wall of one of the cottages.

'Hey! You can't take that!' says the little girl, looking up at the adults like a fledgling blackbird squawking at its parents. 'That's our bath!'

'We require the services of a posterial depository for a few minutes,' Seeker explains. 'If you would be so obliging.'

'Somewhere to park our bums,' Sarah translates. 'We can pay,' she adds, handing each child a penny.

Eyes big as buns, the children look at each other open-mouthed and run off, shrieking with delight.

CHAPTER 44

'When the Devil loosens his grip on thy foul mouth we will talk,' Elmo tells Frank Dent. 'Until then enjoy the brig!'
Dent is shackled and behind bars like a caged animal. Beside him are Jack, arm in a sling, and Henrietta, sporting two black eyes, and the unconscious Bill who lies in a pool of blood, his shirt thick with it, his head bandaged.

'I'll as soon rot in hell than talk terms with thee!' Frank says, spitting on the floor.

'Enough, Mumblecrust! Gag him,' Elmo instructs Pierre. 'His bile can fester in his throat a while. With luck Jack and Henrietta will come to their senses as the grog wears off.'

The ringleaders locked away, Elmo assembles the rest of the crew up on deck.

'It is time to move on,' Elmo announces. 'Until now, we were as lucky as seven-toed cats, but finally this cruel shore has sapped our strength and slain our friends.'

'Though we have not found all we sought on this expedition, we have fortune enough. Our adventures here have paid us handsomely, well enough for each of ye to leave the *Inevitable*, if ye choose, with enough money to turn your backs upon the waves. When we reach Whitby each one of ye will be able to step ashore and buy a house or a tavern and keep it warm and snug and fill it with children, if that is your choice. You will keep cattle and grow potatoes, tell tall tales of our escapades and pity those poor fools who have never ventured upon the seas.'

'Those who wish can stay with me as we leave these dangerous shores in our wake, and the cold towns of England,

and set course for the reefs of the Equator and the sweet spices of the Indies!'

'Before we leave we will plant crosses for each of those comrades we have lost. We will honour them and thank God for life and love shared. One and all are heroes …'

Someone mutters under her breath whether Silas could ever be a hero to anyone.

'No one shall mock or curse the dead while I captain this ship!' Elmo says. 'Whate'er our differences we have served together, supped together, fought together, and must acknowledge same. So let us prepare our service of thanks and then, when it is done, ready ourselves to set sail for the crossover and our future!'

Half an hour later, a boat is lowered and Elmo and seven of the crew pull oars to the beach. The predators that rampaged earlier have gone but the bodies of their victims are strewn about: a partially dismembered ankylosaur lies on the sand, its dead eyes thick with flies, huge mouthfuls ripped from its underbelly; and three of the deer-sized dinosaurs lie on the blood-soaked sand with their throats slashed.

Only when Elmo has satisfied himself that there is no current danger does he step from the boat. He wades ashore through the gentlest of waves and climbs the beach. In his wake follow five of the crew - Noah, Pierre, Thin George, Phin and Newt – carrying the simple crosses that have been hurriedly assembled.

Derek and the others watch in silence from the ship as the crosses, each carrying the name of a lost crewmember, are thrust into the sands at the top of the beach beside the remains of the broken boats. Beneath a cloudless sky upon the golden beach, on the edge of the emerald jungle, the Captain and crew remove their hats and stand a moment in prayer.

Behind them a turtle hauls herself from the sea and begins the slow crawl up the sand to the spot where once, years ago, she hatched. By tomorrow morning, having laid ninety-seven white eggs as round as golf balls, she will have returned to the waves and be many miles away across the turquoise sea.

Solomon and Irish Joe, on the boat, and Beth, on the ship, scan the jungle through their telescopes alert for any signs of movement in the trees. Thankfully, all is quiet save for the never-ending chatter of insects and amphibians and the whispering waves that lick the boat. The cadences of prayers drift in the air.

The ceremony completed the crew walk back to the boat. Above them, hidden in the forest beside a broken palisade, a megalosaur stands silently beneath an incongruous whalebone arch, its head tilted to one side. She stares with cold eyes down towards the sea, the monkey puzzle and cycad trees blocking her view of all but the narrowest slither of the beach. Her nostrils flare as the humans appear beside the boat, climb aboard and head back towards the ship anchored some forty metres from the shore.

Feet trample round the capstan, and the anchor slowly rises until she hangs dripping at the bows. The sails begin to draw and the ship awakens from her slumbers.

CHAPTER 45

'Find those bitches and lock them up. We'll trade them as hostages and if that fails we'll find another use for them,' Sly laughs as he runs a large butcher's knife up and down the whetstone that hangs from his belt. He tests the blade's sharpness against his thumb.

'Aye! And let's not forget that dandiprat bag of mystery, Robert Seeker. They say that he has a room at the White Horse and Griffin,' says Argument. 'Toss him off the top of Saltwick Cliff. See if he can fly.'

'First things first.' Sly has the knife up against the light in the window as he squints along the blade to check it is straight and true. 'Send Tom and Isaac up to Silver Street. Tom's in the store room.'

'Second thoughts,' Argument is still thinking about Seeker. 'That skinny runt will make passable dog food.'

Sly continues scraping and sharpening the knife.

Outside the open window, in the next yard, Sarah and Robert Seeker listen in silent horror.

'We have to warn Amy!' Sarah whispers.

'I fear we will …' Seekers starts in his usual declamatory style.

Sarah waves her hands frantically to shut him up. Just in time. The scraping sound comes to a stop. They sit in silence, scarcely daring to breathe, praying that no one comes to the window.

The knife scraping recommences and Sarah points up the yard, away from the noise. They creep away on fearful shoes but have barely taken a dozen steps when the children reappear.

'Have you finished with our bath?' shouts the little girl.

Sarah puts her finger to her lips and mimes a shushing sound. The children stare wide-eyed as the two adults draw near. Sarah repeats her gesture and presses a sixpence into the girl's hand. The boy seems ready to complain.

'Share it,' Sarah mouths the words silently.

The children grin each other in astonishment; with the pennies from earlier they are rich beyond their wildest dreams.

'Can we get out onto the field that way?' Seeker whispers, pointing eastwards and up the hill.

The children nod. Seeker pats them both on the head and smiles. Sarah makes a dramatic pantomime of creeping away and Seeker follows suit. The children giggle helplessly.

Some fifty steps higher up, the path ends at the foot of a cliff of brambles, bushes and trees. A dead end.

'Confoundations! I'll catch those little rascals and clip their ears and …'

'Please stop, Mr Seeker. We haven't time to chase after children. Look, there is a rope. We can haul ourselves up.'

Some five minutes and an arduous scramble later, they emerge at the foot of Alms House Close where they stand in the wet grass catching their breath.

'Right, let's find Amy.' Sarah says, pulling twigs and leaves from her sleeves.

'I fear we may be too late, dear lady.' Seeker wipes the sweat from his brow. 'There is but one bridge over the Esk and we are sure to be recognised and apprehended.'

'Are you all right, Mr Seeker? Your face is bright red.'

'My coat. A trifle heavy in the unseasonal heat.'

'Can we not find a boat to take us across? Or borrow one? Our lives may depend on it!'

'They will have spies everywhere.'

'We must have allies in the yards,' Sarah insists. 'Rebecca

will find us a boat, I'm sure of it.'

'What about her family and their safety?'

Sarah realises the damage is already done.

'Oh my God, Rosie is on Silver Street with Amy!'

They hurry eastwards towards the Abbey Steps. With luck they will reach the bottom of the steps, sneak round the end of Church Street and get onto Tate Hill Pier unseen, where they will find Rebecca sorting fish.

The sky is getting darker by the minute. In her heavy skirt, Sarah struggles to make progress through the thick wet vegetation.

'Wait. Wait!'

Seeker stops.

'What is that building?' Sarah asks as she catches up. She points up the hill at the ruins beyond the wall.

'Abbey House.'

Seeker sets off again. Strangely circumspect for a man who loves his own voice. Sarah senses he knows more than he is letting on.

'Mr Seeker, please wait!'

He stops again, looks anxiously towards the ruins over the wall.

'Is that building somehow connected to everything?' Sarah asks. 'Have you been there?'

'I would venture that we have but two choices, Madam. We can make a bold, if somewhat improbable attempt to reach Silver Street ahead of Mr Sly's ruffians or we can focus our energies on the nefarious activities of the Architects. Without wishing to sound discourteous I would strongly recommend the former.'

Sarah nods, he has a point. They continue across the field, the rough skeletons of dead plants snagging their clothes, the wind threatening to snatch Seeker's hat. Across the harbour, on the horizon to the south, a sickly slither of yellow light forms a ribbon between the distant hills and the charcoal sky. They exit the field onto Church Lane. Hearing neighing to her right, Sarah turns toward the Abbey ruins and watches a horse and cart emerge from the house grounds up the road. An old man, hunched over, his face hidden in the shadow of his hat, whips his horse as he turns the cart toward the Hawsker Road. The rear of the cart comes into view. It carries but one item, a long lump hidden beneath a pile of sacks. Poking out beneath the hessian is a pale human hand.

Sarah shudders and hurries after Robert Seeker who is already halfway across the churchyard toward the steps.

'Can you see who that is please?' Amy calls out.

She knows exactly who it is but is happy to make Sarah wait. What kind of friend would try to force her to abandon their fiancé in the nineteenth century? The father of her unborn child. It is so selfish. And, frankly, so ungrateful.

Sitting in the light by the window, Amy returns to the romance novel on her lap. Clarence has returned from the hunt, invigorated by the bright alpine air, when he spies Aigline de Venzéles alone in the rose garden, her auburn hair gently …

A second knock on the door.

'Rosie!' Amy calls.

The door to the kitchen opens.

'Sorry, Miss Amy.' Rosie hurries across the living room, drying her hands on her apron as she goes.

It isn't Sarah at the door.

Two swarthy men push past Rosie and stride into the apartment.

'Sorry to disturb you, Miss,' says the first man, with a belly the size of a whisky barrel. 'Mr Robert Seeker has sent us to find you.'

In the background Rosie retreats to the kitchen.

'He asks that Maud and Phoebe of Silver Street join him

for luncheon at the White Horse and Griffin on Church Street,' says the second man, who is holding a large roll of crimson cloth.

'Forgive me for asking but are you Maud or Phoebe?' asks the first man.

Amy is about to reply that she is neither Maud nor Phoebe, when she remembers that those are the very names that Sarah used when they visited the jewellers to sell the diamond bracelet. Robert Seeker must be using those same names to protect their true identities. She tries to remember whether she is Phoebe or Maud, and plumps for Maud.

'I am afraid that Phoebe has just popped out,' she says lightly. 'Can I ask how you know Mr Seeker?'

'Through the amateur dramatic society,' says the second man, turning to smile at his accomplice. It is a smile largely devoid of teeth.

'Romeo and Juliet,' the first man explains. 'We were all ... angels.'

Amy is struggling to see either man, or Robert Seeker, acting in a play, and does not recall the story including angels.

Why isn't Sarah here?

Was that the back door?

'Please thank Mr Seeker; I will let Phoebe know as soon as she returns,' she says. 'We accept the invitation and will join him at two fifteen.'

The two men don't move.

'I'm sorry, is that all?' Amy asks.

'Isaac and I are to accompany you both. Mr Seeker is concerned to ensure your safety, there having been a few unfortunate incidents of late down by the harbour.'

Alarm bells are finally ringing in Amy's head. She stands and heads toward the kitchen. 'Will you excuse me for a second?'

Before she can reach the door Amy is grabbed from behind,

gagged, her arms tied behind her back. The roll of crimson cloth turns out to be a large sack, which is pulled over her head. While the first man slings Amy over his shoulder, the second man throws open the kitchen door. The back door is open.

'The other one's done a runner!'

'Shit!'

Moments later the two men come out onto the street where their bundle is dumped unceremoniously onto the back of the waiting cart. The men climb aboard and the hand brake is released. The horse doesn't need telling the way back to the bridge.

Three minutes ahead of them and already halfway down Flowergate, Rosie is racing towards the drawbridge across the Esk.

Rosie is no fool. She immediately recognised the two bruisers sent to grab Amy and Sarah. Tom Allison and Ripley (she doesn't know his Christian name) live at the other end of Church Street and are regularly involved in brawls. There's even talk in the yards that the two men side with the press-gangs to punish families they dislike, handing men and boys alike over for a few shillings and condemning mothers and bairns to the workhouse.

That she was not recognised can only be down to one thing, they weren't expecting to see Rosie working as a housekeeper in a better part of town, with a clean apron and her hair up beneath a bonnet. She practically slides down the steep Golden Lion Bank and emerges a stone's throw from the bridge.

If the sky has ever been darker at one o'clock, Rosie cannot remember it. A thin rain leaks from the heavens as if the sagging black clouds are bulging waterskins sewn from giant cows hides, with seams that might unravel at any moment to dump their entire contents upon the town.

Her shoes clatter over the bridge. Rosie dives left onto Sandgate, across the town hall square and in less than a minute reaches home where she scoops up her children and makes her way in through open windows and out of side doors, across yards and through ginnels, past bubbling cauldrons of whale blubber, and an old man sorting rags for a grandson who beats him if he doesn't work fast enough. She dodges a chimney pot that has fallen off a roof as the wind starts to pick up ahead of the storm that is surely coming. Finally she is far enough from home to feel safe. Entering a cottage with a broken front door, Rosie hurries along a dark corridor, dragging the children after her.

'You're hurting me!' Vera cries. 'Mum!'

Simon is snivelling. Rosie ignores them both. She knocks on the door at the end of the corridor. A little old woman answers and ushers them in.

'What the matter, my loves?' asks Margaret Bowson, putting her arms around the crying children.

'I need you to look after t'bairns, Margaret,' Rosie says, struggling to catch her breath. 'Those bastards, Tom Allison and Ripley, the ferret-faced one with the belly, always getting into fights. Anyroad, they're out making trouble. And Mum must be out on t'pier.' She gets down on her knees to talk to the children. 'Auntie Maggie will look after you both while I fetch Nanna Bec.'

With that she kisses Simon and Vera on the foreheads, nods her thanks to the old woman and races out.

CHAPTER 46

A stiff breeze fills the sails and the *Inevitable* is making good headway northwards up the coast towards Crossover Cliff. The sea that has for days been as flat as a village pond, now swells grey with waves. With the breeze and the sun having disappeared behind huge clouds, the air is cooler. Away from shore, the sound of the jungle has been replaced by the creaking and groaning of the rigging and tearing of the booms against the blocks.

The decision having been taken, everyone wants done with the crossover, no matter how hard it will be with so many of the crew lost or sick.

Ezekiel, Flora, Jack, Henrietta and Newt and the others who joined Bill's mutiny are back in harness, ashamed and subdued, eagerly volunteering for the toughest and dirtiest jobs. Elmo has spoken with each of them in turn and told the rest of the crew to let bygones be bygones; they all live or die together as one crew.

Only Bill and Frank remain in the brig. Aside from the risk that they pose to the unity of the crew, both men are injured and will be of little use on deck.

The ship's deck has been cleared of clutter, the remaining boats secured, a meal prepared and eaten, and now Elmo sits in his cabin discussing how they will lower the masts with a third of the crew gone. With him are Big George who has been chosen to replace Chisholm, Beth who will be Big George's second, Noah, and Pierre.

'We will have to start half an hour early,' says Big George, 'to give us time.'

'We'll be too slow,' counters Pierre. 'We'll never reach the cliff with enough momentum to push through.'

'What do you think, Beth?' Elmo asks.

'I'm with Big George. But I'd drop the mizzen sooner. As long as we keep full sail on fore and main we'll be fine.'

'That's madness! Do that and sky sails, royals and stays will all be lost, we'll never raise them in time. She has lost her head, Jean-Jacques!' Pierre insists.

'We can afford to lose a few sails, Pierre, it's the masts we have to protect,' Beth counters.

'That's right,' Elmo intervenes. 'But we will also drop the stays as soon as we are able, to save them from damage. Set to! Before this day is out we will have toiled harder than any crew before!'

In less than an hour the sea turns rough, the ship is heaving with the swell. Solomon the cook extinguishes the stove, there will be no fire until the ship is through the tunnel and safe. Everything that isn't nailed down is on the move, down below bottles and biscuits roll underfoot while, out on the blustery deck, landlubbers like Derek stagger on dizzy feet.

Focusing on the task in hand, Derek pauses for a few seconds to look at the horizon whenever he feels sick. He has not been sent up into the rigging, more experienced hands are needed up there where the motion of the ship is more pronounced. His task is to work with the team ready to brace the sails should the wind shift about, and to man the capstan when the time comes.

Derek has little understanding of how his activities are helping maintain the ship's course but he has huge respect for Big George and Beth's ability to turn almost any wind from any direction to their advantage. He watches Beth, her red hair billowing in the breeze, co-ordinating with Big George at the other end of the ship and barking out orders to the crew; there is something awesome about commanding a ship that can circumnavigate the globe without oil or coal or GPS or satellite communications.

'Are you asleep, Octopus?'

'Awaiting orders. You're amazing; you know that? Ma'am.'

Beth laughs. 'We'll make a sailor of you yet, Derek. If you survive long enough.'

A tug at Derek's sleeve. He looks down to find Lizbet at his side.

'Captain wants a word with thee,' she says.

Beth nods and Derek stands down and follows the girl to the hatch and below deck.

Nat, sitting beside his sleeping sister, waves weakly as Derek and Lizbet pass by on their way to the captain's cabin. Derek waves back.

They pass the steps that lead down to the brig, from which a snoring sound can be heard. Lizbet stops at the door of the captain's cabin and indicates to Derek that he can enter.

Elmo sits at the table that has been screwed back to the floor, one leg braced with wood where it was broken in the melee during the night. In front of him is the map that charts their course back to the Crossover Cliff. Also on the table, secured with a rope, is the brass helmet with the three disc-mounted telescopes.

'We have less than an hour before the chaos begins,' he tells Derek, without looking up. 'I need to understand what you want and to tell you a little about the situation we will face when we enter Whitby.'

'How did the others get back to their time?' Derek asks. 'The woman, Angelique.'

Elmo looks up, his facial expression unreadable.

'Her driving licence is in one of the boxes on the top shelf behind the secret wall.'

Elmo studies Derek; so he *did* peer into the boxes after all. What else has he learned?

'She was French,' Derek continues since Elmo has said nothing. 'Did you take her from Whitby, or somewhere else? Where is she now?'

'Sit down,' Elmo points at a chair. He rubs his hands over his face. 'Some years ago I made a deal in Whitby. At the time I thought only about the money I needed to transform my ship and too little about the people willing to lend me it. I thought them glad of the work because Whitby lives on shipbuilding and the appetite for whaling ships is dying.'

'They created this wonderful ship, to my specification, and in exchange I agreed to repay our debt in pearls. They have not asked the source of the jewels. The deal has been mutually beneficial. When we needed more hands on deck the group, they call themselves the Architects, said they could find us new people. Strong healthy people with …'

'Sorry, I just want to know about the woman,' Derek cuts Elmo off mid-flow.

For a second it seems as if Elmo might lose his cool. The moment passes.

'She came from Whitby,' he tells Derek. 'We found her surrounded by drunken men during an electrical storm at night. We rescued her. She stayed with the ship until four years ago when she disappeared on one of our visits to Whitby to trade our pearls. We searched everywhere but could not find her, and thought her dead. Then last year we received a message that she had been kidnapped. The Architects, the very group we are trading with, demanded an outrageous ransom for her release. They requested that we provide them with living monsters from this side of the crossover and declared that if we don't deliver on this voyage they will kill her.'

'How would they even know of the dinosaurs' existence?' Derek says dismissively.

'All on board this ship are sworn to secrecy as to where we fetch our pearls. But tongues are like caged birds, Derek. Open the door and they fly away. Buy my crewmembers a few pints in a tavern, write off a gambling debt, or offer the men twenty minutes fun on Grope Lane, and the peloothered tosspots will boast and blabber without restraint. Anyway, that is not your problem. When we reach Whitby you, Nat and Aleka are free to leave.'

'How will we get back to our own time?' Derek asks.

Elmo shrugs. 'I only know that heavy storms create strange phenomena in the town. There is someone who may help and I will …'

'Captain! The sea is boiling!' Noah stands in the doorway. 'Big George needs your counsel on deck!'

Elmo leaps to his feet. 'We will talk again after the crossover,' he reassures Derek.

Derek follows Elmo and Noah.

A gale is blowing and heavy rain is lashing the ship. Big George and Beth have already ordered the crew to drop several sails to steady the ship and slow her down. The stays are down and safely stowed.

'Permission to drop the spanker and fold the mizzen, Captain!' Beth shouts above the flapping sails.

Elmo nods. 'Derek and three of Big George's team can help.' He glances up at the crew high on the masts; uncoordinated and rocking perilously on the footropes rigged beneath the yards as they wrestle the sky sails and main sails.

Elmo strides forward and bursts into song.

'Heave Ho! Heave Ho!'

In a flash the whole crew, up in the rigging and down on deck, join him, glad of a rhythm for their work.

'Heave Ho! Heave Ho!
Haul them in and tie them down
Brace your backs and heave the sails
Pull in the slack and steady the stays
Jolly the jibs that ride the waves!

Heave Ho! Heave Ho!'

Elmo turns to Big George and Beth. 'Don't *watch* them, *lead* them!'

'Aye, Captain.'

'We cannot afford any more deaths on this ship! Remember Chisholm's way with the crew.' He slaps them both on the back, 'Be your best selves! And pay attention, you've sails flapping. Pull them round and luff up.'

With that Elmo returns below deck to conduct final checks.

With the spanker sail down, the ship requires more work to hold her heading. As the mizzenmast is folded back, half the crew are busy bracing the fore sails and main sails. It takes six crew to man the capstan and slow the mast's descent. And six more to position the yardarms and rigging as she comes down.

Finally the mizzenmast is part resting on the poop deck, part trailing over the back of the ship

'Ahoy!' shouts a voice high in the crows' nest. 'Crossover cliff ahoy!'

The warm rain at his back, Derek thinks about what is coming; it was snowing when they left Whitby. If the ship survives the crossover they'll sail a very different sea. The approach is as frightening as before. The seafloor rising beneath the ship and sea room diminishing with every passing minute, the waves become choppier, less predictable. Elmo has reappeared, his brass helmet in place, one of the three telescopes over his right eye as he scans the cliff ahead.

'Steady her round or she'll be rolled over!' he barks at Big George. 'And make sure we keep enough speed to hold our course.'

The depleted crew, already exhausted from lowering the mizzenmast, turn to the mainmast. The sails are dropped – sky, royal, top gallant, topsail and main – and men and women race down the rigging, moving with the grace and speed of acrobats in a circus. As soon as they are all safely on the deck the locking pins are removed. Ropes are made taut, others slackened off, backs braced, capstan locked and work begins.

'Haul them in and tie them down
Brace your backs and heave the sails
Pull in the slack and steady the stays
Jolly the jibs that ride the waves!'

The first few degrees are tough enough as the crew heave the mainmast off the vertical. Beth shouts their progress.

'Ninety-eight degrees. Ninety-five. Ninety-one. Brace yourselves lads! She'll soon be kicking!'

The eight strongest men are gathered round the capstan, ready for the moment the mast begins to fall under its own weight. Derek eases the tensions in his shoulders. Suddenly the full weight of the mast is there, bearing down on the ropes above the capstan and the men are straining every sinew, desperately trying to control the mast's descent, to slow its fall, to stop the capstan from spinning out of control.

'Heave Ho! Seaward Ho!
Hold the line! Heave Ho!'

Derek feels splinters tear into the soles of his feet as the capstan crew turns slowly, shoulders bulging, calves burning. Tonnes of oak shift back towards the deck against the rock-rolling of the keel in the swell that threatens to throw all the men on their backs on a ship that is still racing towards the cliff.

'Heave men, heave! That's right, my lovelies! My pretty boys!' Beth shouts. 'Heave Ho!'

'Clear the rigs!' Big George shouts to the rest of the crew who are feeding rope and pulling rope and shifting rope.

In the intensity of the moment, as he pushes against the furious will of the capstan, Derek imagines himself in a scrum on the rugby pitch and realises that his whole life has led toward this moment. When Noah beside him slips and falls and another man runs in to take his place, Derek stays calm;

he is built to do this. They will succeed.

'Heave Ho! Heave Ho!' Derek chants and the others join him.

'Heave Ho! Seaward Ho!

Hold the line! Heave Ho!'

And so the mainmast falls in slow motion like a mighty tree in a forest until finally it lands beside the collapsed mizzen-mast. In the last seconds someone shrieks as rough hemp rope wraps round the flesh and bone of Henrietta's thigh, pulls taut and burns the skin. Big George and Jack quickly rush in and take the strain off the rope to release her.

Two masts down and no broken limbs.

The crew lie gasping on the deck. Barely a minute to catch their breaths and take the refreshments brought round by Lizbet and Sam Solomon.

'I've a question for you, Lizbet,' Derek says, taking the cannikin of fresh water from her.

Lizbet stops. 'What?'

'Which came first, ships in bottles or the *Inevitable*'s strange masts? This is how they get model ships into bottles, bending the masts back, isn't it?'

Lizbet shrugs. 'Drink the water. Thou won't get another drop while we're through the other side.'

'Aye, aye, Captain,' Derek salutes her.

Lizbet smiles and runs off to water the next parched sailor.

Elmo is busy organising the bowsprit stays and the braces that will enable them to lower the foremast.

Somewhere to Derek's left a sailor is whistling a hornpipe to himself. The sea breaks against the bows and chases round the ship. As he removes splinters from his feet, Derek thinks back to the moment he lay on the deck of the ship that first day in the snow watching the same operation as they approached the crossover in the other direction. Confused, groggy and lost. It feels a life time away. He wonders how Aleka and Nat are doing, wishes he could tell them they will soon be back in Whitby. If their luck holds.

'Stations! And hurry!'

The same process all over again. They wait for Captain Elmo, helmet on and measuring speed and trajectory towards the cliff, to give the order. They are in luck, the tide is just right. Some four hundred metres from the shore, Elmo gives the order to lower the foremast. All across the ship men and women heave and strain, now having to step over the cordage, masts and yards that are spread across the deck.

Is the foremast shorter than the mainmast? Does it weigh slightly less? Derek doesn't know but the work is slightly less backbreaking. Maybe it is simply the knowledge that the work will soon be done, that there is an end to their labours.

'Haul them in and tie them down
Brace your backs and heave the sails
Pull in the slack and steady the stays
Jolly the jibs that ride the waves!'

The foremast is down. The cliff is now less than a hundred and fifty metres away. The ship has slowed; without the wind in its sails, only the jibs on the bowsprit remain, they are now almost totally reliant on the current to take them in. But this is no ordinary cliff and these are no ordinary currents, rippling, bubbling and chattering around the ship. The *Inevitable* rolls and lurches in the swell, water flung incessantly upon the deck to wash across and pass through the scuppers.

'Quick to the bowsprit! We are almost done!' Elmo shouts above the noise of the sea. 'Before the breakers hit us!'

The jib sails flap violently in the shifting winds and crack like gunshots as they fill then empty then fill again. The crew cling to the rigging with the strength of lions. They haul the jibs even though the keel of the ship is juddering over submerged rocks, threatening to toss them all into the fatal sea.

'Now haul the booms! That's it, my heroes! All rich as

emperors after this, lads! Heave ho!'

Derek joins the battle pulling the flying boom and then the jib boom back towards the prow, ignoring the flying spray soaking them from head to toe over and over.

The job is done. Half the crew, including Lizbet and Sam Solomon, race to the hatch and disappear below deck. The rest lash themselves as best they can to the deck. Derek straps himself down at the back of the main deck close to Beth and Big George.

Forty metres to go, the tunnel entrance now looming ahead and the ship bucking like a horse.

Die with your eyes open!

No one speaks except the helmeted Elmo who barks out orders to steer the rudder. There is no turning back, if their course is wrong they will soon be smashed against the cliff and die each and every woman, man and child, over one hundred and fifty million years from home.

Thirty metres. Twenty. Ten. The cacophony is deafening.

'Steady! Steady!'

In a terrifying scraping rush the *Inevitable* is dragged into the tunnel and the helter-skelter ride begins. A brief moment of incomprehension (how can the current work simultaneously in two directions?) then Derek abandons himself to the ride as he did before, allowing the experience to wash over him, breathing deep the amazing reality of being alive in this place and in this moment.

CHAPTER 47

They arrive at the approach to Tate Hill Pier at the same time from two different directions, Sarah and Robert Seeker emerging at speed from a narrow ginnel between the houses at the exact moment that Rosie is running past the same spot. They all smack into each other and end up in a tumble on the cobbles, nursing spinning heads, bruised ribs, and very sore backsides.

'Rosie, thank God you're safe.' Sarah picks herself off the floor and looks about her. 'Where's Amy?'

'They've taken her, Miss Sarah! Two of Sly's thugs turned up on Silver Street. I slipped out side door. I know I should have stayed but I panicked and …'

'It's okay, Rosie,' Sarah reassures the young woman. 'You've mouths to feed and children to protect. This isn't your fight.'

'I need to warn me mam and …'

'Are the children safe?' Sarah interrupts.

Rosie nods.

'Let's find your mother,' Sarah says.

'Might I offer a propitious interjection?'

'As long as you make it brief, Mr Seeker,' Sarah says.

'And in plain English,' Rosie adds.

'Let Rosie find her mother while we stay out of sight,' Seeker proposes, rubbing the growing lump on the back of his head.

The young woman races off as Sarah and Seeker withdraw to the shadows between the houses, from which Sarah watches the Duke of York Hotel sign on Tate Hill, swinging rustily back and forth in the stiffening breeze. The air is now cooling rapidly. Seabirds race overhead, seeking sanctuary inland.

The storm is coming.

At the other end of Church Street a horse and cart bearing two 'gentlemen' and a wriggling crimson sack turns the corner onto Green Lane, away from the harbour and up the hill towards Abbey Lane.

Sly and Argument's general store on Church Street presents a problem. Every movement through the old town becomes a contortion of ginnels, yards, backdoors and snickets as Sarah, Seeker, Rosie and now Rebecca take care to avoid the risk of passing directly in front of the shop owned by two of the Architects. The locals negotiate these alternate routes with ease, but Sarah knows that neither she nor Robert Seeker could take short cuts through people's homes so effortlessly, in one door and out the other.

No one in the yards questions Rebecca or Rosie as they trespass here there and everywhere. These journeys are the physical manifestation of mutual aid, of lives intertwined by a common experience of hardship; the need to avoid debt collectors and pressgangs, to dodge the bailiff and keep out of the workhouse.

Down in the harbour fishermen work frantically to secure and protect their boats against the storm that will arrive in the coming hours. Everything that can be removed - nets, lines, baskets, ropes and tubs - is taken away for safekeeping. Sacks are wrapped and tied round edges of the vessels to prevent damage as they collide either with each other or against the piers in the surge waters. Some take their boats further up the Esk and tie them up against trees, well away from the harbour. Others join forces to haul their cobles, as they call their small fishing boats, out of the water and up onto Tate Hill.

The God-fearing then climb the 199 steps up to St Mary's Church to pray while the rest go home or retire to the inns and taverns, to smoke, drink and exchange the opinion that this storm will be even worse than the one a few days back.

'I honestly don't know,' Sarah says.

'Time is very much of the essence, Madam. Our American cousins play host to a variety of mesoscale convective vortices but such meteorological events are infrequent on this side of the Atlantic. Maybe Rebecca can apprise you as to how many electrical storms there have visited these environs over the past two years.'

'Mr Seeker is, I think, asking how many thunderstorms there have been in Whitby,' Sarah explains to Rebecca.

The sky is now so dark as to leave the occupants of the small damp room on Wheelwrights Yard barely able to make out each other's faces in the gloom. A musty mountain of damp rags obscures the dirty window. Rosie has gone to find her children.

'There's maybe half a dozen storms a year,' Rebecca says. 'When the boats can't go out we lose the lines and have to muck them and bait them again. We lose so much.'

'How many winter storms, Rebecca?' Seeker asks.

'One. Maybe two. I can't tell thee when there were last more than one. And two in a week is rare as seven-toed cats.'

'So you see, Madam,' Seeker says turning toward Sarah, 'we must …'

'Yes, Mr Seeker, I quite get the point, thank you.' Sarah cuts him off testily. 'It's now or never. Or, at the very least, now or maybe not for another six months.'

The other two wait in silence while Sarah considers her options. She can look after herself and make preparations to leave the 1820s and return back to her own time alone; assuming that time portals do exist and really are brought into existence by epic thunderstorms. She has every right to save her own life, and an obligation to Stephen. God only knows what he has been going through these past few days.

Alternately, she can seek to persuade Amy to come with her by pointing out that if they don't leave now they might be stuck in 1821 for many months or even years. Does Amy really want to give birth in a world without anaesthetics or real doctors and nurses? It makes Sarah shiver just thinking about it. For the first time in her life she is almost grateful that she and Stephen have been unable to have children.

It isn't really an alternative; they don't even know where Amy is or how they might rescue her from the clutches of people who prey on the poor and conduct dubious experiments that are no doubt as bizarre as the nonsense in Dr Frankenstein.

Have these two even heard of Dr Frankenstein?

And finally, there is Derek, the only reason that she and Amy are stuck here, two hundred years from home. If he weren't a drunken lout who has never given a thought for anyone but himself, they wouldn't be in this hellhole. No one knows where he is or even if Derek is alive or dead. He could be rotting at the bottom of the harbour, feeding the crabs, for all they know.

Rebecca's hand finds hers in the gloom. 'Don't worry, love.'

'I just don't know what to ...' Sarah starts.

'Mr Seeker, I have suddenly remembered,' Rebecca cuts Sarah off in mid-sentence. 'What you were doing on the sands by Saltwick Bay this morning? What did you learn at Abbey House?'

'Abbey House?' Sarah says.

'We went up there last night to talk with the caretaker. Mr Seeker hopes that he will help us …'

'Regrettably, Gordon MacCrab will no longer be of succour to anyone on this Earth,' Seeker interjects.

'How?' Rebecca gasps 'You didn't …?'

'Of course not. I am not a murderer! He was shot in the back in the subterranean labyrinth that lurks beneath Abbey House.'

'A labyrinth?'

'More properly, a network of tunnels and caves. Since ancient times according to MacCrab. He was showing me what they were doing down there when they arrived. MacCrab, rest his soul, saved my life at the cost of his own.'

'Could that be where they have taken Amy?' Sarah asks.

'And you escaped from there to Saltwick Bay?' Rebecca says, putting two and two together.

'When the tide was out. It won't be possible to use that route in a storm,' Seeker says, second-guessing Rebecca's train of thought.

'So how *do* we get in Mr Seeker?' Sarah asks. 'If you believe Amy might be there.'

'There *is* a dungeon of sorts beneath the ruins,' Seeker admits, 'but we have too few weapons, Madam. If the conspirators are indeed up there, they will be armed to the teeth and guarding the entrance to Abbey House. I must also advise that there are all manner of occult symbols and other indications of necromancy in those vaults. I fear these scoundrels will stop at nothing, including the most diabolical means, to protect their interests.'

'So *what* do *you* propose, Mr Seeker?' Rebecca asks him, increasingly frustrated with his failure to get to the point. 'Should Sarah abandon her desire to save her friend? Is the whole town under threat? What exactly are these bastards hoping to achieve? If we knew that, I might hope to persuade others to join us. There are plenty of God-fearing folk in the yards who might help.'

Sarah is only half-listening. She feels increasingly detached from reality, stuck in the wrong century with people who are simultaneously very real and very distant. It is as if she were lost in a story or a role-play game. She is overwhelmed with the desire to be able to step through a door and be shot of everything, to be back in bed beside her boring snoring husband on Henrietta Street in twenty-first century Whitby or, better still, back in Dorking. Her head is swimming. If a storm is about to hit Whitby and *if* that storm somehow triggers the creation of a time portal then she needs to be standing beside it waiting for the moment it happens. Sod everything else. It's not her fault that Amy threw a tantrum and it's not her fault that Amy's drunken boyfriend Derek stepped into history then disappeared off the face of the Earth.

'I just want to go home,' she mutters. She smiles in turn at Rebecca and Seeker. 'You're both very kind, kinder than I think anyone has ever been to me, but I can't take much more of this. If you know a way to rescue Amy then let's try it but, if you don't, let's just wait for the storm to hit and hope that some weird Whitby thing happens and I can step back into my own time and leave you to get on with your lives.'

As if in answer, wind rattles the window frame. The rain has turned to sleet that peppers the panes. Robert Seeker produces a tallow candle and his tinderbox from one of the pockets of his voluminous coat. He lights the candle and its meaty smell fills the room as the flame trembles in the draught. Out in the fearful yard, a dog barks itself hoarse at the racing clouds. Darkness settles heavily on the chimney pots as the old town sinks into shadow.

Time traveller, fishwoman and paranormal investigator stare into the flame, each lost in thought. Sarah is shivering.

'Can there really be no way of …' Rebecca starts.

'Wait!' Seeker jumps to his feet. 'How obtuse of me! Dulbert Puzzlehead! Of course … Of course! My dear ladies, there is another way in!'

CHAPTER 48

Wood grinds against stone as the ship kisses the west pier. Tired bodies trudge around a capstan white with snow, muscles burning, alternately facing into the driving elements then into the town. They smell neither the coal fires nor the cauldrons of whale blubber bubbling in the yards; the squalls storming in across a bitter North Sea are sending the Whitby air inland over the moors, purging the town of its fuggy blanket.

Waves of sea foam, churned up in the breaking sea, tumble over the pier like a rough rabble of wraiths. The foam flies in lumps thick across the harbour, spattering the boats and on, up the ghauts and ramps into the shuttered streets, probing the narrow belly of the town.

'Haul them in and tie them down
Brace your backs and heave the sails
Pull in the slack and steady the stays
Jolly the jibs that ride the waves!'
'Heave Ho! Seaward Ho!
Hold the line! Heave Ho!'

Chests heave and bodies turn, drawing the ship close against the pier. The sails have all been dropped and some are now deployed over the side to cushion the ship's hull, bulwark and gunwale. The rigging groans and gyres, the way a gibbet rope cries while a hanged man twitches on his way to eternity.

No one is on the pier to greet the ship; the town's entire population is tucked inside. There are no lighthouses upon the piers, they have not yet been built. No obstructions slow the wind that howls off the angry sea. After the warmth of the land beyond the crossover, this place is brutal, bleak and barren.

'Stand easy!'

The trudging stops and the crew scramble as best they can back on board, disappearing below deck to escape the elements.

The *Inevitable* has limped to Whitby just hours ahead of the thunderstorm that will soon batter the coast. Like the rest of the crew, Captain Elmo is shattered. Ensuring the vessel had sea room while making rapid progress from the crossover and back to Whitby was challenge enough in a rising swell and squalling northerlies, particularly as they passed the headland at Kettleness with its alum works and its village hanging on the edge of the cliff ready to collapse into the sea.

From Kettleness into port was even worse, every second of the journey requiring almost superhuman concentration lest any slip or misjudgement risk the ship and its entire crew. Twice they almost lost steering-way as the current and the wind threatened to turn the ship about and roll her over.

And yet, here they are in Whitby; exhausted and cold, nursing sprains and injuries, the memory of lowering and then raising the masts on a skeleton crew etched achingly into their bodies. Elmo prays that their luck holds, that they can complete their business and leave for warmer climes as soon as the storm abates.

The girl Lizbet sits shivering close to the stove as Sam Solomon boils water and brews tea and coffee. The capstan crew are allowed to sit closer to the heat, to help dry their clothes of sea, snow and sweat. Derek's hands are wrapped around his mug of steaming tea into which has been poured a generous slug of rum. The heat radiates like sunrise in his throat as he swallows.

The gimbal lamps have been lit and hung up. Derek throws a glance towards the unconscious teenagers, Nat and Aleka, covered in a blankets. Beth mops their brows.

For a while everyone is too tired even to speak.

Outside, the ship is enveloped in a swirling blizzard of snowflakes, as if the Milky Way has fallen from the heavens to wrap the vessel in a vortex of stars. The rhythmic rubbing of the hull against the pier becomes the slow snoring of a wooden giant.

And so the evening might end for the crew of the *Inevitable*, in a lacklit drift to dreams and sleep, if it weren't for the first flash of lightning. Derek stirs from his torpor and, bent over beneath the low ceiling of the deck, he steps over and between the resting bodies of the crew towards Nat and Aleka.

'We've made it,' he whispers. 'We're back in Whitby!'

Aleka's eyelids flicker. She mumbles something incomprehensible. Beside her, Nat, in a foetal position, wheezes in his sleep. Both twins are fighting high temperatures and in bad shape, their hands and fingers stiff and bloated.

'What is the plan, Derek?' Beth asks quietly, appearing at his side.

Derek turns and stares into Beth's eyes for a second, lost for words.

'What would you do, Beth? This is your world and not mine. I feel completely helpless. I would take them to a doctor so that they can immediately be taken by helicopter to the Institute of Tropical Medicines and put on antibiotics. I realise that none of that will make any sense to you. What would you do?'

'When I were sick with fever, as a girl, the benevolent society came and ordered me taken outside into the fresh air. The winter air is always a cure for the miasmas that linger in the home. All my clothes were washed and then there were the bloodletting. Leeches are very good for reducing the heat and speed of the blood so …'

'I'm sorry, Beth,' Derek cuts her off. 'None of that works, does it?'

'And there's opium and wine to stimulate the body,' Beth

continues earnestly, her face a picture of worry. 'And to purge the inflammation in the brain the cure is …'

Another flash of lightning is visible through the small windows, lighting up the east cliff across the harbour.

'I understand.' Derek smiles kindly. 'Do you know who might help me carry them both over to Henrietta Street?'

'There's a physician on Church Street.'

Derek has no intention of letting a 19th century quack anywhere near the teenagers but Beth doesn't need to know that.

'Everyone is shattered but maybe Noah or Big George might help you,' Beth says. 'I'm afraid I'm spent, Derek.'

'I'll find the captain.'

Ten minutes later, having received Elmo's blessing, Derek is on the pier with Phin. They wear thick oilskins against the cold and are armed with cutlasses and pistols. Beth and Noah help lift the two unconscious teenagers, well wrapped in thick blankets, over the gunwale.

Some ten metres along the pier, Derek, who is carrying Aleka over his shoulder, stops and turns to look back at the ship, its empty masts silhouetted against the speeding clouds. Snowflakes stick to his face like frozen tears.

If all goes well, in a few hours he will be back in his own century and this insane adventure will be a mad memory.

But can a man ever really escape the *Inevitable*?

'Watch how you go, my drunken octopus!' Beth waves.

Derek wants to reply but knows his voice will be too thick with emotion. So he nods.

The arctic wind hurls the blizzard ahead of them as they walk the length of the pier, slipsliding on stones slick with snow, surrounded on all sides by the relentless clamour of the waves. And still the sea foam surges, sticks and soars.

They reach the relative shelter of the buildings along Pier Road. A chained dog barks harshly in a lacklit yard.

CHAPTER 49

While the storm gathers outside, within the town hall on the east side of the Esk, an experiment is being assembled.

Cramped in the loft space beneath the clock tower Constantine Featherston, member of the Architects, is busy making final adjustments to the measuring devices she has been installing for the past three hours. Encouraged to 'apply herself in physics' by her late and somewhat eccentric uncle Henry Featherston who thought girls 'no more dull-witted than boys', Constantine is a small wiry woman in her forties with sharp features and the determined demeanour of someone who does not suffer fools. If Phlogiston exists then she will be the one to prove it, and she certainly does *not* need the services of an assistant, thank you very much.

Satisfied at last that everything is absolutely in order, she turns to the device that Robert Seeker saw on his visit to the town hall but did not recognise and draws it towards her. It is a speaking tube.

'All connections made,' she announces into the tube.

The tube joins the collection of cables that trail along the floor behind her, and snakes into the stairwell, descending the steps to emerge in the main room above the square where two more of the Architects have plugged the cables into a most curious contraption that rests upon the table in the centre of the room. No lanterns have been lit, the only light comes from the windows.

'All connections made,' says the tinny voice emanating from the speaking tube.

Charles Tate, lardy son-in-law of Marmaduke Bovill,

founder of the Architects, peers carefully at the contraption in front of him. To the naked eye this glass sphere set upon a black box is inert and empty but to Tate, who is wearing goggles with crystal lenses of an extraordinary composition, the sphere is now glowing with a faint and incontrovertibly blue aura.

'Hello!' he expostulates, smiling at his accomplice, Gideon Peat, and nodding.

Peat returns the nod, smooths the handlebars of his large moustache and makes the declaration that they are eagerly awaiting below.

'All systems primed and prone.'

His words disappear down the second speaking tube, installed in the fireplace, following the thick cables down the spiral staircase to street level where they pass through the secret opening set beneath the steps and into the basement hidden beneath the street.

The basement room is almost dark, lit only by a couple of lanterns tucked strategically in a corner. Four people are gathered around the large table in the middle of the room, their shadows obscuring much of its surface.

Zachariah Barton is tired and old, an impatient man and a fidget. 'What was that?'

'It was Peat. He says the systems are primed.'

'Does he indeed? What the hell would that fool understand about systims?' Barton retorts. 'The pup can barely button his flies.'

'Systems, not systims, Mr Barton. And will you please move the brandy? I worry there will be an accident.' The amply framed Elizabeth Hall is determined to ensure that on this occasion all present must apply themselves to the task in hand. She makes to grab the whisky bottle and move it from the table.

'How dare you, Madam!' Barton explodes.

‘She is absolutely right, Zachariah,’ John Kidson steps in, adjusting his hair to better cover his bald pate. ‘There is much at stake this evening and these storms are rare as hen’s teeth. So let’s clear the decks.’

Barton, already in his cups, mumbles and grumbles that Kidson is a tiresome nose bagger, but he does as he is told and takes the bottle off the table. He sits heavily on a chair in a corner of the room, cradling the bottle as if it were his newborn baby.

Marmaduke Bovill glances briefly at Barton, if the old fool weren’t so rich he would have been expelled from the group many years ago. The pompous shot-clog is a blabbermouth. It’s a wonder he hasn’t destroyed the entire project by boasting about it in a tavern or in a melting moment with one of the plumper wagtails on Grope Lane.

‘Look!’ Kidson points at the table. ‘It’s starting!’

In the centre of the table is a weak circular pool of light, maybe a metre across. Elizabeth Hall, now wearing a set of crystal goggles, claps her hands excitedly.

‘How long must we wait?’ she asks Bovill.

‘If we are to unveil the immortal face of nature herself we must have patience, my dear.’ Bovill’s face is completely in shadow. ‘For years we have floundered in the multifarious complexity of our task, let us not squander this moment in impetuous haste. Natural philosophy has brought us this far. We have probed the mysteries of life and laboured tirelessly in our laboratory, explored galvanism and electricity and now, if we avoid deranging the mechanisms of these instruments, we may perhaps glimpse into the soul of the universe itself. I therefore …’

Bovill is stopped in mid-flow by the sound of snoring from the side of the room.

‘John, my good fellow, be so kind as to remove the bottle from that catchfart’s hand before it crashes to the floor.’

Kidson does as he is asked.

'Shall I fetch the cage?' Hall asks.

'Yes. We may yet be waiting many hours but it would be good to have all the apparatus to hand,' Bovill replies. 'I must now calibrate the helmet.'

A loud banging emanating from the corridor sends Kidson, lantern in hand, scurrying to open the door that can only be opened from the inside. He returns moments later with a bespectacled Henry Smales.

'No sign of Watson, I suppose?' Smales barks, somewhat out of breath. 'He was meant to join us at Abbey House.'

'I sent him to Baxtergate and the Wharf to check the nodes were secure,' Bovill tells Smales.

'So what happens if they attack?'

'If who attacks?'

'That ferret Seeker. We've taken one of the women up there. Sly and Argument are convinced there's trouble brewing and ...'

'That's enough!' Bovill cuts him off. 'Do what you must do but here we are focused on the task in hand. If that is all?'

Smales snorts, spins on his heel and strides back down the corridor with Kidson in his wake.

Three floors up in the loft of the town hall Constantine Featherston peers out across the harbour through the tiny window set above the heraldic shield that faces the square. She would love to climb the bell tower for a proper view of the gathering storm but it is dangerous up there; only three years ago her predecessor in the role of upper electricist was vaporised when a thunderbolt struck the tower.

CHAPTER 50

'Shut up! I said, bloody shut up!'

The dog continues barking, trying its best to alert the household to the presence of strangers in the backyard.

Another lightning flash followed a few seconds later by a loud rip of thunder. More frantic barking and shouting. A thwack. A brief whimper and all is quiet on Henrietta Street.

'You've hurt him, dad!' a child's voice protests.

'And I'll hurt you in a bloody minute if you don't shut up! It's just a storm. Now go to sleep.'

Outside the outhouse behind the cottage, Sarah, Seeker, and Rebecca draw breath. While the storm rages, their nefarious activities will pass undetected. Everything is as Seeker described it. They haul the door open and begin to empty the space beyond of its junk: buckets, old nets, the tin bath, ropes, the upturned table, a couple of broken oars, barrel hoops, two chamber pots, a torn sail …

Eventually the outhouse is empty. No door. No tunnel. Nothing.

'What are we looking for, Mr Seeker?' Rebecca asks, arms akimbo.

The snow swirls around them and has already turned the buckets white. Sarah wraps her arms around herself against the cold. The clouds over the sea are pulsing with lightning and the gale is whistling through the chimney pots.

Seeker is disappointed. 'It has to be here. The six-pointed star on the map clearly shows …'

Sarah steps into the outhouse. 'In the film I saw, the door was hidden.' She starts tapping the rear wall of the outhouse.

'It was a pharaoh's tomb in Egypt. The wall looked solid but in fact …'

As she taps along the wall the tone suddenly changes from short and high-pitched to low and hollow. Seeker joins her.

'Heavens above! You are right, dear lady! What strange nature is intelligence that she abandons us when we most need her. See here … and here,' he taps up and down. 'Confoundations! There is a void behind the wall!'

Seeker produces a long knife from one of the pockets of his voluminous coat and stabs the plaster repeatedly. All at once the blade sinks in as far as the hilt. No longer caring if the whole world hears him, though thankfully it cannot, Seeker sets to, plunging the knife into the plaster and rocking the blade to and fro as chunks break off and fall away. In no time at all he has knocked through to create an opening a metre high and forty centimetres across.

Lightning pulses in the clouds above the harbour and the air ripples in the rip of a thunderclap.

'Alacrity is of the essence! The storm is almost upon us!'

'I'm not going in there without a lantern,' Rebecca says.

Sarah produces her LED torch from the folds of her dress and lights it. Rebecca and Seeker leap back, showing the same astonishment as Rosie in the apartment.

'Don't worry, it's quite safe,' Sarah reassures them.

CHAPTER 51

The two men pause at the town hall to take the weight off their shoulders. They lower the sleeping teenagers to the ground. The Tuscan columns around the open ground floor of the town hall do nothing to block the cold but the building does provide some shelter from the snow.

Nat opens his eyes for the first time in a while. He looks surprised, the way babies do when they wake up.

'Aleka,' he whispers.

'It's okay, Nat. She's right here,' Derek reassures him. 'We're going home.'

'I can't feel my arms.'

'I'm taking you to a doctor. A proper doctor. In the 21st century.'

'Cool. They're wicked, doctors.' Nat's eyes are closing.

Beside him Aleka coughs in her sleep.

'Hey! It's snowing!' Nat wide awake again.

Derek nods.

Nat blinks a snowflake from his eyelashes. 'Why wouldn't you?' he mutters about nothing. 'Weird, dude.'

Lightning turns night to day in the square and thunder growls.

'Best keep moving,' Phin advises.

The town men re-shoulder the teens and enter Church Street. For no particular reason Derek looks back. Candlelight flickers in the upper window of the town hall, somebody is staring down at them. A faint blue aura hangs in the air. Like fog or sea fret.

Their boots ring on the cobbles of Church Street.

'This *is* the way to Henrietta Street, right?' Derek's memory of Whitby is fragmentary.

'Past the Abbey Steps,' Phin reassures him. 'Almost there.'

They reach Tate Hill and the foot of Abbey Steps. Two children huddle together in a doorway beneath a pile of rags, their pale thin faces staring nervously ready, as they always are, to leap up and race away to escape a beating. And yet they feel safer out here in the freezing lacklight than they ever do in the workhouse, where they are abused by various adults.

Derek recognises Henrietta Street even though he has only spent a few moments here, and most of those drunk. The blue glow is clearer now; the street is alive with otherworldly energy.

'Up here on the left,' Derek tells Phin.

The street is white-carpeted with snow. The blizzard rushes towards them, driven off the North Sea and thick into their faces. To Derek the snowflakes become a vortex of stars, bending the laws of time as when a spaceship approaches the speed of light.

Up ahead, a chimney pot tumbles down the roof tiles to shatter on the cobbles.

'This way!'

The two men turn into the narrow alley that leads between the cottages. Steps lead down toward the dark surging waters of the harbour.

Is this the way they took me?

A flash of lightning over the sea illuminates the boats moored in the harbour and, in the middle distance, the silhouette of the *Inevitable* hard against the harbour wall. Huge waves smack the pier, sending sheets of spray almost as high as the ship. Water is replacing the air; snow, sea, waves, clouds, fog exploding in all directions to subsume the town.

And there it is, behind a cottage. Derek steps forwards until he stands in front of the open door he passed through a week ago. Was it a week or a hundred million years? Or more? The blue aura around the door is the kind of hue you see under ultraviolet light: fluorescent, ethereal, phantasmal, eerie. Blue as a gas flame.

Beyond the door is a black empty void as deep as time itself. Suddenly Derek is afraid. What if he is mistaken? What if the door does not lead back to the 21st century? What if it leads to somewhere else entirely? What if there is no way back? What if this phenomenon is not benign but malevolent?

Though he has never previously believed in evil, he has never previously found himself thrown back in time to a land heavy with dinosaurs either. In an existence taken over by unimaginable chaos, why would anything make sense?

Phin also looks nervous.

Aleka groans. Derek touches her forehead. Burning. One of her arms slips out from under the blanket. It is red hot. Is her unconscious body responding physically to the place and the moment? The skin of her fingers, hand and arm is so swollen and tight that it might burst. Her breathing is coming in short laboured gasps.

Derek is also breathing more and more rapidly. The adrenalin surging through his body, he is starting to hyperventilate.

In a few moments he may be safe or he may have ceased to exist altogether.

Is it worth the risk?

It's not for you. It's for them. This is their only chance.

He looks across at Phin. 'Wait here,' he says, 'I'll be back.'

Staring into the void beyond the door, the muscles of his jaw so tight that he might crack his teeth, Derek takes six or seven deep breaths.

Four steps and you're in. Go!

He steps quickly forwards, clutching Aleka to him as tightly as he can.

If I'm wrong, Aleka, I am so so sorry.

He passes into the blue light and crosses the threshold.

Funny you can't see it from outside. He is in the basement of the cottage. All light is on upstairs. He climbs carpeted stairs. The air is clean, no smell of tallow. He places Aleka gently down on the sofa opposite the television, his head swimming in the terrifying normality of it all.

Remember Nat.

Before stepping back down to the basement Derek enters the kitchen, pulls open the fridge door and grabs a carton of milk. He takes two long gulps. Spots a tomato. Takes a bite. Cool, fresh, perfectly, frighteningly round.

Remember Nat.

Back downstairs and a brief look into the bathroom. A bathroom! He turns the tap and, in wonderment, watches the water flow, clean and clear. The 21st century! His eyes fill with tears.

A shout from outside.

Derek hurries out of the bathroom and crosses the threshold. In the ethereal blue glow Phin hands Nat over to Derek's arms.

'Take care of yourself, Phin.'

Phin nods. Derek turns back towards the door. In his mind the past is already fading to dust at his back.

A gunshot rings out.

'No! Captain, this way!' a female voice shouts down the street.

'Beth!' Phin runs off without a second glance.

Why on earth are Elmo and Beth out there?

Derek hesitates a second, blinks, then crosses the threshold with Nat. He climbs the stairs up to the front room and places Nat on the ground close to Aleka. He looks around but cannot see what he is looking for. Back into the kitchen where he takes a banana from the fruit bowl. He is so hungry. There, on the windowsill, a stack of large Post-it notes and a marker pen. He scribbles then returns to the front room. Aleka and Nat haven't moved.

'Stephen?' Derek calls out. 'Amy? Sarah?'

There are bags and cases by the door, a coat hanging on a chair. He doesn't recognise anything.

The sound of stirring upstairs.

Of course, they must have left. New people.

Derek places the Post-it note on the sofa by Aleka's head and crosses to the foot of the stairs, leading up to the bedrooms.

'Help! Fire! Help!' he shouts.

A door opens.

A man's voice calls out fearfully, 'Who's there?'

'What is it?' asks a second male voice.

'There's someone down there!'

As soon as he hears footsteps, Derek turns and hurries down the stairs to the basement, charges through the door, across the blue threshold, back into the blizzard, pushing the door closed behind him. With luck they'll be too busy to come down into the basement for a while. With luck he'll be back inside ten minutes and able to explain everything.

Derek runs up the alley and out onto Henrietta Street as a couple in pyjamas make their way downstairs to the front room. One is clutching a bottle as an improvised weapon, the other has his phone in hand and has already keyed in 999.

They stare in horror at the two people sleeping in their cottage. The Post-it note reads:

> *These two kids need urgent medical attention.*
> *They've had allergic reaction to something in*
> *the sea. Call an ambulance and the police.*
> *Parents rented cottage up street. Nov 21.*
> *They're twins. 14 I think. NAT AND ALEKA.*
> *Thanks.*

Derek reaches the foot of the 199 steps. A man lies dead on the ground. His top hat has rolled away, revealing a bald head with a comb-over. Clutched in his hand is a long knife. A bloodstain spreads across his coat.

The two children are still huddled in the doorway.

'Which way did they go?'

One of the children sticks a hand out from under the pile of rags and points up towards the ruined abbey. She watches Derek race up the steps, taking them two at a time.

CHAPTER 52

One hundred and fifty steps further up, Elmo, Pierre, Beth, Noah and Phin are heading towards Abbey House. Elmo is incandescent with rage. His relationship with the shipbuilders of Whitby has not been great but it has at least been straightforward. It is now clearly anything but.

Having left the ship some ten minutes after Derek and Phin, Elmo's party arrived at Marmaduke Bovill's residence on Flowergate, with the pearls and the other deliverable in a large box, as per the agreement, only to learn that Mr Bovill was not at home. The servant explained that he was not allowed to reveal where Mr Bovill had gone. Elmo said he didn't have to; he knew exactly where to find him.

Reaching the town hall, they found the building closed and no one answering, even though lantern light was visible in the upper windows.

Having previously learned of the existence of a meeting room beneath the town hall, accessed from a local tavern, Elmo led the party to the White Horse and Griffin where they hammered on the door until the landlady answered. An ill-tempered exchange followed during which it was alleged that Elmo was mistaken and that there was no passage, secret or otherwise, connecting the tavern with the town hall.

The matter was only resolved when Pierre began sweeping glasses and bottles from the shelves behind the bar. The landlady, now joined by her husband, found herself interrogated at gunpoint as the destruction of her bar continued. Eventually the pair decided wisely that it was not their battle and they agreed to show Elmo and his party the secret passageway and the door at the end of it.

Pierre hammered on said door with the pommel of his sword until finally the door was opened from within.

Noah returned upstairs to the bar with the publicans, to look out for a trap or ambush while Elmo, Beth and Pierre followed comb-over king, John Kidson, along the corridor and into the secret chamber where they found Marmaduke Bovill.

It is fair to say that Bovill and Elizabeth Hall were amazed at the contents of the large wooden box that Pierre was carrying, and tried to take charge of it, but were prevented from doing so by Elmo who reminded them that the exchange could only take place after Angelique was produced. Bovill replied that she was being kept in a prison cell beneath the ruins of Abbey House and that he was currently busy engaged in a singularly important scientific endeavour and that he would be obliged if Captain Elmo could return in the morning when the exchange might take place in better circumstances.

It was at this moment that Zachariah Barton awoke from his drunken stupor, cast a swivel eye toward the newcomers and ordered Bovill to *"have these blackamoors, brigands and buccaneers taken outside and flogged."*

Only Beth's rapid intervention prevented an enraged Pierre from running Barton through with his cutlass.

Elmo decided to head straight to Abbey House, taking John Kidson along as hostage and keeping the box with them. At the foot of the 199 steps Kidson produced a knife, mumbled something vainglorious and inane about protecting king and country, and stabbed Elmo in the arm. Whereupon Beth whipped out a flintlock and shot him dead.

Elmo is worried about the contents of the box. The cold is intense as they approach the top of the hill, they must hurry or they may have nothing to trade. With Kidson dead they no longer have a hostage or a guide.

Everything that could go wrong is going wrong.

CHAPTER 53

'Which way?'

'Upward, dear ladies.'

Shortly after entering the tunnel they reach a bifurcation, one path leading up and the other southwards and down towards Church Street and, perhaps, the town hall. Two thick cables wrapped in cloth run along the floor close to one wall. Sarah, who is more familiar with electric cables than the other two, is shocked that the cables aren't insulated properly but the technology won't exist for another sixty years. They step carefully over the cables and head upwards.

Proof of the danger is soon seen in the desiccated and electrocuted rats lying beside the cables at regular intervals.

The tunnel rises as steeply as the Abbey steps and here, below ground, there are several long sections without steps, forcing Sarah, Rebecca and Robert Seeker to scramble up as best they can over a rough broken surface.

They are soon panting from their exertions but they are at least dry, out of the wind and away from the snow. It's the little things, isn't it, Sarah thinks to herself.

The bright white beam cast by Sarah's LED torch provides Seeker and Rebecca with the incontrovertible proof that Sarah is absolutely from a different moment in history. It crystallises the reality of time as yet unpassed.

For Seeker the torch is more significant than any of his other discoveries: the hidden rooms, the blue glows, the strange helmet with its telescopes, the subterfuge, the maps and all the rest of it. This extraordinary beam of light changes everything. There really *are* new things awaiting humanity in the future and, somehow, Sarah and Amy really do belong somewhere else.

For Rebecca, the light is an adventure. In the midst of a life etched through with hardships, drudgery and struggle, the light is a beacon as bright as Christmas. It lifts her up and transports her to the joy she felt as a little girl racing to the rock pools to gawp at the strange creatures that flinched and crawled and swam beneath the clouds reflected on the water's bright surface on those rare days when she didn't have to work.

None of them knows what they will find when they reach the top of the tunnel but all three are now too wrapped up in the moment to give a damn.

'Can't be much further!' Sarah says optimistically.

'It *can* be! It's last time I listen to thee. I'd no idea this tunnel were lurking at the back of Alice Hobson's. Poor woman will be scared witless!'

'One hundred and three steps so far, if I may interject, ladies.'

'Bloody hell, Mr Seeker, you're not counting are you?'

'An organised mind is a precondition to a successful enterprise, Rebecca.'

'Will you listen to him! He's barely …'

'Shh,' Sarah cuts in. 'The pair of you. We don't want to give whoever is up there any warning of our arrival.'

The tunnel turns to the right, still rising as steeply as before. They tread more carefully, trying to make as little noise as they can. Sarah cups her hand over the end of her torch to constrain the beam. Hemmed in, before and behind, by total darkness, they walk in a narrow shard of light. Down here, deep underground there is no ambient light or night sky to create a sense of space and the roughness of the walls means there is barely any echo either, just the crunching of their determined, careful feet. They are in short like a pupa wriggling in its cocoon, tucked in on all sides and blind to the world.

CHAPTER 54

Not before time, nature is on their side. The combination of warm weather earlier in the day and now driving snow makes their task of finding a way into Abbey House very much easier. The carts have churned up the mud and created a clearly-read path through the snow. All they have to do is follow it.

Through the gates, along the ruins and on past the house and round the corner until, boots, trousers and skirts sodden, they find the entrance. The cart is standing outside, though the horse has been unhitched and presumably led to shelter somewhere.

The party from the ship push open the door and cross the threshold. The fools who have passed this way ahead of them continue to help them as Elmo, Pierre, Beth, Phin and Noah navigate the labyrinthine corridors of the decaying house.

Beth carries the lantern and a cutlass, Elmo, Pierre and Phin primed pistols, and Noah the large box as they follow the muddy bootprints along the same threadbare-carpeted corridors that Robert Seeker walked with Gordon MacCrab. High on the fraying wallpaper, the family portraits scowl at the passing presence of more intruders.

At the end of the passage where plants grow through fractured floorboards Elmo hauls open the door set into the rough boards that keep out the elements and steps through into the collapsed ruin beyond. Snow swirls down through the open roof and first floor joists that have lost their floorboards. Bramble skeletons snatch at their clothes and momentarily the crew lose sight of the footprints they have been following.

'Over here!' Beth says in a half-whisper.

Sure enough, footprints and melting snow beside a door that is tucked beneath a once grand staircase. The door opens noisily. They follow the steps down into the bowels of the earth, moving ever more cautiously, all alert to the possibility that they are walking straight into a trap.

As Elmo's team are descending into the earth, Derek, a little way behind, arrives at the front door of Abbey House.

The door is open. Derek follows the footsteps of others across the threshold and into the building. He has no lantern and has taken only a few hesitant steps when he is struck on the head from behind and crumples unconscious to the floor. His assailant lingers a moment, plank of wood in hand, and decides he hasn't time to do more than place a well-aimed kick at his disabled opponent.

Tasked by Bovill to run through the yards and across Almshouse Close field to reach Abbey House before "that bastard Elmo gets there", Peat is soaked to the skin and very much the worse for wear. Difficult to cross before the snow fell, the field is now treacherous with the vegetation hidden from view, and Peat has measured his length and face-planted several times. He is incensed that Bovill should treat him as a junior lackey and will not forget the slight.

It takes Peat several attempts to light a lantern but eventually he does so. He has no idea of the identity of the man lying unconscious at his feet but it clearly is not Elmo. Aiming a last kick into Derek's ribs, Peat hurries down the corridor in pursuit of the group he saw enter a few minutes earlier, the ends of his long handlebar moustache bouncing in front of his face as he runs.

Elmo and the others have reached the two doors that bear the signs reading:

DO NOT ENTER
upon pain of
DEATH

Thick metal cables wrapped in cloth emerge from under one door and disappear under the other. They choose the second door where the passageway beyond is drier and the walls are painted black. They move forward swiftly and quietly. Beth hides the lantern under her sleeve to stop it lighting the path ahead.

'Look,' Elmo whispers. 'Light!'

Barely visible but he is right. Beth blows out the lantern and they wait for their eyes to adjust. They can just about make each other out in the darkness and now they have stopped moving they hear faint echoing voices; someone is shouting.

'Remember,' Elmo whispers. 'First we find Angelique and make sure she is safe. Then we bargain.'

The others nod.

Moments later Derek comes round, lying on the floor in the entrance of Abbey House, aching all over and none the wiser as to what just happened. He can see next to nothing in the lacklight and does the only thing he can do; fumble along the wall until he reaches a door. This he opens and steps into Gordon MacCrab's office. The room smells of coal fires and sweat and musty fabrics. But the windows, if there are any, must all be shuttered because the room is even darker than the entrance hall. His hands reaching out in front of him, Derek takes small steps and hopes he isn't sharing the room with the hitherto unknown psychotic inventor of the world's first pre-Victorian infrared goggles.

Eventually having knocked over what he imagines to be a couple of glasses that were sitting on what he thinks might be a table, his fingers brush what he decides *must* be a lantern! In his admittedly short visit to the 19th century he has already learnt that in a world that doesn't even have matches, where there is a lantern there will often also be a tinderbox close to hand. Two broken fingernails later he discovers that the table may be a desk, for it contains a drawer and, within the drawer, a small tin that rattles when he shakes it!

He carefully opens the tin and feels the contents. His fingers find steel, a flint and a cloth.

Child's play!

Copying what he saw Lizbet do on board the *Inevitable*, he holds the steel over the open box with the cloth in it and strikes the steel downwards with the flint. Sure enough sparks fly down into the cloth. Bringing the box close he blows gently and in a few second the cloth glows then bursts into flames.

Light!

Now he can see the candle on the table. He lights the candle then uses that to light the wick inside the lantern. The room is revealed. The tatty furniture and wing-backed armchair by the dead fireplace. The painting of a Scottish glen, complete with castle and majestic stag. The mould spreading across the damp wall and, on the floor, two broken whisky tumblers. The lantern is bright now. A quick swig from the whisky bottle and he is on his way.

Captain Jean-Jacques Elmo and his party peer out of the darkness of the tunnel towards the cave, maybe ten metres ahead.

The space is lit by maybe a dozen lanterns. They see the large metal tank, thick coils of cable, tools and winches. They smell the stench of coal dust and molten iron, the acrid smell of cold steel and the sweet smell of hot iron, the faintly sulphurous smell of the acid in the tanks.

'Why feed her?' a voice echoes in the cavern. 'She may be gone in an hour. She's a bargaining tool, nothing more.'

‘She won’t be a bargaining tool if she’s dead, will she?’ replies another voice.

‘She flashed enough jewellery when they came into the shop. Make her pay for it.’

Beth hears the sound of someone sobbing. She tugs Elmo’s sleeve to draw his attention.

Elmo feels a surging rush of emotions, anger and relief; Angelique is here!

A blue glow blooms briefly over the tank as a lightning strike above ground sends a burst of electricity down into the belly of the ground.

‘How many?’ Elmo gestures to Pierre who is standing the furthest forwards.

Pierre creeps forward then turns back and indicates six people with his raised fingers; he can physically see three and guesses presence of the others from the moving shadows on the floor.

Another gesture from Elmo, ‘Are they armed?’

Pierre shrugs.

They all inch forward, their shoes scruffling the loose dust and gravel on the tunnel floor.

One noise hides another.

Out of nowhere Elmo feels the barrel of a gun at his back, hard against his ribs. He turns his head very slowly and finds himself face-to-face with a man sporting a huge handlebar moustache and a sneer.

‘Drop the weapons, you low-life sea scum,’ the man snarls.

The others turn towards the voice.

‘Hands where I can see them. Now move.’

Elmo and the others exchange glances.

‘Any funny stuff and he’s dead. And you, yes you with the package, keep it where I can see it.’

By now Pierre turns and clocks the sudden shifting tide of fortune. They are caught like rats in a cage. All four sailors walk forwards towards Pierre and the mouth of the cave.

One noise hides another.

Gideon Peat keeps his weapon pressed against Elmo's ribs. Everything is going swimmingly …

Until he feels the gun barrel at his own back.

'I owe you for the lump on the back of my head,' hisses a new voice. 'Please move and give me an excuse to shoot.'

Beth turns and sees Derek standing at the back of the queue. The drunken octopus has come to the rescue!

'Lower your weapon,' Derek's pistol is hard between Peat's shoulder blades. 'Very, very slowly.'

Peat does as he is told. As his hand comes into view it is clear he has no gun, all he has is a pointed stick. Noah spins round, grabs Peat's arm and twists it violently behind his back.

'Getting a bit crowded in here, isn't it?' Noah tells Peat.

'Calls us sea scum?' Beth says. 'A pretty rose-bud like you?' She leans forwards, grabs one of the handlebars of his extravagant moustache and cuts it off with a single swipe of her knife.

Elmo puts his fingers to his lips. They still have the advantage if they can surprise the occupants of the cave.

'WATCH OUT!' Peat shouts at the top of his voice. 'YOU'RE ALL UNDER ATT- …'

The shot rings out, deafeningly loud in the restricted space of the tunnel. White smoke blooms like fog as Peat slumps to the ground.

Their ambush now impossible, Derek and the others retreat back into the tunnel. The cave echoes to the sound of running feet as the occupants scramble to collect their weapons. The storm above ground is forgotten.

CHAPTER 55

Above ground the storm is anything but forgotten.

In dozens of the houses squatting in the shade of the east cliff, dogs are barking or cowering beneath tables, children have their dirty noses pressed to open-eyed windows as snow piles high on sills. The whale blubber stops bubbling in the trying-out cauldrons as the biting wind exhausts the fuel beneath them. Thick churning waters in the harbour rock the boats, smacking against each other or forcing them to exchange rough wooden kisses. Even the rag merchants are indoors, unable to push their trudging carts up Church Street.

The eye of the storm is almost overhead.

Urine-yellow gobbets of sea foam roam the streets in gangs like marauding Vikings. Clouds scrape the chimney pots clean of smoke and sheltering gulls. Thunder growls, rips and rages and lightning arcs from sky corner to sky's end over a whimpering Whitby.

In their secret laboratory hidden beneath the town hall, the Architects are locked in the throes of a master plan that will harness the power of these elemental forces.

Her eyes shining with expectation and protected behind the singular crystalline lenses of her goggles, Elizabeth Hall takes another mouse from the cage and feeds it into the wire box at the end of a long wooden handle. She awaits the next bright surge of energy and, when it comes, thrusts the hapless creature forward along the lines of force marked upon the table, towards the centre where the blue glow is thickest.

Scorch marks and ashes mark the spots where half a dozen previous attempts have failed.

All eyes in the room are fixed and focused on the anxious mammal as it receives the full force of the miasmic phlogiston.

'Yes!' she shouts triumphantly as mouse and wire cage disappear. 'YES!'

'My God, Elizabeth!' Marmaduke Bovill blurts. 'We've DONE IT!'

He grabs Charles Tate, his son-in-law, who has been relieved of his duties up above to allow him to witness the experiment, and he hauls him round and round in a jig.

'Hey! Hey!' yells Zachariah Barton as the spinning lardy-butts step repeatedly on his feet. 'I'll have the pair of you shot and hung up over my fireplace if this doesn't …'

'We've *done* it, Zachariah!'

'Done what?'

'The mouse. It's disappeared!' Elizabeth says. 'Do you realise what this means?'

'Cat's got no supper?'

'No, you old mumblecrust. The phlogiston. It works! We've sent the mouse to a different time and place!'

'I'll drink to that.' Zachariah Barton leans forwards to retrieve the whisky bottle from beside his chair. 'What happens next?'

'We're sending you in after t'mouse,' says Charles Tate, much to his father-in-law's amusement.

The mood is not so jolly three floors up, beneath the bell tower, where repeated lightning strikes on the rods above her head are causing sections of the cabling in the loft to melt. Constantine Featherston, standing close to these cables, feels dizzy and nauseous and is convinced that something is wrong with her heart. The time lag between lightning and thunder-claps suggest the storm is not yet at its peak and she fears for what is coming.

CHAPTER 56

Baxtergate on the west bank of the Esk lies empty and shuttered, its inhabitants all indoors. No one witnesses the striking blue glow halfway down Angel Yard, the fifth point of the six-pointed star marked upon on the Architects' arcane map of Whitby. The blue phosphorescence that exudes from a warehouse is bright as a gas flame and growing.

Inside the building are the mortal remains of Thomas Watson who ventured too close to the giant acid battery and was overcome by sulphurous fumes. He will never again sit down in the Freemasons Tavern to play cards and relieve Tobias Jeffers of his money.

A black cat saunters down the street, oblivious to both snow and storm. At the mouth of the narrow yard he senses movement and stops, his tail pointing upward, alternately making an exclamation mark or a question mark above his back. He sniffs the air and peers long and hard into the lacklight. The extraordinary glow loiters in the air but the cat's attention is focused on the two mice nibbling beside a mess of potato peelings and paper beyond the warehouse door.

Belly rumbling, the cat softfoots forward until he reaches the edge of the halo of blue light. Lightning rips the sky, cat and mice suddenly spotlit as if on stage at the Palladium.

The mice disappear into the refuse while the otherworldly glow intensifies.

Obeying the rumble in his belly, his tail weaving slowly back and forth above him like an anglerfish's lure, the black cat settles on his haunches and waits for the rodents to re-emerge. When they do, the cat leaps forward in an action-packed arc of fur, muscle, claws and teeth and … promptly disappears off the face of the Earth.

The mice too are gone … back into the pile of peelings where they will remain, trembling and alert, until the storm has passed.

CHAPTER 57

Both sides are struggling, Elmo and his party unable to get out of the tunnel against a barrage of gunfire from the cave, and the cave's occupants unable to enter the tunnel without easily being picked off by those sheltering within it.

So far Noah has taken a shot in the arm, causing him to drop the package, and in the cave two men are down, Tom Allison shot in the neck and Henry Smales hit in the thigh.

White smoke hangs heavy in the air, unable to escape the confines of the underground labyrinth.

'You cannot win!' Sly bellows into the darkness. 'Give yourselves up or die as rats!'

'He's dead,' says Isaac Ripley at Sly's side and trying hopelessly to stem the blood flowing from Tom's neck. 'They've bloody murdered him!'

'You'll not intimidate them,' Smales advises Aaron Sly. 'They're little more than pirates.'

'You weren't saying that when you built his ship and took his money,' Sly sneers.

Argument keen to get the battle done, goes down on his hands and knees and leans out to peer into the tunnel. A volley of shots rings out, one bullet catching him clean between the eyes. He drops face down without uttering a sound.

'Haul him back!' Sly barks. 'Devils! Bastards!'

Henry Smales and John Camphor, the jeweller, drag Argument back by the feet, away from the tunnel mouth and roll him over. Sly drops to his knees and peers down into his friend and business partner's eyes.

'Come on, Joe, fight it!' Sly orders him. 'You're a warrior, always have been. You and me, thick as thieves! On your feet, lad, and we'll kill them all! These bastards aren't worth spit!'

Joseph Argument stares up at him from far far away.

'We'll hit them harder than a typhoon,' Sly thunders into his friend's face. 'They'll rot in hell for this!' He slaps Argument's cheek repeatedly. 'Fight it, for the love of God!'

'He's gone, sir,' Ripley says quietly. 'He's dead.'

'GET OUT, USELESS GLUEPOT!' Sly screams. 'You'll not get another penny from me. To the workhouse with ye! Cowards! Wretches!'

One noise hides another.

The hammer is drawn back on the firearm that has nestled for months within one of the many pockets of a voluminous coat, its owner convinced that one day it might prove useful.

'Nobody move or this duckfoot will fashion new orifices for each and every one of you.'

Footsteps as three more people enter the cave from a second tunnel. Sly turns slowly to find himself looking into one of the four barrels of a duckfoot volley pistol gripped in the hand of the red-haired pipsqueak he confronted outside the shop. And he recognises one of the women too, a fisherwoman living in one of the yards on Church Street.

'You can come out,' Rebecca shouts to those in the tunnel under the house, keeping her revolver pointing directly at Smales' chest. 'We have Sly and the others covered.'

Sarah stands beside Rebecca sword in hand but not yet convinced she will have the guts to use it. Elmo and the others emerge from the other tunnel.

'And you are?' Elmo asks.

'Robert Seeker, from London. Assigned by my employers to conduct an evaluation of the acroamatic phenomena manifesting contemporaneously in the environs of Whitby.'

'Can anyone understand this gentleman?' Elmo looks around him in puzzlement.

‘Forgive my grandiloquence. You must be Captain Jean-Jacques Elmo of the *Inevitable*?’ Seeker continues.

‘The same. And my crew: Pierre, Beth, Phin, Noah and …’

‘Derek!’ says Sarah staring in total disbelief at the sailor standing before her, armed to the teeth.

‘You know each other?’ asks Elmo.

‘Yes! Well, not really but yes. What are you …’

If Sarah is shocked then Derek is even more so.

‘Do I know you?’ he asks, staring at the woman in front of him.

Noah places the wooden box and a lantern on the floor on the hexagon that lies at the heart of the six-pointed star and, in doing so, covers the image of the town hall with the eye of Horus radiating at its core. Phin finds ropes to tie up their captives while Seeker and Rebecca continue pointing their weapons. Elmo, Pierre and Beth meanwhile walk off further into the cave.

Derek’s head is swimming. How can he possibly know someone from the 19th century? But her voice …

Sarah removes her headscarf, revealing her 21st century brunette boy bob hair.

‘Oh my God!’ Derek says in astonishment. ‘Sarah? What are you …?

‘We came looking for you.’

At the other end of the cave, Elmo, Pierre and Beth have passed the second of the large metal tanks and reached the entrance of the chamber that contains the prison cells. Through the iron bars, Elmo sees a human form lying in a foetal position on the floor facing the far wall. She wears the rough clothes of a fisherwoman. On the wall above her the initials A.V. are scratched into the stone. Elmo’s heart soars. It’s true! He has found her, the mother of his daughter Lizbet! He grabs the bars and rattles them.

‘Angelique! *C’est moi!* It’s me!’

Beth appears at his side, holding the keys that were hanging on the wall. Elmo takes them, unlocks the door and steps into the cell. He gently touches her shoulder.

'*Mon amour! Je suis la! C'est fini.* It's over. You are safe!'

The woman slowly unwinds and lifts her head.

Elmo lets out a huge wail of despair.

Beth grabs Elmo's sleeve. 'Captain, you frighten her!'

'This is not Angelique!' Elmo cries. 'Who is she?'

Pierre drags an utterly bereft Elmo back as Beth kneels beside the cowering woman.

'I am sorry Madam. Please,' Beth says softly. 'We mean you no harm. You are safe, I assure you.'

Beth waits and slowly the woman turns again to look up into the green eyes that smile kindly beneath the billowing curls of red hair.

Elmo has stepped back into the main chamber of the cave and is shouting, 'They've tricked us! She's not here. They have a different woman locked up in there! We must hurry back to the town hall or all is lost!'

Bound hand and foot, Smales and Camphor are propped up against the cave wall. Isaac Ripley and Aaron Sly are next.

At the very moment that Pierre and Beth re-enter the cavern, supporting the blond woman from the prison cell between them, Aaron Sly takes advantage of the multiple distractions. He rolls to his right, dropping out of the line of sight of the pistols trained upon him, and grabs Noah's cutlass off the floor in one movement. Back up on his feet, Sly throws himself toward Rebecca intending to take her hostage or kill her trying.

'NO, YOU DON'T!' roars Derek, drawing his cutlass and leaping to his left.

Surrounded by so many bodies Robert Seeker is unable to use his four-barrelled duckfoot volley pistol for fear of killing half his own side.

Derek and Aaron Sly lock swords. Only Noah's serrated blade pressed against his throat prevents Isaac Ripley from joining the fray.

The others step back as Sly slashes his blade about furiously. Derek dodges and parries.

'Let's see the colour of your entrails,' sneers Sly. 'There's not a man on God's Earth can beat me in a fight!'

Sly is a big man, not quite as tall as Derek but built like brick house. Derek is the fitter faster man. He lets Sly tire himself out, side-stepping the increasingly wild slices and thrusts, slashes and hacks. As Sly tires, his footwork becomes increasingly sloppy and predictable and Derek is able to step forward, slash the big man's arm and retreat to a safe distance. Blood blooms on Sly's sleeve.

'FIGHT ME, YOU COWARD!' screams Sly, his face red with rage as his blade finds only fresh air for the fiftieth time.

'Drop the sword, old man,' Derek retorts. 'You'll give yourself a heart attack!'

Sly roars lunges forward and slashes as Derek spins away then catches the older man with a hefty blow on the back with the pommel of his sword. Winded, Sly gasps and loses his balance, face-planting on the stone floor of the cavern. Derek is onto him in a split second, pinning him to the floor with his knee as he pulls Sly's head back and slides his cutlass under his neck.

Noah, who has finished trussing up Isaac Ripley, steps forward, kicks the cutlass out of Sly's hand then grabs his ankles and ropes them together. The fight is over.

Derek is not yet on his feet as the woman from the prison cell breaks away from Beth and races across, past the box and over the occult symbols on the floor and throws herself into Derek's arms.

'Amy?' he gasps in disbelief.

'Oh Derek. You won't believe what we have lived through

in this awful place! It's unimaginable. The filth and squalor. Where have you been? We thought you were dead. And what are you doing with a sword?'

As Amy pours her heart out, Derek glances at Beth.

Amy notices Derek's head movement and turns and sees Beth, who smiles and nods encouragingly.

'And Sarah's been here with me. We had to sell the bracelet to get some money because we had no idea how long we would be stuck here. Do you know how much candles cost? It's ridiculous. First of all, they stink of boiled bones or whale blubber or something and then the light is so rubbish you need five or six of them lit at once just to read a book. And then there's the heating. Or total lack of it. You would not believe how …'

Amy is interrupted in full flow by a movement in the middle of the room. The wooden box has started rocking back and forth, slapping heavily on the floor. All conversations stop. The rocking becomes wilder, as if the box is possessed by a demonic force. The glow above the tanks intensifies. Eventually the box falls over, the lid breaks open and those who are trussed up against the wall begin to call for help.

The light of the lantern on the floor beside the box throws huge shadows of one of the world's most terrifying predators up onto the roof of the cavern. A young, agitated and very hungry megalosaur looks around, its feathers soft-haloing its body, its head jerking this way and that. Aaron Sly now trussed up with the others can only wriggle and shout as the baby dinosaur rushes at him and sinks its sharp teeth into his thigh.

'They wanted it,' Elmo says. 'They can have it!'

'Is that what I think it is?' asks Sarah, eyes wide as hubcaps.

'Let's go. Where does *that* lead?' Elmo asks Seeker, pointing to the tunnel they emerged from.

'Back down to Henrietta Street,' Rebecca tells Elmo.

'And that one,' Seeker points across the cave, 'takes you to

Saltwick Bay but, with the sea so rough, we would …'

'Let's go down to Henrietta Street. Leave them a couple of lanterns so they can enjoy their reward from the land beyond the crossover.'

'Hello? Why is no one listening?' Sarah says. 'What is that animal? Derek?'

'It's a dinosaur.

'A *what*?'

'A bloody dinosaur. Now come on.'

No sooner have they all stepped into the tunnel down toward Henrietta Street that they hear an explosion ahead of them. The air fills with smoke and the orange glow of flames lights the walls.

'The wrapping round the cables has caught fire!' Seeker says.

'Back the way we came,' Beth says, stepping into the tunnel that leads back to the house.

CHAPTER 58

Halfway down the 199 steps the snow has slackened off and they can all finally see across the harbour. The storm is in full spate. Monstrous waves hurl themselves at the pier sending waves and spray flying up as high as the masts of the *Inevitable*. Lightning rips the sky and a constant barrage of thunder shakes the town as if it were in the thick of a bombing raid.

Blue phosphorescence pools the darkened streets, across the harbour, in the distance on Church Street, above the town hall, and on Henrietta Street. Behind them as they descend the steps an orange glow in the sky suggests that the Abbey House ruins have caught fire.

Amy clings to Derek's arm. Seeker walks beside Sarah and Rebecca. Weapons are out and primed, everyone knows the battle is not yet done.

'Over there!' Phin points toward the ship. 'Lights in the captain's quarters! Someone is messaging you, Sir.'

Jean-Jacques Elmo produces a telescope from within the folds of his coat and raises it to his eye. Phin is right. 'You have good eyes, Phin.'

'What's happening?' Pierre asks.

'Mutiny aboard!' Elmo replies, deciphering the message in the flashing lights. 'Bill and Frank must have escaped and are attempting to seize the ship! We must hurry.'

'What about the Architects and Angelique?' Noah asks.

'We were duped,' Elmo tells him. 'The Architects have troubles enough of their own. Our ship comes first.' Elmo turns to the others. 'Mr Seeker I thank you for your help and you Rebecca. With good fortune we may see each other in the morning. Derek, you are worthy of any crew upon the seas. I salute you, Sir.' Elmo raises his hat. 'Ladies.'

Beth and Derek exchange glances.

'So long, my drunken octopus! May your seas run smooth and the rum forever warm your heart, Derek.'

Before he can reply, Beth has spun on her heels and is charging down the steps, cutlass in hand, after the other members of the crew.

Which leaves Sarah, Amy, Seeker, Rebecca and Derek. They walk slowly, exhausted, each lost in his or her own thoughts. With every step the perspective changes. One minute they are overlooking the small town as if it were a map: staring down at snow-covered roofs and smoke sputtering from a hundred chimmey pots, and the *Inevitable*'s masts silhouetted against the foaming water beyond the pier.

Then the perspective changes. The streets come up to meet them, the harbour disappears from view and they become part of the small town that flanks the river Esk. And finally the chimney pots on Henrietta Street are above them.

Amy squeezes Derek's hand. Derek wonders if Nat and Aleka have already reached a hospital.

The roar of the sea is now clearly audible, or is his imagination playing tricks?

That building over there is still a pub in 2022. In two hundred years I'll be sitting in it, getting blind drunk.

Suddenly Derek is more lucid than he has ever been in his life.

'I know that this will sound insane and maybe …' he starts hesitantly, turning toward Amy. 'I can't really explain it but, the thought of going back to a world where I work in insurance, where the biggest physical challenge I ever face is in a scrum in the Second XV on a rugby pitch in Dorking, TV dinners, Pub quizzes. Everything so boring and safe and predictable.

Mapped out from cradle to grave.' He is speaking so quickly now that the words are blurring together. 'I can't do it, Amy. I can't go with you. I belong here. You don't need a miserable millstone around your neck.'

'You don't know what you're talking about,' Sarah says. 'Amy, tell him that you're …'

'Stop it,' Amy says.

'He has a right to …'

'Don't you dare!' Amy retorts. 'That's enough!' She looks Derek in the eye. 'I am so glad we found you and know you're okay. I sort of know what you mean about here, it *is* an adventure. I couldn't deal with it, but you are more alive here in this place than I have ever seen you.'

'Amy …'

'Shut up, Sarah.' Amy turns back to Derek. 'We have to hurry or we will miss the chance to get back.'

They reach the foot of the steps.

'Thank you for coming to find me,' Derek tells Amy. 'I really didn't deserve that.'

'Yes, you did. And you deserve to live your best life.'

'So do you.'

Amy nods. 'Yeah. And I will.'

There is a strong blue glow behind the cottages on Henrietta Street.

'You'd better hurry,' Derek tells her. 'The door is open behind the cottage.'

Amy is confused. 'How do you know?'

'I took Nat and Aleka there earlier.'

'Who?'

'You'll find out,' Derek smiles.

'Amy, are you going to tell him …' Sarah starts.

'Sarah, for the last time, will ... you ... shut ... up?' Amy lets go of Derek's hands. 'You'd better hurry. I see you can use that sword and they need all hands on deck! Is that how you say it?'

Derek shrugs. 'No idea!'

They smile and kiss briefly and Derek turns and races off down Church Street and out of sight.

'So *that's* Derek,' says Rebecca.

'Yeah, that's Derek.' Amy says, her voice thick with emotion. 'Glad he's all right. Come on, let's find that door while there's still time.'

They are on Henrietta Street when a vicious lightning strike explodes against the bell tower on the town hall, the thunderclap so loud their ears are ringing.

Robert Seeker, who has said nothing at all for over ten minutes, happy to observe the extraordinary goings-on, finally finds his voice.

'Ladies, I must thank you all for this marvellous adventure! If I die tonight I die a satiated and contented man if only for having had the occasion to finally make use of my duckfoot volley pistol. I have been carrying the weight of it for three years and had all but given up on finding a use for it!'

'You didn't even fire it!' Rebecca taunts him.

They turn into the alley between the cottages. The blue glow is brighter than ever.

'You are right, dear lady. Here goes!' Seeker produces the four-barrelled duckfoot pistol, points it towards the harbour, cocks the trigger and fires. The noise is as loud as the thunder and the recoil such that Seeker is blown over as his arm flies up above his head.

'I have officially now seen everything!' Sarah announces as she helps him to his feet.

The others laugh.

'Look! The door!' Amy says.

'Thank you from the bottom of my heart,' Sarah says to Rebecca. 'Take this, you've more than earned it. You and Rosie deserve everything good that life has to offer.' She presses all the money she has left into Rebecca's hand.

'And take this too.' Amy splits her money, giving half to Rebecca and half to Robert Seeker. 'Thank you to you both. For everything. And have a wonderful Christmas! We'll be thinking about you all!'

The three women hug and include a clearly embarrassed Mr Seeker.

'I've never hugged a man with so many guns in his pockets!' winks Rebecca.

By the time Sarah and Amy reach the door, Robert Seeker and Rebecca have gone. Their faces lit in the blue aura, the two women open the door and disappear into the future.

Rebecca and Robert Seeker walk down Church Street both feeling slightly numb. Rebecca is keen to find Rosie and the children. Seeker is worrying whether it will be safe to enter the White Horse and Griffin or whether he should seek out new lodgings.

Another huge lightning strike slashes the sky.

By the time they reach Arguments Yard smoke is billowing out from the town hall, the bell tower is alight and the snow has turned to rain that now pours from the heavens like Falling Foss waterfall. With luck the rain will quench the flames.

Within the town hall the lightning has melted the cables. Fumes and fire have killed Constantine Featherston up in the loft and asphyxiated all the Architects down in the basement.

Derek races along the West Pier, praying he is not too late. He glances across the harbour at the huddle of cottages on the East Cliff and hopes there is no longer anyone there he knows.

'You're late, landlubber! They're already back in the brig.'

Derek looks up at the ship. Beth is up on deck, her lantern lighting up her red hair and green eyes, her smile as wide as a yardarm.

EPILOGUE

'There are more of them!' Andrew shouts. 'Call the police. I can't handle any more of this, Wolfy. And the stench! There's mud everywhere!'

'Calm down. We'll ring the agency. Let them deal with it.'

'The whole weekend is ruined! And the power is still down in the basement. We just have to find a hotel.'

Sarah and Amy close the door and look about them. Everything seems pretty damn normal. Carpet on the stairs. A bathroom! Electric light pouring down the stairwell.

Beaming from ear to ear, the women hug.

'Spoiler alert! Two tramps are making out in our basement.'

'Stop it, Andy! Why do you always have to …'

'I'm telling you! I can see them! Oh ... my ... God!' Andrew is shouting from the top of the stairs.

The women climb the stairs towards the two men, a trembling Andrew, in his pyjamas and dressing gown and a bemused Wolfy, in pants and vest.

'Are there ... any more of you?' Andrew asks.

'No. I don't think so,' Sarah says.

'The children have been taken to hospital,' Wolfy explains calmly. 'And the police have been and gone. Would you like a coffee before you head on?'

'The *children*?' Sarah says.

'Girl and a boy. There was a note,' Wolfy hands Amy the Post-it note.

Amy reads it. 'Oh God! Sarah, Derek came right inside earlier and left two kids. He crossed the threshold then went back!'

'There was another note,' Wolfy says, remembering. 'Found it face down under the sofa.' He takes a note from the table beneath the television and hands it to Amy. 'Did one of you write this?'

Stephen,
Popped out to find Amy and Derek who have stepped through a strange door in basement.
They aren't even wearing shoes!
Tried to wake you.
Back in a few minutes, I hope.
Sarah XXX

Amy passes the note to Sarah.

'Stephen has never seen this? Sarah asks.

Wolfy shrugs.

'We *will* have that coffee, if you don't mind the smell of us.' Sarah points down at her tatty clothes. 'We've come rather a long way. Do you have a phone we can borrow?'

'What's the date?' Amy asks.

'This is freaking me out, Wolfy. I bet they haven't even had their booster shots. You haven't, have you?'

'Andrew doesn't do mysterious or Gothic, I'm afraid. Do you take sugar?'

'I can even love the dreadful drapes,' Amy says, looking around her in wonderment. 'We really *are* back!'

As Wolfy steps into the kitchen there is a knock on the door. Andrew arches his eyebrows, the sooner they are back in Manchester the better.

'Do come in,' Andrew says throwing open the door and abandoning any attempt to maintain control of the situation. 'It's party night. Apparently. Tea or coffee Or something stronger?'

A wet and bedraggled man with grey hair and grey eyes and a facemask steps in out of the storm. He removes his coat and hands it to Andrew.

'Am I the butler?' Andrew asks exasperatedly.

The new arrival looks like he belongs in the 1950s, nylon shirt, cardigan, maroon tie.

'Hello, I'm Brian,' he says to the two women. 'I'm a reporter with the Gazette and I know who you are.'

'At least this one is wearing a mask,' Andrew mutters approvingly.

'Derek said she was healthy, beautiful and strong and quite the smartest kid he'd ever met,' Sarah tells Angelique.

They are sitting with Amy and Stephen on a bench close to the whalebone arch, looking out to sea. It is the middle of December and they are all in hats and coats. Festive garlands stretch between the lamp posts. Across the harbour, the old town is spangled in lights and pretty as a Christmas tree.

'They call her Lizbet. And she remembers you. The captain has your driving licence in a box hidden in a secret cupboard so Lizbet knows what you look like and …'

'I know the cupboard! In the captain's cabin!' Angelique interjects. Her eyes are full of tears but she is smiling.

'We didn't have more than a few minutes together,' Amy says, 'but Derek told us that the Captain almost sacrificed everything to rescue you. The gang, the bad guys, I'm sorry I don't know their names, they pretended they had kidnapped you and demanded a ransom.'

'A ransom?'

'The strangest ransom you could ever imagine. It was a baby dinosaur!'

Angelique laughs. 'At last I am no longer the only mad woman in Whitby!'

'It's true,' Amy protests. 'They carried it in a wooden box.'

'I can believe it. But who will believe us?' Angelique turns to Stephen who hasn't said a word. 'You must be so pleased to have your wife back.'

He nods bewilderedly. He has been doing a lot of listening.

'Nat and Aleka are recovering and the parents have arrived at the hospital,' he tells Angelique. 'You might like to meet them sometime.'

'I have a confession to make, Stephen. I told you that Jean-Jacques Elmo had tricked me and thrown me over the threshold and back into the twenty-first century without Eliza Bethany. It was a lie. We were like sheep that pass in the night, Jean-Jacques and I, but he never did me harm, he is a good man. The Architects did kidnap me and locked me up in a cave beneath a ruined house."

'Ships.' Stephen says.

'Ships?' Angelique says.

'Ships. Ships that pass in the night. Not sheep.'

'After a few months I broke out,' Angelique ignores the interruption. 'During my incarceration I had learned about the link between the electrical storms and the portals and when the chance came I seized it and escaped back to the present. I was so ashamed of my behaviour, of saving myself and abandoning my daughter, that I lied. I have lied to everyone ever since and it has eaten me up. I beg you to forgive me.'

A man hurries past the bench with his shopping, whistling *Hark! the herald angels sing*. As his shoes clatter on the steps that lead down to the harbour bandstand, Amy is transported back to a table in a house on Silver Street where she and Sarah shared teacakes with two friends from a different time.

'When my daughter is born I am going to call her Rebecca Rosie Whitby,' Amy says quietly, turning towards Angelique, 'and I will bring her to meet you.'

'Shame her dad won't be …' Sarah starts.

'Don't lecture me,' Amy snaps. 'I know it's not a perfect

start. I get that. But trying to spend your life with someone who doesn't want to be here isn't any better. Plus it's not every child whose missing parent is a buccaneer on the high seas!'

Angelique recalls the sea washing against the bow of a ship called the *Inevitable* and a jungle coast 165 million years away … and smiles.

"And I'm telling you that ammonites biofluoresce at night. Huge shoals of them come up towards the surface. They make these waves of rippling blue light to communicate. It's magical.' Nat stands his ground.

'Yeah, right and you know what fossils did a hundred million years ago because …?' Brad Rowley, the class bully has Nat pinned against a locker outside the school hall.

'No wonder he spent a week in hospital,' sneers Jess, one of the *popular* girls. 'Surprised they let him out.'

'Loser,' Brad shouts into Nat's face.

Nat spots his sister. 'Tell them, Aleka.'

Aleka arches an eyebrow, steps forward, grabs Nat's arm and pulls him away from the group.

'Natty Watty needs his nap,' someone calls out after them.

Peals of riotous laughter.

'I've told you,' Aleka says. 'We pass our exams, go to university, become professors of palaeontology *then* we tell the world that ammonites fluoresce in the dark.'

The moon is full. The sky is inky blue and full of stars. North of the town hall on Church Street the erstwhile businesses premises of Aaron Sly and Joseph Argument - pawnbrokers, general store and tallow chandlers – has changed hands and become:

Rebecca Anne Johnson & Daughter

GENERAL STORE

Fisherfolk go about their business in the yards, skaning the lines and baiting the hooks that will be dropped over the sides of the fishing boats in the morning if the weather holds. There's hardly any whale blubber boiling grey in cauldrons, whaling being less and less profitable and, because it's summer, hardly a black whiff of coal smoke either. But the rag carts still trudge up and down and the destitute still nip out of the workhouse to earn a few pennies on Grope Lane.

In the lacklight, a thousand barrels of fish await collection on the piers while the sea laps the stones as gently as a kitten at a saucer of milk.

Lanterns are glowing in the windows of the town hall that has had its clock tower restored. It is 1823 and up the spiral staircase the town hall is hosting its first meeting of the Whitby Philosophical Society. A heated debate is taking place on the subject of petrifications and snakestones.

'They're not snakes and never have been,' Rebecca tells the gathering. 'They are the remains of creatures that died millions of years ago. Creatures that once swam in the sea but have long since vanished.'

'What betwattled nonsense!' says a white-whiskered old gentleman across the room. 'Chair, can I insist that only the educated are allowed to take the floor?'

Robert Seeker, who is seated at the back of the room, is tempted to interject. Instead he smiles at Rebecca; she's more than capable of fighting her corner.

'The world is changing, you old mumblecrust,' Rebecca retorts. 'It always has and it always will.'

'And whaling has to stop before we kill every last creature in the sea!' Rosie says getting to her feet. 'Come on, mam. This lot don't have a clue!'

The view from up in the crow's nest is vast and blue. The sun has set and Ireland is behind them as the ship sails towards the pink rope of sky that lingers on the horizon.

'Hey! HEY!'

Derek peers down. Beth and Lizbet are on the deck way below, waving.

'What can you see, my lover?' Beth shouts up.

'Nothing much,' Derek shrugs and smiles. 'Some sea, a bit of sky .... and my whole life ahead of me.'

ACKNOWLEDGEMENTS

Thanks to my partner Mary for reading the draft and offering her comments and suggestions; to Peter for proofreading and insightful comments; to Chris, Fran, Fiona, Angela, Jenna at our wonderful independent bookshops in Whitby, Saltburn and beyond for their support; to Dominique for her art; to Megan for her expertise on the palaeontology of the Jurassic Coast; and to you, the growing band of readers of my Whitby books. We all share a love of the tales that lurk and linger the lacklit narrow streets and yards nestling around the harbour where the river Esk meets the North Sea. That magical Whitby trap has snared us all.

I am grateful to have had the opportunity of diving into the historical archives available at the Whitby Museum to learn more about the natural history of the coast and the social history and the tough lives of the fisherwomen and fishermen.

There are many amazing, strange and eccentric things in the museum: fossil plesiosaurs and ammonites, ships in bottles, old photos, costumes ... and George Merryweather's utterly lunatic *Tempest Prognosticator* or leech barometer.

The Jurassic world conjured up in this story no doubt contains many errors. These are my own. It all happened a very long time ago and my memory is not what it was.

For much of the Jurassic period the area that is now Whitby was under the sea ... but between 175 and 165 million years ago there was land! Beaches, rivers, and forests. Monkey puzzle trees, horsetails and cycads. From the east cliff in Whitby down to Saltwick Bay and beyond, the rocks contain fossils of a wide variety of plants and trees, crocodiles other reptiles, and dinosaurs, including megalosaurs and sauropods. The footprint of a nine-metre-long megalosaur was found in Filey. And of course, there are armfuls of ammonites.

I am not aware of insect fossils from Whitby but beetles, dragonflies, cockroaches and other insects certainly existed during the Jurassic period.

Could plesiosaurs walk on land? Until 2010 it was thought that yes, they dragged themselves up the beach to lay eggs, just like turtles. Then a fossil of a pregnant plesioaur turned up and everything became more complicated ...

Did the oysters of the Jurassic contain pearls and could the crew of a bizarre time travelling whaling ship have made a honest living from diving for them? Who knows? Oysters and clams have existed for hundreds of millions of years.

Duckfoot pistols - lethal contraptions just as eccentric as the Tempest Prognosticator - very much *did* exist (there are even versions with up ten barrels). And certain fashion conscious dandies in the 1820's *did* think that wearing two waistcoats in different colours, one over the other, was the height of cool.

Does the old town hall really have a basement?
It ought to!

If you have enjoyed reading *The Whitby TRAP* we'd love your review on our website at **www.injinipress.co.uk**

Lastly, one of the characters, Rebecca Anne Johnson, features in **The Whale Bone Archers**, a collection of short (but decidedly tall) stories that also offers a different take of a scene in **SCRAVIR - While Whitby Sleeps**.

Also by C.M.Vassie

SCRAVIR

While Whitby Sleeps

The best-selling contemporary gothic horror story is an explosive reimagining of Whitby's darkest hour!

The Famous Goth Weekend is in full swing. But while a mysterious guest star's music rocks the Pavilion, emaciated corpses are appearing in the streets. Dark forces are mingling with the thrill seekers.

Outsider Daniel Murray has never believed in the supernatural. Local girl Tiffany Harrek is not so sure. If they are to survive the next 48 hours they must wise up. Fast.

A few readers' reviews of Scravir

"A dark brain-itching blend of gothic and contemporary"

"Brilliant. I was hooked & stay in bed all day reading it."

"Intelligent, intense, packed with twists and genuinely original."

"An eerie brew of supernatural energy, antiquity and intrigue, Scravir is a real page-turner."

"Love this book ... absolutely fantastic, cannot wait for the next installment."

"Well the plan was to read this on holiday this week but silly me started it and finished it before we'd set off. Great read, loved that it was set in Whitby. Can honestly say it's my favourite book."

"Wow, read this in 3 sittings. Great use of character viewpoints between chapters and flows well. Story turned out not how I thought but still scary in the end. It actually answered questions and tied everything off in the end which I truly enjoyed about the book. Hate when the ending is flat but this was great. Perfectly executed."

"Being a fan of gothic horror, urban fantasy and of the beautiful, enchanting town of Whitby, this book appealed to me from the outset ... I started reading and half way through realised how late it had got! From the perfect descriptions of the town to the complex characters it's a book I was hooked on from start to finish ..."

"Wow! The only reason I put this book down was to go to work. Decided to take the bus home so I could read uninerrupted for 50 minutes on the journey. Loved it ❤"

"This fast-paced supernatural thriller is a cracking read. Full of surprising twists and turns. Evidence of a monstrous crime accumulates as we follow first-hand the sequence of events, the blur between fiction and a documented moment in the hidden history of Whitby adding to the excitement."
ESK VALLEY NEWS

"The central characters are very engaging and the novel is told from different viewpoints which helps with the exciting plot twists and also creates the suspense and tension that keeps the reader on the edge of their seat."
WHITBY ADVERTISER

Tall Stories of Whitby

The Whale Bone Archers

These sixteen short stories by C.M.Vassie provide an alternative guide for exploring Whitby.

Can you find Dracula's bootprint on one of the piers? Does a ghostly fish and chip shop haunt the town? Is there a bed of nails on Henrietta Street? What does whale blubber feel like?

A map shows you where each of the stories is set and the endnotes at the back of the book help you distinguish fact from fiction.

"The nuggets of truth tucked away in these madcap tales had us all thinking about Whitby's fascinating history."

"A magical mix of humour, hauntings, and history that had me in stitches."

"Vassie fabricates some wildly imaginative tales that combine Whitby's fascinating history with ghost stories and made-up "historical" accounts. His novel weave of history, mystery and humour make an enjoyable and informative read - and gives you a ready stock of tales to regale visitors on a fun day out round town.
ESK VALLEY NEWS

"The easy to read madcap tales made me think twice about the sights of Whitby I see nearly every day!"
WHITBY ADVERTISER